A Heart Made New

KELLY IRVIN

HARVEST HOUSE PUBLISHERS
EUGENE, OREGON

Cover by Garborg Design Works, Savage, Minnesota

Cover photos © Chris Garborg ; Bigstock/lawcain; iStockphoto/JenniferPhotography Imaging; edcorbo

A HEART MADE NEW
Copyright © 2012 by Kelly Irvin
Published by Harvest House Publishers
Eugene, Oregon 97402
www.harvesthousepublishers.com

Library of Congress Cataloging-in-Publication Data
Irvin, Kelly.
A heart made new / Kelly Irvin.
p. cm.--(The Bliss Creek Amish ; bk. 2)
ISBN 978-0-7369-4383-3 (pbk.)
ISBN 978-0-7369-4384-0 (eBook)
1. Amish—Fiction. 2. Homeless families—Fiction. 3. Kansas—Fiction. 4. Domestic fiction. I. Title.
PS3609.R82H43 2012
813'.6—dc23

2011048733

Printed in the United States of America

12 13 14 15 16 17 18 19 20 / LB-NI / 10 9 8 7 6 5 4 3 2 1

To Tim, Erin, and Nicholas
Love always

ACKNOWLEDGMENTS

The same village that raises the children helps an author write the book, it seems. My thanks to family and friends for your enthusiastic support of my writing journey. Tim, Erin, and Nicholas, you can't begin to imagine how much your support of my dreams means to me. Not to sound like a broken record, but I don't think I can ever say thanks enough to my agent, Mary Sue Seymour, for encouraging me to try something new, and to my editor, Kathleen Kerr, and all the folks at Harvest House Publishers for helping me to do a better job of telling the story. To my writing buddies in Alamo Christian Fiction Writers group, I offer my humble gratitude for the opportunity to be a part of such a wonderful group of writers and prayer warriors. For all this and all of you, I give thanks to the One responsible for all blessings, Jesus Christ, our Lord and Savior.

Give thanks in all circumstances;
for this is God's will for you in Christ Jesus.
1 Thessalonians 5:18 (niv)

This is the day which the LORD hath made;
we will rejoice and be glad in it.
Psalm 118:24

Chapter 1

Annie Shirack wanted to count her blessings, but she didn't have time. Customers had been lined up three-deep at the bakery counter when she returned from a quick sack lunch with her friend Miriam. Annie pushed the cash register drawer shut with a quick snap of her wrists. Inhaling the sweet scent of baking cinnamon rolls, she turned to face the last customer of the early afternoon rush.

"At this rate, you'll have to give me the day-old price. Four dozen snickerdoodles and that carrot cake." Mrs. Johnson pointed, then glanced at the gold watch on her skinny wrist. She wrinkled her long nose and tilted her shiny, hair-sprayed head. "That should be it for today."

Ignoring the pique in her customer's voice, Annie grabbed a sheet of wax paper and began depositing the cookies in a white paper bag. She threw a quick glance at Miriam, who grinned, shrugged, and bit into a brownie—a treat after the cold sandwiches they'd just shared on the bench at the park across the street. Annie grinned back, enjoying the look of bliss on her friend's face. One of the joys of being a baker. Besides, Miriam was right. Nothing to do but grin and bear difficult customers.

"I'd better get back to the tack shop." Miriam brushed crumbs from her oval face. "*Daed* will need my help."

"Wait a minute or two and I'll get that recipe I told you about for the double fudge cookies." Miriam had a special soft spot for chocolate. Annie loved that about her friend. "Your daed won't mind if you're a few minutes longer."

"I'll take him one of your brownies." Smoothing wisps of brown hair that had escaped her prayer *kapp*, Miriam settled onto a bench along the wall. "That'll soften him up."

The bell hanging over the double glass-plated doors tinkled as one of them swung open and closed with a bang. A young man Annie had never seen before slipped into the store. He looked around, saw Annie, ducked his head, and began to peer into the display case that contained a dozen kinds of pie.

Curiosity got the better of Annie. He didn't look like the typical tourist visiting Bliss Creek for a glimpse of prayer kapps and buggies. She sneaked another glance. His jeans sagged on narrow hips. He had both hands stuck in the pockets of a denim jacket that had to be plenty warm for this late spring day in Kansas.

Definitely not from around here. Not that it mattered. Her boss, Sadie Plank, owner of Plank's Pastry and Pie Shop, delighted in the brisk business. Many of the local *Englisch* ladies did their grocery shopping on Fridays in preparation for their husbands being home all weekend. That usually included a stop at the bakery.

If only every day could be like this. Otherwise…No, she wouldn't go down that road. Things would get better. Business would improve. David would get better. To think otherwise would be a lack of faith. Annie had plenty of faith. She'd just like to have some control over her life too.

Stop it. "That will be forty-eight dollars, Mrs. Johnson."

Mrs. Johnson scribbled a check with a fancy silver pen and handed it to Annie. "I'll be in Monday to pick up the cake I ordered for my parents' anniversary," she called over her shoulder as she walked to the door in heels that clicked on the wooden floor. "Remember, chocolate buttercream frosting on white cake."

How could Annie forget? Mrs. Johnson had given her instructions

five times. She glanced again toward the young man. He sidled closer
to the display case, seeming intent on the selection of cookies. The
schtinkich of cigarette smoke he brought with him threatened to drown
out the scent of cinnamon wafting in the air.

"Are you ready to order, sir?"

He didn't answer. He didn't even look up. All right, not ready yet.
After a quick tug to straighten her kapp, Annie washed her hands.
Wiping them on her clean apron, she went to the kerosene-powered
refrigerator and pulled out the butter and a carton of eggs. Time to
make gingersnaps. She'd let the ingredients come to room tempera-
ture while she looked for that recipe for Miriam.

"Annie, did you get Mrs. Rankin's order for the birthday cake?"
Sadie trudged from the backroom, carrying a twenty-five-pound bag
of flour over her shoulder. "It should be next on the list."

"Let me do that." Annie rushed to help her. "The doctor said no
heavy lifting for you."

"You're so skinny; the bag weighs more than you do." Sadie dropped
it to the floor with a grunt and straightened, one hand on her back and
a grimace on her wrinkle-lined face. "Mrs. Rankin wants it by five
o'clock. David will be here by then—he can deliver it."

David had a treatment today. He tried to act like it was nothing so
his mother wouldn't worry so much, but Annie knew different. She
saw how hard he tried to hide his discomfort. "He doesn't have to do
that. Josiah and I can deliver it on the way home. The cake is ready—"

"Ma'am." The man's hoarse voice had a soft Southern twang to it.

Annie turned to face him and smiled. "How can I help you today?"

The young man didn't smile back. He didn't even make eye contact. He shoved his black hair from his eyes with a hand that had grease
under its fingernails. He had the bluest eyes Annie had ever seen. She
tried again. "I have cinnamon rolls in the oven. They'll be ready in
about two seconds—"

"I'm really sorry about this."

His voice cracked. He stopped, the corners of his mouth twitching.
A pulse pounded in his temple.

Annie tried to catch his gaze. "Sorry about what?"

"My kid's gotta eat."

He drew his hand out from the pocket of his denim jacket. A silver gun appeared.

Sadie's gasp told Annie she'd seen it too. Out of the corner of her eye, Annie saw Miriam stand. Annie wanted to scream for her friend to run, but she knew better. *Stay there. Stay there.* Annie backed toward Sadie without taking her gaze from the gun. She'd seen plenty of hunting rifles, but this was a handgun. A gun made for shooting people. She clasped both hands in front of her to quiet their trembling.

"You can have whatever you want." Annie crowded Sadie, who grabbed her arm and held on tight. The woman's touch steadied her. She swallowed her fear and lifted her chin. "You don't need a gun. We'll share what we have with you."

The man waved the gun toward Miriam. "Get over there with them."

Panting as if she had run a race, Miriam scurried toward Annie and Sadie. They grabbed hands, holding on tight. Whatever happened, they were together. "It's all right," Annie whispered. *No it's not. God, please.*

"Put the money in a paper bag." The man pointed the gun at the cash register. "Then lay it on the counter."

Annie moved toward it. Sadie and Miriam didn't let go. They stayed together. *One step, two steps, three steps.*

The sounds of ragged breathing and the dragging of their shoes on the wooden floor filled the bakery. No one spoke. Annie forced herself to let go of the two women so she could open the drawer. Miriam nodded in encouragement. "It's all right."

It was strange to have her own words of encouragement repeated back to her. They sounded just as silly coming from Miriam's mouth. Annie's hands shook so hard she dropped the bag and had to retrieve it from the floor. Sadie grabbed her arm and helped her straighten.

"Hurry up!"

The note of hysteria in the man's voice frightened her more than the gun. Tugging free of Sadie's grip, Annie stuffed the bills into the bag.

The smell of singed bread wafted through the air. The rolls were burning. She almost laughed. Burned cinnamon rolls—surely the least of her problems right now.

Biting the inside of her lip until she tasted salty blood, Annie tried to hand the bag to the man.

He waved the gun at her. She fought the urge to shriek and plunge to the floor.

"The coins too." His gaze met hers finally. He looked as scared as she felt. The realization startled her. "Everything. I need everything you've got."

He had the gun, but he was scared. More than scared. He looked terrified. The thought steadied Annie, and her shaking stilled.

"You can have it all." She slapped the rolls of coins they used to make change into the bag and turned to him. "What about food? You said you needed to feed your child. Let me give you some bread. Some cookies too. Do you have a son or a daughter?"

The man snatched the bag from the counter. He started to back away and then seemed to waver. "I…a girl…she's three. She'd really like a cookie. I'd like to be able to give her a cookie. She ain't eaten nothing but bread and cheese today."

"Does she like peanut butter? I have peanut butter cookies. And I'm sure she'd like this banana bread. I just made it this morning." Surprised that her voice hardly shook at all, Annie picked up another bag and started packing it with the cookies, a loaf of whole wheat bread, and a loaf of banana bread. She breathed. *God, help me. God, help him. He needs Your help. Show him a better way. Open a door for him. God, take care of his little girl.* "What's her name?"

He shook his head. "Forget the food. There's no time."

"We have some raisins, bananas, and apples," Sadie spoke up for the first time. Her voice sounded high and tight, but she looked determined. "Take them too. Fruit is good for her. For you too."

"I have to go. Count to fifty before you call anyone." He started backing toward the door. "Count to fifty. If you don't, I might have to come back."

His half-sob took the sting from the threat. Annie breathed in and out. In and out. "We won't call anyone."

"Sure you will." The gun dipped and came back up. "The second I'm out the door, you'll call the cops."

Suddenly light-headed, Annie gripped the edge of the counter to steady herself. Purple spots danced at the periphery of her vision. Miriam's hand touched her shoulder, rubbing in a comforting circular pattern. Annie swallowed bile that made her throat burn.

"No, we won't. We don't have a telephone."

He snorted and backed toward the door. "Right."

The vision of a little girl with dark hair and eyes the color of heaven pierced Annie's heart. He had a little girl who needed to eat. "Take the food." She rushed around the counter, the bag in her hand. "Please."

"What are you?" His mouth open, face puzzled, he accepted her offering. "Nuns or something?"

Annie's heart was banging hard against her rib cage. Surely he could hear it. "No. We're…we're Amish."

"I'm sorry I had to scare you like this. Thank—"

The door opened. The bell dinged.

The man whirled, and a deafening blast filled the air all around Annie. She clapped her hands over her ears and sank to the floor. Someone screamed as more shots filled the air. The *bam-bam* made Annie jump each time as if it were a new, unexpected sound. Shattered glass rained down on her. Shards pricked the skin on the back of her fingers and pinged against her kapp. *God, ach, God. God.*

Time slowed until the seconds lingered like syrup poured from a bottle held high over the plate. Unable to draw a breath, she gasped, the sound hollow and muffled by her fingers over her ears. An acrid smell that reminded her of her brothers' hunting rifles filled the air. She didn't dare look up.

Miriam? Sadie? Were they hurt? *Look, just look.*

Annie managed to raise her head a fraction of an inch. They were huddled behind a chair by the storage room door. Miriam had both arms around Sadie, covering her with her own body. Were they hit?

Annie couldn't tell. She fought to make frozen muscles move. She dragged her hands from her ears and slapped them on the floor. The rough wood felt solid and dependable under her fingers.

Move. She wanted to crawl toward her friends, but her leaden legs and arms refused to cooperate. *God, help me.*

Footsteps pounded. The sound cracked the ice that immobilized Annie's entire body. She looked back. The man shoved Gwendolyn Haag to the ground and fled through the shattered glass door.

Bliss Creek's mayor scooted on her hands and knees until she reached the bench along the wall. She cowered there, her face contorted with terror. "I just came for my brother's birthday cake," she whimpered. "I can come back later."

Chapter 2

David Plank swallowed back the lump that threatened to rise in his throat. Some days were better than others. This wasn't one of them. He slapped his hat on his head and pushed through the door of Bliss Creek's fancy new medical clinic. The air outside seemed cleaner and fresher, nothing like the stale, sterile room where they gave him his chemo.

On legs that felt like wet noodles underneath him he trudged down the sidewalk, each step away from the clinic a step in the right direction. Four more weeks and he'd be done—with this round. He tried not to think about what lay beyond that milestone. He'd been down that road before. No point in stewing over something he couldn't control.

At the corner he turned right and clomped to Bliss Creek's blacksmith shop. The owner, Caleb Shirack, waved from behind the window of a small room that served as the office. David waved back and headed toward the forge. Apparently oblivious to David's entrance, Josiah Shirack smacked a molten horseshoe with a hammer several times, each blow shaping the shoe a little more. From the size of it, the shoe must be for a workhorse.

"Josiah. Josiah!" David hated to startle a man with a hot poker in his hand. "Hey!"

Josiah stuck the shoe in water until it stopped sizzling, then laid it on the anvil. "You look mighty green."

"Funny, I feel more purple." David adopted the same light tone he always used when talking about his health. Talking about chemo was boring, yet people seemed to want to have long conversations about it. "A little yellow, maybe."

"You're the funny man." Josiah wiped sweat from his whiskerless face with a torn, semiclean towel. Josiah had been David's closest friend since they'd been old enough to chase tadpoles with fishing nets and make mud houses in the shallow end of the pond on the Shiracks' farm. He wouldn't push. Not about the Hodgkin's lymphoma, anyway. "So today is the day."

Here we go. David didn't have the strength to spar with Josiah right now. His friend had spent too much time among the Englischers in his *rumspringa*. Their ways of talking everything to death had rubbed off on him. "What do you mean?"

"The day you'll ask Annie to take a buggy ride with you."

"Your sister rides with me all the time."

"I'm not talking about making deliveries in the wagon." Josiah growled, his brown eyes hot with irritation. With his dark curly hair poking wildly out from under his hat and his tall, solid frame, he looked just like his older brother, Luke. And a lot like his father. David considered telling him that, just to get him riled up, but Josiah didn't give him a chance. "You know what I mean. Time to pony up."

"I think you talk too much." David adjusted his hat. Since the chemo, it was too big without any hair to hold it in place. One nice thing, though, about wearing a hat all the time—it covered up his bald head. "I saw Miriam at the tack shop yesterday. Now that school is out, she'll work there every day. You'll see a lot more of her."

"It's possible." Josiah grinned. It was fairly common knowledge that Josiah and Miriam Yonkers, who had taken over as the school's teacher after his sister Emma married in November, had left a few singings together at the end of the evening. "But this is about you and Annie, not Miriam and me."

"Courting is private."

"In other words, mind my own business?"

"*Jah.*"

"How long have we all been friends—you, me, Annie, Luke, Timothy, Jonathan, Emma—all of us?"

Josiah liked to ask questions to which he already knew the answers. The habit irritated David. "Since as long as I can remember."

"So you know Annie well enough to know she doesn't care about the cancer."

The heat of the forge stoked David's nausea. If he didn't get his horse and leave soon, he'd lose his lunch on his friend's boots. "Did you get Rosie taken care of? I need to hitch her up and get going. *Mudder* has some deliveries for me."

"She's ready." Josiah's tone was curt. He strode toward a row of stalls. "I just never took you for a coward."

The unexpected word smacked David in the face. Anger whipped like the flames in the forge, sending heat coursing through him. Josiah didn't know what he was talking about. Despite the doctor's orders to the contrary, David went to his treatments on his own. He struggled through them alone so that his family didn't have to see him like that. Annie didn't have to see him puking and heaving until nothing came up anymore.

Breathe. Breathing brought more nausea. Light-headed, David swayed. Concern on his face, Josiah took a step toward him.

David backed away, both hands up. "The first round of chemo didn't work. The remission didn't last. There's a chance I'll die. Is that what you want for Annie? To be a widow before she's really a wife?" He brushed past his friend and tottered to the stall that held his mare. "How much do I owe you?"

"Annie told me the doctors said the prognosis for Hodgkin's is good." Josiah slipped up next to him. "Besides, you don't know God's will for you. Don't pretend you do. Your daed died young. My daed died young. I figure we've had our share of grief."

"It doesn't work that way. You're like Annie—an optimist. It must run in your family."

"She's an optimist because she has faith. From faith comes hope. She's waiting for you."

David faced his friend. "I never asked her to wait. How much do I owe you?"

"No charge for a friend—even if he is pigheaded." His face grim, Josiah started toward the door. "I'm going to the hardware store," he yelled, apparently for Caleb's benefit. Josiah's cousin waved a pencil and went back to the ledger in front of him.

Feeling like he'd let a friend down, David led Rosie from the stall. Josiah couldn't know what it was like. Having faith meant accepting, didn't it? If he really believed, he had nothing to be afraid of, right? Why was everyone so afraid of death? It seemed like a lack of faith. He was fighting to accept his lot, whatever it turned out to be. Pain wrapped itself around his heart and squeezed at the litany of things he would never have, never experience. Marriage. Fatherhood. Annie.

Annie had pretty green eyes and that faint dusting of freckles that made her look younger than her twenty years. Some might find fault with her daydreams, but David found himself mesmerized by the girl who wrote poems and played Mary in the school Christmas pageant. No girl smiled as often as she did. While she worked, while she walked, while she baked, while she prayed. He'd never known anyone so intent on finding the good pieces of fruit among the rotten. She believed in the possibilities of the future so much it almost made him believe in her dreams too. Almost.

The sounds of sirens jerked him from his agonizing reverie. They didn't get many sirens in Bliss Creek. Just for heart attacks and the like. David tried to shake away the image of his father gasping in pain, his face darkening to a shade of purple as he thrashed on the barn floor. Who was it this time? Not Mudder, surely. She took her medicine every day and ate the foods the doctor said were best—David saw to that.

"David, come quickly!" Josiah threw the shed door open wide. "Quickly!"

His hands fumbling, David tied the reins to the stall railing. "What is it?"

"Michael Glick says someone robbed the bakery. Shots were fired."

Gunfire.

Mudder.

Annie.

Chapter 3

Annie flew to the oven and tugged open the door. Smoke poured out. The cinnamon rolls were blackened, unrecognizable blobs of burnt dough. She coughed, and her eyes teared up from the smoke. She sniffed hard, grabbed a hot pad, and pulled the pan out. "What a mess. I'll have to start all over again. It's such a waste."

"They're just cinnamon rolls. We'll make more. The main thing is we're all right." Her kapp askew and a clump of wiry gray hair hanging in her eyes, Sadie reached for the broom. "I guess I'd better clean up the glass before someone steps on it."

"You sit down and rest a minute." Looking not the least bit worse for wear, Miriam tried to tug the broom from Sadie's grip. "I can take care of the cleanup. Daed will understand. He'll be glad I stayed to help when he hears what happened."

Annie suspected differently. Solomon Yonkers might want his daughter as far away as possible from the scene of a shooting.

Sergeant Dylan Parker put one huge hand on the broom, making both women let go. "This is a crime scene. We need to leave it as it is until we can take some pictures." His gaze encompassed Annie. "You too, Annie. Could you go outside and have a seat on the bench out there?"

"Burnt cinnamon rolls are evidence?" Annie instantly regretted her tart tone. Sergeant Parker had never been anything other than courteous when he came in for a bag of pastries to take to the staff at the police station. He liked to joke about having a sweet tooth that he planned to have pulled before he went broke at the bakery. Annie tried again. "We need to clean up. Customers like a tidy store."

"We can't have customers stepping on this glass." Sadie tried to take back her broom. Sergeant Parker didn't let go. "I need to clean up."

They engaged in a tug-of-war that made Annie want to smile, in spite of everything. Sergeant Parker towered over Sadie. He appeared to eat well and probably went to one of those gyms she'd heard about where men lifted weights. Plain folks built muscle with work. Other folks used heavy things. That always struck Annie as funny. Sadie was sixty if she were a day and despite lifting huge sacks of flour and sugar every day, she was a little on the sparse side.

"You can't clean up until we've documented the scene." Sergeant Parker won the tug-of-war easily, but he had the good grace not to gloat over the victory. "You're closed for business for now."

"But we need the…" Annie stopped. She couldn't share their problems with this Englischer, however nice he seemed. "For now. Just until they ask their questions."

"Then I guess I'd better run back to the shop." Miriam started for the door. "Daed will wonder where I—"

"Again, I'm sorry." Sergeant Parker held up a hand, palm up. "I need you to stay until I can take your statement."

"You don't need our statements. We won't press charges." Sadie shook a finger at the man. "The poor man just wanted to feed his little girl."

"Oh, ma'am." Sergeant Parker shook his head, a funny look on his face. "Ma'am, he committed armed robbery. He fired shots at you."

"That boy didn't shoot at me. It was an accident. The mayor startled him. He shot the door and the windows. They can be replaced." Sadie frowned and crossed her scrawny arms. "Besides, he seemed to need the money more than we did."

"He didn't shoot at me," Miriam chimed in. "We were all the way across the room when it happened."

If the situation weren't so sad, Annie might have mustered a smile at the indignation in her friend's voice. "He didn't shoot at me either."

A snort from across the room made Annie shift her gaze to Mayor Haag. She jumped up from the bench, her face red with indignation. She marched right up to Sergeant Parker and pointed a finger at him.

"He shot at me. That's attempted murder. This is armed robbery. Don't stand there—go catch him! What do we pay you for?" Mayor Haag smoothed short tufts of silver hair with a shaking hand. She needn't have—not one hair was out of place. They wouldn't dare move. "I'll press charges whether these women like it or not. That turn-the-other-cheek thing works well for their kind, but I have a town full of citizens to keep safe."

"He didn't mean to shoot at you. You scared him and he shot at the door and the window." Annie managed to keep her voice soft, respectful. "It was an accident."

"Whoa! Whoa! Everyone stick a cork in it, okay?" Sergeant Parker held up a massive hand. "Mayor, you sit back down. Annie, do me a favor and take a seat on the bench outside, please. Miriam, you're over here by the cash register. Mrs. Plank, let's put you in that chair back there by that storage room for now."

Annie didn't understand why they couldn't stay together and give each other comfort. But Sergeant Parker was a man of authority. She laid the hot pads in a neat stack on the counter and headed to the door. She nearly ran into Officer Bingham. He was another regular visitor to the bakery. Unlike Sergeant Parker, he could use a few visits to that gym—or better yet, some time in the fields. Gasping for air like a catfish tugged from the creek, he dragged the robber into the bakery.

Blood caked the young man's nose and trickled down the front of the dingy white T-shirt he wore under the denim jacket. His hands cuffed behind him, he wove back and forth, a little off balance. Officer Bingham held onto him with both hands. "We grabbed this guy running down the alley with a gun in one hand and a bag of money in the other." The way Officer Bingham panted suggested he didn't run very often. "I had to tackle him to get him to stop, boss. He put up quite a struggle. I think we can add resisting arrest to the charges. This is him, right, Mrs. Plank? Is this the guy who robbed you?"

Sadie couldn't lie. None of them could. But something about the man's anguished face spoke to Annie's heart. She shook her head ever so slightly. Sadie's shoulders rose and fell. She frowned. "It was very fast—"

"That's him! Why are you asking them?" Mayor Haag's hands flailed in the air. "That's the man who tried to kill me." She marched over to him. "You will have a lot of time in jail to think about how smart it is to take a shot at an elected official, mister."

"That would be a positive ID, then." Sergeant Parker stepped between the two of them. He turned to Officer Bingham. "Get him over to the station and get him processed." The officer nodded and turned the man around roughly.

"Wait." Annie wrapped her arms around her middle. She took a tentative step toward the man in handcuffs. "What's your name?"

He raised his head. His hair hung in his eyes and Annie wanted to push it back like he was a little boy and she was his mother. His lips trembled. "Why?"

"Why what?"

"Why do you want to know?"

"I want to pray for you. It helps me to have a name."

His white skin went red as a radish. "Logan. Logan McKee," he whispered.

"What about your daughter?"

"Grace. We call her Gracie."

Annie smiled. "That's a pretty name."

Sergeant Parker cleared his throat. "Outside, Annie, please."

Annie complied. Her legs still soft as strawberry preserves, she sank onto the bench in front of the store. Sergeant Parker's black police car sat next to the curb, red and blue lights on top still flashing, one door open. It felt…untidy. Ignoring the curious gazes of more than a dozen people—all Englischers—who were loitering outside the yellow crime scene tape Sergeant Parker had strung across the front of the bakery, she scurried over and shut the car door, then went back to her seat.

"Annie, Annie, are you all right?"

Long legs pumping, David raced across the street, Josiah right behind him. David's hat flew off, revealing his smooth, bald head. He stopped long enough to retrieve it. A car horn blared and the driver shook a fist. Both men kept going. Annie shot from the bench. They were going to get themselves killed over nothing.

"Is Mudder all right? They said shots fired. Shots fired!" David ducked under the tape and skidded to a stop so fast Josiah almost ran into him. "Who would shoot at you and Mudder?"

"*Ach*, David, you shouldn't be running! Sit down." Annie offered him her spot on the bench. He staggered away from her, put both hands on his knees, and gasped. She followed him. "We're fine. Your mother's fine. Miriam's fine. Nobody was hurt."

"Miriam? Miriam was in there?" A look of near panic on his sweaty face, Josiah started to push past Annie. "Is she hurt?"

"Listen to me." Annie grabbed his arm. "Everyone is fine. Sadie. Me. Miriam. The mayor. You can't go in there. The sergeant says it's a crime scene, and he's interviewing each one of us—taking statements, he calls it."

"The mayor was in there?" His face stony now, Josiah crossed his thick arms over a chest made broad by almost a year of working the anvil. "Police statements? Luke isn't going to like this. Maybe you should go back to working at home."

"It was an accident. The mayor scared him." A chill ran up Annie's arms. Surely she wouldn't be forced to give up her independence and a job she loved because of this. If Luke agreed with Josiah, she wouldn't be given a choice. "Don't tell Luke you think I should stay home. I'm fine."

Josiah picked up his hat, revealing his wild mop of brown curls, and slapped it back down hard. "I don't know—"

"*Ach!*" David sagged against the wall, his breathing so noisy that Annie started. "I think I…"

"What is it? What do you need?" Annie took a step closer to him, longing for the freedom to offer him her hand for support. "Didn't you have your treatment today? Shouldn't you lie down?"

"I don't want to talk about chemo!" Still hunched over, David stared up at her, his dark eyes full of emotion. His flaring anger didn't surprise Annie. David never wanted to talk about his illness or admit the slightest weakness. He didn't trust her enough for that. "Where's Mudder? Something like this could give her another heart attack."

Annie understood his fear. He'd already lost his father to a heart attack. Sadie's first one had been mild, but still scary. "She's fine—"

David ducked past her just as Officer Bingham came through the door with Logan McKee. David stopped moving. "Is this him?" He scowled at Logan. "Why would you do this? Shoot at women who never hurt you?"

Logan hung his head. "I didn't mean—"

"You could've given my mother a heart attack—"

"But he didn't." Sadie squeezed past Officer Bingham and approached her son. Her arms went up, but she stopped short of giving him a hug. "We're fine. This poor boy didn't hurt anything but a window and the door—and that was purely an accident."

David's gaze went from Sadie to Annie and back. "*Gut.* That's *gut.*" He crumpled to the ground.

Chapter 4

The darkness enveloped David like a heavy blanket. Hot. He felt hot. He struggled to fling it off him. His arms weighed so much he couldn't lift them. He managed to open his eyes, and a bright light nearly blinded him. He blinked and tried again. The light sent a jagged pain pinging through his head. *"Ach."* He tried to raise his hand to rub his forehead. Tape tore at the hair on his arm. "Ouch. What is this? Where am I?"

"Good, you're awake." The fog lifted and Doctor Corbin came into view. He adjusted the IV tube taped to the inside of David's arm. It snaked over his head to a bag filled with clear liquid hanging on a rack. "Feeling any better?"

The medical clinic. The brown fake leather chairs and the smell of medicines mingled with antiseptics and cleansers were all too familiar. David struggled to sit up. "Where's my mother? Is she all right?"

"She's in the waiting room. I'll send her in after we talk."

David pushed away the sheet and swung his legs over the side of the bed. His head swam, making the room rock like a boat on a pond. "I'll go to her. She should be at home resting after what she's been through today."

"I checked her over thoroughly. She's fine." Doctor Corbin put his fingers on David's wrist and glanced at his watch. "You, on the other hand, are dehydrated. Until you get some fluids in you you're not going anywhere. Do you think you can eat?"

David sank back on the bed. "It's hard to eat when everything tastes like sawdust, and it all comes back up anyway."

"Did you refill the prescription I gave you for the nausea?"

Prescriptions cost money. Money they could ill afford to spend. "I will. As soon as I get out of here."

"You passed out. I'm keeping you overnight." Doctor Corbin tapped his pen on the folder in his hand. "I'll ask the nurse to get you something from the cafeteria. Any requests?"

David stared at the window over the doctor's shoulder. No sun backlit the blinds. How long had he been out? A night at the clinic only meant more bills. "I did too much. That's all. I promise to go home and rest."

"Since I've heard that story from you before—too many times— I'm sticking with my original plan." Doctor Corbin smiled and stuck the pen in the pocket of his white coat. "How about a cheeseburger and maybe some green beans? Some chocolate pudding for dessert? I know you like a good burger."

"I don't lie."

"I'm not saying you do, David. I'm saying I'd rather you stay where we can monitor your condition overnight. When I see some improvement, you can go. Not before."

David clamped his mouth shut to keep from saying something ungracious. Doctor Corbin accommodated the Plain ways, as much as it was obvious he didn't understand them. He never pushed the cancer support group on David. Once Bliss Creek's first and only full-service medical clinic opened in the fall, the doctor never asked David to go back to Wichita where they had places that specialized in cancer treatment. "Fine."

"Do you want to see your mother now?"

"Yes."

At the door, Doctor Corbin looked back. "Lie down."

"I won't try to escape."

"I know. I'm asking you to lie down."

David did as the doctor asked. The door closed with a soft squeak.

He stared at the ceiling, wishing he could do something, anything to ease the constant ache where his heart once resided. All of this meant nothing. He'd struggled through the first round of treatment with the certainty that he would be cured. Hodgkin's lymphoma had a good recovery rate, according to Doctor Corbin. Every reason to have hope. The day Doctor Corbin announced he was in remission, David had asked Annie to a singing. Six months later, Doctor Corbin had sat across his desk from David and told him the cancer had returned.

That was that. He refused to get his hopes up again. Worse, to get up Annie's hopes. One person out on the crashing waves was enough.

"Hi."

Startled, David rolled over to face the door. A young child, maybe six years old, peeked through the door. Given the bald head and non-descript hospital nightgown, David couldn't tell if it was a boy or a girl. The child pointed a finger at him. "Who are you?"

"David. Who are you?"

Uninvited, the child padded barefoot into the room and climbed up on the chair, the gown so long it tangled up. "I'm Kinsey. Do you have cancer too?"

Kinsey. Boy or girl name? Probably a fancy girl name.

The shadows around her eyes and the gaunt look on her face were all too familiar. "Yes."

"I knew it." Head cocked, Kinsey grinned. "You don't have hair."

David ran a hand over his slick head. He hoped his hat wasn't lost. Last time he'd been in overnight, it had disappeared somehow. "It grows back."

"That's what Mommy says." Kinsey crossed her legs and scratched her nose with stubby fingers. "I don't care. It's nice not to have to wash it and brush it. Besides, Grammy gave me some really cool kerchiefs to cover it up. One's purple. Purple's my favorite color. What's your favorite color?"

She covered all that without taking a breath. David wanted to smile. Instead, he carefully considered the question. "Green. I think it's green."

"Why?"

"Because it's the color of grass and things that grow." And Annie's eyes. "It reminds me of being outside."

"Instead of being in here."

Smart little girl. Being outside instead of looking at beige walls and shielding his eyes from glaring, fluorescent lights. "Yes. Instead of in here—"

"Kinsey Rene Navarro!" A round woman in the brightest purple dress David had ever seen burst through the door. She swooped down, grabbed Kinsey's arm, and tugged her from the chair before facing him. "I'm so sorry. Kinsey, apologize to the man. You know better than to barge into other people's rooms. I've told you a dozen times to stay put."

"This is my mommy. Her name is Willow."

Willow had long, shiny brown braids and dimpled cheeks. She exuded health in the middle of a building full of sick people. David tried not to resent that fact. "It's nice to meet—"

"Don't interrupt, Kinsey." Willow's tone said she had to admonish her daughter about that particular fault quite often. "The doctor wants you to stay in bed. Your immune system is weak. There are germs."

"Grammy says there's germs everywhere. I get bored." Kinsey's lips drooped. "I'm exploring."

David tried to get a word in edgewise. "It's no problem—"

Willow shook her head so hard her braids bounced. "This is a hospital—"

The door opened again. This time Mudder and Annie filed into the room. Willow put both hands on Kinsey's shoulders. "Again, I apologize. You have visitors. We'll get out of your way."

His face on fire, David gripped a pillow to his chest. "Mudder, I told you before. No visitors."

"Annie was so worried." Seemingly oblivious to Kinsey and Willow, his mother rushed to his bed. She clutched a paper sack in one hand, the faded green canvas bag that served as her purse in the other. "She just wants to make sure you're okay. We brought you some crackers."

The woman squeezed past Annie, headed toward the door. Kinsey threw out an arm. Her little hand touched Annie's arm. "You have green eyes."

"I do." Annie smiled, a smile that was better than any pain medication Doctor Corbin could offer. "Yours are blue."

"Like the sky—"

"Kinsey! Enough." Willow bustled her out of the room.

David gave the quiet a second to settle around them. Annie took two steps toward the bed. Then another. And another. She smoothed back her blonde hair around her kapp, even though it didn't need it. "The little girl was sweet. Who is she? Are you—"

David met her gaze. "You have to go."

"I want to stay." She sighed. "I only want to help."

"Go." He couldn't keep looking at those sad green eyes. He would waver. "Go home."

"I'm going." She paused at the door. "If you change your mind or you need something, send Josiah for me. I can read to you. I found an old copy of *The Oregon Trail* at the used bookstore. Remember when we used to read that in school? Or if you just want someone to sit with you…"

He couldn't let the tears in her eyes or the entreaty in her voice sway him. Hurt her now and she'd get over it sooner. Later would be worse—for her.

"No."

"David!" The disapproval in his mother's voice only added to his shame. "How can you be so stiff-necked?"

"I—"

Annie let the door close behind her without a sound.

PLANKS PASTRY & PIE SHOP

Chapter 5

Despite being anxious to reach the buggy and start home, Josiah slowed his pace on the sidewalk that led to the shop. Annie had been lagging behind ever since they left the hospital. It wasn't like her to be a slowpoke, but given the events of the day it didn't surprise him. Having a stranger shoot at her. Having the man she loved—if he interpreted her stiff-jawed attempt to bottle the sobs correctly—collapse at her feet. It had been a long day and they still had chores to do at home.

If David weren't already in a world of hurt, Josiah would be tempted to straighten him out. Not exactly the frame of mind Luke or Deacon Altman expected of him as a Plain man, but honest all the same. He had committed himself to the principles of forgiveness and grace, but he remained as human as ever. This was his sister, after all.

She needed to go home, get some food in her, and go to bed. Things wouldn't look so bleak on the other end of a good night's sleep. That's what Daed always said. The thought of his father didn't rip out Josiah's insides the way it had for the last year. The pain had subsided to a deep, unending ache.

Annie stumbled. He grabbed her elbow and steered her around the corner onto the street that led to the blacksmith shop. "I'll get Mooch. You wait for me at the buggy."

Her wordless acquiescence spoke volumes.

He picked up his pace, then slowed. Miriam leaned against the side of the buggy, her head down as if she were studying the ground. As the sun descended in the west, her skin glowed against the dark navy of her dress. Despite the long white apron, he could tell she filled out the dress. The thought caught him off guard and sent hot blood coursing to his face. He might have learned to think that way in the Englisch world, but Miriam didn't deserve it. He owed her an apology without having opened his mouth. A new low for him.

At the sound of their approach she looked up, straightened, and smiled. "Daed had my brothers board up the broken window and door at the bakery. He says not to worry—they'll put in the new glass tomorrow first thing. Paul is going over to the hospital to tell Sadie right now. What an awful thing to happen. It's so strange…we ate our sack lunches together at the park, and it was a perfectly normal, average day. Next thing I know we're getting shot at and robbed. I'm just mystified at how things happen sometimes, just mystified. Mystified! And how is David, by the way? What did the doctor say?"

That was Miriam. Running at the mouth, bubbling over with words and energy and never quite running down. Usually, Josiah liked that. It kept him from having to keep up the conversation, but today it added to his own, well, *mystification* when it came to women. Where did she come up with all these words? Probably in those library books she liked to read between customers at the tack shop.

Still, the way Annie's face brightened relieved him. His sister rushed over to Miriam. "David's all right. The doctor says it's a common reaction to the treatments and not being able to keep food down. He hasn't been taking the medicine he needs for the upset stomach."

A friendly face. As always, Josiah tried to identify why Miriam's unwavering friendliness—near perfection—unnerved him. They'd sat in the same classroom for years, walked the same path home from school every day. He'd teased her about her the funny way she ran the bases, her long dress flapping, when they played baseball. She'd helped him with his multiplication tables and his English. He'd fixed her ice skates. When had their easy give-and-take turned into something awkward? Her eyes, warm as hot chocolate, always seemed to be asking a question—one he couldn't answer.

"I'll get Mooch."

"At least say hello." Annie's tart tone matched her frown. "She won't bite."

"I know that." Josiah tugged at his too-tight suspenders. He'd gotten taller in the last month. When would he stop growing? It made him feel like a kid. "Miriam, are you all right?"

She shrugged and nodded.

He took the time to look at her more carefully. His hand came up. He dropped it just in time to keep from touching her sleeve. It gaped with a long tear. "You tore your dress."

"I caught it on something. It's nothing a few stitches won't fix. How about you? Have you talked to Luke about getting back to farming yet?"

"Not yet."

"I'm not surprised." Miriam's brown eyes were more like chocolate ice cream than hot cocoa now. "You always were one to put off until tomorrow what you could do today."

That was Miriam. No beating around the bush. Spontaneous with her words. Generous with her affection. How she survived in—Josiah stopped himself right there. Plain people might reserve their show of emotions, but that didn't mean they lacked feelings. *We*, he reminded himself. *We don't lack feelings.*

"I reckon." The words sounded stiff in his own ears. "I'd better get Annie home. A good supper and a good night's sleep and she'll be right as rain."

"Let me be the judge of that." Miriam pushed back from Annie and made a show of surveying her from head to toe. "Hmm, I don't see any new holes."

Annie giggled, the color returning to her face. "Silly girl."

"Daed says I may be cheeky sometimes, but I'm a good girl." Miriam grinned, but some underlying challenge in the words rang in Josiah's ears. "Daed always tells the truth."

Did Miriam know how blessed she was to still have a father to tell her the truth? Solomon Yonkers didn't mince his words, and he protected his three daughters like a faithful shepherd. Josiah edged toward the shed. "We'd better get going. Luke will wonder why I'm not there to do the chores. I expect Leah is wondering the same thing about Annie."

"If he's heard about the shooting, he's probably looking for you right now."

"He's planting Sudan grass today."

"My brothers are doing the same." Miriam nodded. "Will you be at the horse auction tomorrow?"

Josiah shrugged. "I imagine so. Ned can't pull his weight on the plow anymore, and Luke is thinking of replacing him." Here he was on firmer ground. Talking with Miriam like they used to talk, just a boy and a girl. "It's a question of money."

"I know exactly what you mean. Anyway…" Her dimpled cheeks turned pink. She turned to Annie. "Will you be at the singing Sunday night? Maybe Josiah can bring you."

"I haven't been to a singing in months." Annie's voice cracked. She turned her back on them and hoisted herself into the buggy. She swiped at her face with her sleeve. "Not since…well…I'm too old for that."

Miriam's sideways glance was an open invitation. Josiah shifted and cleared his throat. Singings were fun. Not his idea of great music and there weren't any instruments, but he had found his peace with that. "I might—"

"Joe! There you are." The voice which had haunted Josiah's sleep many nights during the past year caught on the moist breeze and drifted over him. "I thought I heard you. I've been waiting forever."

Chapter 6

Josiah went still at the sound of that voice. After a year he'd finally learned to turn it off, tune it out, see it as white noise left over from a season in his life that had ended with him clinging to life, tubes taped to his arms, machines beeping around him. But this was no dream. His boots were rooted to the ground in front of the blacksmith shop, mired in his reluctance to turn around and look at the girl who'd inspired the entire experience.

Annie glared at him from her spot in the buggy, but Miriam slipped past him and approached their visitor.

"Hello, Sarah. It's nice to see you again."

As usual, Miriam had far more grace and courage than he did. Wiping sweaty palms on his pants, Josiah pivoted. "Sarah."

She looked different. Her hair, usually running like a red river down her back, had been caught up in a thick twist not quite covered by her kapp. She wore a long, dark blue skirt and white blouse instead of her favorite jeans and T-shirt. Only the pink tennis shoes reminded him of the New Order Mennonite girl he'd courted and once asked to marry him in an alcohol-induced haze.

With a quick but friendly nod, Sarah ducked past Miriam and grabbed his hand. "I need to talk to you." She glanced at Annie. "Alone."

"That's not a good idea." Annie stood, her hands knotted in the material on either side of her dress as if she would leap from the buggy. "Luke said—"

"Annie, just give me a minute." He glanced at Miriam, hoping she would see the apology in his face. "It'll only take a minute."

"Or two." Sarah tugged at his sleeve. Even without looking back, he could feel the cut of the two women's disapproving glances, sharp as knives between his shoulders. *You promised*, they said without opening their mouths.

Inside the blacksmith shop, Sarah stepped into the light of the kerosene lantern that burned on a table in the corner. For a moment, she simply stared at him as if drinking in the sight. He could find no words to sum up everything that had happened since the last time their paths had crossed. He could still feel the warmth of her hand when she covered his one last time. And the way his heart had squeezed and exploded when the hospital room door slammed behind her.

"Caleb went over to the diner to get some supper." The light breathlessness of her voice caught at Josiah. She remembered too. "He said I could wait here for you. He said to tell you not to bother with closing up; he'll take care of it when he comes back."

"Why are you here?"

"I missed you." Sarah smoothed the starched material of her skirt. "I wrote you a couple of times, but I never heard back."

Because he'd kept his promise to Luke. No more contact with the people who'd made his journey back to faith so complicated. Not that he blamed anyone—least of all Sarah—for his weakness of spirit. "Sarah, you know I can't—"

"Don't! Please, don't!" She raised thin fingers and touched his lips. "Let me talk first, okay?"

Her fingers were warm and soft, just as he remembered them. *Stop.*

"Annie's had a rough day. She needs to go home. We both have chores to do." Before he could give in to the urge to hug Sarah, he strode to the stall and opened the gate. "Come on, Mooch. Let's go."

He walked the horse past her. She stood, not moving, watching. He forced himself to meet her gaze. "Go home."

"You don't really want me to go home. We both know that."

Sarah knew him better than any other person in the world, even Miriam, as hard as she tried. He picked up his pace. Mooch snorted and tossed his head, straining at the halter and forcing Josiah to hold on with both hands. He felt just like Mooch, struggling against restraints he couldn't understand.

"Joe, please, I came here to tell you something." Sarah tugged at his sleeve. "Stop for a minute."

Joe. Only she called him that. He slowed.

Sarah slipped around him so he was forced to look into her blue eyes. "I'm willing to do whatever it takes for us to be together."

"Whatever it takes?" His heart squeezed in a painful hiccup. "What are you talking about?"

"There's not a big difference in what we believe."

"Only in the way we live." Josiah grabbed the string of her kapp and tugged. It slipped from her head and her loose bun threatened to come undone. "I remember running my hands through your hair. It felt like…like the down on a baby duckling. That's not something a Plain man should do. Not this side of his marriage vows."

He held out the kapp and she snatched it back. Ignoring the tears in her eyes, he plowed ahead. "Did you drive here? Did you borrow your brother's truck? Did you listen to the radio on the way? I'm thinking there's a cell phone in that bag and probably an iPod."

"Joe, please!" Tears welled up in her blue eyes. "Why are you acting like this? I took the bus. I left my phone and my music at home. I'm serious. I thought you were serious. If you're not…"

"You can't become Amish just because of me. You have to join the faith. You have to live the way we live."

"I believe what you believe. You just don't believe in me." She whirled and stumbled through the door.

Josiah stared at the empty space where Sarah had stood. She had once represented everything he thought he wanted. A way out. Now she wanted a way in.

"Sarah, wait!" He tugged Mooch through the door and into the evening sunlight. The horse whinnied, high and tight. Miriam still stood at the buggy, one hand on the front wheel. She didn't move. Neither did Annie. He tried to ignore their furious gazes. "Easy, boy, easy. Sarah, come back here. How long are you planning to stay in Bliss Creek? And where?"

She whirled and marched back, stopping within inches of him. The familiar smell of roses tantalized him. "I'm staying indefinitely." Sounding as if she'd been running, she slapped the kapp back on her head. "How long depends on you. I could stay forever...or not."

The tears were spilling down her cheeks now. He couldn't help himself. He brushed them away. Her hands came up and captured his fingers. Ever aware of watchful gazes, he tugged them away. "Where will you stay?"

"I'm visiting my cousin Rachel and her family. They live out on Voelcker Lane."

Voelcker Lane was on the other side of town, but Bliss Creek was small. Luke would run into her. Or Emma. Or worse, Leah. But it didn't matter—Annie would spill the beans to Luke the second they returned to the house. As she should. He couldn't blame her for remaining true to the *Ordnung* even though he could never seem to abide by it.

"I have to get Annie home." Josiah swallowed against emotions that threatened to choke him. "I'll...we'll...we'll talk soon."

"Thank you, Joe. Thank you."

She threw her arms around his waist in a tight, familiar hug. Josiah closed his eyes.

"No, no." He jerked away, leaving her standing with her arms limp at her sides. He wanted to assure her somehow. He leaned in and whispered close to her ear, "I'll come when I can."

She nodded and walked away.

Miriam started forward. Neither spoke as her path crossed Sarah's. As Miriam approached Josiah she smiled, a sad, sweet smile. "Goodbye...Joe."

Chapter 7

Annie wiped at her forehead with her sleeve. The heat of the day hadn't dissipated yet, and the evening sun was shining directly in her eyes. The heat billowed off the blacktop. Josiah still hadn't said a word since they pulled away from the shop. He held the reins so tightly his knuckles had gone white. She couldn't stand the silence anymore—he had to tell her what was going on. Otherwise, she'd be forced to tell Luke that Sarah was in Bliss Creek. And not just in Bliss Creek...at the blacksmith shop with Josiah.

How could he do this to Miriam? Again. Poor Miriam. Annie's heart ached for her friend as much as it did for her own situation. How had the two of them managed to fall in love with wayward men? "Well?"

"Well what?" Josiah slapped at a fly that buzzed in his face. "Well, nothing."

"Don't be dense." Annie was too tired to pick her words with care. "You've made so much progress. Luke is so happy. We're all so happy you're back, and now it's starting all over again."

"No, it's not." His face morose, Josiah turned the buggy onto the dirt road that led to their house. "I didn't know she was coming back."

"You didn't ask her to come here?"

"Why would I ask her to come to Bliss Creek?" The bitterness in his voice sliced through Annie. She'd been so sure Josiah was content back where he belonged. His tone said differently. "If I wanted to be with Sarah, I would've gone back to Wichita. And we all know how well that turned out for me the first time. I'm not an idiot."

Annie fended off memories of sitting in a hospital, waiting for the doctor to tell them if Josiah would live. "Are you sure? Because if you aren't, you need to tell Miriam. Now."

He jerked on the reins. Mooch snorted and halted by the front porch. "I'm sure."

Annie stood, anxious to get out of the buggy. She was too tired to think clearly. "Then you need to tell Luke that she came and you sent her home."

"She's not going home. She's staying with her cousin for a while." He fiddled with the reins in his hands. "And you can't tell Luke."

"He needs to know. He can talk to Sarah's father."

"She's eighteen. He can't stop her from coming here—or staying here." Josiah's gaze dropped. He adjusted his hat. "She says she's come here to join our faith."

Annie missed a step and almost fell out of the buggy. She caught herself and stepped down. "Join our faith?" Her mind's eye flashed to Sarah in the hospital waiting room. Purple flip-flops, jeans, a tank top, working a cell phone with both thumbs, her face intent underneath a kapp that didn't begin to cover her flaming red hair. "The bishop will never allow it. Not unless she can prove she's embracing the faith, and not you."

"Don't you think I know that?" Josiah clucked and snapped the reins. The buggy started forward. "Don't tell Luke. I'll convince her to go home. Soon. Right now, I'm going to do my chores."

Annie watched him drive away. Poor Miriam. Annie wouldn't have put up with her brother's shenanigans. But then he was her brother, and not the man she loved. She put up with David's stubbornness and his inability to tell her what was on his mind or in his heart. He insisted on carrying his burden like a big, fat log on his shoulder.

Irritated all over again, she glanced up at the house. It was sturdy and simple, like her. The clean white walls and green trim invited her into a home warm with welcome. The thought brought tears to the surface again. All the way home she'd swallowed tears so that Josiah wouldn't see her crying over David. Not that he would notice, so deep in a funk was he over the scene with Miriam and Sarah. But Miriam hadn't made a scene, Annie reminded herself. She'd simply said her goodbyes and trudged away, shoulders back, her head held high.

Annie recognized that posture. She used it herself. Every day. Calm and quiet strength on the outside, but on the inside, a heart that was breaking. Determined not to let the first tear spill, Annie gnawed on her already raw lower lip and strode across the porch to the door. It opened before she had a chance to reach for the knob. Luke stood in the doorway. "It's about time."

"Jah. It's been a long day." She brushed past him, not wanting to see the disapproval in his eyes. "I'm sorry I wasn't here to help with supper."

"Leah needs you to be here, *schweschder*. The girls are teething and fussy." His frown fierce, Luke tugged at his beard with an enormous, callused hand. "But that's not my concern right now. *Onkel* John stopped by. He told me what happened at the bakery."

"I guess everyone in the countryside has heard by now." Annie summoned a smile. She needed to tell him about Sarah. First things first. Let him recover from one shock before she delivered another blow. "Everything is fine. No one was hurt."

"You were shot at." Luke's inflection didn't change, but the furrow over his eyes deepened. "He missed. A poor shot?"

Annie repeated her story again.

"Mayor Haag is involved." Luke winced. He sank into the hickory rocker. "The Englischer brought a gun into the bakery with the intent to rob you. That was no accident. I'm concerned about you working in town. Every day more outsiders come. Too many."

"Most are tourists who want to take our pictures or buy something Amish. They mean no harm. This was an...unusual circumstance. It could've been any store in Bliss Creek." Annie sat in the other rocker and gripped her hands together. She kept her voice respectful. Since their parents' deaths, Luke was the head of the Shirack household. He had the final word. "Are you saying I'm not to work anymore? We need my income."

"You could go back to selling your baked goods at the produce stand." He rocked back and forth, his gaze directed at the windows, even though the dark green blinds were drawn against the setting sun. "Then you would be at home. With two sets of twins and three boys to oversee, Leah's working her fingers to the bone. Not that she complains. The cooking, the cleaning, the laundry, the sewing, the canning, the garden…and now the little ones are teething."

The recitation of Leah's tasks and the slight note of entreaty in her brother's voice surprised Annie. Luke had never given much thought to women's work, she was certain of that. Leah must have said something about Annie not helping enough. That had to be it. On top of everything else, Luke had to listen to Leah's opinions about his family. He'd held them together by sheer force of will since the accident. If taking care of his brothers and sisters as well as his own four children overwhelmed him, he never let it show—until now. Leah had a hand in it, to be sure.

"I'll cut back on my hours and do more work before I leave in the morning. I can get up earlier." Annie didn't want to add to his burden. She chose her words carefully. "I'll make sure I'm home in time to fix supper and clean up the kitchen."

"Mary and Lillie can clean up." Luke pursed his lips, making his beard bob. "It's the cooking. They're not old enough to handle that without close supervision. They're cutting the grass now and cleaning the chicken house, but their work on the laundry isn't up to Leah's standards yet. They're too short to hang clothes on the lines."

Leah *had* complained. At least Luke didn't disagree with Annie's plan. Hope coursed through her, bringing with it the courage to speak. Luke was still Luke, her big brother, protector, and defender.

"Don't worry about the bakery. Sergeant Parker called it an isolated incident." Those words had stuck in Annie's mind. *Isolated incident.* She hadn't felt isolated. She'd felt exposed. A chill shook her. "I'll get home earlier. I'll do the baking and leave the counter work to Sadie. She'll understand. I'm going to fix myself a bite to eat and then I'll do some sewing."

Luke rocked once and the chair squeaked under his weight. "Leah saved you a plate—stuffed pork chops and mashed potatoes. You weren't hurt? Flying glass?" He looked as if he were imagining the scene. "No bumps or bruises? Leah has a salve—"

"The man apologized before he took the money." Annie had been trying not to remember the ear-shattering blasts or the prickly shower of glass. "He said he needed to feed his child."

His forehead wrinkled, bushy eyebrows raised, Luke leaned forward and gripped his knees. He looked so much like Daed, she would never have to worry about forgetting her father's face. "Did you tell him we would give him food?"

"Jah. We offered him food from the bakery."

Luke shifted in the chair again. "Sometimes people start down the road and take a wrong turn. Then they don't know how to get turned around again."

Like Josiah, who had come back but still seemed mesmerized by the road he'd traveled.

"They need the rest of us to show them the way." Annie couldn't bring herself to tell Luke about Sarah, not when he looked so tired and worn from the weight of his responsibilities at home. "There's one other thing. Sergeant Parker made it sound like we would have to testify in court. Against the man."

"No." Luke's frown deepened. "We hold no grudge against this man. I'll speak to the bishop about it tomorrow when we have the meeting."

"He says I don't have a choice. I'm a witness. Sadie, Miriam, and I all are witnesses."

"Don't worry about it. I'll speak to the bishop."

Luke leaned back and closed his eyes. Annie stood in the doorway, unsure whether to leave him. She did worry about it and a lot of other things. Like her brother aging before her eyes.

"Luke?"

He opened his eyes. "What?"

"Is something else wrong?"

"Something beside my little schweschder getting shot at?"

His half-chuckle sounded weak. When was the last time she'd heard him laugh? "You seem…worried."

"Worrying is a sin."

How often had she heard that rule? She'd yet to hear someone explain how to stop worrying. "I know."

"It's nothing new." He sat his hat on his knee and ran a hand through thick curls. More forehead showed these days. His voice dropped to almost a whisper. "With our methods of growing crops, we have difficulty producing enough to cover our costs. We need to become more cost efficient or we could begin to see farms lost."

"Farms lost." Annie grabbed the doorframe and steadied herself. "Our farm?"

"It won't come to that." He looked up at her, his tone firm, his expression determined. "We will manage. We will learn."

Annie didn't know what that meant. She only knew she couldn't imagine her life without this home she'd grown up in. She couldn't imagine living in town. "Is there something I can do? Work more hours?"

"You do plenty. Pray for God's guidance and follow the *Ordnung*. Nothing more is asked of you."

"What will you do?"

"The same." Luke rubbed the spot along the ridge of his nose until it turned red. "And I've been considering switching from wheat to beef."

Cattle. Annie knew little about such things. "There's more money in that?"

"There are a lot of start-up costs, but the margin of profit is much greater and there are fewer issues with weather."

Start-up costs. Margin of profits. These things meant nothing to Annie, but she would raise the cattle herself if it meant staying in the home she'd grown up in and visiting with neighbors she'd known her whole life.

Before she could speak, high-pitched squalling whipped down the stairs and drowned out the silence. Luke opened his eyes. "That would be Esther. She'll wake Martha any second now."

"I can take them into my room." The way he could tell the cries of his daughters, one from the other, warmed Annie. "You two need to get some rest."

"Leah will put some ointment on their gums. They'll go back to sleep—God willing." He rose and started up the stairs, his steps heavy on the wood. "Don't worry about what I told you. God will lead us where He wants us to go." He stopped midway. "And David?"

"The same."

He nodded and tromped out of sight.

What else could she say? Annie contemplated the chasm that separated her from David. She had no idea how David was. He wouldn't tell her. Wouldn't let her in. Didn't even want her in the room. What did he fear?

If she'd learned anything from Mudder and Daed's deaths, it was that life consisted of a brilliant flash of light, like the sun as it peeked from behind the thunderheads or lightning rippling on the horizon. It faded before a person had a chance to reach for it, let alone touch it. If she closed her eyes—whether from fear or uncertainty—she would miss the golden, shiny God moments. Walking along the pond, skipping rocks and watching the turtles sun themselves. Playing volleyball with the children. Picking strawberries. Feeding the chickens. Rocking baby nieces. Baking bread. Eating watermelon. Sweet moments.

With pain came joy, blossoming, magnificent joy. Like baptism. Like marriage. Like giving birth. Annie remained as certain of that as she was of the wooden floor under her bare feet. Time shot forward in leaps and bounds, making each moment something to be cherished. She wanted to cherish time with David before it ran out. However short or long it turned out to be.

He didn't feel the same way. She should stop waiting for the time in which he would. If God's plan for her did not include marriage to David, she had to learn to accept it and move on. Luke expected her to marry and start a life of her own. She could not continue to add to her brother's burden. She didn't want to be a burden to anyone. She only wanted to marry, have children, and grow old with the man she loved. Wasn't that what every Plain woman wanted? Why wouldn't God want her to have that? She didn't have the temerity to ask. Her lot was to accept and obey. Somehow she had to accept the possibility that God intended her for another. She had to bury her feelings for David.

If only she could figure out how.

Suddenly too tired to eat or sew, she followed in Luke's footsteps. At the top of the stairs, she hesitated. The crying had ceased to pour from Leah and Luke's room. She trudged down the hallway, intent on slipping into bed.

Tomorrow would be another day. She would catch up on the darning of socks and letting out the hems in the boys' pants tomorrow. From little Joseph and William all the way to Josiah, the boys seemed to get taller every day...and needed clothes to match. Lately Mark looked like he planned to go wading in the pond, with the bottoms of his pants not coming close to reaching his ankles. The mountain of work never receded.

A plaintive, half-muffled sob stopped her. It came from her sisters' room. Lillie and Mary should have been asleep by now. Annie opened their door a crack and peered in. Mary knelt by the bed, her hands clasped in front of her.

"God, I just wondered if you could maybe help me." Another little sob. "Leah is mean to me and Lillie. All the time. I know you saw her yell at us today. I didn't mean to spill the flour. And Lillie tried to stand on a footstool to hang up the pants on the line. Josiah's pants are bigger than she is. They only got a little dirt on them. Maybe you could help the twins sleep more so Leah wouldn't be so tired. I'd like that a lot. Thank you. Amen."

Mary laid her head on the quilt and sobbed. The sound shattered Annie's heart and scattered the pieces across the heavens. She slipped into the room and knelt next to her little sister. "*Ach*, schweschder, Mary, it's all right."

The girl threw herself against Annie's chest. "Shhh. Leah will hear you. She's mad at us."

"Why?"

"She says we just make more work. We don't help. We hinder. That's what she says."

"I'm sorry I haven't been here more. I'll be here to help more. I promise." Lillie and Mary were six years old. They were growing up without a mother and father. Leah had a responsibility to teach them, not terrorize them. Annie's resolve grew. "I promise."

Mary wiped her wet face on Annie's apron. "I miss Emma."

"Me too."

"And Catherine."

"Jah."

"Can Emma live at home again?"

"No, little schweschder, she's married to Thomas now. You know that."

"But Catherine could. She didn't get married. She doesn't have a husband."

They really didn't know that. Catherine had been gone more than a year. Not one word in all that time. As was to be expected. After being baptized, she'd chosen to forsake the Plain ways and seek an education in the Englisch world. "She's not coming back."

Mary wiped at her face with the back of her arm. The tears ceased. She crawled under the sheet next to Lillie, who slumbered peacefully, an occasional little snore the only noise in the room.

"Goodnight, Annie."

"Sweet dreams."

"You promise?"

"I promise."

Annie closed the door without a sound. Less time at the bakery. Less time with David. It was for the best. Her sisters needed her. Her family needed her. David didn't. She would learn to accept that.

Somehow.

Chapter 8

D avid signed the last piece of paper with his neat, careful signature and pushed the paper across the counter to the discharge clerk. She acknowledged the gesture with a quick smile. "You're good to go."

"What about the bill?"

The clerk made a show of studying a computer screen that he couldn't see from his side of the counter. "Well, it shows here that your mother took care of it, Mr. Plank."

He didn't like to be called Mr. Plank. Not even his father had used that courtesy title. They were simple folks. No need for titles. He also disliked that his mother tried to carry his burdens for him. She shouldn't be using her funds from the bakery to take care of his medical bills.

"How could she? When?"

"She made arrangements before she left yesterday. In fact, it looks like we'll owe her some money. She insisted on paying a lump sum in advance." The clerk smiled again. "Sweet woman, your mother. She said you would be upset and to tell you not to take it out on me."

Sounded like his mother. He would straighten this out when he returned to the house later. Right now, he had to get to the horse auction. Making an appearance would reassure his brothers that he could still carry his weight—at the farm and at the bakery.

Ignoring the disapproving glare of the nurse, he sidestepped the wheelchair and strode down the hallway. He couldn't get to the door fast enough, and he didn't need a wheelchair to do it. His desire to flee the building propelled him quicker than wheels could.

"Mister. Mister David!" The sound of a small, high voice brought him out of his reverie. A head covered with the slightest brown peach fuzz peeked through a doorway. "*Pssst!* Over here!"

David slowed. Kinsey looked both ways down the long hallway. Empty except for the nurse who was headed in the opposite direction. Holding pink rabbit-eared slippers in her hands, Kinsey traipsed barefoot across the space that separated them. "Hey, where are you going?"

"Home."

"No fair." Her bottom lip protruded and her sky blue eyes turned stormy. "I want to go home."

"Your doctor knows best." The door to freedom beckoned only a few feet away. Apparently, Kinsey was trying to make a break for it. David sidled past her. "He'll send you home soon enough."

Or God would take her home. David mentally banged a hand against his head. *Stupid.* He had no idea what Kinsey's prognosis might be. Whether she would go home at all. Not every cancer patient did. He had no right to get her hopes up. He sucked in air and faced her. She looked so sad. "How long have you been here?"

"This time?"

This time. He knew that feeling. "Yes."

"I mark the days off on the calendar in my room before I go to sleep at night." She wrinkled her nose. "Last night, it was seven."

Seven days. A lifetime for a child—or an adult, for that matter. He glanced at the empty wheelchair still parked in front of the discharge station. "What floor are you on?"

"Second."

"Come on." Her mother was probably searching frantically this very moment. "How about I give you a ride?"

"I ride in those things all the time." Her face turned morose, but she made an effort to smile. Her lips were chapped and cracked. "I want to ride on a horse. A black stallion. Named King. I wanna ride real fast and jump over big logs and rivers and gallop all over the place."

"Horses are okay too, but you've never ridden in a chair pushed by me." David had ridden horses his whole life. They were simply a form of transportation to him. She spoke like a city kid who read a lot of books. He bowed and swept his arm out in an exaggerated flourish. "Your buggy awaits you."

Kinsey's gaze strayed toward the double doors. Her shoulders slumped, she climbed into the chair and stuck her slippers on her feet. "Whatever."

The discharge clerk frowned. David leaned over the desk and whispered, "I'm taking her back upstairs. Her mother will be looking for her."

"I should really call a nurse—"

"I've been coming here for how long?"

"Too long, Mr. Plank. Just go directly there." She pushed her glasses up a long nose and smiled. "Do not pass go. Do not collect two hundred dollars."

He smiled back. Even Plain folks got that reference. "Promise."

He grabbed the handles. He would be late for the horse auction, but his brothers would hold a spot for him. "We're off!"

He pushed her as fast as he could safely. His stomach lurched and his legs trembled, but he didn't slow down.

"Faster!" Grinning, Kinsey clapped her hands. "Faster, faster!"

He wanted to oblige her, but his body wouldn't let him.

Fortunately, the elevator door loomed. He slid the chair sideways and slapped the button. *Thank You, Lord, for short hallways and long elevator rides.*

Strange prayer for a Plain man. God would understand. So would the deacon, were he here. Thankfully, he wasn't.

On the second floor, he gave Kinsey a repeat performance. They were at her door in seconds. Gasping, he tugged it open. "Home sweet home."

Home it was. David got a quick impression of walls covered with pictures—some torn from magazines, some hand-drawn—all of horses. The bed was covered with a bright green and blue quilt and stuffed animals of every variety. In the middle of all that chaos stood Kinsey's mom, hands on her hips. The purple dress was gone. Today she wore a waitress uniform with the words *HomeTown Restaurant* embroidered over the white shirt pocket.

"There you are. I was just coming to look for you—again. You're making Grammy crazy!"

"I'm sorry, Mommy." Kinsey climbed out of the chair and crawled into bed. She closed her eyes. "I'm sleepy now. Go away."

Willow's face crumpled and her hands went to her mouth.

"Goodnight, Kinsey." David backed toward the doorway. "I'd better return the chair."

To his chagrin, Willow followed him to the door.

"Thanks for bringing her back." Her voice barely above a whisper, she sniffed and wiped at her face with a wadded-up tissue. "Her Grammy doesn't have the energy to keep up with her—it's like herding a cat. She called me, said she had a migraine. I came quick as I could."

"Kinsey said you were at work." David didn't remember seeing Willow around. Bliss Creek was a small town. Not that it was any of his business. "I'd better go."

Willow kept talking, seemingly unaware of David's hand on the door or his desire to flee. "I got a job waitressing to try to cover the bills. It helps some, and my aunt helps too. She's so sweet to us."

"What about your...husband...Kinsey's father?" David wanted to reel in the question before it escaped his mouth. It was none of his business. The Englischers didn't always have family the way Plain folks did. A father and a mother married and together. "I'm sorry. It's none of my—"

"He's not in the picture. I didn't have insurance so I had to sell everything we had to help pay the medical bills. When that was gone, I came here to stay with my aunt. Kinsey calls her Grammy. She's a godsend."

No husband. No father. No man to carry his share of the load. It wasn't right. David glanced at the walls covered with horses. "She said something about riding horses."

"She hasn't been able to go to school much since we moved here so she spends a lot of time reading books. You know, like *Black Beauty*." Willow touched a drawing that featured a purple horse wearing a ribbon around a long stick neck. "She thinks we should get a horse and she should get to ride it. Like we could afford that. She just knows she read a book and it sounded like fun."

David couldn't imagine not being able to ride a horse. Around Bliss Creek, children learned to ride before they learned to muck the stalls and feed the chickens. "You don't know how to ride?"

"Me? I grew up in Kansas City. I can handle a Harley, but a horse? And even if I could ride one, how would I afford it?"

"When she gets better, when she gets out, maybe...I mean...every farm around Bliss Creek has horses." David plucked at his suspenders. He was the youngest child in his family. He had no experience with children. "There are a couple of stables where you can take lessons—"

Willow motioned him into the hallway. He followed, drawn by the excruciating pain in the woman's face. It looked so familiar. She sank against the wall, her hands to her cheeks. "She's not getting better. I don't think she's getting out. Not permanently, anyway."

David contemplated her choked, tear-soaked words. He understood the depths of her desperation, but somehow seeing it on her face made him realize how it must look to others. Like giving up. Such a lack of faith and hope. "Doctors can do so much now."

Willow shook her head, her hands still glued to her face. After a few moments she straightened and dropped them.

"Kinsey has acute myelogenous leukemia. Usually adults get it, not kids." Willow wrapped her arms around her middle as if the clinic's refrigerated air chilled her. "She needs a bone marrow transplant, but we haven't been able to find a match. Her dad was Latino. I'm Caucasian. Which makes her a hard match."

Even with his own experiences David knew little of this sort of thing, but he nodded. "So you'll keep looking until you find this match."

"If only it were that easy." She blew her nose hard with a sodden tissue, the sound loud in the empty hallway. "I'm sorry to dump all this on you, practically a stranger. You have your own problems. Go home to your family. To that pretty girl with the green eyes. She must be waiting for you."

"No. She's not waiting." At least he hoped not. "If there is anything I can do…"

He stopped. The urge to help was too strong to ward off. If nothing else, it would take his mind off his own problems. Clear away the wooly cotton in his brain. "We have horses. I could give her lessons."

"Oh, I don't know." Worry and fear creased Willow's face. "Her immune system is weak from the chemo. I don't want her to be exposed to a lot of germs."

"I understand." David tipped his hat. Kinsey's mother had the last word on what was best for her daughter. "I'd better go, then."

He started down the hall.

"Wait."

He glanced back.

"Do you have a black horse?"

"No. But there are black horses around."

"She's seven years old."

Small for her age. Her growth stunted by her disease.

"Yes." He waited for Willow to marshal the words. She seemed to be having an argument with herself. She had to convince herself. He had no part in that fight.

"She hasn't done one fun thing in over a year. Not one. Just needle pokes and tests and medicine that makes her throw up and pain and more pain."

David nodded. Nothing to say to that. He could picture every stage. The feeling sick and not getting better. The doctor's appointments. The tests. The diagnosis. The downward spiral into a never-ending series of new lows brought on by milestones in the treatment. He waited.

"Maybe I'll think about it. The riding, I mean." Her fingers wrapped around her thick braids and held on tight, her knuckles white with the force of her grip. "I want her to have some fun, you know. She should have some fun."

"I'll see if I can find a black horse."

"A stallion?"

"A beauty."

Her already wet eyes filled once more with tears. "A beauty," she agreed.

Chapter 9

Tugging Mark along, Josiah followed Luke past the booths selling produce, tack, and crafts to the doors of the fairgrounds arena. Mark wanted to stop and look at things, but Josiah didn't want to lose sight of their older brother. In this crowd, they might not find each other again until the horse auction ended.

"Stinks around here, doesn't it?" A mischievous grin on his face, Mark put two fingers on his nose. "*Pe-uuu!* Smells like you after a day at the shop."

Josiah grinned, refusing to take offense. He breathed deeply instead. The smell of manure, horseflesh, and sweat mingled with the aroma of sweet hay in the hot, moist air. It reminded him of long summer days when he was younger and Daed told him to muck out the horse stalls. Things had seemed simple then. Before the rumspringa and girls and decisions about baptism.

"It's the smell of prosperity for a farmer." Josiah grinned at his younger brother. "Breathe it in, *bruder*. This is your future."

Mark skipped back a step and bumped into an older man with a cane.

"Watch it, little boy." The man managed to stay upright and he didn't sound too upset. "Us older folks aren't as spry as we used to be."

"Sorry—"

54

"Keep up!"

Luke's terse tone made Josiah jolt forward, Mark in tow. Luke had been grumpy from the moment they left the house, totally ignoring Mark's excited chatter. The boy had never been to an auction and Luke seemed bent on spoiling it for him. Josiah kept waiting for him to say something about Sarah. His demeanor meant something had happened, but whatever it was, Luke didn't seem to want to share it.

They squeezed in between a couple of Englischers who were deep in a conversation about combines and grabbed a spot against the railing. They'd have a decent vantage point.

"See, there's the sorrel I told you about." Luke pointed to a sturdy-looking mare. "Samuel Hartenstein says she's trained and reliable. She's a little on the small side, but he says she's a good worker."

Josiah simply nodded. Luke didn't really need his opinion. His brother had checked out all the available livestock the day before. He was a good judge of horseflesh. He had plenty of experience. "I—"

"What do you think?" Exasperation made the words sharp. "Or do you have an opinion on anything that matters?"

Stung, Josiah felt his face heat up. His brother might be strict, but he was rarely unfair. The two men next to him shifted away, their voices loud as they argued the pros and cons of different brands of farm implements. Josiah leaned closer to Luke, trying to make himself heard over the din.

"She's a good-looking horse. You checked her out. The problem will be everyone will want her. The price may go too high."

"She's a beauty—" Mark began.

"Hush," Luke interrupted. "I asked Josiah his opinion. Josiah, you haven't seen her up close, and you haven't seen any of the others. Did Daed teach you nothing about buying horses?"

Luke hadn't asked him about the others. "What is wrong?" he asked in a low voice. "Did you hear something? Did someone say something about me to you?"

"Why? What have you done? Never mind. Not now." Luke gripped the railing so tight his fingers turned white. He glanced around, then moved closer. "After the auction, I want you two to go to a meeting with me."

"A meeting?" Josiah's plan to visit Sarah at her aunt's house after a stop at the blacksmith shop faded away. He had to talk to her—he had to send her home before her presence did more damage. "I told Caleb I'd take a couple of jobs for him this afternoon at the shop."

"So push the time back. The bishop wants us to talk about farming practices—all of us together as a community." Luke's gaze glanced off Josiah. "I figure you might know a bit about that, what with the time you spent at community college. Mark needs to hear this too. We must all work harder, work better, if we are to take care of our families."

Mark's expression said he was as baffled as Josiah. The boy was eleven. A hard worker, but far from ready to shoulder family responsibilities. He was barely tall enough to handle the plow. Fear stabbed Josiah in the gut. Strange as it seemed, considering the sudden, irrevocable loss of their parents, he'd never entertained the notion that something could happen to his solid-as-a-railroad-tie older brother. "Why? Are you not going to be around to do it? Are you sick?"

"No. I'm not sick." Luke stopped, his beard bobbing up and down as he struggled for control. "It's time for you to step up and have a voice in those decisions. You have an interest in more modern ways of farming. Or at least you did."

Luke had never wanted to hear about those modern methods before. His back had to be against an immovable wall for him to consider them now. Josiah didn't crow over this bittersweet victory. Too much was at stake. A way of life he'd learned to appreciate after his sojourn into the Englisch world. "I'll do whatever I can, but you know that I never finished a course—"

"Hey, the Shirack brothers!" Timothy Plank, David's oldest brother, wormed his way through the masses. Jonathan and David followed. The men could've been triplets. "You have your eye on the sorrel, do you?"

Luke's expression told Josiah to close his mouth. Timothy was Luke's closest friend, but he apparently didn't want to discuss these changes in front of him. Josiah stifled his questions. It would have to wait.

Instead, he studied David. His friend's face glistened with sweat. Knowing him, he'd left the hospital too soon. Again. As Timothy and Luke discussed the sorrel, Josiah edged his way toward David. "Did they let you out of the hospital, or did you escape? You don't look like you feel better."

"Not you too." David rolled his eyes. "Don't make me say it."

"Say what?"

"Do you know how many times a day I say I'm fine?"

"I'm guessing a lot."

"Hundreds."

"You exaggerate."

"Not really."

"Could it be people want to know? You know, like out of neighborly concern?"

David shoved his hat back on his head. It hung precariously loose, and he clamped it down with one hand. "Or they're nosey."

"Plain folks are never nosey."

A small grin flitted across David's face. Finally. Josiah grinned back. "Now that you're feeling better, are you going to bring Annie home from the singing tomorrow night? Take her on a little buggy ride?"

The grin faded. David edged closer to Josiah. His gaze traveled to Luke and Timothy, the scowls on their faces too intense for a horse auction. "You should mind your own business. What's this I hear about Sarah Kauffman being in town?"

For closed-mouthed people with no phones and no fast transportation, the Plain sure knew how to make news travel. Josiah glared at David and shook his head. *Not in front of Luke and Mark.*

His eyebrows raised, David frowned. He started to say something, then stopped. "There're the Yonkers brothers."

Josiah swallowed against the roiling of his stomach. He hadn't done anything to anybody. Made no promises. He watched as Miriam's brothers passed by. Paul's gaze met his, and both men nodded carefully.

"Friendly." David inched closer. "What do you suppose they've heard?"

"I can't believe Miriam told them."

"Why should she protect you?"

"Because I didn't do anything. It isn't my fault—"

"All right, folks, let's get this show on the road." The auctioneer's booming voice filled the arena. "We've got some outstanding horse-flesh on the auction block today. Get your numbers ready. Who wants to take home this gorgeous Morgan? He's a beaut, folks, stands sixteen hands high, comes from an owner who's retiring. He's road and ride ready. Not a thing wrong with him. Who'll give me twenty-five hundred? Come on, anybody?"

Jonathan's number went up. So did half a dozen other white plac-ards with black numbers on them. The bidding contest heated up. Relieved, Josiah concentrated on the auction and tried to forget the accusing look on David's face. For this moment, at least, he could lose himself in the business at hand. Horses were a critical factor in the suc-cess of a farm, and even more so for Plain businesses. Horses were their mode of transportation. They were a substitute for the motor-driven equipment that gave *Englischers* an advantage when it came to plant-ing and harvesting. Of course, horses were much less expensive to buy than farm equipment and feed was cheaper than diesel.

Josiah wondered how far the bishop would be willing to go—how far the community would be willing to go to make sure their farming operations continued to support their families. Once he'd dreamed of attending junior college and learning about agriculture so he could produce crops in a more efficient, cost-effective way. That plan had been dismantled when he'd chosen to return to his community. It sat on a shelf in the corner of his mind, gathering dust. Maybe now he would be allowed to call upon some of that knowledge to help his fam-ily and his friends. Leave the heat of the forge behind and return to the land.

His happiness at what price? The community forced to change practices that went back generations?

Determined, he focused on the sale.

Two hours later Josiah trudged from the barn, trying to keep up with Luke's long, determined stride. Mark followed at a run. "Well, there's always next time."

"Yes, next time. If we'd had more cash on hand…" Luke's distracted response trailed away. "Let's go."

"Go where? Where's the meeting?"

Timothy, David right behind him, surged through the huge double doors, pushed forward by a sea of people still chattering about who'd bought what. "See you at Bishop Kelp's house," Timothy called. "As soon as we pay up and load the horse. Sorry you didn't get the sorrell."

Luke shrugged. "See you at the bishop's."

"The bishop?" They were going to the bishop's house? Josiah's stomach heaved. What if someone had seen Sarah in town? What if it came up at the meeting? "Luke, couldn't you just tell us what the bishop says?"

"Get in. It's time you stepped into a man's shoes."

Chapter 10

Josiah stood in the back of the room, Mark next to him. His brother's mouth hung open in a wide yawn. Josiah elbowed him and Mark grunted, then slapped his hand over his mouth. Josiah sneaked a quick look around to see if anyone had noticed. All gazes were on the bench where Bishop Kelp sat, arms crossed over his paunch. His sober expression did nothing to calm Josiah's nerves. Nor did the faces of Deacon Altman and Deacon Pierce, who sat tall on either side of him.

Bishop Kelp's house looked exactly like the Shirack house. As did every other home in the community. No better. No worse. All the other benches were full. At least one representative from every family in the district had come. As one of the youngest men in attendance, Josiah would be expected to leave the discussion to his elders. He wasn't sure why Luke had wanted him and Mark there at all.

"Two years ago many of you lost your crops to the tornado." Bishop Kelp's sonorous voice carried to every corner. He didn't beat around the bush. "And this year we've had almost no rain. Many of you are struggling to make ends meet. There's been talk about using newer... more modern methods of farming in order to have a greater margin of profit."

Surprised, Josiah peered to his left, then his right. No one moved. They barely seemed to be breathing. Was Micah Kelp saying he would agree to this? If that were the case, Josiah would have to help Luke. Although he'd never completed the courses he started at the junior college in Wichita, he'd learned a lot. He'd read about the use of chemical pesticides and fertilizers to increase yields. He could use that knowledge.

"Such talk is not to be tolerated." Deacon Altman chimed in, his gaze somber. "Each one of you has the responsibility to hold your neighbors, as well as your family, to the Ordnung."

So much for that question. Josiah sank back against the wall. Things did not change. He shouldn't chafe against that. This was his lot. To be a blacksmith and to yield to the Ordnung. When would that become natural to him? Others took to it like breathing. For him it was like trying to breathe underwater. Always a struggle. Always gasping for air in order to live for one more moment, one more day.

"No motorized tractors. No rubber tires. No engine-driven combines or threshing machines. No computers for tracking expenses or researching new pesticides or ways to increase yield." Bishop Kelp joined in the chorus started by Deacon Altman. "We have used manure for three hundred years and it costs us nothing. It's been proven over and over that our ways work."

Then why were they teetering on the edge? Things might change in other communities, but not here in southern Kansas. Josiah willed himself to keep his face passive and his mouth shut. This conversation belonged to his elders. They were wiser. They understood the long-term impact of change on their way of living better than he.

"What we can do is talk amongst ourselves about other, more traditional means of maintaining our way of life through hard work and careful use of our resources," Deacon Pierce said. "Who has ideas?"

The room remained quiet for several minutes. Bishop Kelp leaned back in his chair, his face passive. He didn't seem the least bit bothered by the silence.

Peter Blount stood, his chair scraping against the wooden floor in a startling screech. His bony face turned red. He took off his hat and smashed it between his two weathered hands. "There's been talk that maybe we should concentrate more on livestock, less on crops. Pigs, cattle, sheep, chickens." He cleared his throat. "I'm not much of a talker in front of everyone, but I thought it was worth bringing it up."

"That's fine, Peter." Deacon Altman's voice was gentle, just as it had been at all of Josiah's counseling sessions. He was the only man Josiah knew who could make a person feel like he'd been to the woodshed for a whipping without raising a hand or his voice. "I've heard that too. Switching to cattle, raising them for beef."

"I've talked to some of the Englischers about that." Luke spoke up, surprising Josiah—both that he had spoken and that he had talked to Englischers about farming. "They say the start-up for raising cattle for beef is steep, but they're doing much better than they were with the wheat. They quit farming wheat a good fifteen, twenty years ago when wheat prices hit rock bottom."

"I don't know. I think it's risky to invest our small reserves in cattle right now." Solomon Yonkers shook his massive, white-haired head. "We're barely holding on as it is. Plus there are a lot of regulations involved in raising and selling livestock. Regulations that make it more expensive and bring us closer to the Englischers who must inspect and review and tell us how we must keep our buildings and our animals. It will affect us in ways we cannot see right now."

"If we don't do it now, those reserves will be gone and we'll have nothing to start over with if we lose our wheat again next year," Paul Yonkers countered, disagreeing with his daed. Again, a surprise. These meetings were full of them. "The younger folks need to have some way of supporting our new families when we start them. Farms have been divided among sons for so many generations now that they've become too small to support us. It's the big farms that are making money in this day and age."

"That's true," Luke said. "Maybe we split up. Some stay with wheat. Others experiment with starting new herds."

"And some continue to work in town," Thomas added. "Those jobs in town supplementing our income are important."

Easy for Thomas to say. He had his own farm. A good-sized one at that. If Luke split the Shirack farm with Josiah and Mark, they would be down to thirty-five acres each. Josiah wanted to raise cattle. He wanted to raise crops too. He wanted to farm. But a person didn't always get what he wanted. If anyone knew that, he did. *Keep your mouth shut. Keep your mouth shut. Keep your mouth shut.*

"Could it be this drought is God's way of telling us to diversify? To use better, more modern methods, more modern equipment?" The questions burst out of him of their own accord. Luke shook his head vigorously, but it was too late. Josiah plowed ahead. "I mean, how do we know that isn't God's plan for us?"

Bishop Kelp steepled thick, hairy fingers. "We must not presume to know what the Lord's plan for us is." His stern gaze traveled the room. "None of us. Our focus must be on the Ordnung. On keeping our children on that path that steers them far from worldly ways. Breaking from our tradition now will not serve that purpose."

Bishop Kelp's gaze came to rest on Josiah. He swallowed and forced himself not to look away. After a second the bishop moved on. "What thoughts do the rest of you have?"

No one spoke. The curtains rustled in a faint breeze that passed through the open windows, providing the only sound.

"There are more and more influences battering us now." Paul Yonkers finally broke the silent stalemate. He spoke rapidly. His features—so like Miriam's—were drawn tight with nerves or excitement, Josiah couldn't be sure which. "Perhaps a move would be better for all of us. I've heard there's land to be had in Montana. New districts have started in Colorado. Parties have been sent out by other districts to Alaska and even Mexico. There are those among us who seem to delight in bringing worldly influences to our community, like snakes poised to strike."

"Let's speak our minds here." Bishop Kelp's sharp tone said he'd reached the end of his patience. "If you have something to say, say it straight out."

Paul shifted from one dusty boot to the other. "Maybe it's Josiah who should say it. Tell us, what was that Mennonite girl Sarah Kauffman doing in the blacksmith shop yesterday?"

Chapter 11

Annie wiped damp palms on her apron and put her hand on the door to Bliss Creek's police station. She'd never been in this building before. She couldn't ever have imagined a time when it would be necessary. Luke would not be happy—if he found out. But he would never know. For now, he was still at the horse auction. The thought made her feel sneaky. Still, she had to do it. She'd been thinking about it all morning through the noise of the older Plank brothers, along with Samuel and Paul Yonkers, putting in the new windows at the bakery. She couldn't bear the thought of Logan McKee all alone in a cell. Maybe he felt guilty. Maybe he felt sorry.

Go on. Go in. She peeked inside. A ceiling fan whirred overhead, making a gentle, monotonous sound. She slipped over the threshold. Officer Bingham sat at a desk, his feet propped up, a *Hunting and Fishing* magazine draped over his belly. Music, tinny and indistinct, dribbled from a clock radio with big red numbers on it that set on a shelf over his head. His eyes were closed. She cleared her throat and let the door shut with a heavy click.

Officer Bingham swung his feet from the desk and sat up with a startled snort. "Yes sir! Yes sir!" The magazine slid to the floor. He bent over and smacked his forehead on the desk. "Ouch!"

Annie swallowed a giggle. It wasn't nice to laugh at people in pain, but Officer Bingham reminded her of a steer who'd mistaken a house for the barn. Suddenly she didn't feel so nervous. "Sergeant Bingham, it's just me. Annie Shirack."

Rubbing his forehead, he righted himself. "Sorry, ma'am. I was just…I mean, I…just keeping up with the latest information on firearms, ma'am."

Unless that information was written on the insides of Officer Bingham's eyelids, Annie doubted that. "I'm here to see Logan McKee."

"Pardon me?" Officer Bingham's eyes widened and his mouth dropped open. "You can't see the suspect. You're a witness."

"No, I'm not. I told Sergeant Parker I wasn't—"

The door swung open so hard it banged against the inside wall. A young woman trotted in with a little girl in tow. The woman had long, stringy blond hair and a silver stud in her nose. The girl's hair was a thick mat of dark curls that hadn't seen a brush in a long while. They didn't look much alike, but both wore pink T-shirts. The girl's had something purple and sticky-looking all over it and seemed to be a size too big. The woman's, on the other hand, stretched tight over a large belly. She was expecting. Both T-shirts made Annie long for a washtub and some soap.

She averted her eyes, aware that she'd been staring. She didn't care for it when people stared at her long dress and kapp. But why would someone bring a small child into the police station?

"I'm here to see Logan McKee." The woman spoke with the same southern drawl Annie had noticed in Logan's speech. "I'm his… we're…we're together." Her face turned the color of ripe tomatoes. "I'm Charisma Chiasson. I need to see him."

Charisma Chiasson. What a beautiful name. Annie rolled it around in her head. Plain people choose plain names. Biblical names most times. That way no one put on airs or became too fancy. But the name Charisma Chiasson wasn't fancy; it reminded Annie of the earth. Like David did with his eyes the color of wet, freshly plowed dirt. *No.* As of last night, she had set aside thinking of David as any more than Josiah's closest friend. "I also would like to see Logan McKee," she said firmly.

Charisma eyed Annie. Annie smiled at her, but didn't speak. What did one say to the friend of someone who'd pointed a gun at you?

"You're from the bakery, aren't you?" Charisma's face turned an even deeper shade of scarlet. "You're the one he—"

"Whoa, now." Officer Bingham raised both of his big hands. "Just back up the train, both of y'all. Hold on." He hitched up the belt that held his gun and lumbered around his desk. "This isn't visiting hours, ladies. You'll have to come back in the morning. Nine to ten. Except tomorrow is Sunday so you best wait until Monday."

Annie glanced around the office. Empty. Knowing Bliss Creek as she did, she could be almost certain Logan McKee was the only person currently in the jail. "I work in the mornings. Would it be a terrible problem to allow me to see him now—just for a minute or two?"

"Why do you want to see him?" Charisma tugged the little girl away from a crumpled soda can she was attempting to pull from a wastebasket. "Stop it, Gracie."

Grace. Just as Annie imagined, she had blue eyes, fair skin, and dark hair. It was for her that Logan had committed this crime. "To see if he needs anything."

"Gracie, stop it!" Charisma hoisted the girl on to her hip. Then she winced and rubbed her stomach. "Why would you do that?" she asked, turning back to Annie.

Annie searched for words to explain her desire to be charitable. Upbringing. Grace—the other kind of grace. Would the woman understand that? "He's in jail."

Seeming to ignore Annie's response, the woman took a step closer to Officer Bingham.

"I really, really need to see him." She swiped at her face with a crumpled tissue. "I need to talk to him. Please."

"Rules is rules, ma'am. Ain't a hotel we're runnin' here. He made a phone call. That's about all he's allowed for now. The judge will come in from Wichita to hold court on Tuesday morning." Officer Bingham pawed at the stubble on his double chin. "I'm sorry. Come back Monday."

"Did he call a lawyer? Ouch, Gracie, stop it!" Charisma ripped Gracie's hand from her tangled hair. "He needs a lawyer."

"The judge will assign him a public defender when he's arraigned, since he's indigent and all."

Indigent. Annie searched for the meaning of the word. Didn't have money. Of course he didn't have money. If he had, he wouldn't have been robbing a bakery. Never having been in this world of guns and laws and courts, she hadn't thought about the money Logan McKee would need to defend himself.

"Then he'll get out on bond?" For the first time, Charisma looked hopeful. Tears welled up in her blue eyes. "He'll get out?"

"Depends on how good his lawyer is. And whether he can come up with the money for bail." Officer Bingham didn't sound like he held out much hope of either. "Plus he don't live around here. That makes him a flight risk."

The hope on Charisma's face faded as quickly as it had appeared. She started to back toward the door, her lips pressed together in an obvious attempt not to cry. Sergeant Parker strode in just in time to nearly mow her down. Mayor Haag traipsed in behind him so he had no place to go. "Whoops, sorry!" He grabbed Charisma's arm and steadied her. "Easy there."

"Whoops!" Gracie crowed. She clapped her hands. "Whoops!"

"Don't worry about it." Charisma rushed past the newcomers and disappeared through the door.

Mayor Haag frowned and rubbed her arm as if she'd somehow been damaged by the encounter. "Young people. No manners these days. Absolutely no manners."

"That was the prisoner's girlfriend," Officer Bingham threw in, his chest puffed up in a self-important pose. "And I'm guessing that was his kid."

Frowning, Sergeant Parker removed his hat and ran a hand through short hair. "He said he had a family here, but he wouldn't tell me where they were staying—not that they have a lot of choices here. Did she tell you anything?"

"Well, no. I, mean, I was gonna ask, but she got all out of sorts on account of the fact that I wouldn't let her see the prisoner—"

"He has a name." Annie couldn't help herself. "The prisoner has a name. It's Logan McKee."

"I'm sorry, Annie." Sergeant Parker massaged his hat with both hands. "If this seems harsh to you, I apologize, but we're just doing our job."

"I would like Logan McKee to get out of jail now." Annie took a deep breath and called upon her small reserve of courage. "He's had time to think about what he did and repent. I know he's very sorry."

The mayor laughed, a high, irritating cackle. "Good grief, child—"

Sergeant Parker held up a hand. "Mayor, please." He turned to Annie. "I know your people do things differently, but Officer Bingham and I have to uphold the law. People can't just go around trying to rob innocent ladies like yourself, Miss Miriam, and Mrs. Plank. We have to make sure Bliss Creek is safe for everyone. Otherwise, the crooks will come in and take over."

"I don't think Logan McKee is a crook." Annie straightened, drawing herself up to her full five feet. "He made a mistake. I'm sure if you ask him, he'll tell you he won't do it again. I could vouch for him."

Sergeant Parker slapped a big hand to his mouth, Mayor Haag snorted, and Officer Bingham laughed right out loud. "Vouch for a criminal you'd never seen before? Aren't you the silliest girl—"

"No need to call names," Sergeant Parker interrupted the officer. "Nothing wrong with a little compassion, even if it is misplaced."

"That man does a mighty fine imitation of a crook." Mayor Haag tapped a long painted fingernail on the counter that separated the foyer from the office. "And he's staying right where he is until the judge comes in."

Sergeant Parker stepped closer to Annie. "I'm sorry, really I am. Is there anything else I can do for you?"

Something about his gentle tone reminded Annie of the way Luke talked to a spooked horse, or little Joseph when he had a nightmare. Annie edged toward the door. Sergeant Parker's height always made her feel young and small. Or maybe it was the gun on his hip. "I should go now. It'll be time for fixing supper soon. I'll work something out and come back Monday morning."

"Absolutely not!" The mayor wedged herself between Annie and the door. "You can't be seeing him period. You're a witness. I want to make sure you'll be at the courthouse on Tuesday. McKee will be arraigned. The city attorney wants all the witnesses there. We don't want this criminal getting out on bond before his trial."

Feeling like a deer caught in a hunter's sights, Annie looked to Sergeant Parker for help. He gave her a slight shrug and an apologetic smile. No help from that quarter. She faced the mayor. "I'll have to talk with my brother about that."

Mayor Haag didn't budge. "Missy, we need to show people that crime will not be tolerated in this town. Tourists will stop coming if we don't. We need tourism to grow the town's economy. Bliss Creek is going to be the next Lancaster County."

"I thought farming was the mainstay of Bliss Creek's economy," Sergeant Parker said, finally speaking up. "Not gawking at our Amish neighbors."

Given courage by his kind words, Annie squeezed past Mayor Haag. "I'll not be speaking in court." She lifted her chin and looked the mayor square in the eyes. "I've forgiven Mr. McKee. Maybe you can find it in your heart to do the same."

Her own heart pounding, she slipped through the door. The mayor's exasperated huffing followed her, but the woman didn't. Could she make Annie go to the hearing? Could they make her speak in front of a judge and lawyers? Anxiety made it hard to breathe. Luke would know. He would talk to the bishop. They would work it out.

Annie set her dilemma aside and concentrated on the bigger problem that interested her a whole lot more. Charisma Chiasson looked desperate...as desperate as Logan had been at the bakery yesterday. What were they doing in Bliss Creek? Did they have family? It was none of Annie's business, of course, except that Logan had chosen the bakery to rob.

The sinking sun reminded her that she had to get home. She'd promised Luke she'd be there to help with supper. More importantly, she'd promised Mary she'd be home more. The twins needed her. The needs of her family tugged her in one direction, the needs of a young woman with child tugged her in another. If her *Aenti* Louise were here, she'd say Annie should do what Jesus would do. Family would take care of family, but who would take care of a woman and her child in a strange place with no family to help?

Unable to answer that question, Annie hurried along the sidewalk, intent on reaching the blacksmith shop. Josiah would give her a ride, as usual. She would come back tomorrow and look for Charisma and Gracie. Sadie would give them food to eat. They were probably staying in the town's only motel—the bed and breakfasts cost too much. She'd look tomorrow.

Resolute in her plan, Annie turned left, ducked past a lady pushing a double stroller, and took another left. Two pink shirts bobbed in front of her. Charisma was holding Gracie on one hip while she tugged open the door of a dusty green minivan. Gracie screamed and kicked. "Stop it!" Charisma glanced around, her face red from exertion and something else—fear. "You have to get in."

"Don't wanna get in. No. No. No!" The little girl's screams got louder. Gracie's flailing arm connected with her mother's cheek and a bare foot landed in her stomach. The woman doubled over and let go of the child. Gracie landed on her backside on the hard cement. Screams turned to wails.

Charisma plopped down on the curb next to her daughter and put her face in her hands. "Gracie, please, please, you have to get in," she sobbed. "For Mommy. Please."

Annie sidled up to the van and peeked in. Food wrappers and paper bags cluttered the front seat. The middle overflowed with blankets. In the rear sat brown sacks stuffed with clothes. No wonder Gracie didn't want to get in. It looked like a dirty, cluttered, makeshift home. If they were staying in the motel, why were all those bags of clothes still in the car?

Annie knelt down next to Charisma and put her hands on the weeping woman's shoulders. "Are you all right?"

Charisma didn't look up. She started to rock back and forth. "Please, Gracie," she whispered.

"Sorry." The little girl threw her chubby arms around her mother's head. "I sorry, Mommy. I sorry."

Charisma cried harder.

Annie squeezed her shoulders. "Can I help you?"

"You again." The woman raised her tear-stained face. "Why would you help me?"

"You're living in your van. You need help."

Charisma's face went from red to white. She popped to her feet. "We are not living in our van. It's just messy. We're messy people, okay? Have you ever taken a cross-country trip in a car with a three-year-old? They're messy. That's all. You can't tell people we're living in our car."

"I'm sorry...I didn't mean...I won't tell anyone anything." Annie stood. "Who would I tell? I just want to help."

"You're not gonna tell SRS?"

"What is SRS?"

"Come on, you can't be that innocent! Even with the dress and the bun and the bonnet, you have to know about SRS. Social and...something services. They take kids away from parents who don't take good care of them."

"Are you not taking good care of Gracie?"

Charisma nodded toward the van. "What do you think?"

Gracie stood on her tiptoes and patted her mother's belly. She giggled. "Baby, baby, baby!"

Charisma squeezed the girl's hand without seeming to realize it. "Don't you see? They might not understand about the van. You can't tell. Promise me you won't tell!"

"I won't tell. I want to help."

"Why?" Charisma sat Gracie on the front seat and handed her a ragged brown monkey. "You don't know me. Logan tried to rob you."

"You need help. I can help."

"How? Are you going to give me money so I can put gas in the car? Are you going to give me money for a motel room?"

"I don't have any money." Annie gave everything she made at the bakery to Luke. She fumbled for a way to help. Something. Anything.

It hit her. "You can come home with me. We have room at our house. We have lots of food. We can share."

Charisma's mouth dropped open. "Are you crazy? Or like some kind of nun or something?"

"I'm not crazy and I'm not a nun, I promise."

"I couldn't just go home with a stranger." Despite the words, Charisma's expression said she was thinking of the alternative. She glanced at Gracie, who tossed the monkey over the back of the seat and grabbed a dirty plastic fork with an equally dirty hand. Charisma licked cracked lips. "Could I?"

"My name is Annie Shirack. Now you know me. Come with me to my brother's shop. We'll come back in the buggy for your things or you can drive the van to our house. Josiah will tell you how to get there."

"I can't take the van. It's out of gas."

"Then we'll get your clothes and come back for it later. My family will help." Annie sent up a little prayer that she wasn't overestimating Luke's charitable instincts. He had so many children to support already. "We all will."

Her face pensive, Charisma traced a square in the dirt on the car window, then added a roof and a door. "Won't your parents think it's weird, you coming home with a pregnant girl and a little kid?"

The question stung. It shouldn't. It had been more than a year. She should be used to the idea by now. "My parents passed away. I live with my brother and our family. We have lots of children at our house. One more won't make a difference."

Charisma chewed a ragged fingernail.

"Mommy, I want PBJ. PBJ." Gracie rapped on the seat with the fork. "PBJ."

"PBJ?"

Tears rolled down Charisma's face. She smeared them on the sleeve of her T-shirt. "Peanut butter and jelly. She wants a sandwich." Charisma choked back a sob as she tugged Gracie from the car. "She's hungry and I can't feed her. All right? I can't feed her."

"I happen to be a very good cook." Annie took the bag Charisma had draped over one arm. "You're going to love my sandwiches."

Now she just had to convince Luke this was a good idea.

Luke…and Leah.

Chapter 12

Is it true?" Bishop Kelp's harsh tone scraped across Josiah's ears like sandpaper. "The Kauffman girl is here in Bliss Creek?"

The stares of every man in the room bored into Josiah. David shifted next to him. Josiah took a breath and let it out. He had done nothing wrong. He forced himself to straighten. Ignoring Luke's furious face, he met Bishop Kelp's gaze head on. "It's true, but—"

"You saw her?" Luke stood. "Why am I just hearing about this?"

"Luke, sit." Bishop Kelp pointed to the bench. "Sit quietly."

Luke subsided.

"She arrived yesterday. I didn't talk to her before she decided to come here." In the silence as the men waited for Josiah to explain, David cleared his throat. His breathing sounded ragged. "I didn't know she was coming, and I didn't ask her to come."

"Did you advise her to return home?"

Josiah wiped sweaty palms on his pant legs. "I did, but she...she seems to have other plans."

"Other plans?"

"She's coming to see you." Josiah took a deep breath. "She says she wants to join our community."

Bishop Kelp leaned back in his seat and exchanged glances with Deacon Altman. No one spoke for a moment.

Luke squirmed on his bench. "That's just—"

The bishop held up a hand. "Luke, we will have no further discussion about this until the girl comes to me." His gaze whipped back to Josiah. "You will have no contact with her at all. Until we know what her true motives are, nothing has changed. This girl brought you nothing but trouble. You've come a long way, Josiah, but the road back is short."

"This wasn't my doing—"

"But you said nothing to us. That leads me to believe you were considering your options."

"I…" Had he been considering his options? Despite the urge to storm out, Josiah forced himself to stand still. A rustling sound made him glance toward David. His friend had slipped past Mark and was angling for the door. Some friend. Probably didn't want to be associated with the black sheep of the community anymore. Fine. "I told her she should go home."

A true statement. But had he meant it? Josiah's gaze caught Paul Yonkers's. Miriam's brother's stare made his skin turn icy. Josiah forced his gaze back to Bishop Kelp. "She said she's spending the summer with her cousin over on Voelcker Lane."

"Then we'll not see your buggy on Voelcker Lane this summer."

Josiah forced a nod. "I have plenty of work to do."

"See to it that you do it and nothing else." Bishop Kelp stood. "These are difficult times. Circumstances force us to spend more time doing business among the Englischers. We must not lose sight of the Ordnung. Each one of you is responsible for making sure your families remember that. They look to their husbands and fathers to set the example. To follow the Ordnung."

His gaze traveled to Luke, then Josiah. "Don't let them down."

He strode from the room and the deacons followed close on his heels. Silence reigned for a long moment. Then men began to discuss the situation among themselves. No one looked at Josiah, for which he was supremely grateful.

Then Luke wormed his way through the crowd. His face contorted with anger, he leaned in close to Josiah's ear. "Get out to the buggy. Now."

Chapter 13

Annie put her hands on her hips and surveyed the street in front of the blacksmith shop, first left, then right. Bill Cramer drove by in his old green pickup truck. Michael Glick waved as he passed in his buggy. She waved back. No sign of Josiah. She nibbled at her lower lip, trying to decide what to do next. She needed Josiah to take Charisma and Gracie out to the farm. The longer it took, the more likely Charisma would have second thoughts. The idea of little Gracie sleeping in that van during these hot, humid nights caused a feeling of dread to settle in her stomach. She had to help them. She turned to her cousin Caleb, who leaned on the stanchion where horses were usually tied. "When Josiah dropped me off this morning he said he would be here after the horse auction. Have you seen him?"

"After the auction we all went to the meeting at the bishop's." Caleb lifted his hat and resettled it on his head. "He's probably licking his wounds after the talking-to the bishop gave him."

"Talking-to?" The dread whirled in the pit of Annie's stomach. Someone had mentioned Sarah Kauffman's visit to the blacksmith shop. It had to be. "For what? What did the bishop say?"

"I best leave the telling up to Josiah and Luke." Caleb chewed on a toothpick, then tossed it in a nearby trash can. "I reckon I better get those horses shod. Josiah was supposed to do them, but I've got a feeling he may be mighty late by the time Luke gets through with him."

Gracie squatted on the sidewalk and picked at a green blob of chewed gum. Charisma swooped down on her and swatted her hand away. "Gross! Gracie, stop it!"

"Let me take her." Annie hoisted the little girl to her hip. "Caleb, do you think you—"

The clip-clop of hooves against the asphalt made Annie swivel. Josiah? No. She adjusted Gracie's squirming body. David. Josiah's friend. Nothing more. God's plan, she reminded herself. God's will. She forced herself to smile and wave.

David pulled up on the reins and brought the buggy to a halt. His gaze wandered over Charisma, who crossed her arms and adopted a bored look, and then Gracie. "Did Josiah get back from the meeting yet?"

"Everyone seems to be looking for Josiah. He's a popular man." Caleb chuckled. "You probably know better than I do where he is."

"I had to leave the meeting a little early." David didn't smile. "Tell him I was looking for him, will you?"

"He'll be here—soon as Luke gets done with him."

"Horsie, horsie!" Gracie crowed. She struggled to get down from Annie's arms. "Pet horsie."

Annie held on tight to the girl, but her attention centered on David. "What happened at the meeting?"

David wiped his pale, sweaty face with a white handkerchief. "It was pretty short." He stopped, his fingers tight on the handkerchief. "I wish I'd been able to give Josiah some support, but I had to leave."

"You were sick?"

"I'm fine now."

Naturally, he wouldn't talk about it. Not to her. Dread leaped and plummeted, making Annie feel ill herself. "What exactly did the bishop say to him?"

David shook his head. "You'll have to ask him."

Annie silently counted to ten. She didn't want to ask David for any favors. He'd made it clear how he felt about her being in his life. But she couldn't afford to let Charisma stand here much longer. She could ask for David's help, friend to friend. They'd been friends since their days at school, hadn't they? She quickly made the introductions, then turned back to David. "I need your help," she said.

"To do what?"

"We need a ride. But first, we need to pick up Charisma's things from her van."

"They're going to your farm?" David's eyebrows lifted and his shoulders rose in the slightest of shrugs. "Why doesn't she drive her van to the farm?"

Annie didn't want to embarrass Charisma, but she didn't want David to argue with her about taking them home. "There's no gas and there's no money to buy gas. Besides, I can't very well ride in the car with her—not without asking Luke first."

"And you're sure you don't want to ask Luke about your plan…in general?" A faint smile flittered across David's face. "What exactly *are* you planning?"

"Charisma and Gracie need a place to stay."

David gave Charisma another once-over. Charisma's chin went up and her lips down. "Never mind," she said. "I don't need no charity. We'll be fine."

She tried to tug Gracie from Annie's arms. Gracie threw her small body against Annie and started to cry. Amazing how loud a three-year-old could scream.

"Whoa, hold on!" David's hands came up as if in surrender. "I don't mind giving you a lift at all. Come on, everyone, all aboard."

Charisma looked as if she might protest, but Annie scurried to get Gracie into the backseat and then offered Charisma a hand. The woman wrinkled her nose, but then accepted the help. Annie settled onto the seat next to David. "The van's parked on Walnut Street."

Gracie began to sing a song about a farmer in the dell at the top of her apparently healthy lungs. David glanced back once, then snapped the reins and clucked. "Does Luke know you're bringing home the wife of an armed robber?" His voice was low, pitched for her ears only. "The wife and child?"

"How'd you know?"

"I know you, Annie." His voice cracked on her name. Annie couldn't fathom why. No emotion showed on his face. "Bliss Creek gets a lot of tourists, but they don't live in their vans."

"She's not his wife."

"That makes it so much better."

"They're living in a van."

"Your motives are pure." David's gaze never wavered from the road. "But you're not taking into account everything else that is going on."

"No matter what is going on, shouldn't we be helping our neighbors?" Annie schooled her voice. David only said what Luke would be thinking. She tried to ignore that thought. "Why were you looking for Josiah? What happened at the meeting that affected him?"

"Paul Yonkers told the bishop Sarah is in town. Did you know she was here?"

The dread was back, this time at the thought of what might happen to Josiah if the bishop decided he'd had something to do with the Mennonite girl's appearance in Bliss Creek. Not only that, Luke would be in a terrible mood. This would not be a good time to tell him she'd offered their home to a stranger and her baby. "What did Josiah do?"

"He agreed not to see Sarah."

"So where is he?"

"I told you I don't know. I had to leave the meeting." David glanced her way. "You knew Sarah was here, didn't you? And you know why she's here?"

"Jah, I knew, but—"

"You should've said something to Luke. He was blindsided at the meeting, which made it worse for Josiah."

Annie closed her eyes. He was right. Luke tried so hard to fill Daed's shoes. This wasn't his fault, but he would see it as another failing as the head of the house. "You're right. I wanted to give Josiah a chance to fix the situation. He told me he would."

"He won't get a chance now. They'll be watching his every move."

"Don't you feel a little sorry for him?"

David's mournful gaze shied away from hers. He lifted the reins and clucked again.

"David?"

"I do. But that's neither here nor there."

He couldn't understand because he didn't feel about her the way Josiah felt about Sarah. The realization made Annie draw farther into the corner of her seat. So be it.

"Does everyone always stare at you like this?"

Annie twisted to look at Charisma, who sat with Gracie on her lap in the backseat of the buggy, bags of clothes tucked on either side of her. She followed the woman's gaze through the square buggy window to the crowded produce stand at the turnoff to the Shirack farm road. Eli Brennaman waved from his spot behind the wooden counter. When had the nine-year-old gotten so tall? A miniature Thomas. Annie waved back. "They're not staring at us. They're staring at you."

"Huh?"

"They're used to seeing us in buggies. But not Englischers."

"Englischers? Is that like foreigners?"

Annie exchanged a look with David. He smiled—that boyish smile she had known and loved since he and her brothers were little and they all ran around catching lightning bugs and frogs and turning them into pets. Annie smiled back. Their gazes locked for a long second. Then the light in his eyes faded, and he turned back to the road.

Annie's throat ached. She turned back to Charisma. "Something like that. Ladies in pink T-shirts don't usually ride in our buggies."

"Horsie, horsie, horsie!" Gracie continued to crow. "I want horsie!"

Charisma grabbed her just in time to keep her from hurtling from the seat. "They're taking pictures."

Annie faced forward and clasped her hands in her lap. At this angle those photos would only catch a glimpse of her kapp in the window. Which suited her fine. "You get used to it."

"You don't like to get your picture taken?" Charisma held Gracie up and the little girl waved both hands. "What's wrong with photos?"

"We don't need to look at pictures of ourselves. Pictures make people vain and proud."

"Pictures help you remember good times. You mean you don't even have pictures of weddings?"

"No."

Charisma frowned. "Weird."

Annie let the comment go. Sometimes she wished for photos of Mudder and Daed and of Catherine too. But she need only look at her brothers and Emma to remember what her parents and her younger sister looked like. Besides, memories of them were locked in her heart.

The rest of the ride was punctuated by Gracie alternately singing "Farmer in the Dell" and clamoring to pet the "horsie."

At the front porch, Annie hopped down and turned to help Charisma with Gracie. Before she could thank David, the front door opened and Mary flew out. "You said you'd be home early today. You promised!"

Annie took in her sister's red eyes and tear-stained face. "I'm sorry. Something unexpected happened. What's the matter?"

Mary slammed to a halt on the steps. "Who's this?"

Gracie skipped over to the older girl. "I'm Gracie. I like horsies." She held up both arms. "Pet horsie?"

Mary's frown melted. The girl's normal sunny disposition reappeared in the two seconds it took her to take the younger girl's hand and trot toward David's horse. "I like horses too." She smoothed the horse's long forehead. "Pet him. He's soft."

Annie turned to David, who had begun unloading Charisma's bags onto the porch. "Would you like to come in for some iced tea or lemonade? You must be thirsty."

"You just want company so Luke will be less likely to yell at you." The grin came and went so quickly Annie almost missed it. "Sorry, you're on your own on this one."

"It's a simple offer, no strings attached." Annie couldn't help it. A little of her hurt and impatience bled through the words. He couldn't even accept a friendly invitation. "Just something cool to drink before you go on your way. It doesn't make you beholden to me—to anyone."

"I need to get back to the farm. Timothy bought a horse today and he wants me to take her through her paces. See what work she'll need to be field-ready."

"You're working the farm again?"

"Contrary to what Mudder would like to believe, I'm a farmer, not a baker."

Annie's face burned. "I know."

He tipped his hat to Charisma. "I'm sorry for your troubles. You're in good hands here."

Annie watched him pull away. Despite what Logan McKee had done at the bakery, David had shown grace to Charisma. He was a good man.

Shaking off the storm of emotions, Annie started up the steps, Charisma in tow. "Let's get you inside. There's a lot of people to meet. Mary, keep track of Gracie, will you? Don't let her eat the flowers or get too close to the rooster. He'll peck her. And make sure Mutt gets the chance to sniff her before she pets him!"

"Rooster?" Charisma looked uncertain. "Who's Mutt?"

"Mary Shirack, get in here, now!" Leah stormed onto the porch. "Mary!"

Her gaze swung from Charisma to Annie. Her mouth shut, then opened. "I'm sorry, I didn't know we had company." She wiped her hands on her apron. "I'm Leah."

Implicit in the introduction was Leah's question. Who was this and why had Annie brought her home? Annie quickly made the introductions. "Is Luke here?"

"He hasn't come back yet." Leah eyed the bags. Her eyebrows raised, she stared at Annie. "Nor has Josiah. I heard the buggy and thought it might be them."

"David gave us a ride." Annie started forward. "Would you like some sweet tea?" she called back to Charisma. "I don't know about you, but I'm parched. Come on in. This is our home."

It was her home as much as Leah's. More. She'd grown up here. Leah had moved in after Daed and Mudder died. Annie accepted that fact, but Leah didn't have the final word on anything. Luke did.

She moved quickly through the living room where Leah had set up a playpen that held Esther and Martha. Lillie dangled a teething ring in front of Esther. "Come on, baby! It'll make your gums feel better. I promise." She looked up. "Annie!" Lillie smiled. "You're home! Can you—"

"Keep the twins occupied." Leah cut her off. "Where are William and Joseph?"

Her smile gone, Lillie's gaze went back to little Esther. "Feeding the chickens."

"*Gut*. You can set the tables."

Lillie gave Annie a beseeching look. Annie altered her path so she could give her little sister a squeeze on the shoulder. "We'll talk later." She quickly introduced Charisma. "Mary has another guest for you to meet—you're going to like her. As soon as you set the table, you can go outside and meet her."

Lillie loved taking care of the smaller toddlers. She and Mary would be good playmates for Gracie.

Ignoring Leah's dark look, Annie invited Charisma to take a seat on the bench at the prep table. She poured tea into big plastic glasses, added heaping teaspoons of sugar, and then cracked some ice from the bag in the gas-operated refrigerator. Regardless of what the older folks in the community said, she liked having ice in the kitchen. A small thing, perhaps, but a blessing as the sun ushered in the heat of a long Kansas summer.

Charisma took a tentative sip. "That's good."

"Sun tea. We brew it in big jars in the backyard."

Charisma looked around, her curiosity obvious. "A wood-burning stove?"

"We have a gas oven too. I do a lot of baking."

Charisma's face colored. "Obviously."

Annie smiled in spite of herself. Sooner or later, they would have to talk about what happened at the bakery. And about Logan. But right now, she needed to make her guest feel comfortable. "I love to cook. Do you cook?"

"I make grilled cheese sandwiches—"

"That's not necessary. Supper is already on." Leah stood in the doorway. "Annie, can I see you out here for one moment?"

It wasn't a question, really, but rather a command.

"Coming." Annie arranged cookies on a plate and set it on the table. "To hold you over until we eat."

Charisma grabbed the cookie and took a huge bite. She moaned. "These are so good! Gracie will love these."

"Don't spoil her supper—or yours."

"Annie!" Leah tapped a finger on the doorframe. "Now."

In the dining room crowded with long tables and benches to accommodate their growing family, Leah paced near the playpen. Esther rolled around on the blanket and began to cry. "Take her to the front room." Leah pointed at Lillie. "Where's Mary? She's supposed to be helping you."

With another glance at Annie, Lillie cuddled Esther to her shoulder. "I'll get her." She disappeared through the doorway.

"You're gone all day. You're gone all the time now. We have our hands full here." Leah sank onto the bench. She did look tired. "Who is she?"

"A guest."

"For how long?"

"I'd rather talk to Luke about it."

"Luke? Luke doesn't do the cooking and the cleaning and the caring for the children around here."

"No, but he is the head of this household." Luke's baritone reverberated through the room. He tromped into the room, his shirt soaked with sweat and his face ruddy from the sun. "What's going on here? Mary and Lillie are outside trying to keep a little girl in a pink shirt from eating the sunflowers by the front step. It looks like she may have wet herself."

Leah folded her arms and leaned back, the look on her face a challenge.

Annie swallowed hard and moved toward her brother. "They're living in a van. They need a place to stay, Luke. I couldn't let that little girl spend another night in the backseat of a van. Not in this heat."

Luke's eyes closed for a brief moment, then opened. "No, you couldn't."

"That's all you have to say? You don't think we have enough mouths to feed?" Leah stood, her hands planted firmly on her hips. "That I don't have enough cooking and cleaning and washing to do?"

"Annie did the only thing she could. She offered help to a woman and child in need."

Knowing Leah's habits, Annie figured the confrontation would last about one minute. When Leah figured out Luke wouldn't budge, she'd give in to his place of leadership in the house. "You don't even know who she is."

Luke backed away from the accusing finger his wife waved at him. "I don't need to know."

"Her...she's with the man who robbed the bakery."

"So she exercised poor judgment in her choices of company."

"I'm sure she was in on planning the armed robbery." Leah's voice rose. She rubbed her stomach as if it hurt. "She could be a bad influence on the children."

"We don't know what she may or may not have done. It's neither here nor there. She needs a place to stay, and the children have to learn to reject worldly ways. If they're never exposed to these things, how will they learn?"

"You take everyone's side except mine."

Annie couldn't take it anymore. "I'll take care of her and Gracie. I won't let them be a burden to you, Leah. I'm sorry I didn't ask first, but her need was so great, I couldn't bear it."

"When will you take care of them? On the two days you're not at the bakery? That leaves me with the other five. If only you could see the need in your own home as clearly."

Leah brushed past her and left the room without a backward glance. Annie turned to Luke. "Charisma's an adult. She can help out, and she will take care of her child. She can babysit the little twins." She moved closer to her brother. "I'm sorry to add to your burden."

"My shoulders are wide, but Leah is worn out. You need to help her more, as I said last night."

"I will."

Starting right now. She rushed to the kitchen. Charisma wasn't in the room. She'd probably heard the argument and slipped out the back door. Annie longed to go look for her, but she didn't dare. She stirred a pot of navy beans. Leah had forgotten to add the bacon. She pulled a slab from the refrigerator and set a skillet on the stove. "What did the bishop say about moving from wheat to cattle?"

Luke poured a tall glass of water and downed half of it before he answered. "He listened to everyone's thoughts on it and said he would confer with the deacons. There's a lot to consider."

"It's better to do that than lose the farms altogether, isn't it?" She dumped pieces of chicken into a plastic bag of seasoned flour and began to shake it while the lard heated in a second skillet. "Or move to another state where things are cheaper?"

"Jah." Luke bent over the sink and splashed cold water on his face, then straightened. "The bishop agrees with that. The question is how the change would affect our ability to take care of our folks. The older ones, the sick ones, those who cannot work. There is a cost for that."

"I'm sorry if I'm making things more difficult for us by bringing Gracie and Charisma here." She focused on laying the chicken in the hot grease without burning her fingers. "More mouths to feed."

"We have enough. Smells like something's burning." His words were muffled through the towel he used to dry his face. "Cheese, I think."

"What?"

"You're the cook and you don't smell it?" He jerked his head toward the oven. "Food burning."

He was right. So caught up in the burdens of the day, she hadn't even noticed the faint scorched smell mingling with aromas of frying bacon and chicken. She rushed to the oven. Macaroni and cheese casserole. "It's just a little singed around the edges."

"Like me." Luke chuckled, his features lighter for a brief second. "Don't ever worry about showing charity, little schweschder. You did right to bring them here."

The tight grip worry had on her throat eased a bit. "What about Leah?"

"She's tired. She'll be better in the morning."

Annie appreciated her brother's optimism, but she didn't share it. Leah might put on a happy face for her husband, but she had seen the real Leah at work with the twins. "I don't mean to speak out of place, but I think Leah is being too harsh with Lillie and Mary."

Luke frowned. "Spare the rod, spoil the child."

"They're good girls. Their life is hard without Mudder and Daed."

"Their life is fine. They have me and Leah. And you."

"Mary cries at night."

"She needs to toughen up." Luke adjusted his hat and started for the door. "I have neither the time nor the inclination for coddling. It does them no good in the long run. It's time for you to get supper on the table."

Annie wanted to groan. As a man, Luke didn't understand the need for a soft touch, a bit of affection now and then. "They're just little girls," she whispered to his retreating back. He had two of his own.

Would Leah treat them the same way?

Chapter 14

Annie slid the platter of fried chicken onto the table between Luke and Charisma's plates. Gracie, seated on her mother's lap, squealed and reached for it. "No." Her expression uncertain, Charisma grabbed her daughter's hand and pulled it back. "Wait until you're served." She squirmed in her chair, her gaze skipping from Luke to Annie. "Sorry, she's not used to sitting at a table anymore."

"Don't worry. We're used to little ones at the table." Annie picked up Esther from the playpen, plopped her into a high chair, and strapped her in while Leah did the same with Martha.

"Yes, they have to learn. Better to start young," Leah added. She marched toward the kitchen without looking at either of them. "Mary, Lillie, help me bring in the rest of the food."

The older twins scurried after her, but not before Lillie sent Annie a *help-us* glance. Annie wished she could. She needed to make sure their guests were welcomed properly. Luke would never be rude, but Leah was proving to be a leaf of a different color. She had been increasingly agitated during the preparations of the food. Every question from Charisma seemed to send her deeper into a funk. Charisma couldn't seem to comprehend the lack of a microwave oven, the lack of an electric can opener—which wasn't needed since they ate nothing out of a can. Even the use of cloth napkins and placemats intrigued her. And Leah seemed to have no patience or any ability to be kind to a guest.

Annie gave up trying to figure it out and put a bowl of fresh sliced peaches on the table. Gracie squirmed and tried to escape from Charisma's grasp. Annie glanced at Luke. His face showed nothing. Leah bustled back into the room and slapped the slightly browned macaroni and cheese casserole on the table next to the chicken. Annie patted Gracie's cheek. "I'm sorry we don't have another high chair. It would make it easier for both of you."

"That's okay. She's really too big for a high chair. She uses a booster seat…" Charisma's voice trailed off. "We really haven't had much in the way of furniture in a while."

Leah's disapproving *humph* did nothing for the conversation. Annie scurried around the table and sat between Mary and Lillie. Luke closed his eyes and lowered his head.

Annie did the same.

"I want chicken. I want KFC. I want KFC!" Gracie's shrill voice broke the silence. "Hungry. Eat now!"

"Okay, okay! How about a drumstick?"

Annie raised her head just as Charisma grabbed a piece of chicken with her bare fingers.

"Amen."

Luke packed plenty of irritation into one word.

Charisma dropped the drumstick back onto the platter. "Oh…oh, I'm sorry, I didn't…"

"We pray." Luke held up his plate and Leah slid a huge chicken breast onto it. "Then we eat."

Her face red, Charisma nodded so hard the silver hoops in her ears shook. "I…my grandma used to do that."

"Where's your grandma?" Annie passed Charisma a basket of hot rolls. "I mean, where's home?"

Charisma stopped Gracie from dumping all the rolls on the plate they shared. "The last place I really lived was Baton Rouge."

"You're a long way from home." Josiah scooped a pile of macaroni and cheese on a plate and handed it to Luke. "What brings you to Kansas?"

"Besides robbing bakeries." Mark slipped in the comment between bites on a drumstick. Mary and Lilly tittered.

"That's enough. I'll not have rude people at my table." One look from Luke silenced them.

Red blotches stretching all the way from her forehead down her face to her long neck, Charisma smoothed Gracie's matted curls. "It's a long story."

"And it's none of our business." Luke took a swallow of water. "Josiah, did you take care of those appointments at the shop this afternoon?"

Annie breathed. Luke was too kind a person to make a guest in his home uncomfortable. Unfortunately, he'd chosen Josiah for the spotlight instead. From the look on her brother's face, he didn't want to talk about work or anything else. He picked at the macaroni. "By the time I got there, Caleb had already taken care of them."

"So what did you do instead? You were gone a while."

Josiah pushed back his plate. "I cleaned up the shop and picked up some supplies."

"You didn't decide to do some visiting?"

Josiah's face went red as a radish. Annie held her breath, waiting for him to smart off the way he used to do. His jaw clenched and he tossed his fork on his plate. "I helped Caleb. I came home."

"Horsie, horsie!" Gracie clapped her hands. Her drumstick went flying and landed in Luke's lap. "Chicken, I want chicken."

With two fingers, Luke lifted the drumstick from his lap and laid it on his plate. "I think you'd better have a new piece."

"I'm so sorry, so sorry!" Charisma held out her napkin. It was covered with cheese and grease. She snatched it back. "Let me get you a clean napkin."

"It's all right. I work in the fields. I reckon no one cares about a little grease on my pants."

Silence reigned. Annie rushed to finish her food. Everyone else seemed to be doing the same. Anything to end this meal.

Leah stood first and grabbed a plate still half full of food. She stalked from the room without a word.

"I should help load the dishwasher." Charisma stood and hoisted Gracie on her hip.

"You're a guest." Stifling a giggle at the look on Luke's face, Annie hustled around the table and took Charisma's plate from her. "You can keep me company while I wash, but no doing dishes."

Charisma tagged along after her, Gracie whining about cookies the whole time. "I don't want to be a drag on you."

Annie shook her head. "What's one more plate, a fork, a spoon?"

"Where's the dishwasher? I can load it. It's no trouble."

This time Annie couldn't help it. She laughed aloud. "You're looking at it."

Charisma didn't laugh. She was looking over Annie's shoulder, a troubled frown on her face. Annie turned. Leah was bent over the kitchen sink, retching.

"Leah, what's the matter? Did something disagree with you?" Annie rushed to her side. "Do you need a seltzer?"

Leah raised her head. She tugged a washrag from the counter and wiped at her face. "I don't think a seltzer will help. It'll right itself in a few months—or more."

The look on her face made Annie take a step forward. "You're…oh, you're…are you?"

Leah nodded. Then she shot from the room like a coyote was after her.

Another baby. Another blessing. Annie clung to that belief despite the knowledge that the Shirack house overflowed with that particular blessing at the moment. "*Wunderbar*," she called after Leah. "Congratulations."

Leah didn't reply. She was long gone.

"She didn't look too happy about it." Charisma rubbed her belly. "I know that feeling."

Chapter 15

Annie rolled over, then sat up in bed, listening. The sound of someone pacing on the front porch floated through her open bedroom window. She had no idea how long she'd been asleep. Not long if the burning of her eyes meant anything.

"Shhhh, hush, honey, hush, you're gonna wake everyone up!"

Charisma. Charisma and Gracie.

Annie slipped from her bed and grabbed a robe from the rack on the wall. She tiptoed down the stairs and eased the front door open. A cool breeze born of the dark night draped itself over her shoulders. She inhaled its relief from the heat of the day. And something else. The smell of tobacco. "Charisma?"

A cigarette dangling from her lips, Charisma turned and marched the length of the porch, sidestepping two hickory rockers. In the stark light of a nearly full moon she appeared to be in the middle of a wrestling match with Gracie, who was struggling to get down. "Stop it! You're not getting down." She let go of the girl with one hand so she could grab the cigarette. Her voice rose, then dropped. "You'll wake up everyone in the house."

"Having trouble getting her to sleep, I guess."

"You think?" Charisma muttered. "It's the quiet. She can't go to sleep in this quiet. Do you have a radio of some kind, anything I can play some music for her on? She loves music."

Annie reveled in the silence at the end of a long day. Not silence, really. Birds called to each other. Crickets chirped. Toads sang. A medley of sounds that were drowned out by hustle and bustle during the day. "Wouldn't noise keep her awake?"

"Are you kidding? She's used to the radio. I play music to get her to sleep…in the car, you know." Charisma flopped down in a rocker. Gracie squirmed and whined, still caught in her mother's arms. "Sometimes, if we had the money for gas, I would drive around until she fell asleep. I'd put on some R&B, and she'd be out like a light."

Annie had no idea what R&B was. "Let me take her."

"You don't ever listen to music?"

"We sing a lot. At school and at church. We have singings. Just no instruments."

"Why can't you have recorded music? It's great for dancing. I love to dance."

She sounded so wistful. Annie searched her brain for an answer, for a memory that told her why these things weren't allowed. "We don't dance. We don't use instruments to make music. It's against the Ordnung."

"The what?"

"The rules." Honestly, she didn't know why. It just was. The Ordnung had been handed down for many generations. "It's against the rules."

"You sure have a lot of rules. I thought my mom had a lot of rules, but this is crazy. What harm could music do?"

Annie shrugged. She sometimes heard music in the stores and when they ate in restaurants. It was nice. But she didn't miss it around the house. Gracie's whines grew louder. "Give her to me. I'll rock her."

"She's gonna cry and wake everyone up."

"The cigarette smoke is bad for her. Let me try." Not to mention bad for Charisma and the *bobbeli* she carried inside her. To Annie's surprise, Gracie came to her without hesitation. "Come here, sweetie. It's way past your bedtime."

Way past everyone's bedtime. Daylight and the prayer service would arrive before they knew it. At least there would be no chores. Of course, there was the singing later. If she decided to go, that is, and she *hadn't* decided to go. "If you want, you can lie down. I'll bring her to you."

"As if I could sleep." Charisma dropped the cigarette on the porch and stubbed it out with her rubber flip-flop. At Annie's look, she nudged it with her toe until it slid off the porch into the rose bushes. "Satisfied?"

"As long as you don't light another."

"What are you? The tobacco police?"

"I've heard people talk about how much they cost. How can you afford them?"

"I can't. I'm hoarding my last pack, but I really needed one."

Annie relaxed and began to rock Gracie. The child laid her head on Annie's shoulder and stuck her thumb in her mouth. It felt so perfectly natural and Annie fought the sudden urge to cry. "You are a sweet baby."

"You made a friend." The words sounded grudging. Charisma wiped at her face with the back of her arm. "Coming here was a mistake. I should leave."

"And go where?"

The words were out of Annie's mouth before she could consider how they would sound. She didn't want to make her guest feel worse. She didn't understand how Charisma could consider leaving with no money, no place to go, no food. On her own was one thing, but to take an innocent child was another. Annie rubbed Gracie's back. She felt the little girl's body relax against hers. Her head lolled to one side. "Maybe you're just homesick."

"Homesick?" Charisma snorted.

The noise brought Gracie's head up with a jerk. Annie patted her back. "Sleep, little one." The girl's head dropped again. "Tell me about where you're from."

"I ran away from home when I was fifteen. I ain't been home in four years."

Annie did the math. Not since before Gracie was born. "Where is that? Where did you grow up?"

"Shreveport. That's in Louisiana."

Annie might not have received much geography in her time at school, but she knew that much. "Is that where you met Logan?"

"No."

Both women were quiet for a long minute. Annie began to think the conversation had ended before it really began.

"I met Logan in Baton Rouge the next year."

"Is he Gracie's father, then?" Annie stopped. It was none of her business and the last thing she wanted to do was embarrass her guest, but Gracie had Logan's dark hair and blue eyes. She didn't look a whole lot like her mama. "If he's your husband, why don't you and Gracie have his name?"

"You're so naïve. People don't always get married. I can't believe you're judging me." Charisma's voice rose, its tone shrill. "I don't see any wedding rings on your brother and his baby momma."

"Baby momma?" Annie felt a giggle burble up inside her. And shock that anyone would think Luke and Leah would have children outside the boundaries of marriage. "We don't wear jewelry."

"Even wedding rings?"

"No."

"Then how do you know who's taken?"

"Married women wear black kapps and the men grow beards."

Charisma batted away a dragonfly that buzzed and hovered near her face. "So. Josiah is single then?"

A chill ran up Annie's arm. Just what they needed. Another girl flirting with her brother. "He's spoken for."

"Don't worry. Suspenders don't do a thing for me."

Reassuring if not a little insulting. Annie liked their clothes. It saved a lot of time not having to pick out outfits like the Englischers did with their matching this and matching that. Easier to sew too. "That's good. We don't marry outside our faith."

"What about you? You like that David guy, don't you? He's a little puny, if you ask me, but if the pale and bald look does it for you, then that's cool."

That was one way of putting it. Annie chose not to tell her about the Hodgkin's disease. David would prefer Charisma's disdain to her pity. "David has nice brown hair and plenty of it. It'll grow back and a summer working in the sun will take care of his complexion." Not that it mattered to Annie what he looked like. Her feelings ran much deeper than looks. "It's not his looks that count. Anyway, courting is private."

If only they *were* courting. They were friends, she reminded herself. Friends.

"Courting?" Charisma scoffed so loudly Gracie jumped and whimpered. "I suppose you have beaus too."

Annie stuck a finger to her lips. It was time to change the subject before it got any more unseemly. In any event, Charisma's past was far more interesting than Annie's life. "Why did you run away?"

"It's not important."

Charisma's tone said differently. Annie tried to imagine what might have happened. To leave home and not go back for four years. To not see parents. If Mudder and Daed were still alive, she'd never leave them. "To be so far from family...that seems important."

Charisma stretched out her long, skinny legs and leaned back in the rocker. Her eyes closed for a few minutes. Maybe she would be able to sleep after all. Annie resigned herself to not knowing why Charisma left home.

"I met Logan on the street in Baton Rouge. I was panhandling." Charisma opened her eyes. "He walked right on by me like he didn't hear me ask for money. I called him a nasty name. That's the way I was then. I didn't care what people thought. Anyway, about fifteen minutes later, here he came. He had one of those cup of soup things, you know, like you buy from vending machines." She glanced toward Annie. "You know what a vending machine is, Amish girl?"

"I know. You put money in it and get food out of it." Mark had been fascinated with them at the hospital where Josiah had been treated after his accident. "Candy bars too. And not very good coffee."

"Exactly. He also brought me a candy bar, one of those ones that have a bunch of peanuts in it because he said I needed protein." Charisma smiled a little, her gaze distant. "He sat down on the curb next to me and handed me that hot cup of soup. He looked at me with those big blue eyes and he smiled and I don't know…he made me feel safe. Nobody ever made me feel that way before."

"Just like that?" Annie mulled it over. She'd loved David since she was twelve. A steady, certain, knowing kind of love that she couldn't tell anyone about because they were too young. They couldn't even see each other as anything more than friends until the singings when she turned sixteen. Charisma's encounter with Logan couldn't be the same thing, could it? "Because of soup and a candy bar with peanuts?"

"Because he bothered. With me. No one else had in a long time."

"He showed you kindness."

"I guess."

"Then what?"

"Then he asked me if I wanted to go home with him, so I did."

"Just like that?"

"Just like that." Charisma shrugged. "Beggars can't be choosers. He was nice and he was clean and he didn't hit me or yell at me. He had an apartment where I could get out of the rain and sometimes he had money so we could buy food. He took care of me. That's why I stayed with him even though…that's why I have to stand by him."

Even though what? Annie tried to read between the lines. "Why didn't you get married?"

"Because…lots of reasons. After I realized I was…that Gracie was coming, he asked, but I couldn't. Just because." Charisma wiped at her runny nose like a small child. "But I still gotta stand by him."

Annie understood that part. She wanted to stand by David too. He wouldn't let her. She had to give up now or she would never have the chance to rock a baby of her own to sleep. If she did give up, that child wouldn't be David's. The thought sat like a stone in her stomach. She couldn't imagine having a child with anyone else. "What about your parents? Do they know about Logan and Gracie?"

"No."

Annie tried to fathom the wrenching anguish in that one syllable. "Don't you want them to know they have a grandchild?"

Charisma shook her head and a half-sob slipped out. She slapped a hand to her mouth. After a second, she heaved a sigh. "I'd like for my mom to know, but not my dad. I don't care if he ever gets to see his granddaughter. Not everybody has a family like yours, Amish girl." She squirmed in her chair as if unhappy memories pressed upon her. "My dad is…I ran away because he beat me. One night he broke my arm and my nose. I couldn't take it anymore."

Annie felt chilled to the bone on a hot, summer night. Her community believed in corporal punishment. The Bible said spare the rod, spoil the child. But not this. Not violence, especially directed at a little girl. "I'm sorry," she whispered.

"It's okay. Anyway, I started living with Logan. One thing led to another and the next thing I know, I'm stuck in Kansas in an Amish house with no TV and no radio. And a dishwasher named Annie."

She giggled, a half hysterical sound. After a moment Annie joined her, softly so as not to wake Gracie. "Why did you come to Kansas?"

"After Gracie was born, we were living with Logan's dad and his brother, Sam. They got into it. Logan busted a bottle over Sam's head. We had to leave."

"But why Kansas?"

"My brother wrote me a letter. He says my mom and dad separated. I guess she couldn't take his temper anymore either." Charisma began to tap her flip-flopped foot on the porch as if she were about to take off running. "Anyway, she came up here to some town called Wakefield to live with her sister."

"Wakefield. That's not so far from here. You almost made it."

"I don't know if she'll take me back." Charisma's voice cracked. "I've been gone four years. I'm coming back with two more mouths to feed and another on the way."

"She'll want to meet your beau and her grandchild, I'm sure of it."

"I don't know. Logan said it was worth a try, and we didn't have no place else to go. No place at all." Her bitter laugh fell around them like broken glass. "So that's how I ended up in the middle of nowheresville. No offense."

"None taken." Annie inhaled the sweet scent of roses that clung to the trellis on the other side of the porch railing. "I like it in the middle of nowheresville. I like it a lot."

"I have to get Logan out of jail. I have to get to Wakefield to see my mom. Before the baby's born."

"When is that?"

"I haven't exactly been to the doctor much—just the free family clinic in Baton Rouge, but I think it's probably about a month or so." Charisma shifted in her chair. "I should go on to Wakefield to see if my mom will take me back."

So they had a month to get Logan out of jail. Annie tried to imagine what Leah would say about having guests for that long. Was it even possible to get a person out of jail who tried to rob a bakery? The Englischers' court system was a mystery to her. "So we'll get Logan out of jail, and you'll go to Wakefield."

Said aloud it sounded like a grandiose promise. Annie had no idea how they could make it come true. *God,* she breathed silently, *it's up to You.*

Chapter 16

Annie stifled a yawn and rubbed her eyes. The sound of the deacon's droning voice made her want to nod off. She had no idea how long the prayer service had been so far, but the state of her behind said too long. She immediately lifted a contrite prayer. It was a privilege to be able to worship. She never allowed herself to forget that. Their copy of the *Martyr's Mirror* in the front room reminded her each day of the persecution her ancestors had suffered. She straightened and tried to focus. Next to her, Lillie wiggled on the hard wooden bench. Leah frowned and pinched the girl's arm. Lillie's face crumpled. Annie put an arm around her, ignoring Leah's glare.

Sweat trickled down her temple and tickled her cheek. She inhaled air heated by the many warm bodies crowded into the Glicks' barn. Her stomach growled so loud it sounded like an angry cat. Mary giggled.

"*Shhh,*" Leah hissed as she leaned over Lillie and gripped Mary's arm so hard Annie could see her fingernails digging into the flesh. "No."

Shaking her head, Annie plucked Leah's hand from her sister's arm. They exchanged glares.

To Annie's relief, Deacon Altman began the final prayer. Leah's focus shifted to the front of the barn again. When his voice stopped, everyone rose and began to file from the Glicks' barn in an orderly, quiet manner. Once outside, the chattering began. Annie loved the after-service fellowship. Good food, good conversation, a chance to catch up with what everyone had been doing during the week.

"If you two can't behave yourself in the service, you'll be making a trip to the woodshed." Leah shook a finger at the girls, her tone deflating Annie's joy like a cake taken out of the oven too soon. "I'll have your brother take a whip to you. Do you hear me?"

"Yes, Leah." Lillie and Mary hung identical heads. "We're sorry."

"You should be sorry. You showed a lack of respect for the minister. You're far too old to be misbehaving in the prayer service. It won't be tolerated—"

"They weren't the only ones wiggling, Leah." Annie took Lillie and Mary's hands in hers. "I saw more than one person nodding off. Between the heat and the extra-long sermon, I think everyone was a little sleepy."

"And you! You're one to talk." Leah's voice was a furious whisper but that didn't keep her from spitting the words out. The spray hit Annie's face, making her recoil. "You weren't paying attention yourself. That's what happens when you stay up late gabbing with a guest who has no concept of early rising, prayer, or hard work."

Getting out of bed before dawn had been a challenge, but Annie refused to complain or criticize her guest. "Maybe that is something we can share with her. Maybe that's what we're supposed to do. Show her a better way for her and for Gracie."

Leah opened her mouth, then shut it. She whirled and strode toward the house.

Annie turned to the twins. "Don't worry about her. She's just cranky because it's hard to take care of babies."

"We know." Mary frowned. "The worse she feels, the worse we feel."

Lilly scuffed at the grass with her shoe. "I'm going to wait a long time to have babies."

The twins would never romanticize the idea of having babies. Just as well. It was hard work, but worth it to have the blessing of a child. They would understand that when they were older. Annie's heart ached at the thought. She scanned the clusters of men gathered in the yard.

Engaged in conversation, most were headed for the picnic tables and food. David was here somewhere. Purposely avoiding her. Trying to ignore the hurt that realization brought her, she put her arms around the girls. "Come on. Let's go find Miriam and help bring out the food. After we eat, we can play volleyball."

Together they started across the yard.

"Annie, wait!"

Emma's sweet voice wafted across the yard. Delighted, Annie turned. Emma sat with Thomas's mother and sisters during the service now. The Brennaman family had arrived just as it was beginning, so Annie had had no chance to greet them. She flew across the yard. "Emma, how was your week? I didn't see you one time. I thought maybe you'd come by the bakery—"

"My week? How was your week? You were robbed? I couldn't believe it. I thought Thomas was teasing me at first. And you brought home the man's wife and child. Leah must've been fit to be tied."

"Yes, yes, and yes." Annie linked arms with Emma and they followed the twins, who were skipping across the yard to the Glick house. "We're fine. Only Charisma is not Logan McKee's wife. She's his... girlfriend."

"You do love a challenge, schweschder." Emma laughed. She looked so happy. Annie took a second to savor that. Emma deserved to be happy after all she'd been through. Her sister tilted her head, the picture of inquisitiveness. "Where is she this morning?"

"Asleep, I reckon. She couldn't sleep last night. She said it was too quiet."

"So you stayed up with her. That is so like you."

Annie shrugged. "We're going to play volleyball after we eat. Want to play?"

"I don't think so." A strange, almost dreamy look passed over Emma's face. Her free hand patted her stomach. "I've been feeling a little queasy lately."

Annie studied the hand on Emma's flat belly. "Emma Brennaman. Have you been holding out on me? Are you expecting?"

Emma beamed. "Yes."

"You're expecting!" Annie couldn't contain a shriek. Her sister had waited so long, endured so much disappointment. Finally, God had answered Emma's prayers. Annie threw her arms around her sister. "Wunderbar!"

Emma returned the hug. They danced around, laughing and crying at the same time, and ignoring the amused looks of their neighbors as they streamed past. "It's a dream come true, really." She clapped her hands. "A dream come true. Sometimes I'm afraid I'll wake up and it will be just that—a dream."

"You're not dreaming. You're wide awake." Annie pinched her arm, but not too hard. "When? When do you think the little one will arrive?"

"I don't know exactly. I haven't been to a doctor yet." Emma's face colored. "I wish *Aenti* Louise could deliver this baby. Her poor gnarled hands can't do it anymore."

"Josephina Belnap is a good midwife, I've heard." Only heard because she herself had no use for a midwife. At this rate, probably never would. *Oh, ye of little faith.* Surely, Emma had thought the same thing during those long years after Carl left her, then returned only to leave again, and Thomas's on-again, off-again courtship. "You should go talk to her, make arrangements."

"It's a little early. I only just realized…"

Annie shared an embarrassed look with her sister. Time to change the topic. "We'd better get to the kitchen and start helping. The twins have left us behind." She took the porch steps two at a time and opened the door for her sister. "Thomas must be so pleased."

"You know Thomas. Not much with words, but the look on his face…" Emma's smile grew even bigger. "It made me think of Daed when Mary and Lillie were born."

"Emma Brennaman, I've missed that smile!"

Miriam's cheerful voice interrupted their conversation. Annie turned to receive her friend's warm hug. "I didn't see you at the service."

"I was late." Miriam rolled her eyes and wrinkled her upturned nose. She glanced around the room. The din of dozens of women chattering as they made sandwiches and prepared dishes in the Glicks' kitchen meant no one was listening to their conversation. "My daed chose this morning for a heart-to-heart talk. Which, you know, means I listened and he talked."

"About what?"

Miriam twisted a towel in her hands. "What else?"

"Josiah?"

Her face miserable, she nodded. "He says I must move on or I'm going to end up alone. He expects me to marry and make my own home. There's nothing I'd like to do more. I love teaching as much as you did, Emma, but I don't want to end up in the school forever."

"You won't. You're only twenty." Emma squeezed her arm. "You're still young. I was twenty-two when I got married. Now I'm expecting my first baby at twenty-three. You have plenty of time."

Smiling again at the thought of Emma with a baby, Annie began to slap together sandwiches, placing thick slices of ham and roast beef on homemade bread. "I guess by Plain standards you were a little older, Emma, but not that much. Look at the Englischers. They marry so much later. My friend Melinda who works at the library—she's twenty-four and her sister just married. She's twenty-eight and her new husband is thirty. Can you imagine?"

"That's way too late when you have a farm to run and chores to be done. Imagine not starting a family until you're thirty. How would you work the land without sons to help?" A perplexed look on her face, Emma arranged the sandwiches on a platter. "Of course, they go to school so much longer, don't they?"

Miriam stuck a knife in the mayonnaise. "Do you ever miss being at school?"

"Not really." Annie tried to recall the days when she'd trudged to the schoolhouse to do arithmetic, learn English, and study basic science. "I used to beg Mudder to let me stay home and do the cooking for her. I'd much rather be baking and sewing and gardening. It seems so much more useful."

"Since I started teaching, I realized I sort of missed school. It's fun teaching the little ones English and to read. I think I like it better than the tack shop." Miriam flipped the knife too fast. Mayonnaise flew through the air and landed on Annie's sleeve. "Whoops! Got carried away there."

Peals of laughter drowned out the other women's conversation for a second. One or two looked around, smiles on their faces. "You'll have more opportunity to run into Plain men at the tack shop, though," Emma pointed out.

"I know all the Plain men around here." Miriam's expression darkened. "And apparently the Shiracks have all the tack they need. Haven't seen one of them in the shop since I came back to work."

Annie sighed. There wasn't a thing she could do to help Miriam. She could take a switch to Josiah for being so stubborn and so silly, but she knew he wouldn't budge until he was good and ready. With Sarah in town, who knew when that would be? "Did you ever think it would take this long for us to marry?"

Miriam's somber expression made Annie's heart hurt. "Never. I thought…"

"You thought Josiah was the one." Emma patted their friend's back. "He is the one. I know he is. Just give him time. It takes men a lot longer to grow up, apparently."

That observation lightened the mood as Emma surely intended. All three of them giggled. Annie slapped one last sandwich on the platter. "These are ready. We'd better get them out to the picnic tables before the men start eating the benches."

With a quick nod, Miriam slid the platter from the table and Emma grabbed a bowl of pickled cabbage and a stack of napkins. Following their lead, Annie corralled an enormous basket of cookies—cookies she'd made for this occasion—and headed toward the door.

Annie waited until they were on the porch to continue. "There's something else we need to talk about."

"What?" Emma raised her eyebrows. "Is Leah giving you grief?"

"Not me." Annie leaned toward her sister and her best friend. "Mary and Lillie."

"She's mistreating them?"

"Did you know Leah is expecting again?"

"Luke told Thomas who, of course, told me. What does that have to do with the twins?"

"I don't know. She's tired? Worried?" Annie lowered her voice, wary of others hearing her complain about her sister-in-law. She should be more compassionate, but somehow Leah's attitude goaded her into irritation instead. "All I know is she expects them to take care of her twins and do chores that are beyond their years. I believe in children doing chores as much as the next person, but she has no patience and never a kind word."

"Poor things, they're only six and so little." Miriam shook her head, her face a picture of sweet empathy. "I'm sure they try hard."

The memory of how tiny and light Lillie had felt in her arms a few years ago assailed Annie. They'd been tiny mites, the two of them. "They're old enough to weed the garden, and pick the vegetables, feed the chickens. But not hang men's pants on the clothesline."

"Not when the men are as tall as Luke or even Josiah." Miriam's face went dreamy—like she was imaging just how tall Josiah was. "Even if they stand on a stool."

"I don't know what to do to help them. I try to be home more, but the bakery takes so much of my time. Which is the problem. There's no one at home to help Leah so she expects the girls to take up the slack."

"Maybe I could…" Emma chewed her lower lip. "Do you think Luke would consider letting them come to stay with Thomas and me for a while? I am their sister."

"But then who would help Leah?"

Annie trotted down the front steps and dodged Leah's boys racing across the yard. The basket of cookies nearly went flying. Miriam held up the platter of sandwiches to keep it from spilling.

"Joseph! William! Slow down!" Miriam cried in her best teacher voice. She sounded a lot like Emma when she was the teacher. "Slow down right now!"

"Sorry, teacher!" They didn't slow at all or look the least bit sorry. "Food!"

"They mind you about as well as they minded me." Emma shook her head. "Does Luke know the boys are running wild?"

"That's the thing. Leah is so hard on the girls while her boys are turning into mischievious little rascals. She used to be so strict," Annie said. "Now she seems overwhelmed. I want to help more, but we need the money I earn at the bakery."

She closed her mouth as they approached the picnic tables crowded with men eating and talking about the price of wheat and the unusual heat wave so early in the summer. The question seemed to be how that would affect the upcoming harvest.

Josiah sat at one of the picnic tables, shoveling food into his mouth like he hadn't eaten in days. His predicament over Sarah and the bishop's orders to stay away from her certainly didn't seem to have affected his appetite. At eighteen, he was still a growing boy—one with grownup problems nevertheless. His gaze encountered hers, then skipped to Miriam. Annie saw the instant that the girl's presence registered. He ducked his head and dropped his fork on his plate.

Annie smacked the basket of cookies on the table in front of him. "Miriam brought more sandwiches. Do you want another?"

"No." The pause stretched. Finally he added, "Danki."

"Come on! How about a cookie? Look, these are chocolate chip pecan. They're your favorites."

"Danki." He snatched one from the basket as if a snake might hide in the midst of the bounty.

"Miriam has the recipe for these." Annie nodded toward her friend. "She makes really good cookies too."

"I'm sure she does." He stood. It always amazed Annie that her little brother now towered over her. He squeezed between the benches.

Annie grabbed a handful of cookies and handed them to Miriam. "I'm sure he'll want another one."

A petrified look on her face, Miriam shook her head, but she accepted Annie's offering. Annie jerked her head toward Josiah's retreating back.

"But my daed—"

Annie glared and jerked her head again. Miriam turned and scurried after Josiah.

Annie grinned at Emma, who put her hand over her mouth as if to stifle a giggle.

"Doing a little matchmaking, eh?" Peter Blount helped himself to a cookie. "Dangerous game."

Her cheeks burning, Annie smiled. "But worth it."

He shrugged and went back to his glass of iced tea.

Now, to solve the twins' problem. Annie grabbed her sister's hand and steered a course toward the road that led to the corral and barn. The men had already finished clearing the benches. The barn would be empty. This was a conversation better held in private.

"I don't see why Leah can't ask her sisters for help. They're older and their daughters are doing most of the work around the house by now," Emma said after they were out of earshot. "All she has to do is ask and all three of them will run to help her."

"True. I think she's too proud to ask. She doesn't want Luke to think she can't handle the household." Annie tried to imagine Luke's response. And Thomas's. "What about Thomas? Do you think he'll agree to bringing the twins into his home? You already have Eli and Rebecca. And the bobbeli on the way."

"Mary and Lillie are my sisters, and it's my home now too." Emma linked arms with Annie. "Mudder would want me to watch over them. Daed too. Besides, they are very helpful with small chores. Rebecca is older than her years. She already sews and bakes pies and helps me with the washing. Being without a mother until a few months ago made her grow up a little more quickly."

"Still, she's seven," Annie said. "She can't be any more help than the twins when it comes to cooking and laundry."

"It's different with Rebecca. She was alone with Thomas for a long time and she so wants to please him. Sometimes I think she's a little too grownup for her own good. It would be good for her to have Mary and Lillie to share chores and play." Emma smoothed her apron in a soft, circular motion. "By the time the baby comes, Rebecca will be eight and the girls seven. Eli will be eleven. Old enough to be very helpful."

"Then it's settled."

Emma giggled. Annie joined in. Nothing was settled until the men said so. Besides, Annie could imagine Leah saying no simply because she didn't know how to be agreeable. Then Luke would feel obligated to take his *fraa's* side. She took a deep breath and exhaled. "Will you ask Luke or should I?"

"Let me talk to Thomas first. If he says yes, we'll ask you all to come to supper. We can talk about it over the meal. Have a family meeting."

A family meeting. Those words brought back the dark days after Mudder and Daed's accident. And then Catherine's decision to leave. So many empty spaces at the table.

Sending Lillie and Mary to live with Emma would mean more empty spaces, but it would be best for them. That was what mattered. Not the empty spaces in Annie's heart.

≈

"You know you actually have to go up to her and say hello or she'll never know you're here."

David turned at the sound of Thomas Brennaman's voice. Sudden heat told him his neck had flamed red. He'd been caught leaning against a fence in the shade of a tree watching Annie walk by with her sister. He could only hope his longing had not been naked on his face.

Thomas chuckled. He leaned against the trunk of the old oak tree, shaded under its heavy boughs of leaves. David shifted and propped his boot on the bottom rung of a nearby fence. Annie and Emma had already passed, so engrossed in their conversation they hadn't noticed him in the shadow of the tree.

"What do you mean?" To his dismay, his voice sounded raspy. He cleared his throat. "I'm just getting some peace and quiet."

"Admiring from afar doesn't get you anywhere. I learned that the hard way."

It had taken Thomas forever to ask Emma to marry him. Now they seemed the picture of marital accord. David straightened. "I'm just enjoying a good day."

"A fine prayer service, good food, fellowship, the sun on your face. Blessing upon blessing. It is indeed a good day."

Thomas had lost his first wife to cancer. He understood about good days and bad days. David leaned down and plucked a long blade of grass. He rubbed it between his thumb and forefinger. "And fleeting."

"Exactly."

"What are you getting at?"

Thomas ambled over to the fence and leaned against the railing. "I never regretted one day of my marriage to Joanna. Annie won't regret marrying you—cancer or not."

"If Joanna were here, she might see my side of it." David trod carefully. Thomas might be remarried, but those wounds surely remained tender. "She might have wanted to spare you the pain, if she had the chance to do it over again."

"No."

"How can you be so sure?"

Thomas pointed toward the open pasture across the road. The children were tugging at volleyball net stands, setting them up. Their high-pitched voices mingled with laughter. Balls bounced back and forth before the net even straightened. Thomas's son and daughter were in the thick of it, Rebecca with her kapp in danger of blowing away and Eli scampering after a ball that rolled toward the road.

Finding no words, David simply watched the play for a few minutes. Thomas seemed to need to say nothing further. After a while, he stretched and started toward the road. "I thought I saw a cherry pie up at the house. Now that the sandwiches have settled I might have room for a piece."

"Wait for me."

The other man slowed. David fell into step beside his tall form.

"You still have that black stallion you bought at auction a couple of years ago?"

"No. I sold him to a farmer up by Emporia last year. He didn't take to the plow very well. Why do you ask?"

David tossed the blade of grass aside. "There's a little girl at the hospital who has a wish. Something about a story and a horse named Black Beauty."

"I think the Glicks had a black horse." Thomas grinned. "You ought to go in the barn and check."

David heaved a sigh. The last person he expected to start match-making was Thomas. "You're not coming?"

"I don't think you really want more witnesses. My experience has been it's embarrassing enough."

He was right. David picked up his pace.

"God be with you."

Thomas's words poured over David like early morning sunlight. This was Annie, after all. And he wasn't alone.

≈

Annie stood and brushed hay from her dress. Emma remained seated on a bale, her back against the barn wall. She looked so relaxed, so happy. Annie longed for that contentment. She strode over to the stalls. "Do you still miss Mudder?"

"Yes." Emma shifted. "But I'm more at peace than I used to be."

"That's because you have Thomas and his children."

"Have you seen David?"

"He gave us a ride home yesterday."

"That's a start—"

The barn door opened with a squeak. For a moment Annie couldn't tell who stood in the opening, silhouetted against the bright sunlight behind him. She held a hand over her eyes. "Josiah?"

"No, it's me. David." He eased into the barn, moving like a man afraid his horse might bolt and take his buggy with it. "I wanted to…I wanted to look at the Glicks' horses."

"Why?" Emma stood. "I mean, they're very similar to your horses."

Annie laughed. Emma joined in. David snapped his suspenders, a small grin on his face. "You always were a smarty-mouth, Emma. I don't know how Thomas puts up with it."

"He likes my cooking."

"I'm sure that overcomes many obstacles." David edged toward the stalls. "They don't have a black stallion. Do you, by any chance?"

He knew they did. Her heart raced in a funny pitter-patter that made her feel breathless and light-headed. He had sought her out. Well, he'd come to the barn to see the horses and she was here. He might have known that and come anyway. Inhaling the odors of manure and hay and old leather steadied her. This was David, Josiah's friend. Her friend. "We do. He has a very original name too. Blackie."

"A good name for a Plain man's horse."

"For any man's horse." Annie sidled closer to the stall. Closer to David. "Why are you interested in a black horse in particular? Ours isn't for sale. Luke is trying to buy another horse, not sell one."

David smoothed a hand over the Glicks' sorrel. The horse nickered and tossed his head as if joining the conversation. "I need to borrow a black horse."

"You need to borrow a black horse? Why black?" Annie glanced at Emma. She shrugged and cocked her head toward David. He couldn't see her pointing a finger at him and smiling. Annie glared at her and shook her head. David had come to look at a horse. Nothing else. "Have you talked to Luke about it?"

"It's just that…well, I think you might understand better." He stuck both hands on the stall railing and stared at his scuffed work boots. "You, with your homeless woman and child living in your house."

Annie leaned against the railing, close to him, yet still a proper distance. "Why? What is this about?"

"Kinsey, the little girl at the hospital." David's face reddened. He ducked his head. "The one you saw the other night."

"Before you kicked me out of your room?" Annie couldn't keep the tartness from her voice. She ignored Emma's scowl. "Before you told me you didn't want me to read to you from our favorite book from when we were schoolchildren?"

"Annie, we're not schoolchildren anymore." David stopped. He swiveled and glanced at Emma. She smiled as if to encourage him. Traitor. "This little girl, Kinsey, she has cancer. She's a city girl. Her dream is to ride a black stallion like she read about in some book called *Black Beauty*."

"Black Beauty." Annie and Emma spoke the words in unison. Annie could already see little Kinsey on the back of Blackie. He wasn't a beauty, but he was a good piece of horseflesh, as Luke liked to say. "So you want to make her dream come true."

"I want to give her riding lessons."

"Teach her to ride." Emma clapped her hands. "Make her dream come true."

"No. Dreams are the stuff of fairy tales." David smacked both hands on the railing, a hard rap that must've hurt. "I just want to give her what she wants. Not what the doctor or her mother thinks she needs."

"You want her to believe she will be coming back for more lessons, and someday she'll own a horse and teach her children to ride." Annie dared to put the words on his lips. He might not be able to put his feelings into words, but she knew him. He believed. He had faith. He had hope. At least, there had been a time when faith and hope were tightly woven into every part of his being. "You want her to live."

He didn't look up. He shook his head, then cleared his throat. His jaw worked, making the pulse in his temple jump.

Annie fought tears. Couldn't he see? Those with faith—true faith—always had hope. Knowing and believing in God's plan—that was the faith that led to hope. The events in their lives weren't random. Annie found great comfort and hope in that belief.

The familiar ache in her throat made it impossible for her to speak. She gave Emma an imploring look. Her sister stood. "What a nice idea. I think Luke will agree. It's a charitable thing to do. Just tell him you'll have the lessons when he's not in need of Blackie. Luke has a soft spot in his heart for all children. I know he'll want to help Kinsey."

"*Gut.*"

Apparently that one syllable was all David could manage to utter. It was so full of relief, the ache in Annie's throat eased. He needed her faith and hope to be enough for both of them. He brushed past her, his long strides putting space between them far too quickly. "David, wait. Wait!" She followed him without thinking. "Don't go."

He stopped and turned, and they nearly collided. "What?"

"I need help from you as well."

His expression suddenly wary, he nodded. "I always want to help, if I can."

Annie could almost feel Emma's curiosity swell and fill the room. She lifted her chin and stood straight. "I'd like you to go with me to take Charisma to talk to her mother. In Wakefield."

"Wakefield? That's northeast of here, isn't it?" He scratched his chin, his forehead wrinkled in puzzlement. "She has a van. Can't she drive herself?"

"I suppose she could, but she's expecting and we don't know when the baby is coming, and she shouldn't go by herself, and her mother might not welcome her, and then she'll be all alone, and what if the van breaks down, and Luke will never let me hire a driver and go without a chaperone—"

"Whoa, whoa! All right. It's fine." To Annie's utter amazement, a smile flashed across his face. Then that smile that could chase away all the darkness that threatened to creep into her world disappeared. "You are something, Annie Shirack."

Something? Was that good or bad? Because she wanted to help Charisma? Annie clasped her hands tight. "Does that mean you'll help?"

He touched the brim of his hat with one finger. "Good day, Emma. Tell Thomas he was right."

"He was right about what?" Emma asked.

"He'll know."

"Will you go with us to Wakefield?" Annie intervened.

"When you have permission from Luke to go, let me know." David spun and headed for the door. "I'm sure we'll see each other at the bakery."

He disappeared from sight.

"He's right, you know."

Annie turned to her sister, who had a big grin plastered on her face. "Right about what?"

"You are something."

Something? But what did that mean? What was that something to David?

And was it enough?

❧

Still savoring the last bite of his third cookie, Josiah held out his hand for more. He seemed to have a hollow leg when it came to eating these days. Miriam flashed empty palms at him. It was just as well. He couldn't continue to use a full mouth as an excuse for not talking. They'd walked all the way around the pond. Mostly without talking. He didn't know what to say, and Miriam seemed content to keep quiet. He searched for a topic of conversation. When had it become so difficult for them to talk?

"Good cookies."

"Your sister is a good baker." Miriam brushed crumbs from her hands and apron. "But you know that."

Why were they talking about Annie and cookies? He pointed to a fallen tree trunk in the shade of a few old oaks, out of the heat of the afternoon sun. "Do you want to sit down?"

"I suppose so." Fanning herself with long fingers, she sank onto the trunk. "Annie means well. She thinks we're meant to be together."

He tried to fathom her expression. Half sad, half exasperated. Like an adult scolding a child. He was no child. "Haven't you had enough of this already?"

"Enough of what?"

"This! Me!" He jabbed at his chest with his thumb. "I know I'm hurting you, but I can't seem to stop. I'd think you would want it to stop."

"I really just want you to react to me."

"React? Like how?"

Her face beaded with perspiration, she stared at the pond. "Like any how. You don't seem to not like me, but you don't seem to like me either. I'm just here. You don't take any more notice of me than that rock over there on the ground."

"That's not true."

"Face it, Josiah. I have. I'm not the one who has your heart."

"But you could."

She gave a halfhearted laugh. "Really?"

He propped his elbows on his knees and studied his boots. "I'd like to think so."

She picked up the rock, stood, and lobbed it into the water. "It would ease your conscience if I would find someone else and you wouldn't have to feel guilty about me."

He always admired her throwing arm. She'd been one of the best players in their baseball games. "I wish we could go back to the way it was before."

She turned and faced him. Tendrils of damp hair escaped her kapp and curled on her forehead. He fought the urge to smooth them back in place. From the look on her face, she might smack him. She sighed. "When? What way?"

"When we were friends."

Her face crumpled a little. "Aren't we friends now?"

"Not with this hanging between us."

She whirled and marched toward the edge of the pond, did an about-face, and marched back. "People who love each other should be friends."

Josiah let Sarah's image wash over him. They'd studied together, played video games together, gone to movies together. But the entire time he'd never stopped being aware of the tension between them.

Sarah's brother had called it chemistry. Josiah never acted upon it, never considered acting upon it. Mudder and Daed had brought him up better than that. But it didn't matter what they were doing, the physical attraction saturated the air around them. Not so with Miriam. His heart reared up to protect this girl with the brown eyes flecked with gold and the impressive throwing arm. He wanted to make sure no one ever hurt her or made her cry. Did that make her a friend? Or another sister?

"All right, I take it back. We are friends."

She sank onto the trunk, so close Josiah could see the tears that wet her eyelashes. "But nothing more?"

Her shoulders tensed and her face contorted with confusion and sadness. Without thinking Josiah grasped her fingers and held on.

Her lips parted and her earth-colored eyes grew large. They stared at each other, the only sounds her ragged breathing and birds bickering in the branches overhead. Josiah held her heart in his hands. "I don't know," he whispered, trying to fathom the sudden fluttering of his own heart. It seemed familiar, yet oddly different. It made his bones ache. "I truly don't know."

She jerked her hands away and stood. "When you figure it out, let me know."

She stalked away, her dress flapping behind her. The utter quiet left by her absence overwhelmed him. He tried to imagine his life without Miriam Yonkers in it. If he let Sarah in, Miriam would be gone forever. He couldn't have both. "Easy for you to say," he whispered to her retreating back.

Even though he knew it wasn't.

Chapter 17

Josiah turned the buggy onto the road that led to the Miller farm. His hands felt slick on the reins. This was a bad idea. In the first place, he didn't know if Miriam would even show up for the singing. She usually came with her brother Paul. Then she and Josiah would slip away sometime later when the singing was in full swing. They would take a long, meandering route to her parents' farm that gave them plenty of time to talk and enjoy each other's company. After the scene by the pond earlier in the day, he doubted that would happen tonight. So why had he come? Because of the strange sensation that had lingered inside him long after she stalked away? Because of the way her hands had trembled in his? Because of the catch in her voice when she told him to let her know when he figured it out?

He couldn't answer any of those questions. His feelings for Miriam were nothing like what he'd experienced with Sarah. That sense of drowning, of not being able to catch his breath every time she slid her hand down his arm and caught her fingers in his. Holding Miriam's hand had been different. Like being wrapped in a warm, comfortable quilt on a cold winter night.

He could be himself. Miriam would accept him exactly as he was. With Sarah, he had to be bigger, stronger, surer than he was. A man. With Sarah, his feelings were all over the place. With Miriam, they were steady on. Which was right?

He pulled up next to a dozen buggies already parked in neat rows outside the barn. Noah Kale waved as he jumped from his two-seater. A beauty of a courting buggy. "Good to see you, Josiah."

Noah would leave the singing with Mary Barton—everyone knew that. There would be at least one wedding in the fall. "I think Miriam's inside." Noah had always been a good friend—one who would understand that Josiah wanted to do the right thing. "I saw them on the road earlier."

"Gut." Not knowing what else to say, Josiah tied the horse near a hay stanchion and waited for Noah to go inside. He patted Mooch's forelock. "Bravery, my friend, bravery." More bravery was needed in affairs of the heart than on any other battlefield. He sucked in air, the smell of hay and dirt and manure mingled in a calming medley. *Stop standing around.*

Inside, the kerosene lanterns gave a soft glow to the high ceiling of the barn. Bales of hay and a few benches served as seating. The place was already full. Sunday night singings were popular among the younger teens. Still new to them. The novelty had worn off for Josiah. He surveyed the crowd. Boys on one side, girls on the other. They wouldn't start pairing off until much later, after the first round of singing ended and darkness gave cover. Where was she?

There. She wore that dark green dress that made her brown eyes seem almost hazel. He started toward her. Their gazes connected for a long moment. Then she turned and slipped into a cluster of friends, her back to him.

Josiah changed direction. Paul Yonkers stepped in his path. "Hello, Josiah." His tone was casual, even friendly, unusual for him. "Can I have a word?"

He stopped. "Jah."

"Outside."

The underlying command wasn't lost on Josiah. He followed Miriam's older brother through the door, jostling against the flow of friends who hollered and waved and moved on, intent on the fun sure to follow.

Paul led the way around the corner, out of the light and frivolity. His earlier smile had disappeared. "Courting is none of my business—"

"Then why are we standing out here?" Josiah wanted the words back as soon as he said them. Antagonizing Miriam's family did him no good. "I mean, I'm just here for the singing."

"I want you to know that Miriam has said she wants me to drive her home tonight."

"That'll make it hard for you to court Susannah, won't it?"

Paul didn't answer. He stared, his gaze hard and direct.

Josiah scuffed at a patch of dirt with his boot. "I'd rather Miriam told me what she wants herself."

"You have one foot in the fancy world. You can't keep your thoughts from another woman." His gaze was steely, but Paul's voice remained even. "You know it would be best for Miriam if you left her out of your dilemma."

"I didn't ask Sarah to come here, and I gave my word to the bishop that I won't see her."

"You said yourself she plans to stay. She wants to be a part of your life."

"The bishop will not allow her to join the community and even if he did, I have made no promises to her. Or to anyone."

Paul flexed massive arms and crossed them. "That's the problem, my friend." He brushed past Josiah. "You don't make promises so you don't have to keep them. Stay away from Miriam. She's here tonight because she's trying to do what's right."

"And what's that?"

Paul stopped. He turned. The moon cast harsh shadows on his smooth face. "She's trying to get on with her life. I'm asking you to let her."

Josiah stood in the shadows for a long time after Paul disappeared around the corner. Paul was right. Miriam had been caught in his indecision for far too long. Time to let her go. It was the right thing to do.

Chapter 18

Stifling a huge yawn, Annie strode into the front room, looking for Charisma. The woman stood by the front windows, staring out. She'd been subdued all morning, hardly speaking at all. As if she was embarrassed about their long conversation Saturday night. She'd spent most of Sunday sleeping in her room while the twins played with Gracie. When Annie had attempted to talk to her about going to see her mother in Wakefield she'd said she wasn't ready yet. Since then she'd been morose and silent. Now her hands rubbed her huge belly in a circular, absentminded motion.

Annie stopped a few feet away. "We don't have to go see your mother, if you don't want to see her." No trip to Wakefield with David. Annie struck down that selfish thought. "You can stay here as long as you like."

"I can't go until I know how long Logan will be in jail. If it's very long…"

Her voice trailed off. She looked so sad, Annie wanted to help. "You always have a place here, if you need it."

"We're just more work for your sister-in-law. It's obvious she doesn't want us here. I don't like being a pain." Charisma grimaced and rubbed her stomach again. "Maybe I could get a job. Like at the restaurant or something. I could waitress."

"Have you ever done it?" Annie tried to ignore the more obvious issues. Charisma was about to have a baby, and who would watch Gracie? "It's awfully hard to be on your feet for an eight-hour shift when you're carrying a baby."

"I've done it before. A long time ago…" Charisma's fleeting enthusiasm for the idea seemed to melt before Annie's eyes. "I just thought if I could get some money, it might help get Logan out of jail."

Annie moved closer. Maybe a change in topic would help. "The breakfast dishes are done. The floors have been mopped and the garden tended. Everyone will be here soon for the quilting frolic. It's really fun—"

Charisma turned. Her fingers went to a wayward strand of her tangled hair and began to twist it. "I'm telling you—this quiet is going to make me crazy."

"It's not really quiet. I can hear the mower outside and the children playing and the chickens squawking."

"Even after I finally go to bed, I can't sleep. The quiet is huge. Like buzzing in my ears." Charisma waddled to the rocking chair and sat with a loud thump. The chair creaked. "At least you could listen to the soaps while you do all these chores by hand. Don't you miss TV?"

It was hard to miss something she'd never had. "No."

"No TVs. No soap operas. No movies. No sitcoms. No reality TV shows. Nothing for the kids to watch."

"They don't need anything to watch. They have too much to do already."

"When we…before we left Baton Rouge, Gracie used to watch *Sesame Street* every day. She was learning to count. I got a lot done while she watched TV."

"We teach our children to count. We don't need a TV for that. And they help with chores so we don't need a babysitting TV."

"It's just so much easier."

"Easy isn't always best." Now she sounded like Luke. The thought tickled Annie, but she didn't laugh. Charisma looked far too unhappy. Annie didn't know how to help. This was how they lived. "Since I'm off from the bakery today, we're doing something fun. We're having a quilting frolic. We'll make quilts for the babies."

Charisma's lifted eyebrows signaled her disbelief. "Quilting? You mean like sewing? That's what you guys call fun?"

"It's loads of fun." Annie rushed over to the table, intent on convincing her guest. She began cutting blocks. "It's easy, really. You just sew the squares together in rows. The different colors make the pattern."

Her steps heavy, Charisma joined Annie at the table. The other woman fingered the green material, but she didn't look convinced. "You mean like with a needle and thread?"

"You've never sewn?" Annie cut another block. "Never? Not even a button or mending a hole in a sock?"

Charisma lowered her head like a schoolgirl in trouble for passing notes. "Sorry."

"Don't be sorry!" Annie pointed to a chair. "Sit. I can teach you. Then you can make clothes for Gracie. And for yourself even. It's much less expensive. We can make clothes for the baby. Even diapers."

"Diapers? You mean like cloth diapers? No one uses those anymore." Charisma grimaced. "And besides, Gracie will never leave me alone long enough to actually do something that complicated."

Everyone Annie knew used cloth diapers. "The diapers are the easiest. You just hem the blocks of material. I'll show you. Just because you've never done it yet doesn't mean you can't."

"Yeah, but then you have to wash the stinky, poopy diapers. Who wants to do that?"

"People who are frugal."

"What's frugal?"

"That's what people need to be when they don't have much money." Annie didn't mean to rub it in. Everyone she knew needed to be frugal. "I mean, people who are careful with their money."

"I guess that would be me—if I had any money to be frugal with. Which I don't." Charisma sighed and shrugged her shoulders. "What do I do?"

Annie handed her a swathe of material. "We'll start with something fun today—a baby quilt. Cut out your squares. Lillie and Mary will watch the babies and Gracie. When she gets a little older, you can teach her too. Later I'll show you how to make a little dress for her—they're super easy. Hardly any trouble at all."

"You're such a Goody Two-shoes." Charisma's smile took the sting out of the words. The smile died. "My dad used to say that to my mom."

Before Annie could respond, loud chatter and laughter poured through the open windows. Their friends had arrived, and the quilting frolic could begin. The thought lifted Annie's spirits. She loved the visiting as much as the sewing. "They're here! This will be fun. You'll see."

The trickle of women turned into a steady flow, all laughing and talking and carrying their bundles of sewing supplies and material. Emma came in the first wave. Annie sidestepped Helen Crouch and her sister Marie. "Emma, am I ever glad to see you."

Emma cocked her head toward Rebecca, Thomas's daughter. "Look who I brought. Rebecca is excited to help make her first quilt."

Rebecca broke into a grin, the spitting image of her father. "I even brought my own material." She held up a bundle of maroon cloth. "Emma helped me pick it out."

"That's beautiful. It will be a nice addition to the quilt." Annie introduced her to Charisma. "Rebecca, show Charisma how to set everything up, and I'll be back in a minute to help you both get started."

Rebecca grabbed Charisma's hand, not the least bit concerned about her new friend's too-tight red stretch pants, bulging stomach, nose stud, or purple eye shadow. "You're going to love quilting. It's so much fun."

Charisma didn't look convinced, but she let the girl lead her over to the table. She glanced back at Annie, who gave her an encouraging smile. "She's right. It's fun."

"So." Emma linked arms with Annie and steered her toward the kitchen. "I talked to Thomas about the twins."

Annie surveyed the kitchen to make sure there weren't any unexpected listeners. "What did he say?"

"He says the more the merrier."

A swift, unexpected pain whipped through Annie, leaving her breathless. From the look on Emma's face, her sister felt it too. "Just like Daed used to say."

"Exactly."

"No wonder you love Thomas so much."

"You'll have this too, Annie. I have faith." Emma patted Annie's shoulder. "For so long, it looked like I would never have this happiness and now I do. That's how I know you will too."

If only it were true. Annie tried to give that burden up. God's will. Another thing Daed used to say. God's will. God's time. Annie's heart constricted. Time could be short, very short, for David. Why did he choose to spend it far from her? Not having an answer to that question, she tried to focus on the topic at hand. The twins.

"Now we just have to convince Luke and Leah." Annie picked up the tea jug and poured two big glasses. "With me working at the bakery, you married, and Catherine gone, Leah's lost her helping hands. And she might not want to rely on her sisters."

Emma added heaping tablespoons of sugar to both glasses. "She's already made it clear she doesn't think the twins help enough."

"Yet they take care of the little ones all the time."

"Can we sit a minute?" Emma handed a glass to Annie and motioned toward the benches. "My breakfast is trying to decide if it should stay or go this morning."

"I still can't believe you're having a baby!"

"It's becoming more and more real to me." She put a hand to her mouth for a second and then exhaled. "Let's talk about something else. Maybe that will take my mind off the morning sickness. What about your visitor? Charisma, you said her name was. What a funny name. When is her baby coming?"

"She doesn't know for sure. She hasn't been to a doctor or a midwife. She thinks maybe a month or two." Annie didn't know how much she should share of those midnight confidences. Charisma's problems were private. "She'll need help with her delivery if Logan is in jail very long."

"Did you talk to Luke about going with her to Wakefield? Surely if David goes with you he won't object."

"Charisma says she's not ready to face her mudder yet. And she wants to see how long Logan will be in jail before she goes."

"And you were so looking forward to riding up there with David." Emma grinned. "Poor thing."

"No. I'm not a poor thing. She is. And poor Luke. Being the head of this household must be—"

"Annie, come quick!" Mary dashed into the kitchen, her bare feet slapping on the wooden floor. "It's a police car! There's a police car coming up the road!"

"Slow down, little one." Annie grabbed Mary's arm. "You're going to knock Emma over."

"Emma!" Mary threw herself at their older sister, immediately forgetting about her mission. "You're here!"

"Help with the quilting, will you?" Annie tossed the words over her shoulder as she rushed through the door. A police car at the door. Leah would love that. Luke too.

She reached the porch just as Sergeant Parker climbed the steps. A man in a suit that hung on him like he'd shrunk in the wash followed. Sergeant Parker snatched his hat from his head, but didn't remove sunglasses so shiny Annie could see herself in them. She didn't like not being able to see his kind blue eyes.

"Miss Shirack, good morning." His tone was businesslike, not the tone he used when he came to buy a dozen maple logs. "I hope you aren't feeling any bad effects from the other day."

"I'm fine." Annie forced herself to stand still, hands clasped in front of her. Sergeant Parker always had the effect of making her want to squirm like a schoolgirl. "Can I help you with something?"

"This here's Bob Moreland. He's the city attorney. He wants to talk with you about the arraignment tomorrow."

Mr. Moreland removed his hat and bowed slightly. "It's about your testimony."

What an interesting name. Moreland. Like more land to farm.

Annie ignored the silly thought brought on by nerves and the word *testimony*. She moved to the porch railing. "I have company. I can't talk about this now."

"Having a party? I didn't think you folks partied much." Mr. Moreland's gaze moved beyond her. "Especially on a Monday morning. Don't you have to toil in the fields or something?"

"It's not a party." Annie smiled to show she took no offense. Most people didn't understand their ways. "It's a quilting frolic."

"I see. One of those women things." He twirled his hat on one hand. His tone said such a thing couldn't be very important in his world. "This will only take a moment or two."

Annie glanced toward the road that led to the highway. Luke and Mark were planting milo. Josiah was at the shop. With any luck, Leah was lying down, resting. Her morning sickness had been bad at breakfast. It would be rude to send these men away. "Shall we talk here or would you like to come in? Would you like tea or lemonade? They're both fresh."

"Don't trouble yourself." Sergeant Parker rested a hand on the butt of the gun hanging from his hip. "Here's fine. Like Mr. Moreland said, it shouldn't take too long. I heard you had a young lady and her daughter staying here with you."

Annie bit back a snappy retort. Having company didn't break any laws. Not that she was an expert on Englischers' laws. "Yes. We have company."

"A Miss Charisma Chiasson."

"Yes."

Sergeant Parker scratched his blond head and sighed. "I wish you hadn't done that."

"She's expecting, and she has a little girl who needs a bed to sleep in. Was I supposed to leave her in a dirty van?" Annie paused for a second, contemplating the scowl on his face. "Why would you care? She hasn't broken any laws."

"Logan McKee is wanted in three other states. He has a rap sheet that goes back years—all the way to juvie court." Mr. Moreland leaned against the railing and fanned himself with his hat. "Charisma Chiasson may be an accomplice in half a dozen thefts, petty crimes, and robberies of habitations. You may be harboring a criminal."

"Charisma isn't a criminal. She's having a baby."

Still frowning, Sergeant Parker moved past Annie so he stood between her and the screen door. She got a whiff of his light, spicy scent. "Did you ask her if she knew what Logan was doing? He didn't have a job, but they had money for gas and food to get them from Louisiana to Kansas. Don't you think she wondered how that could be?"

"I didn't want to bring it up." Annie shifted, the porch rough under her bare feet. The image of Logan's apologetic face floated in front of her. He had broken the law to feed his loved ones. Why didn't he ask for help or try to get a job? Maybe he had. Who was she to judge? "Charisma's upset about Logan being in jail and like I said, she's expecting."

"Her boyfriend pointed a gun at you." Sergeant Parker's tone remained gentle. He removed the offending sunglasses. His eyes weren't so warm now. In fact, they seemed hard. "Don't you want to know how much she knew about it?"

"She wasn't in the bakery with Logan on Thursday." Amazed at her own audacity in talking to these Englisch men, Annie folded her arms to hide her shaking hands. "She doesn't need anyone upsetting her."

"We just want to talk to her. Ask her a few questions."

"She's resting."

"Excuse me, we represent the city of Bliss Creek in this." Mr. Moreland's tone said his patience was thinning. "You are a witness to a crime. Charisma Chiasson may be an accomplice, or at the very least, another witness. I want her out here right now, or I'm sending Sergeant Parker in there to get her."

"Whoa, slow down there, Bob. Let's not get carried away." Sergeant Parker showed no signs of storming the house. "We're just talking here."

"It doesn't matter." Annie took a long breath and gave the officer an apologetic look. "I'm not testifying. Not against Logan or against Charisma. We don't sit in judgment of others."

"Mayor Haag was right. You are a stubborn lot." Mr. Moreland slapped his hat on his head. He adopted Annie's stance, with arms folded. "Do you know what a subpoena is?"

Annie chewed on her lip, searching her brain for an answer. Nothing came to mind. Not from school. Maybe from reading *The Budget*. "I'm not sure. Like a legal paper."

"Yes. It will mean you have to come to court and be cross-examined by the attorneys."

"And if I don't?"

"The judge can hold you in contempt and put you in jail."

An instantaneous raging river of fear coursed through her. Bishop Kelp and the deacons wouldn't like that at all. They would be upset that she brought upheaval to the community by getting involved with Englischers. Luke would be furious. She turned to Sergeant Parker, hoping he would understand. And help. "I didn't do anything wrong."

"I know you didn't, Annie. We're just asking you to do the right thing now." Sergeant Parker took a step toward her. His big boots thudded on the porch. "Tell the judge what happened. Just tell the truth."

"Or you'll be in a jail cell across from your friends." Mr. Moreland straightened. "What's it going to be?"

"Bob, that's enough." Sergeant Parker slapped his hat on his head. "I'll not have you threatening citizens, especially ones who've done nothing wrong."

Thankful for his support, Annie ducked behind him and put her hand on the door. "I have to talk to my brother. You'll have to come back later."

"That's fine. We don't need you at the arraignment, only at the trial. Unless he takes the plea bargain we're offering, he'll be bound over for trial." Mr. Moreland gave Annie what surely must've been his version of a smile. More like a grimace. "You should tell his girlfriend to talk him into taking the plea. It'll save you and your employer and that other girl from having to testify at the trial. If it goes to trial and you don't testify, you'll be arrested. Mark my words, missy."

Sergeant Parker towered over the other man. "You have an eyewitness in Mayor Haag, and Officer Bingham caught the suspect with the money and the gun. You can make your case at trial without our Amish friends."

"The more evidence we can present the better." Mr. Moreland's face darkened to a beet red. "The man is a menace to the community. We have to send a message—"

"Leave her alone. It's me you want."

They all turned at the sound of Charisma's voice. She pushed through the screen door and halted in front of Sergeant Parker. She held out two skinny wrists. "You want me, you got me." She lifted her chin and smirked. "Go ahead. Slap on the cuffs and take the pregnant lady to jail."

Chapter 19

Annie scurried between Sergeant Parker and Charisma. She couldn't let Charisma do something foolish like get herself arrested for no good reason. Mr. Moreland had a grin on his face as if he'd just been given a gift. The porch suddenly seemed very crowded, and the morning sun pressed against Annie's face, making it damp with sweat. She inhaled the sweet scent of roses and tried to get her bearings. Surely they wouldn't arrest a woman expecting a baby. Charisma hadn't broken any laws, but Annie couldn't begin to understand the Englisch way of doing things.

"Sergeant Parker just wanted to ask some questions." She needed to move the conversation off the porch—away from the open windows and big ears of her neighbors and friends. They weren't gossips, but who could resist listening to this particular conversation? "Let's take a walk down to the corral."

"What about Gracie?" Charisma had a mulish look on her face that reminded Annie of Mary when it was time for her bath. "I need to keep an eye on her."

"Lillie was teaching her to dress herself the last time I saw her. They'll keep her occupied."

"Fun, fun." Charisma muttered, but she allowed Annie to lead her away from the screen door. "Whatever."

After introducing Mr. Moreland, Sergeant Parker led the scraggly parade toward the corral that lined one long side of the barn. Mr. Moreland tried to start the questioning more than once, but the police officer's stern stare made his words trail away each time.

Only when Sergeant Parker had slapped both big hands on the fence railing did he say anything. "Miss Chiasson, tell me, did you help Logan rob a house in Baton Rouge, Louisiana, a convenience store in Fort Worth, Texas, and a grocery store in Stillwater, Oklahoma?"

"Don't I get a lawyer?" Charisma's snarl matched her tangled hair. Annie couldn't believe she was the same girl who had whispered her life story on the porch two nights earlier. "Aren't you supposed to read me my rights?"

"You're not under arrest, but if you think you need a lawyer, we'll stop talking right now and you can ride into town with us. I'll call you somebody, and we'll do this official-like in the interview room, video-tape and everything."

Her face shiny with sweat, Charisma crossed her arms over her belly in a protective gesture. "I didn't know."

"You didn't know police were looking for him on half a dozen charges?"

"I said I didn't know."

Sergeant Parker tugged a handkerchief from his pocket and swiped sweat from under his eyes and temples. "Where did you think he was getting the money for food and gas?"

"He said he had some travelers' checks his dad gave him. He was cashing 'em in." Charisma fanned her face with her hand. "Besides, I never saw no money. He'd come back with the van gassed up and a sackful of groceries or he'd come back with a sackful of hamburgers and fries and a six-pack of soda. If I asked him for money for a comb or some shoes for Gracie, he said there wasn't none."

"Where'd he get the gun?"

"How do I know? I didn't know nothing about any gun until after the thing at the bakery."

"It's not registered to anyone. It's not from any of the break-ins. The bakery was the first place he used a weapon. What changed?"

"I don't know." Her voice rose. She turned her back on them and marched up and down in the grass. "Don't you get it? Nothing changed, 'cept we had no gas and no food and no place to stay. Maybe he figured he was in so much trouble now, it didn't matter. I don't know because you won't let me talk to him."

Annie trotted alongside her, back and forth, back and forth, trying to keep up with the woman's agitated stride. "It's all right. You don't have to answer any more questions." She gave Sergeant Parker her own hard stare. Like Emma's schoolteacher stare. She'd practiced it in case she was ever called upon to substitute. "I'm sorry, but you're upsetting a lady who is expecting a child. That's not nice."

"Sorry, ma'am. Didn't mean to upset either of you." Sergeant Parker leaned against the corral fence, studying the three horses nibbling at hay in the corner. "I just don't get it. Why didn't he use the gun before?"

Annie grabbed the fence railing and inhaled the familiar smell of manure, hay, and feed. It grounded her. "Nothing to rob in the houses in Bliss Creek. People don't have much and what they do have, they're willing to share." She kept the accusation out of her voice. As strangers, Charisma and Logan had no way of knowing that. "Desperation. Pure desperation."

Sergeant Parker leaned toward her. "You folks aren't having problems, are you?" His voice softened and his gaze seemed to encompass everything about her. "If you ever need anything, just let me know. We aim to serve at Bliss Creek PD."

Annie swallowed, taken back by the intensity of his gaze. "That's nice of you, Sergeant Parker—"

"Dylan. Call me Dylan, please."

"Sergeant—Dylan, that's very kind, but we're doing fine."

"Could we get past this little neighborly love fest and get back to the issue at hand—where did the gun come from?" Mr. Moreland swatted away a horsefly, a look of disgust on his face. "It smells like cow pies out here and it's hotter than Hades."

The *clip-clop* of horses' hooves against the sun-baked dirt road forced Annie to break the hold Sergeant Parker had on her gaze. Who should be coming up the road but Luke and Mark? The wagon slowed and stopped. Luke jumped down. "What is this all about? What are you doing out here with the police?"

"The sergeant was just telling your sister how much he'd like to help her out." Charisma jumped in before Annie had a chance. She plucked a long weed and twiddled it between her fingers. "I mean, help y'all out, of course, not just her."

Luke's expression went from dusk to midnight.

"What Charisma means..."Annie began.

"What Miss Chiasson means is that we're here conducting an investigation into the armed robbery of the bakery." Sergeant Parker replaced his sunglasses on his nose. "I have here a possible accomplice." His hand waved toward Annie, then dropped before he actually touched her. "And a witness."

Luke removed his hat and slid his hand through his wild hair. "I'd be obliged, Sergeant Parker, if you would allow me to speak with my sister in private."

Mr. Moreland started to protest, but Sergeant Parker held out his hand. "We'll be getting out of your way. I know you folks have work to do." He nodded to Annie and Charisma. "Talk among yourselves. Mr. McKee will be arraigned at ten o'clock tomorrow morning. Your presence is not required for the arraignment. However, I'm sure he wouldn't mind seeing some friendly faces in the courtroom."

"Not needed!" His face red, Mr. Moreland tramped after Sergeant Parker. His legs were too short to keep up. "We need to take their statements. We need to depose them."

Annie watched as Sergeant Parker lengthened his stride. Mr. Moreland trotted faster, almost at a run. She put a hand to her mouth to hide her smile.

"Somebody's got a crush on you!" Charisma giggled as if her problems had dissipated with the departure of the two men. "Do you like him? Sergeant Parker—Dylan—is a hunk. Way hotter than Mister Bald and Tragic. I mean, I feel sorry for the guy and all, but the woe-is-me thing gets kinda old, I imagine."

"He does not have a crush on me. I mean, I've never noticed him one way or another. He's an Englischer." She caught Luke's frown. His shaggy eyebrows were up so high they met over the top of his nose. "He's a police officer doing his job. And just so you know, David has Hodgkin's lymphoma. That's why he is bald. And sad-looking."

"An Englischer?" Charisma didn't seem to hear Annie's explanation. She was too busy looking horrified. "You mean you can't date anybody but guys with blue shirts, suspenders, and hats?"

"You will not go to the courthouse." Luke bore down on Annie before she could answer Charisma. "You will stay out of this. Now get up to the quilting frolic. You have company."

He stormed toward the barn without looking back.

Charisma leaned over and spit. "He's uptight, isn't he?"

Trying to hide her disgust at the spit, Annie focused on the earlier discussion. "We don't court people who aren't Plain because it would be very hard for them to live life the way we do. Most aren't used to working this hard. It's a very simple life, one they don't understand."

"That's for sure. No electricity. It's pretty radical. You must really believe in that God of yours." Charisma did a little two-step to avoid a chicken strutting through the yard. "Kind of narrows the gene pool, doesn't it, though?"

Annie didn't know what that meant, so she focused on the first part of her guest's statement. "God of ours? Don't you believe in God?"

"Have you heard anything I've told you in the last few days?" The bitterness in her voice was so sharp, Annie touched her cheek, sure she'd find blood there. "Look at me. If there's a God, He's one mean guy."

"No, no, no, He's not." Annie grappled for words. Always surrounded by her community of believers, she'd never had to defend God before. "He has a plan."

"Whatever. I'm going to the courthouse tomorrow." Charisma started toward the house. "You coming with me?"

Maybe now wasn't the time, but there would be a time. Charisma, as much as anyone Annie had ever met, needed to know God had a plan for her.

She didn't bother to answer Charisma's other question about the courthouse. Either her visitor's hearing was bad or she still didn't understand the fundamental truth of their ways. Luke said no courthouse. That meant no courthouse.

Chapter 20

Josiah peered through the tack shop window. Miriam stood near the front door talking to Samuel Miller, who held a package in his arms. The conversation looked animated. Knowing Miriam, she was regaling Samuel with stories of the latest foal's birth at the farm where her brothers raised and trained cutting horses. Exhaling, he considered his options. He shouldn't go in there while she had a customer, but he wanted to talk to her. He needed to talk to her. He'd been wrong not to do it Sunday night at the singing.

The memory of seeing her standing outside the Glicks' barn Sunday night, her face smiling as she talked to Simon Gross near the end of the singing when the pairing off had started, burned in his brain. Far hotter than her brother Paul's words. Josiah had forced himself to stay and be a part of a crowd that no longer held interest for him. He told himself he did it to move on with his life, just as Miriam was doing. Instead, he'd found himself watching her the entire evening, unable to take his gaze from her as she sang and laughed and talked to everyone but him.

Paul had no right to tell Josiah to whom he could talk. Both Miriam and Josiah were still in their rumspringas. Everyone seemed to have forgotten that. Everyone except Josiah. He hadn't slept for two nights. Tossing and turning, Sarah to one side, Miriam to the other. He had to talk to Miriam. He couldn't forget the sad look on her face at the pond and the feel of her hand in his. So soft, yet so strong. A paradox. Like Miriam herself. So soft and sweet, but built with a backbone made of steel. No one would sway her from what was right. His moral compass.

"Got a harness that needs mending?"

The sound of Solomon Yonkers's voice sent a chill up Josiah's sweaty arms and jolted him from his uncomfortable reverie. Solomon had never been friendly, but he had grown even colder since Josiah's sojourn to Wichita. "No. I...No." Josiah pulled his hat down and moved away from the window. "Just passing by. We needed a couple of things from the hardware store."

"We don't sell nails and such." Solomon's hard stare traveled to the window. He put a hand on the door. "If you're needing tack, I can help you with that."

The emphasis on the *I* was unmistakable. Leave Miriam out of it. "I...I won't be needing anything."

Solomon brushed past him and let the door close with a hard, final slap.

Josiah sat down on the bench. As much as he respected Solomon's position, he had to talk to Miriam. He owed it to her. He had to tell her he meant what he said about not contacting Sarah. As much as his heart and mind battled over it, he had to keep his word to the bishop. He couldn't put his family through that again. He wished he had someone to talk to about it. It used to be he talked to Emma. And David had made his position clear. He would never waver from the tried and true. David never gave an inch. He held his friends accountable. Josiah respected that, even if it sometimes fit him like a shirt two sizes too small. No need to talk to David when he knew exactly what he would say. Josiah would have to muddle through on his own.

"Well?"

He jerked up. Miriam stood in the doorway. He rose. "I...you... your father said..."

"I'm in my rumspringa. Until I'm baptized I still have some leeway. Daed knows that and so does Paul, despite what he said to you Sunday night." Miriam shut the door. She didn't sit down next to him. Not in broad daylight on a Bliss Creek street. "My father knows he's very blessed. I haven't run around like some others."

"Like me, you mean."

She smiled. "Well, as an example."

"You're not mad about what happened at the pond?"

"Sad, Josiah, not mad."

"So why did you avoid me at the singing? Why were you talking to Simon Gross? His rumspringa has been just as…eventful as mine."

"You have no right to ask me about Simon. I can talk to any Plain man I please." Her cheeks turned pink. She strode a few steps along the sidewalk, her long skirt swishing as she walked. *Swish-swish.* It sounded angry. When she turned, though, she still looked sad. "You're the one who makes it so I can talk to him. By your choices. I can't wait forever."

"I know you've been more than patient."

"Helen Crouch is coming." She slipped past him and put her hand on the door. "You've never had a very good sense of timing. Or propriety. This isn't a conversation you have on the street."

"If you want propriety, you won't get it from Simon. Be sure of that." Why did he keep going on about Simon Gross? Jealousy burned through him like fire fueled with kerosene. He had no right to be jealous. "I'll give you propriety. I'll come for you one night this week. Promise me you'll come out if you see a light in the window."

"Promise me there's no one else and I'll think about it. Promise me you won't break my heart again." She still didn't raise her voice. In fact, it got softer.

"I have to take care of some things before I can make promises." The words sounded hollow and empty in his ears. "It won't be long."

She gripped her hands together, almost as if she were praying. "I'm going to be baptized soon."

Josiah stood. "I understand."

She slipped back into the store and let the door shut gently behind her.

Miriam planned to move forward. She wanted him to go with her. If only he could.

Follow the rules. Why was that so hard for him to do? Simple rules. A conversation he'd had with the deacon around Thanksgiving replayed in his head. He didn't like rules because he wanted to be in control. Until he let go and let God take control, his life would be a constant tug-of-war. Back and forth, until exhausted he would finally fall to his knees. God would never let go. That's what the deacon said. So far, Josiah's shoulders and arms ached with the effort to hang on. He longed to let go.

He had to go back to Bishop Kelp and convince him to allow him to talk to Sarah. She would never leave Bliss Creek until he did. And he would never convince Miriam he could be true to her until Sarah left.

❧

Annie dumped a cup of flour into the bowl with such force a fine white dust blew back in her face. She coughed and slapped a hand to her mouth. Gracie, who was standing on a chair next to her, mimicked her movements. More flour flew through the air, filtering the sunlight that shone through the windows of the bakery. Annie touched the little girl's arm. "Gently, gently."

Gracie giggled and reached for the enormous flour canister. "More, more."

"No, that's enough for our cookies." Annie added the rest of the dry ingredients to both bowls, then began to cream the softened butter together with the sugar. She gathered her wits and gave instructions as if the three-year-old understood. It was never too early to teach girls how to bake. "We do it gently so the flour ends up in the cookies and not on the counter and the floor and our faces."

"She's just following your lead." Her tone tart, Sadie punched down whole wheat dough and began to knead it on the floured counter. "Gently, Annie, gently."

"I'm just so…I really wish…I mean…" Annie didn't dare express her true feelings, not even to Sadie. She wanted to be in that courtroom for the arraignment. She should be there supporting Charisma and Logan. She wanted him to know she bore him no ill will. What was the point of being a grownup if people—people like her brother— still told her what to do? "It's nothing."

"You really wish Luke would let you go to the arraignment with the little girl's mudder." Sadie took care not to say Charisma's name, for which Annie was thankful. As long as Gracie wasn't reminded that Charisma had left her alone, probably for the first time in her life, she didn't fuss. But if anyone said the name she became inconsolable for several minutes. "We don't involve ourselves in such things. You know that. Going to court would only make that lawyer want us to be witnesses even more. Besides, you're needed here to take care of the little one."

True. It wasn't like they could leave Gracie with Leah. Her sister-in-law had made that perfectly clear before Annie could even pose the question. Sadie was so kind to let Gracie be in the bakery at all. They'd agreed to let her make her own little batch of cookies and keep them clear of anything that went to customers.

She cracked four eggs, one after the other, into a separate bowl. The quick snap of her wrist, the clean break, the efficiency of the movements made her feel better somehow. This was something she knew how to do. She was in control.

"Annie, are you listening?" Sadie tapped a flour-coated finger on the counter. "You are right where you belong."

"I know." She added the eggs to her bowl and then cracked two more into Gracie's. "Stir." She put a hand on the girl's wooden spoon. "Gently. You don't want raw egg all over your new dress."

A big grin on her face, Gracie slapped a chubby hand on the green dress Annie had made for her the previous evening. After the scene at the quilting frolic, it had soothed Annie to sew. The *whap, whap* sound as she pumped the treadle sewing machine with her bare feet always made her think of Mudder.

"Pretty. Pretty," Gracie crowed. "Gracie pretty."

Pretty wasn't something Plain women aspired to be, but Annie understood the sentiment. "Very nice. Now stir. Gently."

"You have such patience. You'll be a good mother."

At the sound of David's voice, Annie's arm froze in mid-stir. Her heart sped up, just as it always did. It betrayed her every time. His words sank in and the usual ache caught in her throat, then spread until she could barely swallow. Surely he knew how she longed for that day. Didn't he think of having children with her? Apparently not, if he could make such an offhand remark.

She inhaled the sweet, lovely scent of baking bread. *One. Two. Three. Breathe.* She could be as offhand as he. Without haste, she laid the spoon next to her bowl, and turned. "Good morning. I didn't know you were here."

His gaze collided with hers. Something in his dark eyes said he wasn't as nonchalant as she first believed. She refused to drop her gaze. The seconds stretched and stretched, and then seemed to snap back. Something there in the deep brown of his eyes mesmerized her. He felt something. As much as he denied it, she could see it there in his eyes. She took a step forward. He shook his head slightly, cleared his throat, and the want—the yearning—disappeared, swallowed up by regret. Then he bent over to let bags of sugar slide from his shoulders to the floor. The moment was lost in the thud of their weight against the wood. He began to stack them.

"I came in through the back." His voice sounded oddly hoarse, like he had a cold. "Our shipment arrived."

"So I see." Annie glanced at Sadie. She could've said something. A faint smile on her wrinkled face, David's mother appeared engrossed in shaping the loaves and placing them in the greased bread pans. *Fine. No help there.* "Why are you stacking those here, instead of in the back?"

"Because I don't want you two trying to carry them up here."

"I'm quite capable of carrying a bag of sugar."

"From the sounds of it, you need to add an extra helping of that sugar to your coffee this morning." David headed toward the storage room door. "You know that you gather more flies with honey than vinegar, don't you, Annie?"

"Who wants flies in honey anyway…" She didn't bother to continue. He'd already disappeared through the door. "Men."

"Men." Gracie swung her wooden spoon through the air in an enthusiastic flourish. "Men."

A glob of sugar and egg landed on Annie's cheek. "Gracie!" She grabbed at the spoon and missed. More of the sodden mess deposited itself on her dress. What was the point of wearing an apron if it didn't cover anything? She took another swipe and managed to wrestle the spoon from the girl. "You have to keep the spoon in the bowl, little one."

Gracie's face crumpled. "My spoon. My spoon. Want my spoon."

"Like this." Annie stuck the offending spoon into the mess in Gracie's bowl. "Stir, stir, stir."

"Stir, stir, stir."

Gracie reached for the spoon. Her arm hit the gallon of milk on the prep counter and it toppled. Annie dove, but too late. The plastic container smashed into the floor. Its contents poured out in a *glug, glug, glug* sound. Milk splattered on Annie's face, her apron, her shoes.

Angry words flew to Annie's mouth. She pressed her lips together, forcing them back. Accidents happened.

"Milk. I need milk." Gracie clamored down from her chair, her bare feet making squelching sounds in the puddles. She squatted and slapped her hands in the liquid around her. "Drink milk?"

Annie put her hands on her hips and Sadie appeared at her side. "I think three may be a tad too young for cookie-making." She laughed, a deep-in-her-belly laugh. "What do you think?"

Annie couldn't help but join her. The laughter felt good.

"You all have gone completely daft." David dropped a bag of flour next to the sugar. "You're standing there laughing while that stuff dries. What if a customer comes in?"

Always the practical one. That was David. At that moment, Annie wanted to shake him until she could shake a little imagination, a little sense of adventure, a little fun, into him. "You're—"

As if on cue, the door opened and the bells over it dinged.

Fortunately, Charisma entered instead of a customer. Her red eyes and wet cheeks told the story of how the arraignment had gone before she could open her mouth.

"Mommy, Mommy, Mommy!"

Gracie took off toward Charisma. Her wet feet slid from under her, her hands flew up in the air, and she landed smack on her bottom in the pool of milk. Her mouth opened in a wide circle. A second later, the howls started.

"On that note, I'd better go back to the deliveries before it gets too late." David whirled and headed out the back. "You look like you have plenty to do here."

Men. Always ducking out when the going got tough. Annie started toward the crying child.

"I've got her." Sadie scooped up Gracie from the floor and headed to the sink. "I'll clean up the poor mite. You handle Momma."

Annie thanked God for the blessing named Sadie Plank and rushed over to Charisma. "What happened?" she called over Gracie's wailing.

Seemingly oblivious to her daughter's fussing, Charisma sank onto the bench next to the door. She wiped at tears with her fingers. "They offered him a plea bargain—five years to serve—and then he'd be extradited to one of the other states on the other charges. He refused so they bound him over for trial."

Annie tried to absorb all the unfamiliar words. It sounded as if Charisma were speaking a foreign language. "Is he getting out of jail until the trial?"

"Only if we have a lot of money for the bond, which we don't."

"So when is the trial? Soon?"

Charisma scoffed and began rooting through the faded denim bag she carried everywhere. "The judge set the date for a month from now. He says he can't get back to town for a long enough stretch to do a full trial until then."

Annie plopped onto the bench next to her. Charisma and Gracie would be living in the Shirack house for another month at least. With a baby due anytime. Leah would love that.

Chapter 21

D avid lifted the enormous white cake box from the wagon with a grunt. A layered chocolate sheet cake with chocolate cream cheese frosting and cherry filling, it would be the talk of Mayor Haag's thirtieth wedding anniversary party. The whole thing probably weighed twenty pounds or more. Delivering cakes might not be dig-your-hands-in-the-earth farm work, but it felt good to be useful. The sun shone overhead, sparrows chirped in the elm tree in the mayor's crisply manicured front lawn, and a soft breeze dried the sweat on his face. This qualified as a good day. As long as he could brush away the memory of the look on Annie's face earlier when he'd told her she would make a good mother. What had he been thinking? He'd been so taken by the look on her face as she tried to teach sweet little Gracie to bake, he'd forgotten for just a second he had no right to say such a thing to her.

He couldn't help it. The sight of her standing at the counter, making cookies, a smudge of flour on her nose, had undone him. Everything about her pleased him, from her green eyes to her long, thin fingers to the way she tilted her head when she laughed that low, sweet laugh. Annie. Lovely Annie.

Let it go. Done is done. It can't be helped. It can't be changed. Focusing on the fragile package, he balanced the box on the white picket fence

that guarded the mayor's fancy two-story home and struggled with
the gate latch. With any luck Mayor Haag would be too busy preparing for her party to pepper him with questions and demands that his
mother and Annie appear at the bakery burglar's trial. Of all the people who had to be in the bakery at the time of the armed robbery, it
had to be someone in a position of power in Bliss Creek. Mayor Haag
didn't understand that her kind of power meant little in the Plain people's world.

"Here, let me get that for you."

The voice pulled him from his reverie. David lifted his gaze to his
helper's face. Sarah Kauffman. She smiled up at him, not a care in the
world reflected on her pretty face framed by a carefully placed prayer
kapp that hid most of the fire-engine-red hair she'd wound into a bun.
She didn't look anything like the girl he'd seen driving Josiah around in
a pickup truck back in the height of his friend's wild and wooly rumspringa. That girl wore jeans and T-shirts and played loud music on the
radio so she could sing along to songs that talked about women lik-
ing tractors. That girl called him Dave and tried to get him to join her
friends for a keg pasture party. David tightened his grip on the cake
box.

"So you aren't talking to me? The least you could do is say thanks."

Her tart tone pulled him from the memory. "Danki. What are you
doing here?"

Her dimpled smile disappeared along with the twinkle in her eye
that seemed to say everyone she met could be her best friend. Her bottom lip protruded in a pout that made her look twelve.

"Not you too, Dave Plank." She snapped the gate open and pushed
through ahead of him. "I've been treated like I'm wearing some sort of
red A on my dress by just about every other Plain person in Bliss Creek.
I wasn't expecting it from you."

He adjusted the box in his arms and followed her on the sidewalk.
The man who did the mayor's yard work came around the corner,
pruning shears in his hand. He gave Sarah a curious look and nodded
at David. David nodded back. Mayor Haag had her share of friends,

but Sarah Kauffman? He studied her stiff posture. "The name is David. Why would you think I'd be different?"

"Number one, because you're Joe's best friend, and I'd think you would at least have an open mind on the subject of what might or might not make him happy." She stomped up the steps and then turned to look back at him. "Number two, because you really believe all that forgiveness stuff."

"You don't?"

"Oh, no, I'm not falling for that one." She planted both hands on her slim waist above a long, flowing skirt the color of blueberries. "I'll not say one thing you can take back to your community to prove I'm not serious about joining the faith."

"It wasn't a trick question." David jerked his head toward the door. "Could you knock for me?"

She held up a key. "Actually, the mayor's running late. She asked me to meet you here. She'll be here in a while."

"Why would she ask you to do that?"

"Because…" Sarah slid the key in the lock, turned it, and pushed the thick walnut door open. "I'm her maid."

"Her maid?" David sputtered a little as he followed her into the foyer. Sarah Kauffman, the lazy-daisy girl whom Josiah described as a tomboy, who loved to play volleyball and basketball, who couldn't sew a lick and enjoyed microwave popcorn and pizza rolls for supper, had a job. As a cleaning lady for the mayor of Bliss Creek. "Mayor Haag hired you?"

"Yep." She grinned, obviously pleased with his surprise. "Don't say anything to Joe. I want to be the one to tell him. The deacon knows. He thinks it shows I'm serious about staying here and embracing the life."

"Because you clean bathrooms for the mayor?"

Her frown this time burned a hole in David's forehead. She turned and swished down a hallway with walls covered with paintings of cowboys on horses herding cattle. After a while, the paintings gave way to photographs of the mayor's three *kinner* in caps and gowns. David inhaled the aroma of cherry tobacco. It reminded him of the mayor's husband, who strolled to the bank he owned every morning with a pipe clamped in his teeth.

Sarah laid the key on a spotless granite island in the middle of a huge room outfitted with stainless steel appliances that looked as if they'd never been used. If there was going to be a big party this evening, apparently it didn't involve food. "Set the cake here."

David did as he was told, glad to be rid of the package. The muscles in his arms were starting to quiver from its weight.

They stared at each other for a second. She lifted her chin and smiled. "I know Joe and I can be happy together. We can make a life together as a Plain couple."

"No. You can't."

"What do you know?"

"For starters, his name is Josiah and as long as you call him by an Englisch name, it tells me you don't really understand who he is."

Sarah grabbed a washcloth and wet it under an ornate brass faucet. "It's just a name."

"No. It's from another world. Your world." David brushed his hands together, wishing he could wash them. "And you do it to show people you're closer to him than they are. People like Miriam."

"This is my world now." She slapped the washcloth on the counter and began to wipe with more force than necessary. "Joe—Josiah technically is still in his rumspringa. I don't understand why they won't let him at least talk to me. He hasn't been baptized yet. He should be free to do what he wants."

"Josiah isn't the boy you knew a year ago." David edged toward the kitchen door. He shouldn't be having this conversation. Her sudden appearance had taken him by surprise. "He's grown up now. He's committed to the Ordnung."

"I'm grown up too." She tapped a foot clad in a sensible black sneaker on the slick tile floor. "I'm willing to commit to the Ordnung too."

"Josiah is more concerned about how your presence will affect others than his own happiness. He's worried about your happiness if you decide to stay. He's worried about what will happen if he gives you his heart and you change your mind." David worked to keep his voice kind. She was a girl. She had a heart too. "He's able to see the long-term consequences. That's how I know he's grown up. I don't know if you're grown up enough to see those things too."

Her face contorted with a mixture of frustration and anger, Sarah hurled the soggy washcloth at David. He didn't have time to react, and it smacked him right in the face. It smelled like lemons. Sarah threw her hands in the air. "I hate the way y'all keep judging me."

David bent and picked up the washcloth. He walked over to the sink and dropped it in. When he was sure he could control his voice, he spoke. "That wasn't very grown-up."

"I'm so frustrated. Everyone here treats me like an outsider, a loose woman. I'm an average girl who likes a guy and wants to be with him."

"Likes a guy?" David plucked a tissue from a box on the counter and handed it to her. "If you're not sure, you shouldn't be here at all. You'll end up hurting everyone."

"Loves! I mean loves." She blew her nose so hard it sounded like a duck quacking in the middle of the kitchen. "I love Joe—Josiah. Don't you know how that feels?"

"Like if you had to live without him you'd die?"

She sniffed and nodded. "You do know."

"More than you can imagine."

"So why are you pushing me away?"

"Because sometimes love isn't enough." Not when faith was at stake. Or when cancer reared its ugly head. "You would think it would be, but it's not. Grow up, Sarah. Do the right thing. For Josiah's sake. For Miriam's sake. Go home. Find a good New Order Mennonite man and make him happy."

"That's your advice?"

"That's my advice."

"Josiah told me about Annie." She sniffed hard and wiped at her nose again. "Is that what you're doing for her?"

"Jah."

"Do you think it's making her happy?"

No. He could tell by the look on her face every time he walked into her line of vision. "She will be. One day."

"You're wrong."

"I'm right and you know it."

"Hello, hello, I'm here." Mayor Haag's high voice wafted into the room. "Where is everyone? Sarah, where are you? Why haven't you rearranged the furniture? Or dusted…"

She bustled into the room, bulging shopping bags in each hand. "Oh, David, I'm glad you're here. I have your money, but I want to see the cake first. Make sure you didn't squish it in transit. It's a lot of money for a…"

She stopped. Her gaze swung from David to Sarah and back. "Did I interrupt something?" Her thin, penciled eyebrows did push-ups under her silver bangs. "What are you two up to?"

"Nothing, nothing, Mayor Haag." Sarah rushed over to the cabinet, grabbed a glass, and filled it with water. "David was thirsty. It's sure hot out there, isn't it?"

"In here too." Mayor Haag smiled. "Fine, but get busy. I've got four dozen guests coming this evening, and I want this house spotless. The caterer will be here from Wichita any second. Run along—start in the living room and don't forget the guest bathroom."

Sarah cast a last pleading glance at David and disappeared down the hallway. He picked up the money the mayor had tossed on the counter while she lifted the lid of the cake box. "Oh, it's gorgeous." She dipped a finger with a red nail on it in the frosting on one corner and lifted it to her lips. Her eyes rolled and she sighed. "Ecstasy. Absolute ecstasy. Nobody does frosting better than Sadie Plank. You can tell her I said so."

"Yes, ma'am." He tucked the money in the deposit bag and started for the door.

"David, wait."

He closed his eyes for a split second. Almost made the getaway, but he hadn't been quite fast enough. He turned to face her. "Was there something else you needed? I didn't see anything else on the order."

"No, I had Lou pick up the dinner rolls and cookies this morning." She dropped the lid on the cake box. "You know, I can barely stand to go into the bakery since the armed robbery. That's why I want you to convince your mother and those two other girls to testify in that man's trial."

David backed toward the door, inch by inch. "I can't do that, ma'am."

"Don't ma'am me. I've known you since your mother used to bring you into my sister's shoe store every year before school started. Same pair of boots for each one of you boys."

"I know that."

"It's wrong for a thief to go free. He broke the rules. You people are big on following rules."

Those rules included not judging others. They included forgiving. "Our rules."

"You read the Bible, don't you."

"Yes."

"So you know about the part where it says thou shalt not steal."

"Yes. We also know about the part that says we are to keep ourselves apart from the world." David didn't want to get into a debate with an Englischer over the Ordnung. She wouldn't understand and it wasn't his place to try to convince her. "We also consider the part where it says to forgive not seven times but seventy times seven times."

"Don't get smart with me. I'm the mayor of this town." Mayor Haag pulled paper plates and plastic forks from her bag and slapped them on the counter. "The safety of the people here is paramount to me. That's why you'll do as I ask."

"No, ma'am."

"What did I say about ma'am-ing me?"

"I can't do it. The Ordnung doesn't allow it."

"Don't you want them to be safe?"

"I'll keep them safe. Annie's family will keep her safe. So will Miriam's. Our community is small and united."

"Your mother has a business in my town. Your friends work in my town."

"If you insist they testify neither of those things will be true for long."

She dabbed at smudged lipstick with a napkin, her lips pulled down in a deep frown. "Your father would never have talked to me like that."

Truer words were never spoken. David tried to imagine his father talking to the mayor at all. He was a man of few words who spent most days in the field. He had been content to stay as far from town as possible. This world where they could no longer support their families by farming had forced many changes. "My father would never have delivered a cake to an Englischer's house."

"What are you saying?"

"The world is different now. We work in town because it's necessary to support our families. I'm only asking that you think about what Bliss Creek would be like without the Plain people."

"Pardon me?"

"The Plain people own half the businesses in this town. And the tourists flock here not to see you, but to see us. We understand that and we tolerate it in order to be able to continue to live here."

"What are you trying to say?"

"I'm trying to say…" David hesitated. It sounded prideful, but he didn't mean it that way. It was a simple statement of fact. "Try as we might, we cannot stay totally separate. We need to work in order to support our families. But Bliss Creek needs us too."

"So we have to work together. That's what I've been trying to say." Mayor Haag marched around the counter and stood in David's space. Hands on her hips, she glared up at him. "Work together to keep the town safe, for instance."

"Work side by side. Separately, but side by side." David refused to back down. The bishop might not approve of him arguing with this Englischer, but his mudder, Annie, and Miriam had to be shielded from her. The bishop wouldn't allow them to participate in the trial. "That is what is best for our families. Otherwise, we'll be forced to move to a place where we can protect our way of life."

"Is that a threat?"

"No."

Mayor Haag folded her arms, her stare icy. "Are you sure?"

David stared right back. "It's a fact."

⚘

Josiah raised a hand to knock on Bishop Kelp's door. He hesitated, still trying to work out the words. How could a heart be so torn in two? The door opened before he could knock. Bishop Kelp peered out.

"Josiah. Come in." He sounded as if he'd been waiting for the visit. "There's coffee on the stove. Would you like a cup? Or maybe cold tea would be better in this heat. It's fresh brewed and Susana has ice."

Feeling like a fool, Josiah dropped his hand and followed the bishop into the living room. Despite a parched throat, he declined. Better to get this over quickly. "I needed to speak with you—"

"About Sarah." Bishop Kelp sank into a hickory rocking chair and waved at a second one that faced his. "She was here earlier."

"I didn't know." He perched on the edge of the chair. Hands clasped tightly in front of him, he gathered his thoughts. "I wanted your permission to talk to her."

"I realize you don't need my permission. You've not been baptized yet. You've been running around longer than most." His deep voice gave the words a pall that reminded Josiah of the many funeral services the bishop had led. "With your parents gone, I'm only concerned for your welfare. You went through a bad time last year, but you returned to us. I don't want to see you lose your way again."

His tone was soft, kind, not one Josiah expected or had heard before. He'd misjudged Micah Kelp. He always thought of him as the bishop, but here sat one man concerned for another. Almost like a grandfather. That realization made it all the harder to look him in the eye. "I know that. Danki." He ducked his head. "I don't seem to be able to make a clearheaded decision. It's all muddled."

"Women." Bishop Kelp chuckled deep in his chest, making his beard shake. "They've been known to make men do crazy things."

"Plain men?"

"All men."

Josiah pushed his hat back and gazed at the bishop, hoping for a bit of direction. "I want to talk to Sarah. I need to tell her she shouldn't go through with this. Not on my account."

"I've talked to the girl. I'm fairly certain she's sincere."

Sincere? Josiah tried to rearrange his expression before the bishop saw his disbelief. "She really wants to join the faith?"

"So she says. She has stripped away the worldly things that stand in her way. She's cleaning an Englisch house. She tells me her cousin is teaching her to bake and sew. I'm satisfied with her expressions of faith. Sarah has given this a lot of thought. She's acted on her conviction."

"I know that."

"As she said to me, 'It's not all about Josiah.'" The bishop's grave expression belied the note of humor in his voice. "Sometimes it's not, you know. All about you."

"You think this is best for her?"

"If it brings her closer to God, then yes, it is best, but only God knows. He has a plan for young Sarah Kauffman. Just as He has one for you. Just as He has one for Miriam Yonkers."

The bishop knew too much, saw too much. Josiah stared at the floor, willing the heat on his face to subside.

The sound of Bishop Kelp's chair creaking made him look up. The bishop fixed him with a stern stare. "Never lose your humility. Spend some time on your knees. Listen."

He heaved himself from the chair and plodded toward the door. Josiah's time was up. He followed.

At the door, Bishop Kelp smoothed his beard with a callused hand. He stared at a spot behind Josiah's shoulder, his forehead wrinkled in concentration. At last, he opened the door and stood back so Josiah could pass. "Josiah."

"Yes, Bishop."

"You might be right. A visit is in order. Talk to her. Maybe then you will have a clearer understanding of what you must do. You, not her.

She will do what is right for her. You will do what is right for you. That is not necessarily the same thing. When you know, you will tell me."

It was all Josiah could do to keep from breaking into a run to the buggy. Aware of the bishop's keen gaze on his back, he forced himself to stride forward, every step firm. Once in the buggy he looked back, but the door was already shut.

The bishop thought Sarah was sincere. He might grant her request to join the community. A new start for Sarah. The same old problem for Josiah. It would mean making a decision between two women who were part of his community. No escaping.

Chapter 22

"I still don't see why I couldn't just drive my van."

Annie ignored the pique in Charisma's voice. She'd been complaining for over an hour now. Luke had been adamant. Annie could go to Wakefield to find Charisma's mother only if David went, and only if they hired Luke's Englisch friend, Michael Baldwin, to drive them. Michael did most of the driving for the Shirack family. Josiah needed to work or Luke would've sent him. Annie suspected Luke wanted Michael along to serve as a chaperone in her brother's stead. And because he didn't trust an Englisch girl's driving. Either way, she didn't argue. They needed to find a home for Charisma quickly, before the baby came and Leah had a meltdown.

"Annie, are you ignoring me?" Charisma's voice rose over the sound of the car's engine. Gracie, who'd fallen asleep the moment they pulled off the dirt road onto the highway, shifted in her car seat and stuck her thumb in her mouth. Charisma sniffed. "I still don't see why I can't drive."

Annie exchanged looks with David, who sat in the front seat with Michael. She'd already answered Charisma's questions several times. She leaned against the smooth seat and peered out the window. Everything whooshed by so fast. No time to admire the countryside. With the windows up and the air conditioner on, she could almost imagine summer had ended and the cooler temperatures of fall had arrived. The familiar odors of outdoors couldn't penetrate. Instead the smell of artificial pine wafted from a cardboard tree swinging from the mirror, mingling with Charisma's sweaty feet and the gingersnaps Gracie crushed in her chubby fingers. Was this what it was like in Englischers' houses?

"Annie! Are you ignoring me?"

"Because Luke thought it would be better for you to relax and rest on the drive." She brushed crumbs from the sleeping baby's face with a light touch. "Don't you want to take a quick nap like Gracie?"

Charisma shook her head so hard her ponytail swung in Gracie's face. The girl whimpered.

"Sorry." Charisma patted her daughter's bare leg. Annie would've liked to see Gracie wear a dress for this important visit, but Charisma had chosen a faded pair of shorts and a sleeveless top that read Mommy's Princess for her daughter's first visit to her grandma's house. The outfit matched Charisma's shorts and shirt almost exactly, except Charisma's shirt said: I Love the Lone Star State. "Do you really think I can sleep at a time like this?"

"We've got another hour left before we get there."

"Not nearly long enough." Charisma rooted around in her denim bag. After a few seconds she pulled out a small bottle that she proceeded to squirt on her neck and arms. The overpowering scent of flowers billowed through the enclosed car. The two men in the front seat looked at each other. David cracked his window so the air made a whistling sound.

Charisma didn't seem to notice their discomfort. "I wish I could afford a cell phone. I could call her first. If I knew her number."

"You don't know your aunt's telephone number?"

"No idea."

"At least you have the address. We'll be there soon enough. Have you thought about what you're going to say?"

"I haven't thought of anything else since you forced me into doing this."

Annie reined in her sudden irritation. After Charisma had realized Logan wasn't going to get out of jail anytime soon, she'd been inconsolable at first and then determined to move on with her life. She'd wanted out of the Shirack house just as much as Leah wanted her out. "Don't you want to reconcile with your family before your baby is born? Don't you want Gracie to know her grandmother?"

"It's not all apple pie and quilting at my house." Charisma's voice hardened with each word. She faced the window on her side. "Not everyone lives in a time warp back to the frontier days like you do."

Annie closed her mouth. Better to let this conversation rest. Charisma was nervous. She didn't mean to be ugly; she was just scared. "I know."

They passed a long time in silence, watching the green fields whizzing by the car window. Annie nearly dozed herself a few times, but was always jerked back to wakefulness by Charisma's constant movements.

"I need to use the restroom." Charisma leaned forward and poked David's shoulder. "Hey, can you get your friend to pull into a gas station?"

Annie's face burned. She focused on the back of David's neck and watched it turn red. He swiveled far enough to catch her gaze. His rueful smile told her he didn't blame her, even if she was the one who brought this woman into their lives and then asked him to play chaperone. "Yes, ma'am."

"Ma'am? Who you ma'am-ing?" Charisma's face darkened. "I'm only nineteen, not an old lady."

"Michael, can you pull over at the next town?" David's tone remained even. "We could probably all use a chance to stretch our legs."

"The next stop *is* Wakefield."

Annie closed her eyes in relief. The remaining twenty minutes passed in silence, except for Charisma's long, loud sighs. They pulled into the outskirts of Wakefield and stopped at a gasoline station. It was a relief to put her feet on solid ground and stretch. The car seat and Charisma's attitude made the backseat crowded. She watched Charisma stomp into the bathroom, Gracie on her hip. Michael headed into the store to get some cold drinks.

David leaned against the car next to her. "She's a handful, isn't she?"

He sounded amused. Annie didn't see much humor in the situation. "I wish she could be a little more…"

"A little more like you?"

"I guess I thought staying with us would open her eyes to some things."

"That's a little prideful, don't you think?"

Annie ducked her head. He was right. "I didn't mean to be."

"You have good intentions and besides, you have no way of knowing what seeds are being planted. It's possible God brought her to you for a reason. Not only to take care of that child, but also to sow a seed. God will take care of reaping it."

Annie liked the way he thought. Her whole day brightened. "You're so smart."

"No." He straightened and kicked at a clod of dirt with a dusty boot. "I said some things to Mayor Haag about trying to make you and Mudder and Miriam testify I shouldn't have yesterday."

"Like what?"

His head down as if he were studying the ground, he related the conversation in a swift monologue that kept her from interrupting.

When he finally stopped talking and looked up, Annie moved away from the car. "You were right to tell her."

"It sounded like a threat."

"You were protecting your mudder. And me. Danki for doing that."

"Everything I said was true, but I shouldn't have intervened. It's not my place."

"I'm glad you did. It will relieve Luke's worry too."

He nodded, his face pensive. "There's something else."

His quick summary of his encounter with Sarah left Annie breathless. "She really thinks working for Mayor Haag will show she's ready for our way of life?" she said. "Is she using electrical appliances? Answering the phone?"

"I don't know."

"Have you told Josiah?"

He pulled at his suspenders and let them snap. "Do you think I should?"

"Jah." Of course she did. Men could be so slow. "He needs to know what she's up to."

"It's not our business."

"He's your friend. My bruder."

"He's a man who has to make up his own mind about his future."

Again, David was right. But Annie found it hard to accept. "At least don't let him get blindsided about her working there."

"Here comes Charisma."

Michael converged on the car at the same time, ending any chance of more private conversation with David. Annie sighed and wiggled into her seat next to Gracie, David's words still whirling around in her head. Relief made her bones feel weak. If David was right, she wouldn't have to testify. She wouldn't cause Luke any more grief. If they could just get Charisma settled at her mother's house, all would get back to normal. Peaceful.

Five minutes later they pulled into a dirt drive that led to the front yard of a small, neat-looking wood-frame house surrounded by oak trees and blooming rosebushes. "This is it." Michael turned off the engine and clicked off the GPS. "This is the address you gave me."

In the silence broken only by the ticking of the hot engine, Annie surveyed the scene. Pots of red and pink begonias dotted the sidewalk that led to a porch where a tabby cat slept on a swing. Except for the porch light and the white car parked in the driveway, it didn't look that different from her house.

"Maybe we should forget this." Charisma gripped the door handle. "Maybe we should come back another day."

Annie reached across Gracie and patted Charisma's arm. The woman's skin felt clammy. "We've come this far. Go say hello to your mother." She glanced at the house. A gingham curtain moved in the front window. "I think they know someone is here. We'll wait in the car."

"No. No, I want you to come in." Charisma shoved her door open. "They can wait with Gracie."

The men could take care of the baby? Annie gave David an apologetic look. He smiled in response. She scampered up the sidewalk that meandered through the yard. Charisma seemed to have decided to get it over as quickly as possible. Her sandals slapped against the cement, then the wooden steps, and across the porch. She rapped on the door with a fisted hand.

The door opened. Annie knew at once that Charisma's mother stood behind the screen door that separated them. She had the same blond hair, fair skin, long, thin nose, and wide mouth. Annie knew what Charisma would look like twenty years from now. The woman's tight jeans and tighter T-shirt explained Charisma's taste in clothes.

Charisma's mother's mouth was turned down, her expression questioning. The identity of her visitor hadn't sunk in. Her gaze wandered over Charisma's shoulder to Annie. Annie forced a friendly smile. The woman's eyebrows stretched toward bangs that belonged on a much younger person.

"Mom, it's me." Charisma's voice quivered with nerves. "I've come to see you."

"Who's this with you? Have you turned Mennonite on me or something?" The woman's icy tone chilled Annie to the bone.

"Mom!" Charisma made the introductions. "Annie's not a Mennonite," she explained. "She's Amish."

Mrs. Chiasson still didn't ask them in. Instead, she pushed through the screen door, forcing them toward the edge of the porch. The flowery scent of lilacs hung in a cloud around her. Annie coughed quietly behind the palm of her hand.

"What are you doing here?" Mrs. Chiasson's gaze dropped to Charisma's bulging waistline. "You left four years ago. I haven't heard a single word from you and you show up on my sister's steps looking like this?"

Charisma's face turned scarlet. Annie moved closer so she could squeeze her hand. Charisma jerked away. "I thought with everything that's happened you might want to help your only daughter out of a jam."

Mrs. Chiasson opened her mouth. Squalls wafted from the car in the driveway. She shut her mouth and Charisma brushed past Annie and bolted down the steps. "That would be your granddaughter," she called over her shoulder. "I think you should meet her."

Annie wavered. Stay on the porch with Mrs. Chiasson or return to the car with Charisma to retrieve Gracie? Before she could make up her mind, the screen door popped open again. This time a man dressed in a black western shirt, jeans, and cowboy boots stepped out. Annie stared up at him, mesmerized by his height and the odd menace in his stance. The blue eyes looking back at her from under thinning gray hair examined her from head to toe, the frown on his face growing.

The man thrust a huge white hand at her. "Sam Chiasson. Who are you?"

Annie managed to stutter her name. After a second or two, she remembered to accept his handshake. His skin was damp, and she fought the urge to wipe her hand on her skirt. "My friend and I brought Charisma home…brought her *here*," she corrected. This wasn't home to Charisma. She'd never been to Wakefield before. "To see her mother."

His expression didn't change. She saw no sign Charisma's arrival meant anything to him. No joy. No curiosity. That scared her more than any show of emotion would have. He rubbed a hand over a stubby shadow of a beard. "She ran off a while back. We had no idea where she got to. Been with you the whole time, has she?" He sounded only mildly interested in a response. "How did she know Cynthia moved up here with her sister?"

"We only met recently." Annie saw no reason to tell him how they met. She was more curious as to how Charisma could not have known her father had moved to Wakefield with her mother. "She got a letter. That's how she knew about the move."

Charisma marched up the sidewalk with a dazed-looking Gracie on her hip. The moment when Mr. Chiasson's presence registered was obvious. She stumbled, slowed, then sped up. The determined look on her face faded, replaced by a resignation that broke Annie's heart.

Annie ran down the steps. "Let's go home." She put a hand on Charisma's arm. "Come on. Let's go home."

Charisma tugged free. "I thought you left him, Mom. Ricky said you left him and came up here to live with Aunt Tammy."

"Your dad came after me. He's changed, Charisma. He loves me and this family. We had our problems, but we worked them out like mature adults." Mrs. Chiasson linked arms with her husband. He didn't look at his wife, nor did he move closer. "That's what married couples do. You wouldn't know anything about that, would you? Popping out babies like puppies. Where's your husband? Don't see one coming up the walk with you."

"Charisma, please, let's just go. You don't want to stay here." Annie tried to keep her anger out of her voice. She shouldn't judge. "It's better if we go. It's better for Gracie. And the baby."

"He broke my arm, Mom. My nose is crooked. You really think someone who does that to a little girl can change? Is he still hitting you, Mom? I know he doesn't hit Ricky, because Ricky is bigger than him now. He only hits people who can't hit back, right?"

Mrs. Chiasson's face froze. Sam didn't move. They stood there like statues of a happy couple in front of their happy home.

Blue jays arguing in the front yard shattered the silence.

"He hasn't lifted a hand in anger in the three months he's been here." Her voice shrill, Mrs. Chiasson suddenly slid away from her husband. He didn't try to hold on to her. She stuck her hands on her hips. "He's worked on his problems, and I think maybe you should do the same. Maybe you could take some responsibility for the way you acted back then. You drove him to it. You know that, right? With your back talk and your running around all hours, breaking his curfew, hanging out with bad boys? Maybe he was just trying to straighten you out."

"By breaking bones?" Charisma moved Gracie from one hip to the other. "That will teach me, right?"

"You just best watch your tone, girl." Mr. Chiasson took two steps forward, his hands fisted at his sides. "Your mother's right. It's your back talk that gets you in trouble every time."

As if the tension in the air had seeped into her, Gracie began to sob. "Want Annie. Annie."

"Let's go, Charisma. Please." Annie took Gracie into her arms and hugged her warm body close to her. The little girl's arms went around her neck in a frantic grip. She shouldn't interfere, but how could she not protect a little girl? "You can't stay here."

She started down the sidewalk, hoping Charisma would follow. She should pray for these folks. Pray that Charisma could forgive them. She wasn't sure she could forgive them herself. What did that say about her?

David leaned against the car so that he faced the house. She had the feeling he'd been watching and waiting, not interfering in other folks' business as she surely had, but ready to help. He straightened and strode across the grass. "Let me take her for you."

Gracie's grip tightened on Annie's neck. She whimpered. Annie shook her head. "I'd better hold her. All that yelling scared her."

"What's going on up there?" David rushed ahead of Annie and opened the car door. "Who is that man?"

"Charisma's not staying here." Annie peeled Gracie's arms from her neck and slid her into her car seat. She shushed the little girl's whimpers as she buckled the straps. "It's all right, little one, it's all right. Mommy's coming. Mommy's right behind us."

She backed out of the car and turned to make sure she was telling the truth. Charisma stumbled toward them, tears rolling down her cheeks. Annie looked up at David. "We're not leaving her here, and we're surely not leaving Gracie."

David nodded. He strode toward Charisma. "Let me help you." Charisma threw out her arms like a blind person fumbling in unfamiliar territory. David grabbed her elbow and guided her to the car. "Don't worry. We've got you."

Chapter 23

David thanked Michael for his chauffeuring services, ducked out of the car, and opened Charisma's door first. The ride back to the Shiracks had been a quiet one, except for the woman's occasional muffled sob and thunder overhead as a sudden late afternoon storm caught up with them. Rain, finally. They needed it so badly, but it was really too late to help with the wheat. Besides, by the time they pulled into the yard in front of the house, the rain had stopped. Charisma ignored the hand David held out and heaved herself from the car. He grabbed her elbow to keep her from falling.

"Thank you." Her eyes were red, her skin blotchy and wet with tears. "Thank you for taking me up there. I know you have better things to do than drive around a screwup like me."

"I'm sorry." He cringed at the inadequacy of his own words. How many times had he heard them directed at himself? "I'm sorry things didn't turn out better."

"Why would you be sorry?" She tossed back her tangled ponytail. "It's not like you had anything to do with it."

Because he was sorry about everything. All the time. And he recognized the agonizing pain on her face. Her parents were lost to her, and he understood how that felt. "No, but I am sorry, nevertheless."

"Thank you." Fresh tears rolled down her face. "Y'all are so nice to me. I don't know why. I'm nothing but trouble to you."

"No trouble at all. That's what friends are for."

"You're my friend." She seemed baffled by the idea. "You and Annie."

"Jah. All of us."

"You're too good to be friends with a person like me."

Annie came around the car with Gracie on her hip. The two looked like mother and daughter. David slapped the thought away, like a persistent mosquito buzzing his head, threatening to bite and draw blood. He forced his gaze back to Charisma. "We're just plain folks."

"We're just people like you, trying to be decent." Annie hugged the little girl to her chest. "You have a place here as long as you need it."

"I can't ever make this up to you, but I'll try not to make it harder. I promise I'll be a better guest, Annie."

Annie smiled that beautiful smile. "You're fine."

One hand on her stomach, Charisma turned and waddled toward the house, her sandals making a squelching sound in the wet grass. She clomped up the steps and disappeared through the door without looking back. David waited for Michael to drive away and the sound of the engine to die. The humid air hung wet and heavy around them. He forced himself to look at Annie. She didn't look away and he found he couldn't.

"How about you?" He cleared his throat. "Anything I can do to help you?"

She hugged Gracie closer. The little girl snuggled her head against Annie's chest and sucked on her thumb, a look of bliss on her chubby face. "You could tell Leah that Charisma is going to be staying here a bit longer than I first thought," she said, grinning in spite of herself.

"I'd rather be a fly on the wall for that conversation." David managed a chuckle. "I imagine you'll handle it fine."

"What else can we do?" Annie smoothed Gracie's T-shirt with thin, nimble fingers. The torment on her face made him want to catch hold of her hand and never let go. "She has nowhere to go and a baby is coming. We can't kick her out of the house."

"Luke won't allow that to happen."

Leah was another story. David had never understood Luke's choice for matrimony, but then he didn't understand affairs of the heart in general. His brother Timothy was Luke's closest friend. His explanation had been that opposites attract. Maybe that's how he knew that Sarah and Josiah would never work. They were two peas in a pod, unlike Josiah and Miriam. She would be his lightning rod, his balance beam. Sarah would push him over the edge. David sneaked a look at Annie. In their case, never truer words were spoken. She was beautiful, he wasn't. She clung to her faith. In his anger and disappointment, he clutched at it and often as not, missed. Hope and optimism flowed from her. His stream had dried up.

"David?" She had a puzzled look on her face. "What is it? Please tell me."

"I have to go."

"Why? Timothy is taking care of the bakery today, and Jonathan has the chores at the farm covered. What's wrong?" She swallowed. "Why do you keep pushing me away?"

He wanted the child in her arms to be his. The pain of that truth knocked him back a step. "I have to go."

"It's been a long afternoon. Come in for some lemonade or iced tea." She scurried to keep up with his deliberately long strides. "Supper will be on the table soon, I'm sure. Join us."

"I can't."

"Because we have to discuss Charisma's future? You're a part of this family. We welcome you at our dinner table, no matter what the discussion is."

"I can't."

"Because you're afraid."

The last words were hurled at him with sudden vengeance. First Josiah accused him of being a coward, now this woman he loved. Yes, he could admit to himself how he felt. But she could never know or she'd never get on with her life.

"I'm not afraid, not for me."

She trotted along next to him, matching his stride despite her long dress and the burden of Gracie's weight. He felt compelled to slow, despite the desire to escape before he gave in to the need to tell her the truth and ask her to spend the rest of her life with him. The problem wasn't the rest of his life. It was the rest of hers. He couldn't ask her to face the long years ahead as a widow. She ran in front of him, forcing him to slam to a halt.

They stared at each other, both breathing hard. "Move."

"No."

"For a Plain woman, you surely don't understand the relationship between a man and a woman."

"You mean, you order me around, I do what you say?"

"Not exactly."

"In the end, you will win. I know that, but I won't give up, not without a fight. I thought I could be your friend. I thought God's plan meant I should settle for being your friend. But I can't. Because if I do, that means I've given up on you and I won't do that just because you have."

He bolted to her left. His buggy was parked next to the corral fence. He rushed into the corral and started harnessing his horse. He could feel Annie's stare boring into his back.

He hitched the horse to the buggy in silence, but somehow words, angry and accusatory, still leaped back and forth between them. He climbed into the buggy. "I'm going now."

"That's fine. You do that. Come on, Gracie, let's go see what's for supper." She turned and stared up at him. "I was wrong to consider giving up on us. I have faith. And with faith comes hope."

She began to walk away, her shoulders thrown back, her head held high. Much as he wanted to escape, he couldn't move. He couldn't take his gaze from her figure as she sauntered toward the house, every movement steady and strong, as if she hadn't a care in the world. When she got to the big oak tree that marked the halfway point to the house, she turned and waved. "Where's your faith, David? Where's your hope? Tell me that."

∞

Annie's jaw ached with the effort to hold back the tears. She resisted the urge to slam the screen door. It would only scare Gracie and irritate Leah. She'd lost her temper with David. Instead of using gentle words of persuasion, she'd shrieked at him. No man cared for a woman who sounded like that. Why had she said anything? Why had she allowed herself to give in to the temptation to bare her anger and frustration to him? She had been determined to hold her tongue and be his friend through the treatments and the tests and the results. Instead, she'd driven him far, far away. *Oh, Father, please forgive me. Please help David to forgive me.*

The sound of shouting trumpeting from the kitchen forced Annie from her reverie. Leah's familiar screech said things weren't going well in the house either. She wiped at her face with her sleeve and pulled herself together. There would be time later for self-recrimination and prayers for forgiveness.

Charisma trudged into the front room. "I think you'd better get back there."

"What's going on?" Annie set Gracie on the floor next to a pile of the little twins' building blocks. The little girl immediately took her thumb from her mouth, grabbed a block, and threw it across the room. It pinged against the wall and Annie shook a finger at her. "Don't do that, Gracie. Build something for Mommy, okay?" She handed her another block and turned to Charisma. "Why is Leah yelling?"

"I don't know, but Lillie and Mary are trying to hide in the corner and they're both bawling."

Leaving Charisma to entertain her daughter, Annie rushed into the kitchen. Charisma's description didn't do justice to the scene. Leah, her face almost purple, brandished a long wooden spoon in one hand. The room reeked of burned food. The twins scrunched down on their knees next to the wood-burning stove. They were both sobbing. "Annie, Annie!" Mary jumped to her feet. "It was an accident. We didn't mean to burn supper."

"Accident? Accidents are what happen when you trip and knock a dish off the table," Leah shrieked. Her arms flailed and the spoon dipped and rolled. "You are lazy! Both of you! Lazy slackers!"

"It doesn't help to call names." Annie edged into the fray, stationing herself between the wooden spoon and Mary's head. "Whatever they did, I'm sure they didn't mean it."

Leah smacked the spoon on the prep table. "You run around the countryside with your Englisch friend—who never lifts a finger to help, by the way—how would you know what is going on here?" She pointed the spoon at the twins. "I was sewing pants for William and Joseph. These two were supposed to get the clothes off the line. Instead of doing their chores, they snuck into the barn to play with the new litter of kittens. The rainstorm comes along and soaks the clothes and the roast is burned. What will I give Luke for supper?"

"There's ham left from last night. I'll make a casserole." Annie whipped toward the refrigerator, thankful they had a way to keep leftovers cold. "It's no problem."

"You can't fix everything." Leah stomped across the room and stood in front of the small box refrigerator, directly in Annie's path. "Sometimes there have to be consequences."

"She's right."

Annie turned at the sound of her brother's voice. Luke stood in the doorway. His clothes were wet and his boots muddy, but it was the resignation on his face that poked Annie in the stomach. He looked downright miserable. "Leah, go deal with the laundry. Annie, make the casserole. Lillie, Mary, wait for me in the shed."

Annie edged a step closer to her sisters. "No, that's not—"

"Stop talking and do as you were told." He sounded just like Daed. Looked like him too. Old before his time. His gaze swung back to the twins. "Go."

Their faces terrified, they backed toward the door. Lillie threw Annie one last imploring look.

"Luke!"

He brushed past her. "You're making this harder, don't you see that? I have to teach them. That's my job."

"Can't you do it with compassion?"

"That comes after." He paused, one hand on the screen door. "That comes when I agree to letting Lillie and Mary stay with Emma for a while."

Annie breathed a sigh of relief. The twins would suffer a little now, for their own good, but then they would find relief in a house where they were wanted and not in the way.

"What? No. I thought you agreed with me that we needed to keep them here." Leah dropped the spoon on the table. "We agreed."

"No. You argued. I listened." Luke pushed open the door. "And then I made up my mind. They go."

"How will I get everything done here?"

"You constantly complain they make more work. And now you complain that you can't do the work without them. You can't have it both ways," Luke said. "Try putting our guest to work. It appears she'll be here a while."

Luke let the door slam.

Not wanting to see the look on Leah's face, Annie whirled and threw herself into making the casserole. That way she wouldn't have to think about the girls' punishment or their empty seats at the table.

A shuffling sound told her Leah had left the room. Annie grabbed a knife and sliced ham from the bone. The more she thought, the harder she sliced. Why were things so difficult? The knife slipped. "*Ach!* Ouch!" She dropped it and danced around the room, holding her hand. Blood seeped from the end of her thumb and dripped on her apron. "*Ach!*"

"Looks like you could use some help." Charisma's morose look had disappeared. Maybe she'd meant what she'd said when she got out of the car. Maybe she'd heard the discussion and realized things had to change. "You got any bandages around here?"

"There's gauze and tape on the shelf." Annie sank into the chair and applied pressure to the cut. "Where's Gracie?"

"I put her in the playpen so I could have five minutes to myself. What were you doing? Trying to cut your finger off? You can't make everything better, you know."

"I'm not trying to make it all better."

"Sure you're not." Charisma guffawed, then coughed the gravelly cough of a smoker. "You've been trying to take care of me since you met me. Don't you get it? I'm pregnant. I got a kid. I gotta learn to take care of myself."

Annie dabbed at her bloody thumb. "We're supposed to help each other."

"My mom says God helps those who help themselves."

"*Aenti* Louise says that might be true, but it's not exactly in the Holy Bible."

Charisma shrugged as she wrapped the gauze around Annie's thumb and cut the piece from the roll. "I just know I gotta figure this out."

"You're right." Not about the book, but about putting her life back together. Annie held still until the white tape covered the end of her thumb. "What do you want to do?"

Charisma leaned forward in the chair, looking as if she were contemplating her sandals. "I want to have this baby and get on with my life."

"The baby will get here when it gets here."

"I need a job."

"So let's find you a job." Annie couldn't bear to suggest there would be no job for a girl in Charisma's state. After the baby, yes. But then who would care for the two children? "What do you know how to do?"

"Have babies, apparently."

"Charisma!"

She actually grinned. "Just kidding. I can wait tables. I can wash dishes. I know how to iron. I can babysit."

In other words, she would make someone a good wife. "That's a start."

"Tomorrow, I'm going to town to find a job." Her smile melted into a frown. "Can you loan me five bucks?"

Annie gave all her money to Luke. If she wanted to buy cigarettes, Annie couldn't help her. "For what?"

"Gas. And no, I'm not buying cigarettes. I'm giving them up. Too expensive. And like you said, bad for the baby."

"Good. That's good." What had David said about planting seeds? He was wise for his young years—about a number of things. "But you don't need gas. You can get a ride to town with Josiah and me in the buggy when we go to work."

Charisma nodded. "Good. You think Leah will watch Gracie?"

Annie shuddered at the thought of having that conversation. "I'll take her to the bakery. Sadie will help. We need to start looking for a babysitter for you anyway." She stood. "For now, why don't you practice your cooking skills?"

"Who said I had any?"

"Me. Starting now, you're a cook-slash-baker in training."

Charisma grabbed an apron from the hook on the wall. "Look out, Betty Crocker, here I come!"

"Who's Betty Crocker?" Annie teased. She'd seen the cake mixes and cookbooks in the store. She just wanted to hear Charisma laugh. "A relative of yours?"

Charisma whooped. "You slay me, Amish girl, you truly do."

"Slay you? What kind of talk is that?" Annie shook her head. "Go pick some tomatoes from the garden, why don't you? And pick up some fresh eggs at the chicken coop while you're out there."

"Where's the garden?" Charisma grinned again. "What's a chicken coop? Just kidding."

Chapter 24

Carrying a roll of mesh, hammer, and nails, Josiah strode across the yard toward the back fence. After a long day standing over the forge, the heat of the late afternoon sun seemed almost tepid. It felt good to be outdoors, away from the stifling air that awaited him in the blacksmith shop every day. A strange, resigned look on his face, Luke had stopped on his way out to the old shed to ask Josiah to repair the fence that ran along the back of the garden. Wanting to be far away from the twins' punishment, he jumped at the chance. This fence was meant to keep the varmints out of the vegetable patch, but the wire mesh had some gaping holes it in that meant Leah's precious vegetables were becoming dessert for many a four-legged creature.

This was something he could do, something he could fix. With his blacksmithing job and chores, the opportunity to slip away to see Sarah hadn't presented itself. Maybe later this evening. Maybe Luke would think he was out courting Miriam. Sneaking around was wrong, but Luke would never believe the bishop had given him permission to talk to Sarah.

Josiah sank to one knee to examine the first hole. A loud voice singing high and sure—a pop song he recognized from his rumspringa days in Wichita—startled him into dropping the hammer. What a voice. The lyrics weren't great, but the voice belonged in a prayer service or a Sunday night singing. He stood and surveyed the garden. Nobody. It came from the chicken coop. That nasty little shed despised by the twins, who grumbled every time they were sent to collect eggs.

Laughing to himself, he slipped over to the shed to take a peek inside. Still singing at the top of her lungs, Charisma swung a basket in one hand and snatched an egg from a nest. She wore shorts and a tight white T-shirt that stretched to barely cover her big belly. Too busy performing, she didn't seem to notice the chickens that squawked and scattered around her, their chatter indignant. Or her human audience of one who forced his gaze from her midsection to her face.

"You're scaring the chickens with all that caterwauling." Josiah scooped up an egg she'd missed and held it out. The singing stopped mid-lyric. Charisma jumped back and the egg fell to the floor with a crack and a wet splat. "You definitely don't have the idea. Our women-folk don't scramble the eggs until they get to the kitchen."

"You scared me!" Charisma stumbled back another step, her sandals squelching in the chicken excrement. "You idiot!"

"Idiot? That's a little strong, don't you think?"

"Sorry. Like I said, you scared me." She went back to gathering eggs. "I thought I was alone. Besides, you *are* an idiot if you choose that Sarah chick over Annie's friend. What's her name? Miriam?"

"How do you know about that?" It was Josiah's turn to be startled. "Why would you even be thinking about that?"

"Gotta think about something!" She threw her free hand in the air. "No TV, no soap operas, not even a Hallmark movie now and then. It's crazy. The only romance going on around here is Annie and the bald guy or you and Miriam and none of you actually seem to know how to get it together. How could you not pick Miriam over some girl who'll run off the first time you shake your hat at her?"

Josiah opened his mouth, closed it, tried again. "You've never even met Sarah. You've only been here, what, a month? You don't know me or Miriam."

"Like I said, I hear the talk." Her nose wrinkled in distaste, she side-stepped an irate chicken that had its beak pointed at her bare toes that stuck out from worn leather sandals. "I know the Sarahs of this world. And I know your type."

With that silly statement, Charisma marched from the shed into the sun. Fuming at the loose lips that surely belonged to Annie and maybe even Miriam, Josiah followed. Anything was better than the acrid, putrid smell of chicken excrement trapped in a shed. Time to clean it with a large dose of bleach. A good job for Mark.

Josiah inhaled and tried to get a handle on his sudden irritation. She didn't know what she was talking about. Which explained why she didn't try to explain herself. She set the basket on the ground and began to pick tomatoes as if they'd never spoken.

As Sarah liked to say: *Whatever*. Josiah returned to the fence and went to work patching the hole. She didn't know him well enough to know what his type was. He didn't have a type. Wasn't a type. Whatever.

"Go on. I know you're dying to ask me." Her shadow blocked the sun for a second, then moved to the side. He'd been so busy fuming he hadn't heard her approach. She smelled like flowers. Pretty ones. "Ask me what your type is."

"It's a private thing that doesn't involve you."

"If you weren't Amish, you'd be the bad boy type." Charisma leaned against a fence post and fanned herself with long fingers. Her face glistened with beads of perspiration. She smiled a lazy smile. "Even being Amish, you can't help but be the bad boy. You're attracted to Sarah because you know it's wrong to want her. You're even attracted to me with my big belly."

"You're so full of yourself, I don't even know where to start."

"Is that anyway for an Amish guy to talk? You don't even sound Amish."

"I'm as Amish as any man in Bliss Creek." Was he? The extended rumspringa had changed him. Exposed him to things. He'd done things he shouldn't have, no doubt. But that was the point of the running around. To get it out of his system. It also helped him know what was important. "The way I talk has nothing to do with what I believe."

"You like women you know will make your brother crazy and make the big kahuna bishop guy mad." She wiggled a finger at him. "Naughty boy. You just want to be different, that's all. Be your own person. I've been doing it all my life."

"Funny, I thought you were just the girlfriend of a thief, not a shrink." As soon as the words were out, Josiah wanted them back. They were mean and he wasn't a mean person. He concentrated on nailing the mesh to a fence post well away from the one she occupied. "Sorry. I didn't mean that. You better finish picking the tomatoes. Annie's probably making supper right now."

With a grunt, Charisma knelt next to him. Her blonde hair swung in her face, wisps sticking to her damp cheeks. His gaze was drawn to her lips. He swung the hammer, missed the nail, and hit his thumb. "Ouch, ouch!" He dropped the hammer and shook his hand. "Now look what you made me do."

"See, I told you so." She said the words in a sing-song voice. "Told you so. I know exactly what yanks your chain. I know what makes you tick because Logan is a bad boy too. He makes you look like a choir boy, but you're trying. You have that dark brooding thing going on, but it's hard to make it work when you wear blue work shirts and suspenders and cover that gorgeous curly hair with a hat all the time."

Caught somewhere between embarrassed and ashamed at his unbidden reaction to a woman he had no interest in, Josiah grabbed the hammer and focused on his work. Doing what he should've been doing all along. Working. Maybe she would lose interest and leave.

"Me, I'm like Sarah, bad news." She went on, her voice like the incessant buzz of a bee. He couldn't ignore it, because it might sting. "You need to run away from her. Don't walk, run."

He didn't bother to tell her he planned to send Sarah home—if he could ever get the chance to talk to her. It was none of Charisma's business. The Englischer's tone and her harsh words about someone she didn't even know sent a wave of protectiveness through him. Sarah was still his friend. He hazarded a glance at her. "You don't know Sarah."

"I know her kind. You ask her to sew clothes for you and your kids, make your breakfast, dinner and supper, can vegetables, do laundry by hand, quilt, and show up for a three-hour service every other week, and she'll run for the hills. Maybe not at first, maybe not for a while, but she'll run. She'll run so fast, she'll be a streak on the highway.

"Don't let the package fool you. You can dress up an old box with pretty, shiny wrapping, but what is inside doesn't change." She stood and picked up the basket. "Miriam is a sweet person. A good person. She's in it for the long haul. One look at her face when you're anywhere near her would tell you that. She'll never leave you. She'll never hurt you. Girls like Sarah and me, we're a dime a dozen. Miriam is worth a hundred Sarahs. Take my word for it. When you look at Sarah, see me. See what's on the inside."

She strolled away, swinging the basket and her backside. Josiah tore his gaze from her and focused on the fence, but his mind's eye wouldn't let the image of Charisma Chiasson go. It would be a miracle if the eggs arrived in the kitchen unbroken and the tomatoes without bruises. Like the person who carried them. She was covered by bruises that couldn't be seen. Josiah didn't know how or why they'd been inflicted, but Charisma was a walking wound. Jaded, cynical, and nineteen years old. How did that happen? He mulled over her words. Words spoken by someone who'd experienced life. Experienced pain. Someone who thought she couldn't love or be loved. The thought hung around him like a shroud. He didn't want to end up like Charisma. Despite his gut reaction to her, Josiah was glad Annie had brought her home. Charisma might know the Sarahs of the world, but it was someone like Annie who could help her heal.

He glanced at his bruised thumb. Lesson learned. He'd do well to keep his distance.

Chapter 25

David ran a hand over the horse's long, slick neck, adjusted the lead rope, and led Blackie out of the Shiracks' barn. Pools of rainwater dotted the muddy path that connected the barn and the corral. At least the mid-morning shower had cooled the air. David inhaled. The air smelled fresh and clean. If the showers of the last few days continued, they would have a good harvest after all. The clouds had dissipated, and the sun on his face promised a warm afternoon. He soaked it up, thankful for each minute free of pain and nausea. A great day to be outside teaching a little girl to ride. Finally. Between his obligations at the bakery, the trip to Wakefield, Luke's need to use the horse, and Kinsey's doctor's appointments, it had been tough to find a time for this first lesson. And those obstacles were nothing compared to Willow's worry about her daughter getting hurt or contracting some new bug.

He shoved back the brim of his hat and glanced toward the house. Luke was working in the fields and Josiah was at the shop. Annie hadn't been at the bakery in two days because of some kind of stomach flu. Maybe she would feel well enough to venture out of the house today. Probably not. If their last encounter was any indication, it would be better if their paths didn't cross. They would sooner or later, of course, but only time could heal the wounds caused by those angry words. He didn't want Annie to be angry at him, even if it served the purpose of allowing him to keep her at arm's length. He couldn't bear her being mad at him. It was a conundrum he couldn't fathom.

The horse pranced, his head dipping and bobbing as if he were excited to be outdoors, bringing David back to the task at hand. "Easy, there. Easy, boy."

He'd better keep his mind on Blackie and teaching Kinsey to ride. Willow was depending on him to keep her daughter safe. The idea of Kinsey riding didn't thrill her mother. She seemed consumed with the possibility of germs. David understood. Willow wanted to focus on germs so she wouldn't have to think about what might really kill her daughter.

He shook off the thought and walked Blackie around in a large circle to calm him a little before Kinsey arrived. If she'd never seen a real horse before, she might have second thoughts when she saw the size of this one.

"Good boy." He ignored the ache in his shoulders and arms. His strength still hadn't returned, and fatigue overtook him in the middle of the simplest tasks. *Buck up, buddy.*

"What are you doing?"

Startled, David tightened his grip on the rope and turned. He'd been so engrossed in his thoughts he hadn't seen Charisma's approach. She looked much better than she had after the trip to Wakefield the previous week. No sadness marred her face, and the dark circles had disappeared from under her eyes. She still wore her clothes a size too small, but life on the farm seemed to agree with her. Gracie toddled along behind her, a cookie in one hand and a ragged doll in the other. The doll must belong to one of the twins. David had seen *Englischer* dolls, which were nearly perfect in their mimicry of real babies. This one had no face.

He tied the rope to the fence in a loose split knot and pushed through the gate so he could approach her. "I'm waiting for Kinsey."

"Annie said you'd be out today." Charisma fiddled with gauze and tape wrapped around the index and thumb of her left hand. "Kinsey's doctor finally said yes?"

Annie had been talking about him. David tried to take that fact in stride. Really, she'd been talking about Kinsey.

"Yep. Her numbers are so much better that he's letting her spend a few days at home." He leaned against the fence and studied her hand. "What happened to your fingers?"

"Annie's trying to teach me to sew. I'm all thumbs." She sucked at the tip of her finger for a second and let it drop. "I mean, really. She thinks I can make baby clothes and cloth diapers. All I do is stick the needle in my hand so much it bleeds."

"You'll learn." Or not. Maybe it was a skill that had to be learned early in life. David had no idea. "Anyway, Kinsey has the all clear to take riding lessons."

"That's great news." Charisma's gaze dropped to Gracie, who squatted in the mud, chatting nonstop with the doll cradled in her chubby arms. "I can't imagine having a kid with cancer." Red blotches marred her long white neck. "Or anybody close to me. Sorry."

"It's all right."

The sound of an engine stuttering and coughing drowned out the rest of his response. David appreciated the good timing. He was tired of trying to make people feel better about his disease. And tired of them apologizing for something that wasn't their fault. He shaded his eyes against the sun pouring between glowering clouds that couldn't decide whether to move on or unleash another downpour. A green station wagon that looked as if it had survived a tornado—just barely— puttered along the road, splashing through water pooled in deep ruts.

Willow Navarro waved as she pulled into the grassy area by the corral. At least she wouldn't get stuck in the mud there. David waved back and started toward the car.

"That would be them, I'm guessing." Charisma pulled Gracie onto her hip before she could scamper toward the car. "We'll get out of your way."

She sounded a little wistful. What did she do with herself all day besides stick needles in her thumb? Surely she helped Leah and Annie with the cooking and cleaning. David almost snorted. She didn't look as if she knew a mop from a broom or how to scramble eggs, let alone feed a dozen people three times a day. "You're welcome to stay and watch. I'm sure Gracie will like Kinsey, and someday Gracie might want to learn to ride too."

"Gracie's gonna be a city girl." Charisma sounded very sure of herself, yet she stayed rooted to the spot. "Still, I ain't got nothing else to do, I guess. I spent a whole day in town putting in my applications for jobs. At the IGA, the restaurant, the pharmacy, the convenience store, that little salon. Nobody called the phone in your bishop's barn. Leastwise, that's what the bishop's wife told Annie. Nobody's hiring a pregnant lady who's big as a house. So here I sit. It's not like there's a party going on around here or anything."

David bit back a retort. She didn't sound the least bit appreciative of what Annie had done for her or the allowances the bishop made in letting Annie use the telephone intended for emergencies. "Suit yourself."

Kinsey hopped from the car and scurried toward them. She wore a bright purple bandana today, a neon green T-shirt, jeans that hung on her skinny legs, and the shiniest red cowboy boots David had ever seen. Someone had been shopping at the Waylon's Western Wear.

"Is that him? He's huge. Can I ride him now?" She dashed past David, then slowed down when she saw Gracie. She squatted next to the little girl. "Pretty baby, who are you?"

"Pretty!" Gracie took a swipe at the bandana. Her fingers curled around the material and she tugged.

"No!" A horrified look on her face, Charisma grabbed the little girl's hand. Too late. The bandana slid off, revealing the patches of fuzz on Kinsey's head. "I'm so sorry, Kinsey. Gracie, give it back right now! Bad girl!"

It seemed an overreaction, but then Charisma wasn't used to chemo-induced baldness. Kinsey didn't seem bashful about it or the least bit embarrassed. David plucked the bandana from Gracie's hand and offered it to Kinsey. She ignored it. Instead she shimmied up the fence like a monkey and threw her leg over the top railing. "No biggie. She can have it."

"Slow down." David grabbed her tiny waist. "Stop. Let me get to the other side of the fence and then you can come in."

He slipped through the gate and approached from the other side. "Come on." He swung her to the ground. "You need to be calm and quiet. That way you don't make Blackie nervous. Also, the polite thing to do is to say hello to Charisma and Gracie. Meet them properly." He held out the bandana. "And you don't want your head to get sunburned if the sun decides to stay out."

Grimacing, Kinsey slapped the bandana on her head sideways and stuck her hand through the railing. "Please to meet 'cha!"

Laughing, Charisma shook the hand. Gracie, her face solemn, did the same.

"Yuck, her hand is sticky." Kinsey wiped her fingers on her jeans. "What is that?"

"Probably peach jelly. Annie made her toast this morning."

Despite being sick, Annie had made breakfast. What had Charisma been doing? *Don't judge. It's wrong to judge.* David plastered a neutral look on his face. "So she's feeling better?"

"Oh, yeah, she said she's going into the bakery this afternoon to help your mom bake for tomorrow. Friday being such a big shopping day in Bliss Creek and all."

David studied the trees over her shoulder. "I'm glad she's feeling better."

"I think she misses you as much as you miss her. If she didn't work with food, she probably wouldn't stay at home even when she's sick. She hates not seeing you every day at the bakery."

"I never said I…" He stopped. The grin on Charisma's face told him there was no point in disputing her words. "Why didn't she come out to watch the lesson?"

"Leah's got her mopping floors, dusting, baking a casserole for supper, and who knows what else. She'll probably make her do the windows and scrub the fireplace before the day's over. But I imagine she'll sneak out later, don't you worry."

And Charisma had nothing to do. Why didn't Annie say something to her? It wasn't his place, but he was sorely tempted. Charisma made more work for Annie, plus Annie took a lot of guff from Leah about bringing home this Englischer and her little girl. His mind's eye filled with a picture he couldn't forget, no matter how hard he tried. The picture of Annie walking toward him with Gracie's arms wrapped around her neck that day in Wakefield. What would she look like with his child in her arms? Would their child have Annie's green eyes and fair skin? *Stop it!*

"Now, Mister David, now?" Kinsey tugged at his shirt sleeve. "What are you waiting for?"

"For your mother." He managed to gather his wits about him. "I want to make sure she's ready for you to do this."

Taking her sweet time, Willow sauntered over to the fence. Her reluctance showed on her face. "Grammy says she's been racing around like a crazy person all day." She rubbed at a grease spot on her Home-Town Restaurant uniform. "She hasn't had this much energy since... well, since forever. You'd better get started; I have to be at work at one."

"That's plenty of time for a first lesson. It's good that Kinsey is excited. Getting a little sun and some fresh air will do her good." Being outdoors always made David feel better. "Exercise is good too. She needs to work her muscles and get her strength back."

"I don't know. Her immune system can't fight germs. What if she catches something out here?" With eyes ringed with dark shadows, Willow gave the corral the once-over. "They probably have mice out here and who knows what germs that horse has? And what if she falls off?"

"Are you kidding? I've been here over a month and I ain't seen a single rat," Charisma assured her, butting into the conversation. "This is the cleanest place I've ever lived in my life. That's all they do. Clean, cook, sew, clean, cook, sew. And what's even weirder, they like it."

The astonishment in Charisma's voice made David want to laugh, but the frown on Willow's face forced him to swallow the chuckle. She studied the other woman with a curious look on her face. "I'm Willow."

"Sorry." He'd been so wrapped up in the exchange, David had forgotten to introduce them. He quickly corrected his error.

"So you work at the restaurant." Charisma's full lips turned down. "I put in my application a few days ago. No one's called."

"Naomi—she's the owner—she does things on her own time. 'Sides, I heard she interviewed her niece yesterday. You know how it is—family."

David caught the shadow that flitted across Charisma's face. "There'll be other jobs—"

"It don't matter." Charisma interrupted, her usual smirk anchored on her face once again. "Once she saw this belly, she'd never hire me anyway."

"Come on, Mister David, come on! I wanna ride!" Kinsey danced around on the damp earth, her boots sinking into the mud. "You said I could ride him."

"And you will. Patience is a virtue, anyone ever tell you that?"

"Grammy says the early bird gets the worm."

This time all three adults laughed. It sounded good. He'd done the right thing in bringing Kinsey out here. It would be good for her and for Willow. She needed fresh air and sun too.

In mid-chortle, Charisma winced and gripped the fence post tight with her hand. She leaned over, panting. After a minute, she straightened and inhaled loudly through her mouth.

Uncomfortable, David waited for Willow to jump in. She was a woman. All women knew about these things. She didn't say a word, and he coughed, hesitating. "Everything all right?"

Her nose wrinkled and Charisma rubbed her belly with both hands. "Happens now and then. I looked it up in the baby book Annie bought me. It's called Braxton Hicks."

Willow seemed to come out of her fog. She nodded so hard her nametag wiggled. "I had some of those with Kinsey."

And they were off. Women really liked to talk about having babies. Expecting babies, delivering babies, diapering and burping babies. It seemed a fascinating topic to all females. David gave Kinsey a little push. Now was the perfect time to duck out of the conversation. Together they approached Blackie, and Kinsey's pace slowed. She kicked at a clod of dirt. "He's humongous."

"And that's one of the reasons you have to treat him with respect."

A thoughtful look on her gaunt face, she cocked her head. "What are the other reasons?"

"He's a living creature. He feels pain and sadness and hunger and thirst just like we do."

"I know how to be nice to animals. I had a rabbit. I was nice to him."

"*Gut.* Be nice and respect Blackie. If you do something to scare him, he's going to react. Not because he wants to hurt you, but because it's instinct."

She wrinkled her upturned nose. "What's instinct?"

"Like when you get thirsty, you know to drink." David picked up a saddle blanket from the railing. Blackie snorted and tossed his head, adding his two cents' worth to the conversation. "If you didn't, eventually you would die."

"Like birds know how to fly."

"Yes, they just know."

Kinsey studied the horse. "Can I get on now?"

"No. First, you have to learn some things."

"Learn?" Kinsey frowned. "Is this going to be like school?"

From talking to Willow, David knew Kinsey hadn't been in a schoolroom in a long while. Another thing for her mother to worry about. "Not exactly. You have to know how to bridle and saddle Blackie and what to feed him and how to take care of him. That's part of being a responsible animal owner."

"But I don't own him."

"Don't you want to own a horse when you grow up?"

Kinsey gave him a long, level look. Her eyes were much too old for a seven-year-old. Her gaze went back to the horse, and she leaned closer to him. "My mom doesn't think I'm going to grow up." Her voice was barely a whisper. "Neither does Grammy."

David slid the blanket over Blackie's back, debating how much to say. And what he believed. He wouldn't lie and make life all pretty. Life was messy. And short. Shorter for some than others.

"Mister David?"

"Just David." He leaned down so their heads were close. "It's about what *you* think, not what *they* think. First, we put on the blanket to protect his back."

Kinsey ran a frail hand over the wool blanket. "The doctor always tells me I'll get better, but then he goes outside and talks to my mom. They whisper."

"Your doctor is good at what he does. You have to have faith." The irony of his words pricked at David's skin like a needle, over and over again. Why was he trying so hard to get this little girl to believe when he had so little faith himself? "You have to work at it."

Kinsey touched Blackie's shaggy mane, then ran her hand down his forehead. "I'm going to grow up so I can have my own horse." Her voice was soft, its cocky defiance gone. "And I'm going to ride him whenever I feel like it."

"Good for you." David lifted the saddle from where he'd laid it on the fence. "Time to saddle up."

For both of them.

※

Annie strolled toward the corral with her head high. The floors were mopped, the goulash was simmering on the stove, and Leah was occupied sewing new pants for the boys, who were growing like weeds these days. If only she had the patience to show Charisma how to sew like that. No one sewed as well as Leah. But Annie didn't dare ask. Charisma had less patience than Leah. Between the two of them the project would be like a bonfire in a northern wind.

She stepped on something hard and a pain shot through her heel. That's what she got for not paying attention. She lifted her skirt a little and sidestepped another rock in the road. She picked up her pace, anxious to get that first moment over when her path crossed David's. The first time they would speak since she'd thrown a hissy fit in front of him. She missed him too much not to try to salvage their friendship from the wreckage of dashed hopes and dreams.

"Hey, Annie." Charisma rubbed her belly with one hand and motioned to Kinsey's mother. "This is Willow, Kinsey's mother."

"We met—sort of—in David's hospital room. How is Kinsey doing?"

Her expression troubled, Willow shook her head. "She has good days and bad days. This one seems to be a good one." They all turned to watch David lead Blackie around the corral with Kinsey, grinning from ear to ear, sitting high on his back. "I don't know about this. She shouldn't exert too much energy. She needs to save her strength. And what about the germs?"

"Oh, I'm sure David washes his hands."

"I meant the horse." Willow frowned and flipped her long, thick braid over her shoulder. "What about the horse?"

Not bothering to answer such a strange question, Annie leaned against the fence and watched. Kinsey had her hands wrapped around the reins. Her short legs flopped with every step Blackie took. "When can I gallop?" she called. "I want to gallop. When are we going to leave the corral and jump over rivers and stuff?"

David laughed. Annie closed her eyes for a second. She hadn't heard that sound in months. The carefree, clean sound of a friend enjoying life.

"So the wicked sister-in-law let you out of the dungeon?" Charisma flashed a smirk. "I'm surprised. No more hard labor this morning?"

Her words stung. Charisma had been living with them for more than a month. Her determination to be a better guest after the visit to Wakefield had lingered for a few days and then seemed to taper off. She occasionally carried dishes to the tub for washing, helped wash her own clothes, and sometimes made her bed, but mostly she sat on the porch and stared at the horizon like someone might be coming for her. Who, Annie had no idea.

"Leah's not wicked. She's just a hard worker and she expects everyone else to be too." Annie schooled her voice, trying to be gentle. "She cooks and cleans for you too, you know."

"I know I'm just more work. If I weren't so pregnant, maybe somebody would hire me and I could take myself off your hands. I could get a little place in town with electricity and a TV." Bitterness marred the words. "I'm just glad the trial is almost here. I hate imposing like this."

If Logan went to prison, where would Charisma and her children go? Annie suspected Charisma was avoiding thinking about that outcome. Instead, she kept insisting that Logan would go free. How that was possible, Annie couldn't begin to know. She turned her gaze toward David as he led Blackie in a huge circle. Another problem she couldn't solve.

Charisma nudged Annie. "He'd really be cute if his hair would grow back."

Annie couldn't help but smile. David wasn't cute. Cute applied to little boys like her nephews William and Joseph. Hair or no hair, David was a handsome man. She pushed away the thought. Handsome is as handsome does, her mother would say. David was a hard worker and a man of faith. Those things counted far more than looks. Still, her gaze lingered on his full mouth and high cheekbones. His skin had darkened in the last month, taking with it that pale, pasty look of illness. His clothes still hung on him and he needed to gain a few pounds, but that didn't keep her heart from turning over every time he got close.

David's gaze turned toward her and his smile died. He led Blackie away from her toward the other end of the corral. Angry frustration flowed over Annie. "I don't know. He's stubborn as a mule and not nearly as smart." As soon as she said the words, Annie felt mean. "Forget I said that—"

Charisma gasped and grabbed Annie's arm with a grip that would leave a bruise. She doubled over, her mouth wide open. "I think...I think..." She panted. "I think I'm having the baby!"

"Are you sure?" Joy, fear, and envy intertwined into a thick vine that threatened to choke Annie. "Is it really time?"

"I've done this before, remember?" Charisma groaned. "I didn't want to do it again. It really hurts."

Annie tugged free of her grip and whirled, preparing to run to the barn to hitch up the buggy. Then she caught sight of the bright green car. Of course. God's provision. She turned to Willow. "We need to get her to the clinic. I'm so sorry to impose, but do you think you can drive us—"

"Of course. David, Kinsey, we need to go!" Willow clapped her hands. "Now! Let's go. It's time for the baby. Everyone into the lime-mobile."

The lime-mobile? Annie eyed it. Very green. Very beat-up. But faster than a buggy any day. God did indeed provide, but He also had a sense of humor.

Without hesitation, David brought the horse to a halt. He swung Kinsey to the ground. Her face puzzled, then belligerent, she trotted across the corral as fast as her skinny legs could carry her. "Hey, you said I could do this and now you're changing your mind?" She panted, out of breath even though she hadn't come far. Her white skin seemed to stretch tight across her thin face. "I didn't even get to gallop—"

"Kinsey, honey, this isn't about you," Willow interrupted. "It's not always about you. Charisma is having her baby."

Tears bright in her eyes, Kinsey opened her mouth. A groan from Charisma stopped her response. The little girl's eyes widened. "Will it hurt?"

"I imagine it will." David swung the girl over the fence and his gaze met Annie's. "But it'll be worth it."

The next hour was a blur. Rushing to tell Leah they were leaving—at least under these circumstances she didn't object to keeping Gracie—riding in a lime green station wagon that smelled like sweaty shoes and seemed to hit every bump in the road, listening to Charisma's ragged breathing and increasingly loud groans. "Hurry," Annie whispered. "Hurry."

David swiveled to look back at them. Funny how his hearing seemed to be so finely tuned to her soft voice. "It'll be fine. We're almost there."

At the clinic, Willow dropped them off and went to park the car, insisting she would wait to see if they needed a ride home. A nurse settled Charisma into a wheelchair at the emergency room entrance. "We just need to get some information to the admissions clerk here and then we'll get you up to the labor suite. Who is your doctor?"

"I'm not from around here." Her face shining with sweat, Charisma clutched at her midsection with hands that twitched. "I don't have a doctor."

"You've had no prenatal care?"

"What's prenatal?"

"It's…" The nurse's mouth flapped open and shut in disbelief. "It's very irresponsible to go through a pregnancy without prenatal care—"

"I had my first baby this way and she's fine." Charisma began to cry. "Tell her, Annie. Gracie's fine, isn't she?"

"She's healthy and happy." Annie rushed to defend Charisma. "No problems."

The nurse frowned. Her gaze swung to David. "Are you the responsible party?"

David's eyebrows pumped. "Responsible party?"

"The husband?" The nurse's gaze rested on Charisma's bare fingers. "The father?"

"No." David's face turned brick red under his summer tan. "A friend."

"We're her friends. She doesn't have family here, and the baby's father is…unable to be here." Much as he would like to be. Annie was certain of that. How sad it was that he would miss the birth of his child. "Can you please help her? She's in pain."

Charisma began to sob.

"We'll help her, miss, you can be sure of that, but as I said, we need some information first. What about insurance?" The nurse's frown deepened. "Miss Chiasson, do you have insurance?"

"No." Charisma gripped the arms of the wheelchair and panted. "It hurts, please, it hurts."

"We'll be responsible for her." Annie couldn't stand it anymore. The Plain people always took care of their own. For the moment, that included Charisma. "You know that."

The nurse's gaze went from Annie in her long dress and kapp to

David in his suspenders, black pants, and hat. She pursed her lips. "Well—"

"I'm having a *baby* here!" Charisma's groan turned to a scream. "Could we gab about this later?"

"Someone needs to fill out paperwork." The nurse thrust a clipboard at David and slapped both hands on the wheelchair handles. "Y'all talk amongst yourselves and decide who that will be. In the meantime, we'll find someone to deliver this baby."

Annie grabbed the clipboard from David and strode to the admission desk counter. If she couldn't answer the questions, she would make something up.

"You can't solve all her problems for her."

David's voice was soft in her ears. The admissions clerk didn't look up. Annie smoothed the paper. So much information she didn't have about Charisma. Her medical history. Her permanent address. Telephone number. Social Security number.

"No, but I can stand with her so she doesn't have to stand alone."

"For how long? Until the trial? Until her boyfriend goes to prison? Until he gets out of prison? Leah isn't entirely wrong in considering those questions."

"As long as necessary." Annie heaved a breath and sought to soften her tone. "That is the charitable thing to do."

She turned her back on him and focused on the paperwork. She must think about Charisma only right now. Poor Charisma having her baby alone. Determined to stand in for Logan, she began filling out the forms. The questions she couldn't answer she left blank, the rest she filled in using her best penmanship. When she was done the forms looked reasonably full. And David had left her side. That was fine. Feeling resolute, she strode down the hallway to the waiting room. No David. He really had left her. No sign of Willow and Kinsey either.

She flopped into a chair and picked up a magazine. People she didn't recognize stared up at her. Stories about television shows and celebrity affairs and fashion shows. Not the sort of thing she needed filling her head. She slapped it back on the table.

With nothing else to do and nothing she wanted to think about, Annie closed her eyes and willed herself to think of nothing. Nothing but prayers for a healthy baby and mother. The words filled her mind and her heart. She would not think of herself now and the hole she couldn't fill. The hole left when her dreams of sharing a life with David fled. *Stop it.* She squirmed in the chair. *God, forgive me. Forgive me for being so self-centered. So selfish.*

"Miss? Miss!"

Annie opened her eyes. A nurse stood in the doorway, a big smile on her face. "Are you with Miss Chiasson?"

"Yes, ma'am." She popped from the chair. "Is she all right? Is the baby all right?"

"He's fine and dandy." The nurse clapped her hands as if applauding her own report, two quick little claps. "It's a good thing she arrived when she did. She made short work of it."

"A boy?"

"A boy."

"Healthy?"

"Fit as a fiddle."

Annie had no idea what that meant, but the smile on the nurse's face said all was well. "Can I see her?"

"In about half an hour. They're getting her cleaned up. Will the father be along shortly?"

The balloon of happiness floating around Annie deflated, shriveled up, and dropped to the ground around her. "Not…no…no."

"Well then, she'll be in room two-ten in about thirty minutes. You may visit, if you want."

Annie paced the entire thirty minutes. She wanted to see the baby, hold him, live that moment with Charisma—the moment she couldn't have for herself. She couldn't wait for Emma to experience this happy time. She would get to experience it with her and being an aunt would be the next best thing to being a mother. She would learn to be content with what God gave her.

Finally the time arrived. She managed a sedate trot down the hall to room two-ten. She pushed through the door into a room decorated with wallpaper featuring teddy bears and daisies. Light streamed through windows on an empty bed next to Charisma's. She had the room to herself. Her hair scraggly and wet with sweat, Charisma's head was bent over the baby in her arms. She looked up at Annie, tears streaming down her face. They weren't tears of joy. A hiccupping sob hung in the air between them.

"What is it? Is there something wrong with him?" Annie ran to the bed. "The nurse said he was healthy."

"He is." Charisma sobbed harder. "Don't you see? I don't love him."

Chapter 26

Annie struggled to comprehend Charisma's words. How could a mother not love her baby? How could Charisma hold her newborn son in her arms and declare she didn't love him? "You can't mean that. He's beautiful and he's yours. Don't you know how blessed you are? I would give anything to hold my own baby in my arms."

"Not the baby! Are you crazy?" Charisma hiccupped and squirmed in the hospital bed. She needed a tissue. Annie looked around, spied the box, and handed it to her. Charisma swiped at her nose. "I'm talking about Logan."

"Logan?" Annie couldn't help it. Her gaze dropped to the baby in Charisma's arms. He opened his tiny mouth and bellowed a wail too loud to come from someone so small. "You and he...I mean...you..."

"That's not love. You are so naïve. What we have isn't love. Not for me, anyway." Charisma blew hard and the baby wailed at the noise. "He gave me a roof over my head." She rocked back and forth against the pillows until the baby's wailing died down again. "He took care of me and Gracie. He stole for me. He broke the law for me. How can I abandon him?"

Annie bit her lip to keep her mouth shut. Men and women were meant to marry, then have children. To commit to a lifetime together. Charisma and Logan had gotten everything out of order and now

their children would pay the price. Hers was not to judge. She understood that, but she also understood why things had to be done in the
right order. Charisma and her babies served as an example. A painful
example.

"Now is not the time to make a decision about your future. You
just had a baby." Nothing would be decided now. Charisma and Logan
could still make it. Annie whipped around the end of the bed and
approached the other side. She held out her arms. "May I hold him?"

Charisma laid the bundle wrapped in a soft blue blanket in her
arms. Annie breathed in the scent of baby. Beautiful baby. "Logan's the
father of your children. You're forever linked to him. Don't you think
you'll learn to love him?"

"He's in jail, probably going to prison for at least five years. Not
much of a chance of that." Charisma pulled her sheet up around her
neck and burrowed under it. "Besides, if I don't love him after all we've
been through, what makes you think I'll start now?"

She had a point, but Annie couldn't let go of the image of Logan
driven to steal for a hungry child. She glanced down at the bundle in
her arms. The baby had a blue cap pulled over his head so she couldn't
tell if he had his father's hair. "Love grows over time. It gets bigger and
stronger."

"I don't know what love is. Maybe the way my dad treated me
messed me up so I can't love a man." Charisma tossed the sodden tissue on the nightstand next to her bed. "But then I can't support two
kids, neither."

Annie swallowed against her own tears. Sadness flowed over her in
a river of regret for innocence lost. Surely Charisma wouldn't spend the
rest of her life without love because of her father's actions. "You will
learn to support them. Even if you don't stay together, Logan will have
to help you. It's the Englischers' law."

She didn't know much about law, but she knew that the Englischers expected men to take care of the children they fathered. It was never
a question in her community. Marriage came first, then children, and
divorce didn't exist.

Charisma leaned her head against her pillow. Her face was almost as white as its covering. "From jail?"

Good point. "One thing at a time."

"Even one thing seems like too much right now."

Annie kissed the baby's forehead and laid him next to Charisma. "Rest. Tomorrow is time enough to think about all this."

"Okay." Charisma closed her eyes.

Annie tiptoed to the door.

"Annie?"

"Yes?"

"Seeing as I don't have any insurance and I got a healthy baby, they'll kick me out first thing tomorrow."

Annie understood the question behind the statement. "We'll come get you." Another question floated to the surface. "I didn't even ask. What did you name him?"

"Luke David Chiasson."

Annie smiled. "Very nice."

"I figured he could use some good role models in his life."

Luke David Chiasson was going to be just fine. Annie would make sure of it. She pushed through the door, still smiling.

"How's she doing?" David straightened from the wall where he'd been leaning. In the harsh fluorescent light, his skin took on a yellow cast. Black stains under his eyes looked like bruises. "The nurse told me she'd be moved here. I didn't think it would be…I thought it best I wait out here."

"I thought you'd left." Annie swallowed. "Little Luke David Chiasson is doing fine."

"Luke David?" His sober expression fled for a second, replaced by something like embarrassment. "Why would she do that? She hardly knows me."

"She has a lot of experience with bad people, especially bad men. She knows good ones when she sees them. Now you'd better live up to it. Luke David will look to you as a…what did Charisma call it? Jah, a role model."

"An example? I'm nobody's example."

"I think Kinsey would disagree."

The sober expression reappeared.

"What is it?"

"After you started filling out the papers, Willow came in and told me Kinsey wasn't feeling well." His Adam's apple bobbed as he swallowed. "Willow took her to the restroom and she started vomiting. They readmitted her."

"I'm so sorry, David."

"Me too." He stared at his boots. "She didn't even get to finish one lesson."

⊣⊢

Josiah hesitated. Days had passed, but the words Charisma had spoken in the garden were still echoing in his head. He loosened his grip on the picket fence gate. Knock on the door or leave? He'd come this far. Sarah's cousin said she was working at Mayor Haag's house. It was past suppertime—maybe they had her cooking and serving and cleaning up. That would be a lot of work for a girl who hated to put her hands in dishwater because it dried her skin and softened her long nails. David had made it a point to let Josiah know about his discussion with Sarah. He hadn't said much else about her. Not enough to give Josiah an inkling of what his opinion of her was. That was David.

Fine. He would do the right thing and send her home. Attempt to send her home. Sarah had a mind of her own, which had been one of the many things he liked about her. Josiah pushed through the gate, strode up the sidewalk, climbed the steps, and rapped on the door before he could lose his resolve. They needed to talk and they needed to do it now, while Luke was busy helping Onkel John harvest his wheat. Josiah hated sneaking around. He'd thought those days were over. They ended now.

The door opened. Sarah looked up at him. She blinked and a big grin spread across her pretty face.

"Josiah, you're here!" She squealed and pushed the door open wider. "Come in. I've been waiting and waiting. You notice how patient I've been, right? I've—"

"Sarah. Sarah! Stop." Josiah held up a hand. "We need to talk."

The animation seeped from her face.

"Sure." She made a flourish with one hand toward the hallway. "Come on in. Mayor Haag is at her weekly card game. She won't be back for a couple of hours."

"Is Mr. Haag here?"

"Chess night at his banker friend's."

So he was alone with her. Disconcerted, Josiah hesitated in the foyer. "Maybe I should wait until I can see you at your cousin's—"

"Josiah, it's me. I won't bite you." Sarah took his arm and tugged him into the living room. "Besides, Marcus, their handyman, is working on the kitchen sink. The garbage disposal is clogged. We're not alone."

Disappointment took a shot at Josiah. They weren't alone. The clashing of his emotions gave him a headache. No. Not disappointment. It couldn't be. They shouldn't be alone. Not ever. "This will only take a second."

Sarah took a seat on the brown leather couch and patted the spot next to her. Ignoring the invitation, he planted his boots on the braided rug that covered a slick tile floor. "I don't need to sit...you called me Josiah."

"That's right."

Her long dark green skirt and crisp white apron registered. Every strand of her fiery red hair lay confined under her kapp. She wore no jewelry, no makeup. Her face had a shiny, clean scrubbed look that reminded him of Annie. She looked every inch a Plain woman. Still, he knew better. Looks deceived. Actions would tell the true story.

"I'm trying so hard, Josiah."

There it was again. "So I'm not Joe anymore?"

"No. You're a Plain man and I'm a...I'm trying to be a Plain woman. The woman you want."

"I never said I wanted you to be Plain. That was the whole point. Don't you see? I ran away from this life. I ran to you in Wichita because you were you...not this...this copycat of my sisters and mother and all the other women in my community."

"And you came back because this is where you want to be. This is who you want to be. I saw the way you looked at Miriam that day in front of the blacksmith shop." Her tone hardened. She stared at him with a look that spoke volumes. Jealousy. Frustration. Sadness. "She's what you want. Someone who won't pull you out of your world. I get that."

"You think you can be that woman?"

"Look at me. I'm cleaning houses to earn money to support myself so I won't be a burden to my cousin and her family." She patted her kapp with a self-conscience smile. "I've been talking with the deacon every morning as soon as the sun comes up. Rachel is teaching me to sew and how to bake bread."

"Sewing and baking bread and cleaning the mayor's house won't make you a member of this community."

"No, but I should get a reward for all the stuff I do around here. It's been a week and I'm still finding dirty cups and cigarette butts all over the house from a party the mayor threw days ago. It's gross, but I don't care. I'll do anything that helps me fit in."

Fit in. Charisma's words flitted around inside his head. Miriam didn't have to learn to fit in. She just did. She belonged here.

"Sarah, I don't want you to sacrifice your happiness, your whole life for me."

"I'm not. I'm a believer."

"You're not."

"You're sure full of yourself. You think I'd clean toilets for you?"

"I think you idealize what we had."

"What we have."

"You romanticize the time we spent together. We fought all the time." The alcohol-drenched memory of arguing with her on an apartment balcony made his stomach lurch. "I nearly killed myself over you."

Tears bright in her huge eyes, she stood and sauntered toward him. Every fiber of his being wanted to pull her into his arms. Only propriety kept him from acting on his desire. He'd learned some self-control in the last year. She laid a hand on his chest and his heart pounded. "We fought because we love each other. You jumped off that apartment balcony because I said no when you asked me to marry you. If I had it to do over again, I'd say yes."

"I fell off that balcony because I was drunk." He steeled himself against the wave of nausea that always came when he tried to grasp the fragmented memories of that day in Wichita. "I wouldn't ask you again."

"Maybe not today. But you will. I know you will. Feelings like that don't just go away."

"I'm not that boy anymore. Those were...what I felt for you wasn't love."

"What was it?"

The last thing he wanted to do was hurt her. "It was a boy feeling things for a girl. It was a boy wanting what he knew he couldn't have."

"Life with me will never be boring, Josiah."

He had no doubt of that. She would be the bored one. "Don't you miss your friends and your music and the parties?"

"I miss you, only you."

He studied her beautiful face, then tried to remember what Miriam's looked like. A steamy fog blocked it out.

Sarah laughed, the notes like a birdsong. "Don't look so freaked out. We have time. I still have to do a bunch of lessons and junk before I can be baptized."

"Junk? Junk!" His heart slowed. The fog lifted. "You're just playing along to get what you want. Is that what you're saying?"

"You know what I mean." She grabbed his arm and leaned into him. The smell of roses enveloped him. "The same stuff you need to do. Let's be baptized together."

He couldn't help himself. He leaned into her touch, mesmerized by her scent and her softness. Her hands touched his face and her fingers traced his lips. "Kiss me, Joe, like you used to. Please."

She lifted her face to his and he leaned down to meet her. He drowned in the emotion that poured from her. His own emotions battered him. Could he live without her? Was she the one all along? Her lips parted. Beautiful lips.

His muscles froze. No. Not like this. Charisma's face floated between him and Sarah. The words she had spoken in the garden penetrated the desire he felt. *Look at Sarah and see me.* Charisma's advice. The package did not reflect what was inside the box. Sarah could look like a Plain woman, but her actions spoke of an entirely different woman.

Battered, but still standing, propriety won out. *Thank You, God.* For Luke and David and years of sitting on the bench at Sunday prayer service. For Mudder and Daed and the lessons they had drilled into him. A powerful wave of remorse pounded him. It took every ounce of moral strength he could muster, but he managed to jerk back. "No." He whirled and stumbled toward the door. "No."

"Joe!"

He blocked out the sound of her calling and shut the front door behind him, then leaned against the solid wood. "God, help me." The words sounded desperate spoken aloud. They were. Josiah needed help. "Save me, Lord. Save me from myself."

Chapter 27

Annie swaddled little Luke David and lifted him onto her shoulder. He continued to wail despite having a clean diaper. He certainly had a healthy set of lungs. "Sh-sh-sh-sh." She patted his back and paced the room while Charisma's head bent over the treadle sewing machine. She had a determined look on her face.

"If I can just get this thing to go in a straight line." She pumped the treadle twice. "Oh, no, it's totally crooked and now the thread is tangled. This is crazy. How will I ever have enough to keep this little poop-maker in diapers at this rate?"

She snipped the thread and tossed the cloth to the side. "Store-bought diapers would be so much easier."

"If you could afford to buy them." Annie shifted Luke David so he lay in the crook of her arm. He huffed and wailed some more. Annie talked a little louder. "Besides, these soft diapers feel so much better on your little behind, don't they, Luke David?"

"Then you'll have to do the sewing and let me do the walking-the-floor thing." Charisma stood and tugged at an oversized T-shirt that hung down to her thighs. "Give him to me. It feels like my milk came in. Finally. If he can get some real food, he'll stop fussing."

The voice of experience. Charisma might not know much about sewing and cooking, but she knew how to take care of babies. Annie

203

willingly handed Luke David over. Her shoulders ached and her eyes burned. Between the bakery, chores, and helping with the baby, she wasn't getting enough sleep, but she was determined to make sure no additional work fell on Leah. Luke had been clear about that. Charisma and the baby could stay until the trial was over. After that, the family needed to find their own home. How that would be possible boggled her mind. God would provide, she told herself. And she would help. Somehow.

Charisma sank into the rocking chair in the corner and began feeding Luke David. His crying turned to eager suckling sounds. Charisma grimaced. "Ouch! At least this doesn't cost anything."

Annie moved to the door. Even her feet hurt. "And it's good for him. If you're okay for a while, I think I'll get some sleep."

"Sure, I'm fine." Her tone didn't match the words. "He's my baby. I can take care of him."

"I didn't mean to say you couldn't—"

"I know what you meant."

Annie turned to go.

"Do you think I'm a bad person?"

"What?" Once again Annie turned back.

"Do you think I'm a bad person? I have two kids and I'm not married. I don't even love their daddy."

"We all do bad things. God forgives."

"Back to God again." She snorted. "You think what I've done is wrong. Does that make Gracie and Luke David mistakes? Does it make it wrong for me to have them?"

"I'm not very smart." Annie eased into the chair by the door. She picked her words carefully. "I don't know much about anything, really, but whatever you've done, it's not their fault. God loves them and He has a plan for them. You ask Him to forgive you and He will. In the Bible, Jesus says, 'Go, and sin no more.' You have to stop doing what you're doing. Live your life differently. You ask Him to show you what you should do now and He will."

Charisma grunted and shifted the baby to the other side. He made a happy gurgling sound. "Where was God when my dad was beating on me? Where was He then? Was that part of some big God plan?"

"Do you remember the story about Adam and Eve eating the apple?"

"Sure. Who doesn't? I think they talked about it at every Vacation Bible School I went to. And the nasty serpent. What does that have to do with what happened to me?"

Annie tucked away the concept of Vacation Bible School to think about later. "The point is the world filled up with sin and disease after they did that. God doesn't make bad things happen." Even as the words came to her, Annie knew she believed them. And David needed to believe them too. "He wants us to cling to Him when they do. He helped you get away and He helped you find a safe place to be. You got through it the best you could. It's not the way He would've wanted it, but it doesn't mean He doesn't love you."

Her gaze distant and unseeing, Charisma stroked the silky down on her baby's head. "Maybe you're right. I hope you're right."

Chapter 28

Annie smoothed the tiny outfit she'd made for Luke David as she trudged up the steps in front of the courthouse. Most everyone had gone inside already. Between bathing and dressing the children and the long buggy ride, they were late. Hastily, she handed the sleeping baby to Charisma, who accepted with one arm while keeping a grip on Gracie's hand. "Logan will be so happy to see him. Now go on. Get in there before it's time for them to take him into the courtroom. Sergeant Parker is around here somewhere. He'll show you to the holding room or whatever he called it."

Sergeant Parker had visited the bakery the previous day to offer Charisma a chance to talk to Logan before the trial started. He said Logan was in a bad way—depressed and homesick. He needed to know Charisma would be in the courtroom. Annie couldn't forget the look on Charisma's face that day in the hospital room when she said she didn't love the father of her children. She'd been reluctant to visit Logan now, but Sergeant Parker had persuaded her. Annie found the fact that he cared endearing. She had known he had a heart, but not just how big it was.

"I don't understand why you can't come in with me." Charisma tugged at the dark blue dress Annie had made for her. Her baby belly gone, she didn't look as if she'd given birth only two weeks earlier. "You don't have to come into the courtroom. Come with me to the holding room."

Annie didn't bother to answer. Charisma had been trying to convince Annie since they left the house. She refused to understand Luke's prohibition. He didn't want Annie in the courtroom. Period. So far no one had shown up at the farm or the bakery to serve her papers requiring her to be there. Luke seemed to think seeing her would jog their memories—as if they'd forgotten she, Sadie, and Miriam were witnesses to the armed robbery. Not wanting to cause David any grief, she hadn't mentioned his discussion with the mayor to her brother. Mayor Haag wouldn't want to rock the boat with the Plain people in her community, not when they contributed so much to its well-being.

"Go! The longer you argue with me, the less time you'll have to spend with Logan before they start the trial." She smoothed Luke David's bib so it covered his new shirt. "Bring the children over to the bakery later. I'll watch them or Sadie will until it's over for the day."

"It's probably not going to be a long visit, anyway. I may not even stay for the trial."

Something in Charisma's expression caused the hair on Annie's arms to prickle. "Why? Logan needs your support."

"He may not want it after our visit."

"What are you going to do?"

"I'm going to tell him."

"Tell him what?"

"I have to tell him I don't love him. I can't go on like this. I need to get my life together." Charisma's nose turned red. Big tears teetered in her eyes, preparing to fall. "I can't wait around for him."

"You can't tell him now, not when he's facing prison."

"Better I should tell him when he's actually in prison? Write him a *Dear John* letter?"

A *Dear John* letter? Annie skipped that question. "Can't you just let him hold his son in his arms and enjoy that one moment before you break his heart?"

"You're so naïve. It won't break his heart. He won't have to worry about trying to be a dad from prison. Or supporting me. He'll be relieved." Charisma tugged on the dress again. "Did you have to make this so long? I feel like somebody's grandma."

"It's respectful." Annie cocked her head. Charisma looked young and pretty—too young to have two children and be facing the prospect of trying to support them alone. "It's dignified."

"That's not the look I usually go for."

His steps loud on the cement, Sergeant Parker slipped between two men in suits and pounded toward them.

"All right, he's in the holding cell now." He stopped, a strange look on his face. He took his hat off. "You look real nice in that dress, Miss Chiasson. He'll be happy to see you."

Charisma smirked at Annie. "Annie made it."

"I figured as much. She can cook and she can sew." His face suddenly a blotchy red color, Sergeant Parker twisted the hat in his hands. His gaze whipped to Annie, then back to Charisma. "As soon as I get you in the visitors' room I'll bring him in."

"Well, then let's do it." Charisma grabbed a bag filled with diapers. She glanced at Annie. "You sure you can't come in?"

"You should come in." Sergeant Parker didn't quite meet her gaze. "Logan asks about you sometimes."

"I can't." Annie took a quick glimpse of the officer's face, then lowered her gaze to the ground. Charisma's remarks about him having a crush on her floated through her mind. Silliness. "I have to get to the bakery."

"You don't have to worry. They're not going to call you to testify. I promise."

"How can you be sure? Luke says—"

"Because I'm sure. With the mayor's eyewitness testimony and my deputy's testimony, they've got more than enough to convict. They also have two witnesses who saw him come out of the bakery with the gun in his hand and the bag of cash." He smacked his hand against his chest. "There's no one to come forward and say he didn't do it. Mostly because he did."

"But Mr. Moreland said he wanted Sadie, Miriam, and me to testify anyway."

"Mr. Moreland knows you'll be hostile witnesses."

"Hostile?" Annie felt heat flame her cheeks. "We're never hostile—"

"Whoa, whoa. All I mean is you want Logan to be found not guilty. You won't lie, but you won't say anything to get him convicted. Not if you can help it. Moreland figures he's better off with a bloodthirsty witness like the mayor. An upstanding member of the community who is known and loved by her constituents."

"Yeah, with the mayor testifying against him, there's no chance Logan will get out of jail." Charisma's frown drooped even more. "He's going to prison, isn't he?"

"I'm sorry." Sergeant Parker looked genuinely apologetic. "All the more reason for you to get in there with that baby and spend a few minutes with him."

"You coming?" Charisma directed the question at Annie.

Exasperated, Annie shook her head. "I can't. Sadie needs help at the bakery. Bring us the babies before the trial starts, and then you can watch the whole thing in peace."

She turned to flee.

"Wait. Wait here until I get back." Sergeant Parker tinged the words with a pleading tone that surprised her. "I want to show you something."

Curious at what could be so important to this man, she wavered.

He pointed to a bench at the top of the stairs next to the heavy wooden double doors. "Have a seat on that bench. Please. After I take Charisma in to see Logan, I'll come for you."

"I can't be in the courtroom, Sergeant."

He smiled. He had a kind smile. No shadows on his face. No lines of stress or grief around his mouth. And he had a full head of curly blond hair. "Call me Dylan. I know you can't go in the courtroom. That's why I'm going to show you a place where you can watch the trial and if you're careful, no one will know you're there."

She shouldn't. Yet Annie found herself sitting on the bench, contemplating the guilty feelings that swirled inside of her. She hadn't stayed because of Sergeant Parker. She wanted to be there for Charisma. So why did she feel so guilty?

Sergeant Parker was gone just long enough for Annie to think about whether she was doing the right thing, but not long enough for her to run. He barely paused in front of her bench. "Come with me. This way."

She scurried to keep up with his enormously long stride. "Where are we going?"

"Have you ever been in the courthouse before?"

She shook her head.

Whistling a funny little tune, he climbed a long flight of stairs that ended in a landing, then turned and took them up more stairs. His long legs ate up the steps while she concentrated on not tripping over her skirt. When she did stumble, he grabbed her arm in a firm grip. "Easy there. Sorry, I forget not everyone is the Jolly Green Giant."

Jolly Green Giant? His uniform was a dark blue that brought out the blue of his eyes. Annie did her best to ignore the strange thrill that ran through her at a man's touch. She halted and prepared to retrace her steps before something unseemly happened. She hadn't been thinking properly. To go anywhere alone with Sergeant Parker, even though he was an officer, could be seen as inappropriate. In Luke's eyes, no doubt it would be. "I shouldn't be here. I should go to work."

"Begging your pardon, Miss Annie." The smile on his face died and his hand dropped. "I didn't think. I didn't want you to fall and hurt yourself. No disrespect intended."

"Of course not. And it's plain Annie. No *miss* necessary." Annie breathed. Just once she wanted to see the world from an Englischer's view. She'd never run around on her rumspringa. She'd never courted outside her faith. She'd never drank or smoked or worn Englisch clothes. And where had it gotten her? Alone? "Where are we going?"

"Did you ever see the movie *To Kill a Mockingbird*?" At her confused look, he smacked his hat against his forehead. "Stupid question. Okay, this courthouse was built over a hundred years ago. They used to come from all over the county to have court here. In those days, the public sat in the balcony while the attorneys and their clients and the witnesses sat below in the courtroom. They closed off the balcony years ago, but it's still there."

He opened a squeaky door and threw out his arm in a flourish. "Your seat in the hall of justice awaits you."

Annie slipped past him. An odor like old newspaper and mildew mingled in the air, making her want to bring out her cleaning supplies. Light from windows that ran the length of the far wall filtered across the seats, revealing particles of dust that danced in the air. Rows upon rows of empty wooden seats lined the balcony.

Sergeant Parker whipped a handkerchief from his back pocket and wiped off a seat for her. "Just don't get too close to the railing. If the judge looks up, he'll be able to see you. But if you're quiet, no one should know you're here."

She nodded, touched by his consideration. "Why are you doing this?"

His bulky shoulders rose and fell. A diffident smile fled. "So you can see there's nothing to be afraid of. The justice system is meant to be just. It protects us. Protects you. Amish or not. Besides..." His deep voice faltered and his Adam's apple bobbed. "Besides, I like you."

Heat burned through Annie. She stood alone on a balcony with an *Englisch* man who had just declared his feelings for her. "*Ach*, no, I—"

"Hold your horses there, Missy. I'm not being improper or whatever y'all want to call it." He doffed his hat to her in an old-fashioned gesture that touched her heart. "I'm not trying to make you uncomfortable, but you did ask, and I try to make it a rule to tell the truth."

Shocked, she opened her mouth, then closed it. She didn't even know where to begin. Charisma had been right. "So when you come to the bakery..."

"Do I look like I eat a lot of sweets?"

Not an ounce of fat on the man. He filled out his uniform perfectly. She dropped her gaze to the floor. "Sergeant Parker, you know..."

"Dylan. Yes, I do." Now his gruff voice sounded amused. "Like I said, you asked. I would never do anything stupid. I know we can't go out. I'll just continue to admire you from afar."

Not so far. After all, he visited the bakery a couple of times a week. More than any other man she knew. "Someone like you...I mean, surely you have your pick of the pretty Englisch girls."

A rueful look descended on his face. "I've dated plenty. Just never found the right person, I guess. I'm looking for someone with a sense of humor, cheerful, happy in her own skin, a Christian, someone with my values. Someone who wants children. Someone who puts family first." His eyes were warm with humor. "Doesn't hurt if she's pretty, either."

Annie swallowed hard against sudden tears. She waited so long to hear such a declaration. Now it came from the wrong man. Wrong community. Longing to get away from his amused, admiring gaze, she peeked over the railing. The courtroom was even bigger than she had imagined and filled with dark, ancient-looking wood. Long pews filled more than half of the deep green carpet. The judge's bench set up high above the railing that separated him from the masses. "I'm sorry."

"I know." He turned his hat around and around in his hands. If he kept that up, he would need a new one before the end of the day. "I shouldn't have said anything. I've lived here all my life. I know the rules."

Annie stared at the American flag next to the Kansas flag. Time to steer this conversation to more important things. "I should tell you something."

"What's that?" His voice remained soft. He didn't recognize that she had moved on. "You can tell me anything."

"Charisma doesn't love Logan. She plans to tell him now. Right now. Before the trial starts."

His rueful expression fled into a scowl the likes of which Annie had never seen on his face. "She bore his children, and she doesn't love him?"

"It's a long story." Annie met his gaze. She didn't have time or the right to tell him why Charisma found it so hard to give her heart to anyone. "A chain of events, one thing leading to another down this path, until she found herself stuck on an Amish farm in the middle of nowheresville."

His shaggy eyebrows did push-ups. "You approve?"

"I don't judge." A sudden thought popped up—one she couldn't ignore. "She's going to need someone to take care of her and the babies. Logan won't be able to do that."

"You're suggesting that I…" He threw his head back and laughed. "That firecracker? Didn't I tell you I was looking for someone to make a life with? Not some hard-living teenager with babies on both hips and a cigarette dangling from her mouth."

"We're the same age."

"But there's a world of difference and you know it."

"You would be good for her. She would look up to a man who knew right from wrong. You could protect her…from herself."

"The Lord knows she needs protection. But me? I don't know, Miss Annie, that sounds a little far out there." His expression bewildered, he slapped his hat on his head. "I'd better go make sure Logan isn't having a meltdown. This won't help his case."

His words revealed that Sergeant Parker wasn't just a law man. He saw his prisoners as broken people with problems that needed to be fixed. "You're on his side?"

"I'm on the side of rehabilitation. When you make a mistake, you pay for it, and you learn not to make it again so you can rejoin society and be productive." He adjusted his hat again. "He might come out husband material, you never know."

"For someone, but not Charisma. Charisma is broken. She needs someone who can heal her wounds, someone to look after her. She needs someone on her side too."

"You're a regular do-gooder, you know that?" The softness of his tone told her that was a good thing in his eyes. He tipped his hat to her. "You know your way down, right?"

"Yes."

He held her gaze for a few seconds longer. "Thank you for not laughing at me."

"I would never laugh. I'm…I'm honored." Annie stumbled over the words, heat scorching her face. "I hope you…I hope you find what you're looking for. I hope you'll consider at least keeping an eye on Charisma, if nothing else."

"We'll see—and I hope the same for you."

"I already have my someone."

He backed away. "Then I wish you Godspeed."

He disappeared through the doorway. Annie sank into a chair, her bones like water. Had she told the truth? She put her hands to her face and let the tears seep through her fingers. *God, I'm still waiting.*

Chapter 29

Annie swished the broom across the bakery floor harder than necessary. Tiny plumes of flour wafted in the air. She smacked the dustpan to the floor and stooped to finish the job. Customers would've been a welcome interruption. She couldn't help replaying the scene on the courtroom balcony earlier in the day over and over again. Sergeant Parker declaring he had feelings for her. Why couldn't it have been David?

"You're getting more dust on your dress than in the trashcan," Sadie bustled from behind the counter, a bucket of soapy water in one hand and the mop in the other. The smell of bleach mingled with the sweeter aroma of baking bread. "You act like you have a burr under your saddle. What happened at the courthouse?"

"Nothing." It wasn't exactly the truth. Annie didn't lie. Even little lies led to problems. "I mean, Sergeant Parker, he said some things."

"Said some things?" Sadie dropped the mop into the water, put both hands around the handle, and stared at Annie. She didn't look happy. She looked like Annie's mudder had when Annie decided to cut her hair during her rumspringa. Horrified. "What kind of things?"

"Very nice things. Very respectful. But I couldn't help but think... help but wish..."

"You didn't encourage him, did you?"

"Of course not, but I admit it was nice to know someone likes—"

"Now, you just stop right there." Sadie slapped the wet mop back and forth on the floor with such vigor Annie feared there'd be no finish left. "I know my son hasn't been the easiest man to love. It's been very hard on you. But it'll get better. This treatment will work. You'll see. He's getting better. Don't you let some Englischer with a uniform and a way with words get you all turned around. Your heart is Plain through and through. Patience."

Annie didn't have the heart to tell Sadie she wasn't sure David's health was the problem. If David didn't have cancer, would he shine his flashlight in her window? Would he meet up with her at a singing? It was hard to say anymore. "I told Sergeant Parker I already had someone—"

"And you do!"

Did she? Maybe Sadie knew something Annie didn't. "Why do you think he's spending time with this little girl, Kinsey?" And Kinsey's mother. "What is that all about?"

"He's helping a sick child, simple as that." Sadie smacked the mop against the bucket so hard it sloshed water over the side. "Just like you're helping Charisma and Gracie by giving them a place to stay. Your act of kindness gives them hope. David's gives Kinsey and her mother hope. No big secret there."

Sadie was right. They were both helpers. If only they could help people together. Annie would like that. "You're right—"

The door swung open so hard it banged against the wall. The bell jangled and fell to the floor. Charisma marched in, dragging poor Gracie behind her.

"Take the baby, please!" She thrust Luke David at Annie, who braced the broom against the wall just in time to take the little bundle of joy. "Gracie, stop that howling now. You're driving me crazy."

"Daddy! Daddy! Daddy!" Gracie threw herself on the floor, kicking and screaming. "Want Daddy!"

A thick, aching sadness enveloped Annie. Maybe it hadn't been a good idea for Gracie to see Logan again. Out of sight, out of mind, might be kinder. "Gracie, come here, sweetie." Annie laid Luke David in the carrier they'd bought at the Goodwill store and turned to the little girl. "Come to Annie. You're okay."

"She's not okay. If she doesn't stop that screeching I'm going to smack her behind." Charisma plopped onto the bench by the door and stuck the fat denim bag that doubled as a purse and a diaper bag on the seat next to her. Sweat shone on her face and beaded on her red nose. Her lipstick was smeared. "You'll never guess what happened."

Annie figured she wouldn't have to guess. Charisma would tell her. Knowing Charisma, in great detail. She picked up Gracie and stuck her on one hip. The girl hiccupped, but her sobs subsided. "Cookie."

"We could all use a cookie." Annie patted her matted curls. "Especially Mommy."

"Mommy, Mommy, I want Mommy." Gracie arched her back and threw herself toward Charisma, the movement so sudden Annie almost dropped her.

"What did Logan say?"

"First he went crazy, looking at the baby, saying how it was his son, his boy, his baby, and he needed to get out and take care of him and Gracie."

"And then you told him how you feel?"

"Yeah. And then he wasn't talking to me any more. He told his lawyer he was gonna just plead guilty. That he didn't have a reason to live if I didn't wait for him, but the lawyer talked him out of it. He said they didn't offer a good plea bargain cause they had him dead to rights with eyewitnesses. He needed to take his chances with a jury 'cause they were gonna think he was young and cute. He said I had to be in the courtroom every day with the kids so they could see that he's a family man with kids to support."

"Gracie in the courtroom?"

"I know. There's no way she'll sit still for two minutes, let alone two hours. I don't know what I'm going to do."

Annie scraped a piece of dried dough from her apron with her fingernail. "So you're going back."

"They're picking a jury right now. No sense in being there until

someone comes to get me on account of how they won't let me be in
the courtroom until they actually start the testimony. Sergeant Parker
will come fetch me when it's time, but the lawyer said not until tomorrow at the earliest."

"Testimony?"

"Ain't you never watched *Law and Order*?"

Annie tried not to look stupid. "Is that a movie?"

Charisma waved her hands, showering Annie with cookie crumbs.
"Never mind. Until the lawyers start asking the people questions."

"Is Logan really upset?"

"Yeah, I hurt him bad." Charisma sniffled a little. "Real bad."

Logan's determined blue eyes the day he held a gun on her filled
Annie's head. "Can't you take it back?"

"I don't want to take it back." Charisma dug around in the diaper
bag and came out with a tissue she used to wipe her face. "Seeing him
in handcuffs just made it all the more real. He's going away for a long
time, leaving me to raise two kids by myself."

The consequences of doing the wrong thing, even if it seemed to be
for the right reason. Annie had no answers.

Charisma snatched Annie's hand from her lap and held on for dear
life. "You have to come with me to the courthouse. Don't make me go
by myself. Please!"

Luke would never allow it. But maybe Annie didn't have to tell him.
She'd been in the courthouse this morning. Not in the courtroom,
though. Splitting hairs. Wrong was wrong. The thought stuck in her
throat, making it hard to breathe. Annie never denied Luke's authority. Having him in charge made her feel secure. Everything was right
in her world, but now things were all topsy-turvy. Bringing Charisma
into their home had created a crack in their united front. "I can't. I have
to work. And who'll take care of Gracie?"

"Deborah will do it, I'm sure." Sadie spoke up from behind the
counter. "She's my oldest daughter," she explained to Charisma. "I'll
stop by her house on the way home tonight to ask. Go by there on your
way into town tomorrow morning."

Sadie's daughter had five children of her own. Surprised, Annie shifted Gracie onto the bench and went to the counter. "You think I should go with Charisma?"

"Luke was right in saying we shouldn't testify against that boy." Sadie swished the mop in the bucket of water. "Going to the court-house to support a friend is a different cup of tea."

"Should I tell him?"

"You know the answer to that question." Sadie stopped mopping. "Only, I wouldn't tell him, I'd ask him."

For once it would be nice not to have to do the right thing. Annie picked up Luke David. She inhaled his sweet baby scent as he cooed in her ear. "Come on, bobbeli. Let's go home."

Chapter 30

David lifted Kinsey onto Blackie. Her grin stood out in stark relief against her pale skin. She looked a whole lot better. She'd only been in the hospital four days this last time. Now she had more energy. Enough for the two of them. As her enthusiasm for the task at hand increased, his energy seemed to wane. His regimen of chemo had ended, but he hadn't rebounded the way he had the last time. David tried to ignore the clock ticking in his head. Tomorrow he would go for tests. In a week or so he'd know if the treatment had been successful this time. He refused to get his hopes up. Not again.

This time in limbo made him thankful Annie was still at the bakery. Or maybe the courthouse. Knowing Annie, she'd want to support Charisma. It was a wonder she didn't march into the courtroom and tell the judge to let the robber go free. That would be his Annie.

No. Not his Annie. Not now. Not ever, most likely.

He shook his head, trying to clear the painful thoughts. Why did he keep doing this to himself? Focus on Kinsey. Focus on the lessons. They'd managed to get in two more lessons since the first one and each time Kinsey had done better. Each time, Annie had managed to be at the farm instead of at the bakery. But not today. *Gut*. That was *gut*. He would just keep telling himself that.

"Here you go." He handed Kinsey the reins. "Hold the reins lightly, but let Blackie know what you want him to do. You're in charge. Squeeze with your knees."

"You're letting me handle him by myself?"

The awe in her voice produced a sudden lift in David's spirits. Something so everyday in his life, in the life of most Plain people, served as something special and memorable to this young, sick girl.

"You're ready. Just hold steady and walk him around the corral." He hoped the gruffness of his voice didn't give him away. He cleared his throat. "Easy now. Let him know who's in control."

The *clip clop* of Blackie's hoofs mixed with the sound of another horse. David looked up. A buggy approached. The bishop. What was Bishop Kelp doing here? A ripple of unease ran through David. He wasn't doing anything wrong here. Just helping a little girl through the day. An Englischer, yes, but their lessons were simple and out in the open.

Bishop Kelp hoisted his rotund frame from the buggy and strode toward them, his steps ponderous. "David, I wish to speak with you." His gaze encompassed Willow and Kinsey, who kept Blackie moving right on by. "It might be best if we talk alone."

"Mom, look at me! I'm riding. I'm riding Blackie!" Kinsey's voice sang out, strong and happy. "Look, Mister Whoever-You-Are! I'm riding all by myself!"

David held his breath.

Bishop Kelp's face cracked into the briefest of smiles. "So you are."

David hustled toward Blackie, aiming for the reins. "Kinsey, maybe you should get down for a second while I talk to Bishop Kelp."

"I just got started." Her smile melted into a frown. "You said I could ride as long as I want."

He hadn't said that. David started to protest, but Bishop Kelp held up a hand. "She can ride. I only need to speak with you and the girl's mother. It's not a conversation for small ears."

Keeping an eye on Kinsey's progress, David quickly made the introductions. A puzzled look on her face, Willow shook hands. "David is doing us a big favor by teaching Kinsey to ride. It's something she always wanted."

"I understand that." Bishop Kelp removed his hat and wiped at his forehead. "I'd heard a few murmurings here and there about it and I wanted to see for myself that all the proprieties are being observed."

"Rumors?" An arrow of anger shot through David. For people who were supposed to be full of grace, this community sure knew how to be suspicious and backwards. "Who—"

"Propriety?" Willow slapped her hands on wide hips. "Seriously?"

"You're not from around here, I understand." Bishop Kelp didn't seem the least bit put off by her tone. "We're a small, close-knit community. We want no wedge to be driven between our members. We try to keep the ways of the world from becoming our ways."

"We also try to show a Christlike attitude to those in need." David clamped his mouth shut. Arguing with the bishop would only lead to greater repercussions in the long run. He didn't want Kinsey to suffer because of his inability to keep his thoughts to himself. "I'm teaching her to ride, that's all."

"If you're suggesting there is something going on between David and me, well, you can just think again." Willow's face darkened to the color of an overripe tomato. "That's just…it's disrespectful to me and to him. David's been nothing but a gentleman. My daughter has been so ill and his kindness has meant everything to her. He's making her dream come true."

"Her dream?" Micah Kelp looked puzzled. David knew the bishop had the same thought he'd had at first. What sort of dream was riding a horse? All Amish children did it. "I don't understand. She had a dream that she rode a horse?"

"To ride a black horse. It's what she wants." Willow's voice quivered. "It might seem a small thing to someone like you, people like you who have horses all over the place. But for me, it was an impossible dream. You see, it's just me and her and Grammy. We have no one else. No means of doing this."

The bishop stared at her, his expression thoughtful. "And the girl's father?"

"Not in the picture. Never has been."

"I see." Micah Kelp's expression said he saw a great deal. His gaze went to Kinsey. Both her hands were gripping the horn of the saddle, her grin stretching from ear to ear as she passed them on the other side of the corral fence. "I'm sorry for your difficulties."

"Thank you." Willow straightened her shoulders crossed her arms over her chest. "You won't forbid it, will you?"

"No. I wouldn't do that." His gaze went to David. "I think my work here is done."

"Yes, it is." David couldn't help himself. "There's nothing here to see."

"Watch your tone." The bishop's stern expression did nothing but fan David's anger. "Watch yourself."

"It seems plenty of people are doing that for me."

"For your own good and the good of our community." Bishop Kelp's tone softened. "Your family and friends want what is best for you. We're here to help you see what that is. That's all."

David had no response to that. The bishop believed what he said, no doubt, but David was sure small, fearful minds had more to do with this visit than anyone's good.

Bishop Kelp slapped his hat on his head and walked as fast as his enormous legs could carry him back to his buggy. David didn't watch him drive away. He called out to Kinsey, who waved with one hand and yelled, "Yippee-yay-yah!"

He couldn't help it. He laughed. Her enthusiasm was a salve for his soul.

"Let's ride." He untied Rosie's reins from the fence post and hoisted himself onto the horse. Time to give Kinsey twenty or thirty minutes free from disease, free from thinking about hospitals and shots and tests.

He waved at Willow, who opened the corral gate and stood watching and waving as they rode away. Her smile didn't waver, but he knew how much it cost her to let her daughter go on this journey. She wanted to keep her in a safe, sterile cocoon. Life wasn't like that, much as parents might want it. His own mother wanted it. He knew she grappled every day with letting go of her youngest child. He was a man, but to her, still a child. Such was the role of a parent. He glanced at Kinsey's smiling face. A role he'd never know.

∞

Annie watched Luke scrub his hands in the kitchen sink. He ducked his head and splashed water on his face and head. When he turned and reached for a towel, their gazes met. Annie figured he jumped three feet.

"Don't sneak up on a man like that, schweschder." He folded the towel and laid it on the counter. "Could give me a heart attack."

"I'm sorry. I didn't mean to startle you."

"What are you doing here? You're home early from the bakery."

He was early too. Annie didn't ask why. Farmers came and went, depending on a whole host of factors that influenced what work had to be done. She didn't want to get sidetracked. "I was looking for you. I saw Leah out in the garden and she said you'd come inside."

"I need to repair a part and get back out there. We're almost done with the alfalfa."

"*Gut.*"

"Spit it out, girl. What do you want?"

He sounded so much like Daed. His response likely would be the same. The idea that Luke would give her permission to go to the trial with Charisma seemed mighty far-fetched now that she stood in front of her brother. A sudden powerful thirst hit Annie. She picked up a glass.

Luke brushed past her. "I reckon you can ask me at supper."

"I want to go to the courthouse with Charisma tomorrow." The words flew out of Annie's mouth of their own accord. She didn't even have time to polish them. "She needs me."

"Needs you?" Luke laughed low in his throat, no mirth in the sound. "We're feeding her and giving her and her children beds to sleep in at night. Don't you think we've done enough?"

"She has to testify. She's scared." Annie set the glass back on the counter. "It's not about physical comforts; she has no one to lean on."

"You go into that courtroom and the lawyers will see you. They'll want you to testify. Do you want to get up there and be asked to swear an oath and tell those people that the man robbed you at gunpoint?"

Annie pictured Logan's panicked face. The *pop-pop* of the bullets pinged in her ears.

"No. No, but they won't see me. Sergeant Parker showed me…" The words were out of her mouth before she could stop them. "I mean…"

Luke's face froze. His figure, framed in the doorway, seemed to grow bigger. "Sergeant Parker showed you what? When?"

Annie swallowed hard. She shook her head. "I…I meant to say…I…"

Luke clomped three steps toward her. He towered over her. "Showed you what?"

"He showed me a balcony. He said I could sit up there and no one would be able to see me. They won't know I'm there."

Luke's face darkened with barely contained fury. "Why are you asking me for permission when you've already been in the courthouse? After I told you not to go there."

"I didn't mean to go in. I walked with Charisma to the door so I could carry the baby for her while she minded Gracie. Sergeant Parker came out to take her to see Logan. He said he could show me a place where I could see—"

"You were alone with this policeman on the balcony."

"Just for a minute."

"After everything that's happened with Josiah and Catherine, I expected you to know better." Luke slapped his hat on his head so hard he probably gave himself a headache. "You'll not go to the courthouse. In fact, you will stay here on the farm until the trial is over."

Without giving her a chance to respond, Luke stomped past her. He paused at the screen door. "David's buggy is still out by the corral. I'll stop by and tell him so he can let Sadie know you won't be working at the bakery until the trial is over."

Annie flew after him. "No!"

"No?" His face was hidden in the shadow of his hat, but Luke's tone didn't bode well. "Are you telling me no?"

"I mean, let me tell David." Annie pushed through the screen door and followed Luke down the path that led to the barn. "You have work to do. I'll tell him."

"Gut."

Annie couldn't contain herself. *"Gut."*

Luke glared at her, but to her relief, said nothing more.

She waited until his figure was a speck in the distance before heading to the barn. Willow Navarro's car was gone. The lesson had ended, then. The sight of David's buggy still parked by the corral fence told her he hadn't left yet. She took a deep breath, let it out. If she couldn't go to the courthouse, maybe David would go for her. Still shaking with anger, she covered the distance in less than half the usual time. How could Luke be so unfair? Nothing had happened with Sergeant Parker. Luke hadn't even let her explain. If Mudder and Daed were here...no point in finishing that thought. They weren't here. They never would be. This was her life.

She shoved through the barn door with more force than necessary. "David?"

For a second she couldn't see in the shadowy light cast from the window in the hayloft. As her eyes adjusted, she saw a dark form huddled on a bale of hay. "David?" she asked more softly.

His arm covered his bowed head. "Go away. Now!" The muffled words were filled with an anguish that tore at her heart. "Get out!"

Chapter 31

Annie hesitated, one hand still on the barn door. David sat doubled over on a bale of hay. He raised his head. His pale face looked wet in the shaft of light that held him captive. His expression kept her from rushing toward him. "What's the matter?"

"Nothing. Get out."

Not in a million years. "This is my barn."

"Your barn?"

"You know what I mean." She stopped short of stomping her foot in frustration. David's skin seemed to hang on his bones like clothes that were too big and his cheeks sank into his face under cavernous eyes encircled by bruised smudges. The chemo had ended, but the effects lingered. Maybe he needed a doctor. Maybe he'd passed out again.

Letting the barn door swing closed behind her, Annie barged in. A thought slammed into her. She halted. Her heart hammered in her chest so hard she could barely frame the question. Just saying the word might make it so. *God, give me strength.*

"Did the treatments fail again?"

David wiped at his face with his sleeve. He pulled the brim of his hat down so it hid his eyes, then jerked to his feet. He grabbed the reins of his horse and led him from the stall. "I was just leaving."

"David, answer me. What's wrong? What did the doctor say?"

"Nothing." He said the word with a sharp snap that spoke of contained agony. "I don't know yet."

He shoved past her and through the door, his stride unsteady. Annie stood not moving for a long moment in the still quiet of the barn. Why did he choose to suffer alone in silence and shadow? Why could he not trust in her?

She strode into sunlight so bright she had to squint and raise a hand to shield her face. It seemed to mock her. All that light on such a dark day. David didn't look up at her approach, but he pulled the hat down even farther. Annie smacked her hand on the wheel of his buggy. "Then what's wrong with you? And I'm not talking about your health. Why are you so pigheaded?"

"Pigheaded? It's one thing for Josiah to call me that, but you… you're a…"

"A woman?" Annie tapped her boot on the ground, impatient with his words and his attitude. "Jah, I said pigheaded. Do you need to clean your ears?"

"With the silky way you wield those words, it's a wonder you don't have a beau already." His horse did a little side-step two-step that forced David closer to her. He didn't meet her gaze. "Are you sure you want to be so plainspoken?"

"Fine. Be alone. Be all alone. If it makes you happy to see me like this, forget I ever said anything." His sarcasm fueled her anger like dry grass eaten by flames on a windy day, racing across fields with complete, unfettered abandon. "If you don't like me anymore, that's fine. I'll get over it. Starting right now."

His hands stopped moving on the harness. "Is that what you think?"

"What else would I think?" Annie put both hands in the air as if to push him away even though they did not touch. "You avoid me. You barely speak to me. You'd rather give riding lessons to a little girl than take me for a buggy ride. As far as I can tell, you either lost your flashlight or you've forgotten what it's for."

"That's not fair." His Adam's apple bobbed and he wiped at his nose with his sleeve again, like a little boy who needed a tissue. "You know that's not how it is."

"Then tell me how it is."

"Annie."

She put her hands on her hips and stomped her foot. Now who was acting like a child? He drove her to it. "Don't *Annie* me. What is the problem?"

"I can't love you."

"You either do or you don't."

"I can't."

Annie bit the inside of her lip. She focused on the physical pain, trying to block out the hurt his words brought her. When she thought she could say the words without crying, she posed the question. "Can't or won't?"

"Both. I won't be yoked to you, knowing you're going to end up alone."

"I'm alone now."

"You're young and easy on the eyes and half the men at the singings are in love with you."

"No."

David climbed into the buggy. "Did you come out here for a reason?"

The conversation with Luke flooded back over her. "To tell you Luke won't let me come to the bakery again until the trial is over."

David looked confused for a second. Then he shrugged. "I'll let Mudder know."

"Don't you want to know why?"

"It doesn't matter. If that's Luke's wish, then Mudder will understand."

Men. Always the united front. "Fine."

"Goodbye, Annie."

Annie refused to say it. She stood there, rooted to the ground. She wrapped her arms around her middle and tucked her hands under them, trying to stop the shaking. She'd incurred Luke's wrath, David wanted nothing to do with her, and Charisma still had to face the trial alone.

Finally, she stumbled on weak legs to the porch and sank on to the top step. One of the new kittens, apparently separated from its mother, meandered across the yard, stopping every now and then, one petite white paw in the air as it scanned the horizon. Finally, it made a mad dash toward the porch and climbed straight into Annie's lap. Its pitiful mewing sounded so familiar, like a poem she'd known but forgotten somehow. She smoothed a hand across its soft fur and lifted the kitty to her cheek. "I know exactly what you mean."

Chapter 32

David strode across the field, letting his long legs eat up the uneven ground. He lifted his face to the sun and inhaled the scent of fresh cut alfalfa. It felt good to be outdoors, to look forward to hard physical labor. The time had come to get back to work. It was over with Annie. He had ended any chance of her waiting for him. David tried to ignore the vision of her hurt, tear-streaked face in that moment. The memory banged around in his head and bruised his heart, forcing him to confront the truth. He wanted his own child to teach. Not just riding, but farming, and all the things a child should learn from a father. He wanted that child to be his and Annie's. God's plan didn't seem to include that so it was time for him to move beyond old unreachable dreams.

In the distance, Timothy drove the flatbed and Jonathan handled the hay loader that would pick up the dried alfalfa hay from the ground where it had laid drying since the previous day when they'd cut it. Their shirts were soaked with sweat and their faces shiny. Anxious to escape his thoughts, David increased his pace until he loped up to the flatbed wagon and climbed aboard. He grabbed a rake and began spreading the hay in the bed as Timothy operated the loader, letting the tines pick up hay as the horses moved forward. "Looks like a good haul."

"Jah. We're in good shape." Jonathan brought the horses to a halt and the ground-driven loader stopped. Timothy shoved his hat back and wiped at his face with the back of his sleeve. "What are you doing out here?"

"I told Mudder I'm helping you finish this off so we'll be done in time to start cutting the wheat next week."

"You're supposed to help her with deliveries." His face creased in a frown, Timothy took the rake from David and began smoothing the load. "Mudder needs you at the bakery."

David had prepared himself for this battle. He'd been getting this response from them ever since the second round of chemo started. He was done with chemo. Time to get back to work. "Not today, she doesn't. I checked. No deliveries."

"And no Annie." Jonathan snorted. "She's left Mudder high and dry until that Englischer's trial is over. According to Luke, she got all tangled up in the girl's affairs so he's keeping her home."

"You have a problem with showing charity to those in need?" David didn't expect this from his own family. Maybe the others who didn't know him as well, but not his brothers. "Maybe that's something you should talk with one of the deacons about."

"Actually, the deacons are the ones talking about it. Even the bishop mentioned something to Luke about it, from what I hear." Timothy dropped the rake and came a few steps closer. His brother, older by almost ten years, was several inches taller and a good twenty-five pounds heavier. He glared down at David. "And don't get cheeky with me, little bruder. My point is Annie has not been as reliable as we would like."

"She was there when the robbery happened. She takes good care of Mudder—"

"Except when she's busy taking care of the Englisch girl and her children."

"We are called to help others, are we not?" David felt a little hypocritical, considering how he'd questioned Annie about the wisdom of her decision. "Especially women and children with no place to go and no one to help them."

"Annie has the right instincts, but she's showering affection on that little girl because she has none of her own. It's time you made her your *fraa* and put an end to all this wishy-washy stuff."

"Wishy-washy?" His brother had always been bossy, but he'd never tried to tell David whom to court or when. "I'll not take any woman as my fraa until I know my cancer is gone for good. I won't do that to Annie."

"Mudder says the doctor told you your chances are very good. She doesn't understand why you don't have more faith." Timothy crossed his arms over a thick chest. "Jonathan and I have discussed it, and we want you to have the acreage up yonder west of the wheat fields. It's only a dozen acres, but it'll suit you since you'll be running the bakery. You can build a house there and take yourself a fraa. If not Annie, another."

"Running the bakery?" David found himself stuttering. "Mudder runs the bakery. Neither of you is Daed. I'm of age. You can't tell me what to do."

"Mudder agrees. The time you're spending with this Englisch girl worries her too." Timothy turned his back on David and signaled at Jonathan to start the horses moving again. "She wants to retire to the *dawdi haus,* but she can't because she's worried about you."

"She has no reason to worry. I'll find my way on my own. I don't need your messing in my business."

"It's all our business when the bishop starts asking questions." Timothy started the loader again. "There's also been a lot of talk about how much time you're spending with that little Englisch girl. Folks think it's a little…addled. The bishop is concerned. First we start working in town, then we start bringing the Englischers home with us. The influence is creeping into our kitchens and our living rooms."

"The bishop already paid me a visit. He saw Kinsey and her mother. He saw a sick little girl trying to stay alive. He saw that riding a horse helps her do that."

David stopped, trying to corral his anger. Couldn't they see that the time he spent teaching Kinsey to ride healed him as much as her? He didn't know how to give voice to those things. Or whether they could understand them. Jonathan and Timothy had never been sick a day in their lives. They never said so, but he could see it in their eyes: they thought their baby brother was weak.

"The bishop didn't object?" Timothy didn't bother to hide his disbelief. "Are you sure?"

"He was satisfied. Now, I came to work. What do you want me to do? Shall I take a team and the mower over to the west forty and cut the alfalfa there? It'll be ready for you to pick tomorrow afternoon."

"Go back to the house." Timothy looked so much like Daed, a wave of pain rolled over David. "Mudder said the doctor doesn't want you working out in the sun. You might get dehydrated again. Go home. Or go to the bakery. But leave the lessons to the Englischers. They can teach their own."

"I'm ready to work."

"I understand you have time to fill. You want to work, but you can't. You want to help, but you can't. Not yet." Timothy smiled as if to soften his words. "This isn't your time. But it will come. When you're better. Then you'll work and you'll marry."

He was better. Or he would be if they'd stop babying him.

"Let me work." He hated the begging note in his voice. It had come to this. "I need to get back to work."

"No."

Jonathan stopped the team again. The loader grinded to a halt. "Get down." Timothy's tone said the discussion had ended. "Go home."

David hopped down. He turned and looked back. The flatbed was already moving forward. Both brothers waved, Jonathan without turning around. They'd made up their minds about his future and they expected him to get on board or get left behind. He wished he could. He prayed he could.

Chapter 33

Carrying the cake, a knife dangling precariously from one hand, Annie paraded through the dining room to the table where the whole family sat, expectant looks on their faces. She could get there without dropping anything. The days of forced retirement from the bakery had one upside—she'd had plenty of time to work on Mark's birthday dinner. Plain children didn't expect a lot on their birthdays, but it was a special day, nevertheless. Without Mudder there to direct the preparations, Annie and Leah had to work extra hard to make sure the traditions were observed. And it had taken Annie's mind off the trial. And David.

David. Her mind slid over those two syllables and kept right on going. No looking back. She lifted her chin. *Happy. Content. Peaceful. Blessed. Accepting of God's plan.* She chanted the words silently as she made it to the dining room without a mishap and slipped the two-layer carrot cake with cream cheese frosting onto the table in front of Mark. "Ta-dah! Happy birthday, bruder!"

"Cake! Cake! Want cake." Gracie clapped her hands and squealed. "Me, me!"

Charisma grabbed the little girl's chubby hands just in time to keep her from dipping her fingers in the frosting. Dark circles around her eyes and her cranky tone said the uncertainty caused by the trial

235

invaded Charisma's sleep even more than it did Annie's. "You wait your turn."

Annie patted Gracie's curly mop and turned to Mark. "It's your favorite." She nudged Mark's shoulder and smiled across the table at Emma. Emma grinned back. Her little bump was just beginning to show, but her face glowed with happiness. Annie felt no twinge of envy. Her sister had waited a long time. She would be a wonderful mother. It was such a treat to have her and Thomas, along with Lillie, Mary, and Thomas's children here for the celebration. And *Aenti* Louise. She didn't get out much anymore, but today Josiah had gone to fetch her and bring her to the celebration. She sat between the twins, her gnarled hands resting on the table, a grin on her face that said she too wanted cake and lots of it.

If only Catherine were sitting next to them. No, another thought she must discard. God's plan.

"I added extra cream cheese to the frosting and a little more cinnamon than usual." She grabbed a clean saucer and set it next to the cake. Mark would get the first and biggest slice. "It's very tasty, if I do say so myself."

Mark's face reddened. He ducked his head. "You don't have to make a fuss. Everybody has a birthday once a year."

"What's the fun in that?" Josiah pushed aside a plate that had been heaped with Mark's favorite foods—sausage, green beans, mashed potatoes, brown gravy, macaroni and cheese, and Annie's special hot rolls—only a few minutes earlier. "This way we all get cake and ice cream. Besides, you only turn twelve once."

"I'd like to have two birthdays a year." *Aenti* Louise cackled. She snagged her own saucer and held it up, her wrinkled face gleeful. "Or three or four, if it means homemade ice cream."

"We made the ice cream," Lillie piped up. "I turned the crank all afternoon."

"I helped," Mary put in. "I put in the rock salt."

"Fine, everyone helped." Leah's tone was only mildly disapproving for a change. "Happy birthday, Mark."

She handed him a small package. His face brick red now, Mark ripped it open. "New suspenders." He grinned. "I guess you noticed mine keep falling down. The elastic is worn out."

Charisma gave Annie a puzzled look. Annie shrugged. What did Charisma expect? Video games? Maybe one of those fancy iPods she saw the Englisch teenagers listening to when they were supposed to be studying in the library? Annie pushed her package across the table. "Open this one next. It's from Emma, Josiah, and me."

His enthusiasm apparent in the way he clawed through the paper, Mark obliged. "Oh, wow," he breathed, his eyes huge. "A baseball mitt."

"And a new ball." Josiah pulled the shiny white gem from his pocket and threw it gently across the table. "Think quick."

With a big guffaw, Mark caught the toss. "This is great. We can play after the prayer service."

Amid much chatter and laughter, he made his way through several more small packages—colored pencils and a thick pad of drawing paper to go with them, a new hat, a board game, a comb, a candy bar, and homemade cards from the twins. *Aenti* Louise gave him a history of the Plain people. Annie knew he wouldn't appreciate it now as much as he would later, when he was older. Just as she had when *Aenti* Louise had given her one on her twelfth birthday.

"I didn't expect all this," he said, smoothing his hand over the leather of the mitt. "It's almost like Mudder and Daed…when they were here."

The chatter ceased for a moment. Annie let the memories roll over her of so many birthdays for herself, her brothers and sisters, and then Daed every July fifth and Mudder on December second. Sweet times.

Luke clamped a hand on Mark's shoulder. "That's as it should be."

"Later I'll show you how to oil the mitt so the leather stays soft," Josiah offered. "After chores, we can have a game of catch."

"We want to play," Lillie and Mary said in unison.

"Me too, me too!" Gracie crowed.

Everyone laughed.

"Right now it's time for cake and ice cream." Glad for the diversion,

Annie let the bittersweet moment go. She wanted to play baseball too, but she could imagine the look on Leah's face. At her age…never going to get a husband…undignified…" The ice cream is melting," she said. "Emma, why don't you do the honors?"

Emma picked up the knife and guided it through the first cut. The smile on her face faded and the knife slipped from her hand and clattered on the table. She looked puzzled for a second. "I think…" She grimaced and hunched over, her hands on her stomach. "Thomas…"

In a second less than it took Annie to round the table, Thomas made it to Emma's side. "What is it?"

"Something's not right," Emma whispered, her eyes wet with tears. "It doesn't feel right."

"Maybe you should lie down." Thomas helped her to rise. "It's been a long day."

Annie had never heard that tone from any man. Soft, so full of affection and concern. Thomas spoke so little, but when he did he made it count.

Silence had a stranglehold on all of them as Thomas helped Emma from the bench. She made it halfway across the room, then doubled over, gasping. "No, no!" She grabbed Thomas around the waist. "It can't be. It feels like the baby is…it's pain like the baby's coming. We have to make it stop."

Thomas glanced around the room, his eyes glazed with fear. His gaze met Annie's. She rushed forward, Leah, Josiah, and Luke on her heels. "We need to get her to the clinic."

"*Aenti* Louise?" Annie turned to the woman who had delivered hundreds of babies in her lifetime.

"He's right, child." *Aenti* Louise held up hands so gnarled she could no longer straighten her fingers. "I couldn't deliver a baby now and it's a doctor she's needing, not a midwife."

"Should we call an ambulance?"

"By the time we get to Bishop Kelp's to make the call, we could drive to town," Josiah pointed out. "I'll hitch up the wagon. Leah, get some blankets. She can lie down in the back."

"I'll ride with her." Annie slid an arm under Emma's shoulder. "Here we go, schweschder, one step at a time."

Everyone moved, the cake abandoned, ice cream melting, and presents strewn haphazardly across the table. Annie's gaze caught Charisma's. The woman stood, Luke David in her arms, staring. "Charisma, can you help Aenti Louise take care of the little ones while we get Emma into the wagon?"

"I can't believe there's not one cell phone around here...not one. This is what happens when you live like this." Charisma shifted Luke David to one arm and took Gracie's hand. "If I had gas, I could drive you in the van."

"They'll get there fine in the wagon." *Aenti* Louise picked up little Esther, the last baby she'd delivered in a lifetime of midwifery, and patted her back. "This is the way our grandfathers lived; it's the way our grandchildren will live."

They made it, one torturous step after another, to the porch. Time stretched and stretched as if the moments refused to pass. What was taking Josiah so long? Emma's breathing sounded labored and harsh. Annie stroked her back, "It's all right. It'll be all right."

Finally, Josiah pulled the wagon in front of the porch. Leah rushed forward and climbed into the back where she spread quilts and blankets with a quick, sweeping motion.

Thomas and Luke lifted Emma into the wagon. Annie scrambled in after her, the evening breeze cool on her sweaty face. *God, please. Emma has waited so long for this baby.*

Determined not to cry, she settled a pillow under her sister's head and smoothed her crooked kapp so it covered her blond bun. "Is that all right?"

Emma nodded, but the taut line of her lips and the tears in her eyes said otherwise.

Annie reached for her hand. "Breathe, breathe in and out."

The wagon jolted forward on the pitted gravel road. Emma groaned.

"Sorry!" Thomas turned and gripped the back of his seat with both hands. "I'm sorry."

Emma's hold on Annie's hand tightened. "Not your fault."

Thomas turned back to the road. Emma pulled Annie closer, her voice tight with fear. Annie leaned in. "What is it?"

"My skirt is wet." A sob hung in the air between them. Annie couldn't be sure if it was hers or Emma's. "Is it...is it blood?"

Annie closed her eyes. She had to be brave for Emma. "Don't worry. We'll have you to the clinic in no time at all. They'll take care of you."

Emma writhed on the blanket, her body wracked with sobs. "It's blood, isn't it?"

The wagon rocked and jerked forward. Thomas reached back and caught his wife's hand. The dark hid his expression. "Hang on, hang on!"

The night air rushed around them. Annie tried to pray, but the dark sky pressed in on her. *God, why?* Dare she ask that question? God's plan was far too big for one small Plain woman to understand. Did she intend to take only the good from Him and not the bad? *God, help me to understand.*

Never had a ride into Bliss Creek lasted longer, Annie was certain of that. When the clinic came into sight, she wanted to dive from the wagon. "We're here, Emma. We're here, schweschder."

Luke and Thomas carried Emma into the emergency room. Annie rushed after them, leaving Josiah to deal with the horse and wagon. She looked down to shield her eyes from the harsh glare of the florescent overhead lights. A dark stain on the hem of her apron caught her eye. She touched it. Her fingertip came away wet and red.

↬

David wiggled around on his chair to get more comfortable, then stretched his arm over the Monopoly board perched on Kinsey's hospital bed. "One, two, three, four, five..." He let his little silver car piece dangle over the spot where he must land. "No!"

"Yes!" Kinsey crowed and clapped her hands. The motion caused the board to shake and her hotels to slide from one colored square to another. "Whoops! You're on my hotel. You owe me a million billion bucks."

David forced a smile. He was reduced to playing Monopoly on a hospital bed because his family insisted he wasn't well enough to work. Not working only made him weaker. His body needed physical labor. His muscles were soft, his hands getting softer. Like a woman.

"David!" Kinsey jiggled his arm. "Pay attention. Are you getting tired?"

He straightened. "No."

"Good. Don't chicken out on me now that I'm winning. Fork it over, buddy."

"This game brings out the greed in people." David counted out the small bills. "It's not very nice."

"It's not the money." Kinsey snatched the pile from David and counted it again. "I just like winning."

"Well, no problem there. You have all the hotels and trains. Things aren't going to get any better."

Kinsey plunked the money on the board and sank back against the enormous pile of pillows that kept her upright. She sniffed. "That's what they think about me."

David didn't bother to pretend he didn't know what she meant. The smudges under her eyes looked like bruises, her white skin stretched tight against angular cheek bones. He'd seen animal corpses with more meat on them. The thought made his supper of corned beef and cabbage roil in his stomach. "You're stronger than you were yesterday."

"Sure. Wanna arm wrestle?"

"I might get tangled up in that IV."

"I don't want that. The doctors say the drugs are important." She giggled. "I could beat you left-handed, you know."

David knew about the drugs. They dulled the pain, but never quite vanquished it. He could tell from the way her breath caught and the lines deepened around her small mouth. But she didn't complain. He forced himself to laugh with her. It seemed the weaker she grew, the more her spirit blossomed.

Despite an air of being much older than her years, she still had a sweet, infectious laugh that reflected her childishness. The laugh turned into a cough that deepened and became choking. David grabbed her arm and tugged her forward. He slapped her back. "Breathe, just breathe."

The coughing subsided, but her breathing came in short, ugly gasps. "I'm okay."

No, not really. "You scared me for a second."

"Don't be scared." She leaned back and took a deep, long breath, then let it out. Her gaze dropped to the game, its pieces now scattered across her blankets. "Can I tell you a secret?"

Something in her tone made David feel the need to stand. Whatever secrets she shared would be kept in his heart, come what may. "I'm good at keeping secrets."

The hand with the IV needle taped to its back side plucked at her blanket. She met his gaze and smiled. "I'm ready to go."

"Go where? Your mom says it'll be at least a couple of more days. They want to do another round of tests and then they're looking at a different course of treatment—"

"I thought you'd get it."

She sounded so disappointed.

"Visiting hours are over." He picked up the game pieces and put them back in the box. "Time for you to sleep."

"If I can't tell you, who can I tell?" She flipped the box over with both hands, spilling everything out again. Her face scrunched up in anger, she turned toward the wall. "Go away."

David picked up the pieces again, the red and green hotels, the little metal car—Kinsey thought it was funny that he liked using that piece as his—the bills, and the cards. "God decides when it's time for you to go."

"I've talked to Him about it and I told Him I'm tired of this." Her voice dropped to a whisper. "I know it'll make Mommy and Grammy sad, but I'm tired."

The lump in David's throat grew until he thought he might choke on it. "You haven't ridden Blackie cross-country yet. I still have to teach you to jump."

"Please." The entreaty in her voice made his heart squeeze. "Don't be like them."

"Like who?"

"Mommy and Grammy."

"How are they?"

"They keep saying I have to get better."

David knew where she was going. He didn't want to follow. He owed it to her mother to hold out hope. Everyone always told him faith and hope were necessary to physical healing. "You don't want to ride Blackie again?"

"I'm tired," she whispered. "I want to sleep."

"Rest and we'll talk tomorrow about another lesson."

"Tomorrow." Kinsey's eyes drooped shut. "Maybe."

David set the Monopoly box on the nightstand. He lifted the bed rail, snapped it in place, and stood there, fingers tight around the bar, until her breathing became soft and regular. "It's okay to let go." His whisper sounded raspy in his ears. He breathed. "If you have to go, go. God will hold your hand."

He closed his eyes. *Hold her hand. Hold our hands. Don't let us be so selfish that she suffers one more day because she can't disappoint us. If You think she's ready, take her. But if it isn't her time, strengthen her body. Give her relief from her pain.*

The squeak of the door made him jump. He kept his head down and took a quick swipe at his face.

"Mr. Plank?"

He sniffed and cleared his throat. "It's David."

The night nurse slipped up to the bed. "Out like a light?"

He nodded and moved away.

The nurse took Kinsey's pulse and checked the IV. "Your visits really perk her up. Her mother appreciates it, I know. Gives her a little respite. She or her aunt are here pretty much round the clock." She glanced at her watch. "They'll be back any minute, if you want to go on home. I'll stay with her 'til then."

Still unable to speak, he nodded and fled the room. Kinsey would never tell her mudder what she'd told him. She'd offered him the gift of the sheer honesty of a child. He'd been unable to step up to the task and accept it. Instead, he'd offered her the same platitudes Willow and the doctors did. At seven, she was far braver than he.

Shamed by the thought, he punched the elevator button with more force than necessary. The door opened and he squeezed in next to a nurse and her patient in a wheelchair. Her smile did nothing to calm his spirit. Miracles did happen. God might infuse Kinsey's body with newfound strength and health. Or God might ask David to accept Kinsey's death. He might ask him to accept his own. Acceptance of God's will. Faith in God's plan. Kinsey's words echoed in his head. She'd talked with God. They had it all worked out. All that remained was for her to walk into the arms of God.

The faith of a child. He shoved away the thought and waited for the nurse to exit with her patient. Head down, he shuffled through the hallway, anxious to leave this place with its smells that reminded him of suffering. The sound of a soft sob wafting from a nearby waiting room compounded that feeling. He couldn't help himself. He looked to his left to see who might be making such a mournful sound.

Annie.

Her eyes red, she held a crumpled handkerchief to her mouth as if trying to muffle the sound. The air sucked from his lungs, David reversed course. He stumbled over his own feet trying to get to her. "Annie, what is it? What happened?" He sank to one knee so he could see her downcast face. "Tell me, what is it?"

"David?" She swiped at her nose. Horrible sadness mingled with sudden fear. "What are you doing here? Are you all right?"

"Kinsey's back in the hospital." David peered at Annie's face. Her skin was ashen. "What happened? Is someone hurt?"

"It's Emma." She twisted the hanky. Her gaze dropped. "I think she lost her baby."

A knot in his chest where his heart should be, David sank into the chair next to her. "Are you sure? They can do great things here."

A red blotch on Annie's apron caught his gaze. He sighed.

Annie's finger circled the spot without touching it.

"I don't think so." She managed a faint smile. "But Emma will be fine. She and Thomas will try again."

"*Ach*, Annie."

"What?"

"You don't always have to put on a strong front."

"That's funny, coming from you."

Finding no response to that observation, David glanced around the waiting room. "Where is everyone?"

"Thomas is with Emma. Luke and Josiah went back to the house to get her things. In the morning, they have to do some kind of surgery to…you know. Anyway, she has to stay for another day." Her breath came in a half-sob, half-hiccup. "I want to see her and give her a hug before I go. Thomas will come get me when she's ready for visitors."

David's hands clenched involuntarily. There was nothing he could do to make it better. The depth of his desire to do something, anything, startled him. After all that he'd been through, and all he'd seen, he still thought he was in control. *God, I'm sorry. Please forgive me for my big pride. I can do nothing without You.*

"I'm sorry about the baby." He edged a little closer. The words were so inadequate. "I wish I could do something."

"And I'm sorry about your friend Kinsey." She swayed a little. David doubted she realized it. "I'm sorry about your Hodgkin's."

"Me too." He wanted to comfort her, but he had no right to touch her. And he had so little comfort to give. He couldn't imagine why a godly woman like Emma would lose a baby she wanted so badly. Kinsey. Emma's baby. David's father. Annie's parents. Loss surrounded them. It was wrong to question God's plan, yet every day he did. "Do you ever wonder what all this means?"

Annie went still for a few seconds. "Do you remember the stories Aenti Louise used to tell us?"

How could he forget? She was the best storyteller and every story came straight from her *Deitsch* Bible. She had a great love of those stories, and they had sat on the rug at her feet many cold winter nights, listening to her raspy voice. "Like Jonah in the belly of the whale?"

"And David and Goliath. I think of your cancer as Goliath. God will help you defeat it." A glimmer of her normal bright humor shone through in those words. "Anyway, I was thinking of the story of Job just now as I waited. I never liked it that much when I was little. It seemed mean to take everything away from a man just to prove that he wouldn't turn away."

"But God was right. He knew Job wouldn't turn away. And he didn't. No matter what Satan did to him, he refused to deny God."

"Even when his wife said he should."

"We all should avoid poor counsel."

"Emma will never turn away, no matter what she loses." Tears slipped down her cheeks. Annie blotted them with the hankie. "I can only hope to be as faithful."

"You are equally faithful."

"Not really. I wonder each day what God's plan is for me. Why I'm still alone. Why you don't care enough for me—"

"Annie!"

She twisted her hands in her lap. "I don't understand why I'm still alone."

The awful truth tightened its grip around David's heart. His decision to back away from Annie caused her to question her faith. He was responsible for her doubts. Another wrong he couldn't right.

Some things he couldn't change. Like an uncertain future. But now, in this moment, he owed her at the very least a little comfort. He reached for her hand and her gaze connected with his. Her expression was open, soft, almost as if she would comfort him. "I don't have any answers."

"I know."

Her hand met his midway between them. It was so small and soft. His fingers tightened around hers and he pulled them toward his chest so they rested there. He hoped she couldn't feel the erratic beat of his heart. It would give him away. Without speaking, she bowed her head and closed her eyes. He did the same.

They sat, holding onto each other, silent as Annie prayed harder than she'd ever prayed in her life. *Let David truly live. Let David know it's all right to live. Give him hope. Give him faith.*

"David? What are you doing here?"

Annie opened her eyes. Thomas stood in the doorway. Grief etched his face, aging it ten years. "How did you find out so quickly?"

David let go of Annie's hand. A sense of being cold and alone left her with a feeling so painful she had to remember to draw a breath. He stood. "I was here…it doesn't matter. I am sorry for your loss."

Thomas inclined his head. His Adam's apple bobbed. "She wants you, Annie."

Unable to rein in her own emotions, Annie nodded without speaking. She slipped from the room and down the hall. At the door to Emma's room, she hesitated, one hand on the slick, painted metal. Her eyes closed, she sought words. None came. *God. God. God.*

When she was sure her face would reflect none of her own pain, she entered. Emma lay on her side, her knees drawn up like a small child. Her eyes were closed and her hands clasped under her cheek. Annie drew close and studied her sister. The picture of innocence even at the old age of twenty-three. Not wanting to wake her, Annie eased into a chair. Emma's eyes opened and immediately filled with tears. "The baby is gone."

"I know."

Emma's hands fisted and she drew them down to her chest, clutching them tight against her body as if fearing some unseen blow. Her breathing came in tortured, hiccupping jerks that hurt Annie's ears. "I don't understand."

"Neither do I."

Another jerky breath. "Can you pray?"

"Yes."

"Pray for me. I haven't the heart. Tell God I'm sorry."

"He knows. Sleep."

Emma's eyes closed again. After a while, her breathing came more easily. Annie leaned back in the chair, glad to rest a while. No more talking. No more feeling. Just being.

Mudder and Daed's death had taught her only time could ease this kind of agony. With each day, each week, each month, the white-hot fire would be reduced to glowing coals, then embers, and eventually ashes that would scatter and disappear in the gentlest of breezes. The scars would be brutal, rough, and uneven to the touch. But they would no longer burn and ache. She prayed that Emma could survive until then.

That they all could.

Chapter 34

David rapped on Emma and Thomas's door and waited. He smiled down at Kinsey, who looked a little nervous. Surprising for a girl who raced through the halls at the hospital stopping to talk to anyone who would listen. Used to race. Now she let staff run her around in a wheelchair without a fight. Willow hoped the drive, fresh air, and new scenery might give her a boost. She was wasting away in that hospital bed, a little weaker each day. Too weak to ride. Emma needed company and Kinsey would give the girls someone to play with, giving Emma a break.

Like most Plain people, Emma didn't complain about her loss, but no one could deny she felt it deeply. Being at home with the children while Thomas worked long hours harvesting the wheat meant she had no adults to keep her company in her time of loss. Luke had allowed Annie to go back to work at the bakery to help with the hospital bills. Not being allowed to help with the harvest, David figured he could serve a purpose here. Emma might think it odd a man would do such a thing, but today it gave him a sense of purpose and they had been friends for many years.

"You'll like Rebecca. She's nice." He'd been trying to strike up a conversation with Kinsey since they left the hospital. After talking with Rosie and inspecting the horse from one end to the other, she had climbed into the buggy and proceeded to study the countryside. "The twins are rambunctious. They like company."

"I'd rather visit Blackie." At least she was talking. "I bet he misses me."

"We'll visit him on the way back to the hospital."

"I don't want to go back to the hospital." A note of entreaty in her voice made David's hands tighten on the reins. She looked up at him, her eyes huge in her thin face. "I know what I said before, but I don't want to die there."

"You're not dying." Not today. "The doctor says your numbers have improved a little. So stop being such a worrywart and enjoy the day. Like I said, Rebecca is nice."

Kinsey tugged at the kerchief on her head. She'd chosen red for this trip. It made her face seem all the more pale. "Is she gonna freak that I don't have hair?"

"No."

The door opened. Emma stood there, looking as pale and thin as her young guest. "David. It's good to see you. And this must be Kinsey. I like your red handkerchief. It is so bright and cheerful. Come in, come in."

She tried so hard to be the welcoming, not-a-care-in-the-world hostess. David offered her his best smile in return. "Kinsey wanted to meet Rebecca and the twins. Are they here?"

"They're in the kitchen with Miriam. I seem to have an awful lot of visitors these days." Emma managed a halfhearted smile. "Which is very nice. I appreciate everyone's kindness. But it's not necessary. I'm fine. I've plenty of work to do."

"I know you're fine." David knew about that kind of fine. It came from sheer force of will. She had no choice but to be fine. So she arose each morning and went about her business, telling herself she was fine. It was exactly what he did. "They won't let me work on the farm, and business is slow at the bakery. You're doing me a favor by letting me visit."

"Rebecca is making a pie for supper, and the twins are helping. Miriam is supervising. She's keeping them occupied while I get some sewing done." Emma led the way through a simple, neat living room that looked just like the one he had at home. It even smelled the same, with the sweet scent of baking pastry wafting around him. "Which means the twins are making a mess, and Rebecca is trying to stop them because she knows she'll end up cleaning up most of it. Miriam is drinking the tea they keep serving her."

In the kitchen Emma made the introductions. Rebecca wiped her hands on her apron and shook the hand Kinsey held out. Mary and Lillie followed suit, their matching faces solemn as they examined their visitor from head to foot. "You have cancer?" Mary asked.

"*Shhh*, you don't ask questions like that!" Rebecca scolded. "It's not nice."

Miriam put a hand on Mary's shoulder. "It's all right. I'm sure Kinsey is used to lots of questions. Like people asking you about your kapp and your long dress."

"Yep. People always want to know what happened to my hair," Kinsey conceded in a matter-of-fact tone. "I have leukemia."

"Are you going to die?" Lillie posed the question, her innocence reflected in the way she cocked her head. "My mudder and daed died. A truck ran into their buggy."

"My mudder died of cancer." Rebecca added. "I don't remember her. I was a baby. Now I have Emma so I'm not sad."

David leaned against the door frame watching, amazed at how children took in stride the tragedies life dealt them. They handled it so much better than adults. Maybe because they didn't truly understand what they'd lost. In Rebecca's case, she'd never known a different life. This was the one God gave her. Surely, He had His reasons. And now Emma loved and cared for her and the twins as if they were her own babies. And that gave her solace in her time of loss. God's plan?

Bringing Kinsey into his life. How did that figure into the big plan? *I'd like to know that, God, if it pleases You.*

"I'm probably going to die soon." Kinsey climbed up on the bench and sat down. "Can I have the pie now? Just in case."

Miriam met David's gaze. She smiled, but her eyes were sad. "You must use that excuse a lot." Her tone light, she pushed a pie to the middle of the table. "This one is cooling. We'll cut it so you can try it—see if Rebecca and the girls did a good job. We can make another for supper. Would you like to help?"

"Really?" Kinsey's eyes shone. "The only thing I ever made with Grammy was Rice Krispie treats."

"I love Rice Krispie treats!" Miriam grabbed an apron from a pile on the prep table. "Put this on. We'll make a pie you can take home to your grammy."

Emma leaned toward David, her smile tight. "I think she's in good shape. Come into the living room. I have a mound of sewing to catch up on. With everything going on it seems I'm a little behind. Would you like some iced tea?"

David waited while she poured the tea, then took the glass she offered and followed her into the living room. She sat in a rocking chair and picked up her sewing basket. He settled into the one across from her. Her hands occupied with a sock that sported a hole in the heel, she glanced at him, then back at her darning. "Did Sadie and Annie send you over here to check on me?"

"No. To get rid of me."

They both laughed.

"Aren't we a pair?" Emma leaned over her sewing. The needle plunged in and out of the material without hesitation, but her voice shook. "I try so hard to accept what happened as God's will for me, but I still don't understand."

"Neither do I."

They sat a while in silence. Emma knotted and snipped the thread. She picked up another sock, then chuckled.

"What?" David saw nothing humorous in their situations.

"You remind me of Thomas."

"How so?"

"You're so chatty. Annie never mentioned how chatty you are."

David drew lines in the condensation on his glass. "I'm surprised she mentions me at all."

"Fishing for information, are you?"

Not really. He already knew how much Annie longed for more. So did he. But talking about their problem would take Emma's mind off hers. "Is she all right?"

"She told me about that night at the hospital. The night I lost…" Her free hand smoothed the apron that covered her flat belly. "That night you saw her in the hospital."

"I don't want to be responsible for her losing faith. Nor do I want her to be alone when I'm gone."

"Where's *your* faith?"

"I've known you and Luke and Annie since we were all knee high to my daed's britches." David set his glass on the end table. "You've known me. You know I only want to do what is right."

"And you get to decide what that is with no regard for someone else's feelings?" Emma had a little more perk to her tone now that the conversation had turned to fixing someone else's problems. "You have no idea what God's plan for you is."

"Never truer words were spoken."

It must have been the sheer bewilderment in his tone that made her giggle. The infectious sound caught David unaware. It made him laugh. The more he laughed, the more Emma laughed. He had to hold his side, it hurt so much. Emma had tears running down her face. "We're daft, aren't we?"

"Completely around the bend." He guffawed.

"What is going on in here?" Her face puzzled, Miriam swept into the room. "I thought someone was getting tickled to death or something. Are you two all right?"

Before David could answer, a booming knock sounded at the front door.

"Get that, Miriam, will you? I'm in no condition to greet more company." Emma wiped at her face with a hankie. She chuckled some more. "I needed a good laugh. Thank you, David."

"Glad to be of service."

A bemused look on her face, Miriam opened the door. "Oh. It's you."

"Miriam, is that any way to greet a guest?" Emma set her sewing basket aside and stood. "Who is it?"

Miriam backed away from the door. Josiah strode past her. He didn't look any happier than she did. "I didn't know you had company." His dark gaze flitted from David to Miriam. "A lot of company."

≈

Josiah caught Miriam's light scent as he brushed past her. Like vanilla, only sweeter. He wanted to capture that smell and put it in his pocket for later, when he would pace the floor wondering why he couldn't make one person happy. He concentrated on Emma. This visit was about his sister.

"How are you, schweschder?" Josiah allowed himself a quick hug. His family was more demonstrative than most, maybe because of the losses they'd suffered. "Feeling better?"

"Much better." The dark circles around her eyes and wan face belied her answer. "Don't tell me Luke sent you to check on me?"

"Annie, actually. She knew I had to pick up a part and take it to Luke at our place." He glanced at Miriam and away. "But I need to get back to the shop."

"Ach." One syllable from Miriam. Josiah glanced at her again. She folded her arms and tapped one bare foot on the wooden floor. "Your sister also suggested I pay a visit this afternoon. I had to beg my daed to let me take the afternoon off."

"Matchmaker, matchmaker." Emma actually laughed again. "She's getting good at it."

"If it makes you feel better, it's worth it." Miriam flew across the room and put an arm around Emma. "It's good to see you smile. Isn't that right, Josiah?"

His blood still boiling over Annie's little plan, Josiah managed to nod.

"Gut. Miriam, take Josiah out to the kitchen and give him a piece of that pie you made." Emma patted his shoulder. "Did you know Miriam makes a good pie?"

He assumed she did. Most Plain women were good in the kitchen. They started learning young enough. Nothing special there. Not bothering to fight it, he followed Miriam into the kitchen where the twins, Rebecca, and little Kinsey Navarro appeared to either be making a big mess or cleaning it up. He couldn't tell which. The aroma of baking pastry made his mouth water. It reminded him of his own mudder. She had taught Annie to bake and would've taught Mary and Lillie, had she lived long enough.

"Are you all right?" Miriam tilted her head, her expression concerned. "You look so sad."

"I'm fine."

"Have a seat. There's tea and lemonade and lots of pie. Don't be mad at Annie."

"I just don't like my sister meddling." He sounded like a jerk. He couldn't help it. "Annie should mind her own business."

"She is. She considers you her business." Miriam motioned to a chair at the table. "I'll cut you a slice of cherry pie. You're Annie's brother. She loves you. I'm her best friend. She loves me. She wants…" Her cheeks turned pink and her voice trailed away. "She thinks she can make everything better." Given her problems with David, she should know that wasn't always possible.

"She's not in control."

"She knows God is in control." Miriam set a plate of steaming cherry pie in front of him. "Sorry, there's no ice cream. Annie has faith in people. She believes in good."

"Enough for a dozen people." On that they could agree. He needed some of Annie's single-minded faith. As he picked up his fork, he glanced at the girls. They were busy washing dishes or splashing the sudsy water on the floor. "Things are so black and white for her. Not for me. I'm trying, Miriam, I am—"

"This isn't the place for this. Little pitchers have big ears." Miriam cocked her head toward the girls. She sighed. "I know you very well. You don't have to explain."

She didn't know him that well. She didn't know how caught he felt, one boot in each world. One wrong step and he lost everything. He'd almost done that before, but he'd managed to crawl away from the precipice. He had this sneaking suspicion he liked it out there on the ledge. Here in Bliss Creek it was so safe, so secure. So monotonous. "I don't want to make a mistake again. You know—"

Mary knocked a glass from the counter in her haste to grab another pan to dry. Miriam dove for it and managed to make the catch before it hit the floor. "Slow down."

"We want to show Kinsey the new baby kittens. There are five of them." Mary waved her towel around so hard another glass was in danger. "They're black and white and some are all black and some are all white."

"Work first." Miriam gently turned her back to the drain. "Finish up. It looks like a tornado went through here. You cook, you eat, you clean."

She was good with children. She would make a good mother. Josiah shoved a bite of pie in his mouth before he said something he shouldn't. The tart cherry mingled with sweet, sugary syrup. Like life. Every new, fragile moment framed in bitter sweetness.

Smiling, Miriam turned to Kinsey. "You too. No exceptions for visitors."

Kinsey saluted with her towel. "Yes ma'am." She picked up a bowl from the drain. Her gaze traveled from Miriam to Josiah. "You're David's friend. Is Miriam your girlfriend?"

Josiah opened his mouth and shut it. Miriam's cheeks went from pink to cherry red. "That's another one of those questions little girls and boys aren't supposed to ask."

"Like whether someone is dying?" Kinsey frowned as she wiped at the bowl. "That's pretty stupid. I mean boyfriends aren't forever. Dead is forever."

"Unless you marry the boyfriend," Rebecca pointed out. She had a blob of suds on her nose. "Husbands are forever."

"Not always. I saw something on TV…" Kinsey swayed. "I don't feel…"

The bowl slipped from her fingers and sailed toward the floor. The sound of shattering glass followed. Kinsey took two tottering steps and then collapsed in a heap, her small body sprawled on the wood floor like a rag doll, skinny arms and legs askew.

"Kinsey?" Miriam dropped to her knees and touched the girl's cheek. Her fingers traveled to her neck. "She's fainted. We need to get her to the clinic."

"David!" Josiah squatted next to her. Rebecca and the twins hovered behind him, their tearful questions loud in his ears. "David, get in here!"

Chapter 35

David whirled and leaned his back into the emergency room doors. Kinsey flopped in his arms, her slight body dead weight. No, not dead. Just unconscious, he told himself. Her dress flapping around her ankles, Miriam dashed ahead of him. "Help! We need help," she called out, her voice high and breathless. "Someone, please."

A nurse David didn't recognize among the many he'd met in the last year trotted between the rows of chairs. "Triage is that way." She pointed toward a second set of double doors. She stopped, her chubby face creased in a sudden frown. "Oh. It's little Kinsey again. Best bring her into an examining room."

Ignoring the aggravated looks of the half-dozen people sitting in the waiting area, David plowed ahead. *God, please.* She couldn't go yet. Not without Willow and her Grammy at her side. "She collapsed. One minute she was fine, then she was on the floor. She ate a piece of pie and that was it."

The nurse picked up her pace, surprisingly swift on stubby legs. David struggled to keep up. She glanced back. "Where is Ms. Navarro? And Violet?"

"Josiah…my friend went to get them." David panted. "He's on horseback so it will take a little longer."

The buggy ride had seemed endless. One of those times when

David longed for a phone to call an ambulance or a car. A fast car. Glad the bishop couldn't read his thoughts, David laid Kinsey on the bed in the tiny examining room. She didn't stir. Her face was as white as the sheet underneath her.

The nurse picked up a phone attached to the wall, spoke into it, then slapped the receiver into its cradle. "Doctor Burton is on his way." She grasped Kinsey's wrist and then looked at the watch on her own arm. After a minute, she wrote something on a clipboard and then picked up a stethoscope. "What's your name?"

David backed away until he was up against the far wall. He'd never imagined he'd be in the room at this moment. "Is she…is she going to make it?"

"Sir, who are you?"

After a second Miriam answered the question for him.

"What happened?"

"We were making pie." Miriam's voice trembled. "I told her to help wash the dishes. I never thought…"

"Oh, honey, don't worry about it. This sweetie may look like a little princess, but she's tough as old leather." The nurse patted Kinsey's pie-stained T-shirt. "Now go on, y'all shoo. Have a seat in the waiting room. When her family gets here, send them on back."

Together they trudged back to the waiting room. All his energy gone, David focused on picking up his feet and setting them down. *Step. Step. Step.*

"You look like you may need a doctor too." Miriam settled into a chair next to him. "You're green."

"Blue." It came out automatically.

A faint smile appeared. "At least you still—"

Willow burst through the door and sprinted across the room. "Where is she?"

David stood and pointed. "She's that way."

Willow didn't slow. A second later she disappeared from sight.

Josiah slipped through the doors, one hand on Violet Hawkins's arm. She had tears on her wrinkled cheeks. "Is she…is she still with us?"

David nodded.

"Thank God."

She went on alone, leaving Josiah standing in the middle of the aisle. David went to him. "You made it."

He nodded.

"What did they say?"

Josiah sank into a chair next to Miriam and exhaled loudly. "They were upset."

"I know that."

"Her mother said she should never have let you take her from the hospital again."

David sat. "She's right."

"No." Josiah and Miriam spoke at the same time. To David's surprise, Josiah gripped her hand for a second. Her face turned a pretty pink color. "No."

Miriam tugged her hand gently from Josiah's and folded them in her lap as if she were praying. "She was happy. She was having fun. She liked it at Emma's house. It was good for her."

Kinsey happy. Kinsey having fun. David held on to that image. It might be the last one he had of her.

They sat silently then. Josiah and Miriam huddled closer than he'd ever seen them before. It helped his heart to settle. Hope for them in the midst of the hardships of others helped him to find a balance again. The moments dragged by. In each passing second he waited, sure someone would appear to say she'd left them.

Miriam closed her eyes and napped. When her head lolled against Josiah's shoulder she awoke with a start, her face pink all over again. Josiah bought them coffees from a machine. It tasted like oil. Finally, after an hour, Violet Hawkins returned. She stepped more lightly now than she had before. David tried to read her lined, exhausted face. One part resignation, one part relief, one part hope. "She's conscious and they've stabilized her, but her white blood count is way up and her blood pressure is way down." She twisted the strap of her big purse with both hands. "They're going to admit her."

"*Gut.* That's *gut.*" David had to clear his throat again. It hurt. "I'm sorry."

"Don't be. The child is sick. We all knew the danger of letting her roam the countryside." Her voice broke. "We also know the danger of letting her waste away here, losing her will to live."

"We'll go then."

"No, no, she's asking for you." Violet's watery smile only lasted a second or two. "First thing, when she opened her eyes."

Sucking in a breath, David squared his shoulders and followed Violet into the exam room. Willow turned a tear-stained face toward him, but didn't speak.

David leaned over the bed, letting his total focus be on Kinsey and not the emotions swirling around her family. She raised a hand and grabbed his index finger. "I liked making pie," she whispered, her voice so soft he could barely hear. He leaned closer. "I told my mom not to be mad I made pie today."

He swallowed. "Good pie."

"You haven't eaten it yet." Her head lolled back on the pillow. "Don't be nice to me because I'm dying."

"I wouldn't do that."

A sound came from her mouth that might have been a painful ghost of a giggle. "No, you'd tell me to stop feeling sorry for myself."

"Yes. Time to stop laying around and do some work."

"Soon as I take a nap."

Her eyes closed and her grip went lax. He started to back away. Her eyes fluttered open. "Promise me I'll get to ride again."

David glanced at Willow. Her hand fluttered to her mouth. She nodded. He turned back to Kinsey. "I promise. One way or another."

"I'm tired."

"Sleep."

David turned to slip past Willow and Violet. Willow put up a hand. David stopped. He waited. She had a right to be angry.

"Thank you."

Startled, he couldn't think what to say.

"You gave her one more good day." Willow touched his arm. "Thank you."

One more good day. "Don't thank me. Every day on this earth comes from God."

Willow nodded. David could do no more than nod back.

It had taken him a year to come to this place, but now that he was here, he understood. *Thank You, God, for one more good day.*

Chapter 36

Exhaustion clawed at Josiah. The reins weighed heavy in his hands, and the monotonous *clip-clop* of the horse's hooves on the blacktop and the heat that billowed from the road threatened to lull him to sleep. Miriam looked amazingly awake after the day she'd had. She stared at the passing scenery as if she were at ease. He squirmed on the seat, trying to think of something simple to say. Sitting next to her in the hospital emergency room had given him time to think about how good she was with children and how quickly she reacted to Kinsey's collapse. She had her head on straight. She'd never wavered.

"Penny for your thoughts." She gave him a quizzical look. "You're mighty quiet."

"Tired."

"Me too. But wound up." She patted her kapp and ducked her head. "It's a shame we can't just ride for a while."

The sun hung low in the western sky, playing a game of hide and seek with the clouds on the horizon. "It's late. It'll be dark soon. You've missed supper and we've both got chores."

"True."

It amazed Josiah how much disappointment and longing could be packed into one syllable. He shook the reins and clucked at Mooch. "You know how to handle yourself in an emergency."

She shrugged. "Panic doesn't help."

"Seeing that little girl lying on the floor like that…"

"Imagine how David felt."

Josiah could imagine all too well. "He's lost so much. I wonder about him getting close to a little Englisch girl. It's odd."

"She's sick. He's sick. They met in the hospital. I don't think it's odd at all." Miriam smiled. "I think it's sweet. They both understand like no one else can what it's like to have a scary disease. They've given each other a special gift."

"Do you ever think about how it could end for him?"

"Or for her if he goes first."

"He won't die. She might, but not David."

"Because he's your friend?"

"Because he's too stubborn." Josiah paused, considering whether to voice the thought. "Because I don't pray much, but I prayed about him."

"*Gut.*" Miriam surprised him by putting her arm through his and leaning against his shoulder. "I pray for him and his doctors and for strength and courage."

She was so much better than he. "Me too."

"None of us is perfect, Josiah. I don't expect you to be."

"But you are."

"Am not."

She sounded offended, which amused Josiah for some reason. "Are too."

"Stop it!"

They both laughed, her high giggle mixed with his low growl of a laugh. It sounded good. Nothing stood between them except his own weakness. The clarity of that thought pushed him into taking the chance, bridging the chasm he had created between them. "There's always later."

"Later?" She let go of his arm and straightened.

He snatched a flashlight from the floor of the buggy. "I'll double check to make sure the batteries are still good."

Her gaze went from the flashlight to his face and back. "What about Sarah?"

"Sarah can get her own flashlight."

"I'm serious."

He held her gaze. "So am I. I'm sorry it took me this long to figure it out."

"Daed goes to bed early. My brothers will probably be out and about doing their own visiting." A smile spread across Miriam's face. "I'll catch up with my sewing tonight. I've allowed myself to get behind."

He hoped she was right about her brothers. None would be happy to see his buggy in the Yonkers's lane. Miriam's courting was her business.

And now it was his.

Chapter 37

Annie punched the bread dough with her fist, then rolled it over and smoothed it into a ball. Charisma giggled and did the same with the bread dough sitting on the floured cutting board in front of her. The girl laughed at the strangest things, which made teaching her to bake all the more challenging. She'd rather sit on a stool, watch, and make a running stream of comments meant to amuse herself and keep her mind off Logan's fate. The judge had taken a long recess—something about another court hearing he couldn't postpone. The waiting was making Charisma crazy, and therefore Annie too. Annie used the back of her hand to rub an itchy spot on the end of her nose. "Something tickle your funny bone? What's so funny?"

"Who knew making bread could be such good therapy?"

"Therapy?"

"You know, working out your aggressions."

"Aggressions?"

"Annie Shirack, you can't tell me you don't have the desire to haul off and smack Mr. Bald and Pitiful now and again."

Annie's hand fisted involuntarily. She immediately loosed her fingers and wrapped them around the bread pan. "Grease this pan for me, please." She wiped her hands on a towel and began smoothing Charisma's dough. "We'll put these in the pans and let them rise again before baking them."

"Don't try to avoid the question. Don't you ever get so mad at David that you want to kick his—"

"No. No!" Annie slapped down the image in her head. Sure, sometimes she was so frustrated she wanted to chop some wood to keep from giving David a piece of her mind again. She wasn't proud of her behavior that day in the barn. She needed to learn to talk less and listen more. "We don't believe in violence."

"Never? Not even to defend yourselves?"

"We're peaceful people." That fact gave her a sense of security, a knowing who she was and where she came from. "We don't involve ourselves in strife."

"You don't got any guys fighting in the war?"

"No."

"What if somebody killed your little brothers? Wouldn't you want to hurt him back?"

"Hurting him wouldn't bring back Josiah or Mark."

"You sure—"

The bell dinged over the double doors as a customer entered. The door slammed shut with a bang. It was a wonder the glass didn't break.

"Hello, hello. Annie, are you back there?"

Sarah Kauffman strolled through the aisle and sashayed right up to the counter. Annie hardly recognized her in the long, dark blue dress and crisp kapp. Gone were the blue eye shadow and dangling silver earrings she'd favored in the past. She looked so much younger…and more innocent. Annie knew better. She returned to the front counter. "I'm here. Sarah, how are you?"

"So this is Sarah?" Her face full of curiosity, Charisma jumped down from her stool and crowded Annie. "Josiah's Sarah?"

"Yes. No. I mean, this is Sarah Kauffman." Ignoring Charisma's smirk, Annie made the introduction politeness demanded. "What would you like, Sarah? We have some sourdough bread hot out of the oven."

"Mayor Haag wants two dozen hoagie rolls. She's making—I mean I'm making—sub sandwiches for her campaign meeting tonight." Sarah tapped long, unadorned fingernails on the glass. "And two dozen molasses cookies and two dozen chocolate chip cookies. She says you have the best molasses cookies in the state. Is that right?"

She was trying really hard to be nice. Annie grabbed a white paper sack from a stack on the counter and began filling it. Whatever had happened with Josiah, Annie had to treat this girl with the same respect she would any other customers. Some were more of a challenge than others—even Bishop Kelp would concede that fact, surely. "How are things with you, Sarah? Is your job going well?"

"Everything's great." She picked out a chunk of brownie from the sample platter and popped it in her mouth. "Yummy. I'll take a couple of brownies for myself. Mayor Haag won't care."

Annie glanced at Charisma. She was way too quiet. Her lips were turned down in an exaggerated frown. She sniffed and crossed her arms.

Sarah glanced up from studying the trays of cookies behind the glass. "So you're the girlfriend of the guy who robbed this place, right?"

"And you're the girl who nearly killed Annie's brother, right?" Charisma snatched back the platter of samples just as Sarah lifted her hand to take another piece of a brownie. "You're the one pretending to be Amish."

"I'm not pretending." Sarah's tone mixed irritation with surprise. "I'm trying to make a life for myself. Besides, what do you know about it?"

Charisma squeezed past Annie and sauntered around the display case, not stopping until she stood in Sarah's path. Something about her pose—hands on her hips, chin lifted, scowl on her face—made Annie think of a cat defending her territory against a stray who'd wandered onto her property. "I know girls like you."

"You don't know me."

"Sure I do. You're just like me. When you want something, you go after it. Nothing stops you."

Sarah made a show of examining the trays of cookies neatly arranged behind the glass. "Annie, give me a dozen oatmeal raisin cookies too. I'll take them home. My cousin Delia loves oatmeal raisin cookies."

Annie thrust the bag of cookies and rolls at Sarah. "That will be twenty-one dollars and twenty-five cents."

Sarah dug around in her bag and produced a billfold. With an exaggerated flourish she counted out the money. "There you go. Pleasure doing business with you." She smiled at Charisma. "You may think we're alike, but we're not. I would never waste my time on a guy who is willing to go to jail for the pennies he'll get from robbing a bakery in a little backwater town like Bliss Creek."

She pivoted and traipsed to the door in a leisurely stroll that said she hadn't a care in the world. Annie bit her lip to keep unkind words from spilling out. Logan had made bad choices, but Sarah had no right to judge. Plain people didn't judge.

Charisma chuckled.

"What are you laughing about? You thought that was funny? I don't—"

"Annie, Annie! I just proved my point." Charisma held up both hands. "Actually, I proved your point."

"What are you talking about?"

"No way she's suited to your life. She's faking it."

Uncertain, Annie folded her arms and thought about it. "I already knew that."

"You figured she couldn't be that devious. You wanted to believe she might be joining your community for the right reasons. You wanted to believe she'd do the right thing." Charisma plopped the sample platter back on the display case, selected a chunk of cookie, and inspected it before popping it in her mouth. She chewed deliberately. "Now you know. She won't. You have to make your brother see that."

"He already does. He even took Miriam for a buggy ride the other night."

"That doesn't mean Sarah Kauffman can't still get inside his head." Charisma dusted her fingers off. "I know girls like her. I am a girl like her. You gotta make sure he stays away from her."

"How?"

"You'll figure it out. For Miriam's sake, you'd better."

Chapter 38

David smoothed the blanket on Blackie's back, then adjusted its position before adding the saddle. The evening air hadn't begun to cool, even in the shade of the Shiracks' barn. He hoped it wouldn't be too warm for Kinsey. It had been a surprise when Willow had stopped by the Plank house, her uniform wilted after a long shift at the restaurant, to convey a message from her daughter. She wanted the ride now that David had promised her in the hospital. One last time? Willow didn't say that, but David read the painful air of resignation on her face. The doctor saw no reason to prohibit it. Nothing she did now would change the course of the disease.

David didn't want to give up, even if the doctors did. Even if Willow and Violet were trying to find peace with this ending. A chance still existed. God's plan might still be to give her—to give them—more time. He buckled the cinch, tightened it a little, and then led the horse out into the corral where he used a quick-loose knot to tie the rope to a fence post.

Willow carried Kinsey from the station wagon to the fence. The fact that she didn't walk anymore sent a sharp pain careening through David's chest. He anchored a smile on his face and started forward. "Hello, cowgirl. Are you ready to ride?"

She raised her head from her mother's chest, then let it fall back.

"I want to ride by the creek." Her voice was soft, but clear. "Have you seen any wild animals lately?"

"Only the two-legged kind." He made his tone light. "We could stop and fish at the creek, though. We might see a coyote or a raccoon drinking on the bank. You never know."

"Let's ride a while."

"You have to help me bridle Blackie first." David took her from Willow, whose smile of greeting didn't meet her eyes, and sat the little girl on the top railing of the fence. "Do you remember how I taught you to remove the halter and place the bridle?"

"Sure I do. I'm smart that way. You can go, Mommy. We're gonna ride."

Willow didn't move. Her gaze telegraphed a myriad of emotions, but she didn't say a word. David glanced at Kinsey, who was busy patting Blackie, her face soft and dreamy. She seemed far away. David turned to Willow. "I'll have her back here before dark."

Willow gripped her hands together in a balled fist that made her knuckles turn white. "Behave yourself, Kinsey. No taking the reins and riding into the sunset."

"Mommy, you're so silly." Kinsey looked up at David. "First you hold the bridle over his nose with your right hand, then use your left hand fingers to hold the bit against his mouth and put your thumb in the space so he has to open his mouth."

She spouted David's directions almost word for word. He hid a smile. "You want to do it or should I?"

Kinsey contemplated Blackie's mouth. He whinnied, revealing a set of nice teeth. "You do it. I don't want to get horse slobber on my hand. Grammy says no germs today."

Sure that germs weren't the problem, David grinned and proceeded to make quick work of the bridle. Blackie was a perfect gentleman the entire time, making it easy for David to lift Kinsey onto the horse's back. He waited until she had a firm grip on the mane before letting go. Then he climbed up behind her. "You ready?"

He caught the soft sigh, like the wings of a hummingbird hovering near his ears. "Yeah," she whispered.

They took off at a gentle canter toward the pasture that led to a stand of trees along the creek. The early evening sun hung on the horizon making the shadows long and narrow, but David's hat shielded his eyes. A nice breeze kept it from being uncomfortably hot. The sound of sheets flapping on the Shiracks' clothesline across the way kept time with the clip-clop of Blackie's hooves. The scent of fresh cut grass mingled with Blackie's musky horse smell. After a while, Kinsey relaxed against David. "Are we going to go faster?"

"If you want." He picked up the pace. "Hang on tight."

"There's a cardinal!" She pointed at a red spot high in an elm tree. "And there's his wife. She's not as pretty."

He laughed. "Kind of the reverse of people, right?"

She giggled. "Do you mean I'm better looking than you?"

"I reckon that is what I mean."

"I want to gallop."

David tugged the reins to the left. Blackie followed, taking them away from the path to the creek and toward the open fields that separated the Shirack property from the Plank fields. He waited until the ground was smooth and even before he popped his stirrups and called *giddyup!* to the horse. Their pace increased steadily until they seemed to sail through the grassy plain. Kinsey's laugh, high and breathless, rang in his ears, a sweet little melody. "More! Faster!"

After a few minutes David slowed the horse a little, and then a little more, until eventually they came to a simple walk. "That was fun." Kinsey patted Blackie's mane. "Good job, Blackie. Thank you. You're the best horse ever."

David had no idea how Blackie took the compliment. The horse's sides were lathered in sweat. "I imagine this is a lot easier for him than pulling a plow or a buggy."

"I suppose. You're pretty skinny and I don't weigh much at all," she conceded.

"I'm not skinny." David stopped. Why argue with the child? "Well, I reckon you're right."

They didn't talk for a while. He waited, hoping she would give him a clue as to what was going on inside her head. Minutes passed. Mosquitoes buzzed his face. A bullfrog croaked in the distance. "It's quiet." The strength in her voice faded. "I like that."

"Me too."

"Do you think when you die it's quiet all the time?"

"I don't know."

She craned her head back to look at him. Her lips looked purple against her pale, almost transparent skin. "Is it bad that I wish you could die at the same time I do so I'll have someone to talk to?"

David's fingers tightened on the reins. "It's not bad."

"Would you mind?"

If it gave a little girl something to hang on to in a universe where she would never grow up, never be courted by a beau, never get married, where she had to walk through the dark into an unknown so enormous he found it unfathomable, he could be the brave one. "I wouldn't mind because I'd have you to talk to."

She curled her fingers in Blackie's thick mane. "Do you believe in heaven?"

"Yes."

"Are you going there?"

"God decides that. But I know His Son, Jesus, wants me to be there with Him. I think Jesus will be looking for you too. You can talk to Him anytime you want to."

"That's what Grammy says."

"Grammy is a wise woman." The meadow narrowed. They moved so slowly Blackie stopped. His long neck dropped, and he nibbled at the high grass next to the fence. "Let's ride along the creek, see if we see any of the coyotes that have been coming in to drink water and steal the chickens and piglets."

"Cool. I wanna see coyotes."

He clucked and snapped the reins. Blackie seemed a little reluctant, but he picked up the pace into a nice canter. It was a relief to let the conversation drift away. God had sent him a little girl to teach him courage in the face of the unknown and the uncertain. It shamed David beyond measure that Kinsey knew how to reach out and find comfort. She knew which questions to ask and who to ask. She needed solace and she found it. Why couldn't he do the same? Why couldn't he reach out to Annie and accept the comfort she so desperately wanted to give him? The answer didn't reflect well on him. Pride. Arrogance. Selfishness. He shook his head, trying to clear the thought. A skunk trundled across the clearing in front of him. Skunks qualified as wildlife, he supposed. "Kinsey, look, a skunk."

Her head bobbed, but she didn't respond. "Kinsey, that skunk will make a terrible stink if Blackie scares him."

She still didn't answer. Her head lolled against his chest. She'd fallen asleep. He tightened his grip. "Kinsey, you'll fall off."

Her eyes fluttered, but remained closed. Her tiny body had no more stuffing to it than one of his sisters' old homemade dolls.

"I guess that's enough for today." He turned Blackie toward home. "You look pretty tuckered out."

Enough for one more good day.

Chapter 39

David dumped the last bag of sugar on the shelf next to a dozen more. He slapped his hands together to shake off the stray granules that coated them. The shelves were full again. He plucked the shipping invoice from the spot on the top shelf where he'd laid it before unloading. Studying the numbers, he wove his way through the crowded storage room. Physical labor felt good. It occupied his body. Stocking the storeroom kept his mind off the conversations he'd had with Kinsey the previous day.

The memory of her still, peaceful face as he laid her in the backseat of Willow's lime-mobile played in his mind's eye over and over again. Kinsey had found her peace, and he was determined to do the same.

The crowded storeroom felt like prosperity. It was a false sense of security. The cost for flour, sugar, yeast, eggs, milk, and all the spices and chocolates and such needed to make the fancy cakes and pies the Englischers wanted just kept rising. The invoice in his hand proved that.

Intent on delivering the offending piece of paper to his mother, who kept the bakery books, David pushed through the swinging door and into the bakery. His first thought, as always, was to look for Annie. She stood at the counter, engrossed in a discussion with a customer. *Gut*, she didn't see him. Didn't give him that sad, accusing look. Apparently she and the customer disagreed over which was better—chocolate

275

pudding upside-down cake or pineapple upside-down cake. A flat-out tie as far as David was concerned. Mudder looked up. Her wrinkled face dissolved into a smile, the way it did every time their paths crossed. No matter what he'd done or said the last time they met.

"All done in the back?"

"Jah. Here's the bill." David slapped it on the enormous roll-top desk that his father had made for his mother as a Christmas present the year she opened the bakery. "The cost of flour and sugar have gone up again."

Together they reviewed the figures. Sadie opened a ledger and ran her forefinger down a row of numbers. "We're fine. We're fine," she muttered. "I'll pay this later today."

The bell over the door dinged and David looked up to see the customer disappear through the door. Annie had already started toward them. She had a small envelope in her hand. Before she could say anything, David headed toward the storeroom. "I have to stop by Caleb's shop. Josiah wants me to look at a horse the Glicks are selling. He's shoeing him this afternoon."

"David, wait." Annie waved the envelope at him. If she knew he was avoiding her, her tone didn't reflect it. "Doctor Corbin's assistant dropped this note by this morning. She said it was important."

The ticking of the seconds whistled in David's ears as if time suddenly galloped into a future where he had received the news. Hodgkin's or remission. He stalled, hand on the door. Slower than molasses on a cold winter day, he turned to face her. She held out the note. To his surprise his hand came up and took it. "Danki."

He did an about-face.

"Aren't you going to open it?" Mudder bustled toward him. "What does it say?"

"I don't know." Silly thing to say.

"Open it, son. I'd like to know what it says." Her voice quivered only the tiniest bit. "Best get it over with."

The envelope in his hand weighed barely an ounce, yet it felt like an enormous boulder threatening to knock him off his feet. Mudder was right. Get it over with. Now. He ripped the flap open like a bandage from the skin around a wound. Best do it all at once, so it didn't hurt so much.

Mudder put a hand on his shirt sleeve and peeked over his arm. "What does it say?"

The letters swam in front of him.

> David, your test results are in.
> Please come see me at your earliest convenience.
> Doctor Corbin

"Not much." He handed it to her. His hand didn't shake. "I have to go see Doctor Corbin about the results."

"You'll go now?" Mudder's hand closed over the note. She brought it to her chest. "Before you go to Caleb's?"

"This afternoon. I'll go this afternoon." Fighting nausea, he pushed past her. "I have to stop at Caleb's first."

"David, see the doctor first, please." His mother's pleading voice followed him through the storage room. "And come right back here."

She was right. He should go to Doctor Corbin's office immediately. Instead, he pointed the buggy toward the blacksmith shop. Just a little more time. He needed a little more time to prepare.

⊁

Annie pushed the broom across the bakery floor in a listless back-and-forth motion. She was glad to be doing something. Anything was better than sitting around thinking about David's test results or Emma's loss or Charisma at the courthouse at that very moment, learning Logan McKee's fate. She searched for a bright spot. Sadie's daughter Deborah had agreed to watch the babies during the trial. That was *gut*. She didn't have to ask Leah for help. That was *gut*. Slim pickings for bright spots.

"What do you think is taking him so long?" She picked up the dustpan, then laid it down again. "You'd think he'd want to rush back to tell you what Doctor Corbin said."

"Not David. You know him." Sadie wiped down the countertops with a bleach-soaked rag. The astringent smell overcame the sweet scent of baking bread. "If the results weren't good, he'll need time to lick his wounds in private. To prepare."

"Prepare?"

"To tell me and his brothers and sisters." Sadie dropped the rag in the sink and turned on the water. "He worries about how it will affect us more than how it will affect him."

"You think that's it?" Annie's heart clutched at the thought. "You think the results were bad and he doesn't want to tell us?"

"I think it's in God's hands, and it does no good to worry about it. Finish sweeping so I can mop."

"Of course." She pushed the broom across the floor. Somehow it slipped from her hands and fell with a clang against the wood. "I'm sorry. I'm all thumbs today."

"Maybe you should go home." Sadie's words held no accusation, only concern. "You look a little peaked."

"I'm fine. Just tired." She grabbed the broom and applied it with more elbow grease. She had no answers so she baked and she cleaned, two things she knew how to do. She intended to clean until a customer came through the doors. "We'll have customers any minute now."

Please, God, we need customers. The morning had been too quiet. The rows of fresh loaves of bread cooling on the shelf. Cookies ready for the asking. Only two customers had entered the store the entire time. Luke had allowed her to return to work because Emma's hospital stay and surgery would mean bills. The Shiracks would do their part to help pay them through the community's health fund. Not because it was expected, but because they wouldn't dream of doing otherwise.

The door opened with a bang. Startled, Annie almost dropped the broom again. "David?"

Charisma swept into the bakery.

"Oh, Annie! Annie!" She stopped a few feet away, threw her hands over her face, and wept. Between the hands and the sobs, the words she spoke were unintelligible.

Annie scurried over to her. "What happened? Is it over? What did they say?"

"Let the poor girl collect herself." Sadie guided Charisma to a bench where she gently peeled the woman's fingers from her face. "I'll get you a glass of water."

Charisma clutched her denim bag to her chest like it would keep her from drowning in a sea of tears. "He's going to Lansing State Prison. Not right away, because Sergeant Parker says the prison is full right now. They ain't taking anymore prisoners so Logan has to stay in the jail here for a while—maybe a few weeks. He don't know, but eventually he's going to Lansing."

Her legs suddenly weak, Annie dropped onto the bench next to Charisma. She'd known in her heart this was coming, but yet it still shocked her. "They found him guilty?"

"They gave him five years."

Five years. Gracie wouldn't remember him and Luke David wouldn't know him at all. "That's a long time."

"The lawyer said he might get time off for good behavior. They could let him out on parole in two years." Charisma wiped at her nose with the sleeve of the new dress Annie had made her over the weekend. "He doesn't know Logan like I do. Good behavior ain't in his genes. Especially if someone is making him do something he doesn't want to do."

"He'll have to now, won't he?" Doing things a person didn't want to do was part of life. Every Plain child learned that by age two. "He'll want to get out as soon as possible, won't he?"

"Logan can't help himself. He's a rebel." Charisma drooped against the wall, her hands twisting in her lap. "That's what I liked about him…at first."

Not so much now that he would be in prison.

Charisma took the glass of water Sadie offered her and gulped it down in three swallows. "What I really need is a rum and coke. A big one. I'm not pregnant anymore. There's no reason I can't have a drink."

Annie exchanged glances with Sadie. "What you need is to get Gracie and Luke David and take them home."

"Where is my home? I ain't got one."

"You know you can stay with us as long as you need."

"Leah might not agree with you on that."

The tears started again. Charisma rummaged around in her purse and came up with a rumpled package of cigarettes. Before she could pull one out, Sadie snatched the package with surprisingly nimble fingers. "Not in here."

"Fine. Give them to me. I'll go someplace else. There's got to be a bar in this town."

"You're nursing." How could Charisma think about alcohol and cigarettes at a time like this? She had children. A baby. A baby like the one Emma so desperately wanted. "Gracie and Luke David need you."

Charisma rubbed her forehead. Her lips trembled. "What am I going to do?" She threw herself against Annie. Her head landed on Annie's shoulder. "Tell me, what am I going to do?"

Annie hugged her tight and rocked a little. Then she pushed her back so she could see her red, wet face. "First things first. It's time for you to get a job."

"HomeTown Restaurant has that Help Wanted sign in the window again. I'm guessing Naomi's niece didn't want to work that hard." Sadie handed Charisma a handkerchief. "Wipe your face, girl. Now's as good a time as any. You got your best clothes on. You just need to comb your hair."

"I suppose." Charisma mopped her face. She pulled a brush from her purse and went to work on her tangled hair. "You'll go with me, won't you, Annie? I don't want to go by myself. I was in there once before and she didn't even call me for an interview."

Sadie's slight nod told Annie she had her permission to leave the bakery.

"Naomi is a nice lady, but she probably saw you were carrying a baby at the time. Wouldn't do her any good to hire someone who was about to have a baby. Now it's different." Annie didn't know anything about hiring. She'd never applied for a job herself. "Piece of cake. But I'll go with you, if you want."

Ten minutes later they stood at the cash register in HomeTown Restaurant. The aroma of onion rings and hamburgers frying welcomed them. The place was packed with its usual lunch crowd. Annie's stomach rumbled. She hadn't eaten since breakfast in the predawn dark.

Willow rushed past them, a huge tray filled with steaming dishes held over her head with one hand. "Howdy, girls. Get you a table?"

"Charisma wanted to follow up on her application," Annie called after her.

Willow jerked her head toward Naomi Bolton, the owner and manager. "Naomi will have it on file."

Naomi, her face flushed and fingers flying on the cash register, didn't look up. "Be with ya in a sec."

A second turned into several minutes, but Annie didn't mind. She loved the chance to take a peek at the dishes being served. The gravy looked thick and savory. The stuffed pork chops seemed to be getting a lot of attention by diners. Everyone knew HomeTown did a great meatloaf and an even better chicken-fried steak. Annie's stomach growled some more. She'd love to know what seasonings they used in the breading for the steak.

Naomi wiped her hands on a towel that hung from her yellow- and green-checked apron and then shook Charisma's hand. "You interested in a job, right? I could sure use some help. I had a girl quit yesterday and we've been swamped—"

The door flew open and Violet Hawkins scurried in, moving as fast as a woman of nearly seventy could move. She called Willow's name in a high-pitched, breathless voice. The waitress slid a plate of spaghetti and meatballs in front of a young couple, then turned toward Violet. "What is it? What's happening?"

The lunchtime chatter died in an instant. Necks craned and people stared. Annie shrank against the wall, trying to stay out Violet's path as she rushed toward Willow's table. Willow seemed frozen to the spot. At first her face held only a puzzled expression. Then the confusion faded into a realization painful for Annie to watch. The tray in her hand slammed to the floor. "Aunt Violet?"

"I came to get you, honey. It's time." She gently took her niece's arm. "Come on, sweetie, the doctor says it's time. I didn't want them calling you and you having to drive over there, knowing what's…knowing…"

Willow began to move, slowly at first, then more quickly. She paused only long enough to grab her purse from behind the counter. "Naomi…"

"Don't worry about it, sugar," Naomi called after her. "We'll be praying for y'all and that sweet little girl."

The doors swung shut. After a second or two, the chatter resumed. Waitresses sped across the floor with laden trays. The cook shouted, "Order up!"

The busboy clanged glasses together and dumped dirty silverware in a huge plastic tub. Annie bit her lip to keep from crying. How could life move along like that? Just like it had when Mudder and Daed died. Maybe there was a kernel of comfort tucked away in that thought. Life did go on. She clung to the idea.

Naomi stuck a pen behind her ear and pawed through a stack of applications laying on the counter, then looked up to study Charisma. "You're Charisma Chiasson, aren't you? The one who waitressed in Shreveport a few years ago?"

Charisma nodded. "It's been a while, I know, but—"

"Looks like I'm gonna need some help like right now." Naomi pointed toward the kitchen. "Go wash up. The cook will show you where the aprons are. I'll get you a uniform later."

"You want me now?"

Naomi's thick white eyebrows did push-ups above the skinny reading glasses stuck on the end of her equally skinny nose. "I thought you wanted a job."

"I do."

"Get moving, then." She held out an order pad. "People who let grass grow under their feet don't last too long around here."

Charisma snatched the pad and threw Annie a glance as she trotted toward the swinging double doors that led to the kitchen. "The kids?"

Annie couldn't help but feel tickled pink. Charisma had a job. Leah might relax just a little. "Don't worry about it. I'll tell Deborah. She has bottles of your milk to get by for now and she already said she'd be happy to watch them on a regular basis."

"Tell her I'll pay her with my tips…" Charisma grinned. "I can't wait to get a paycheck. No more cloth diapers. No more sewing stuff. I'll even buy formula. No more nursing. I can have a beer if I want. Yippee!"

She disappeared through the doors still singing about money she didn't have in her pocket yet.

Examining the strange feelings of relief mixed with a sort of envy that she didn't like, Annie turned and nearly ran into David. Her heart pounded like a jack-in-the-box popping up over and over again. She backed away and stumbled into a chair. "I'm sorry, I didn't see you there."

He looked as shocked to see her as she was to see him. "I just stopped by to get lunches to go for Josiah and Caleb. They're swamped and I had time." He stopped. "Anyway."

"Did you…did you talk to Doctor Corbin?"

"No."

He raised a hand and waved at Naomi. She stuck her pen in her beehive hairdo.

"What'll it be?"

David rattled off an order big enough for five people. Who was paying for all that? Annie brushed aside the thought. "Why didn't you talk to the doctor?" Her voice rose a little. She tried to get it under control. "Don't you want to know?"

"I went by." David put both hands on the counter next to the cash register. He seemed to be contemplating the packages of gum, the bowl of free mints, and the toothpick dispenser. "He wasn't in his office."

"Oh. Well." Annie gnawed at her lower lip. She would've waited in the doctor's office or asked his assistant to track him down. But that was her. Not David. He'd do what he wanted to do when he wanted to do it. When would she learn that? "Nice of you to pick up lunch for the boys."

"I'll tell them you're still calling them boys." He graced her with a small smile. "I don't mind. They're busy, and Josiah claims to be starving."

Annie saw no reason to mention Josiah had left his packed dinner on the kitchen table—again. He really didn't like sandwiches much. "Are you eating with them?"

He shook his head. "Probably not."

Searching for something to say, she let her gaze drop to her dusty shoes. Was it always going to be this awkward? "Charisma got hired on the spot on account of Naomi's niece quitting yesterday and Willow having to leave in the middle of her shift—"

"Willow left in the middle of her shift?" David's tone shifted from ill at ease to fear. "When?"

"Just a minute ago. Violet came and got her. She kept saying it was time—"

David whirled and slammed through the door. Annie watched it swing shut. After a minute she managed to shut her open mouth. Of course, David would know exactly how Willow felt.

Which was why he would never let her get close. As if she didn't feel his loss already. She felt it every day.

Chapter 40

David hurled himself from the hospital elevator and sprinted down the hallway. He dodged an orderly pushing an empty gurney and stumbled around a patient propelling himself in a wheelchair. He didn't know why he ran. It didn't matter. Whatever happened, happened. Kinsey remained, as she always had, in God's capable hands. David's presence had no bearing on her fate. Still, a desperate need to be with her filled him with energy that couldn't be denied. To see her face and let her know he knew what she knew. That nothing people said or did could change what came next. Let her be. Let her go. Go in God's grace.

A knot of people stood in the second floor waiting room. He slowed. The pastor from the First Baptist Church was there with some other folks he didn't recognize. Violet saw him first. "David, it's sweet of you to come." Her voice thickened. "I'm sorry. I know how you and Kinsey hit it off."

She raised her wrinkled hands to her face. Pastor Bailey put a hand on her shoulder. David halted, trying to understand her words. She was offering him condolences "Is she…?"

Pastor Bailey nodded. "She's gone."

"When?" As if it mattered. Gone was gone.

"Just now. Willow arrived in time to spend a few minutes with her before she went."

The fierce, agonizing wave of pain nearly knocked David against the wall. As much as he wanted to speak the words he couldn't. *God's plan. God's will.* Believe it or drown in a vortex of bitterness. The pain sucked the color from the room around him and threatened to turn the air black. He gritted his teeth. *Don't do this. Don't do it.* Not in front of them. As much as he wanted to turn, to make his legs carry him away, he couldn't. He bent over, hands on his thighs, and forced himself to breathe.

A hand touched his arm. He didn't dare look up. "It's all right." Willow's voice, raspy with tears, was close to his ear. "It's all right, David. She told me she wasn't afraid. She said you were right, that there was nothing to be afraid of. She said to tell you…"

Her voice broke. He straightened. "Tell me what?"

"To tell you she's been riding Blackie in her dreams every night. They've…they've leaped over rivers and galloped across the prairies every night since you gave her that first lesson."

David fought with every ounce of his small store of strength to keep the tears from forming. "She's a fanciful child, isn't she?"

"Yes, she was."

Willow's gentle correction undid him. "I'm sorry for your loss."

"I'll never lose her, David." Willow smiled through her tears. "The Bible says love never ends. Kinsey's death doesn't change my love for her. I gained so much by having her in my life, loving her, being her mom. Death can't change that."

"I know." He wrapped his hands around his hat and tried to gain control of his voice. "My life was better having known her too."

Using his last ounce of will, he forced himself to walk, head high, down the hallway and into the elevator. He punched the button and waited for the doors to close. Only then, when the elevator began its silent descent, did he sag against the wall and close his eyes. *Thank You, God, for giving her a few more good days. Thank You for using me. Thank You for letting me know her.*

The darkness receded. Willow was right. Love was stronger than death. Nothing could change that. God used him to help Kinsey live her dream. God used Kinsey to do the same for David. To give him a few more good days. To let him know what it felt like to be a father. He wanted more. More good days. More days with Annie. She deserved them far more than he did. He could make her happy for as long as God let him.

When the doors opened, David didn't head for the entrance. He strode toward Doctor Corbin's office. Every day from now on, for Kinsey's sake, would be a good day.

This is the day which the LORD hath made; we will rejoice and be glad in it.

Chapter 41

Annie waved the grocery list in Josiah's face. A little help would be nice. It had been a long day at the bakery and she still had work to do at home. If they split Leah's list, things would go more quickly and she'd still be home in time to help with supper. "Come on, help me, bruder." She hopped down from the buggy and pointed at the IGA. "Leah only needs a few things, but they're heavy."

"I don't see why I have to come in," Josiah groused. Despite his tone, he climbed down and tied the horse's reins to the long post and cable in front of the store. "I'm sweaty and dirty from working all day. They've got Englisch boys working there who get paid to carry out the groceries."

Annie stepped onto the mat and the automatic door of the IGA swung open. She felt funny having those boys carry her purchases. They always looked at her with such obvious curiosity. Like they'd never seen a girl in a long dress and kapp before. Which obviously they had in a town like Bliss Creek. "In the time we've spent arguing about it, we could be done." Annie marched toward the back of the store. "You get the bags of flour and sugar. I'll get the clothes soap."

He frowned. When his forehead wrinkled like that he looked just like Luke. "Where would the baking stuff be?"

He was being deliberately difficult. "That way." Annie pointed toward aisle two. "I'll get the clothes soap and meet you back here."

Annie didn't like shopping after a long day at work, but Leah had her hands full at home and no buggy available to do shopping even if she could get away. Determined to make this quick, Annie trotted through the aisles without dallying to looking at the displays.

A titter of laughter rang out. A high sound mixed with a lower, husky laugh. Somebody was having a good time on the household cleaning items aisle. Intent on her mission, Annie rounded the corner next to a neat stack of cat food in ten-pound bags. Sarah Kauffman stood in the middle of the aisle, her hands on her hips and a smile on her lips, talking to Peter Blount's son, Daniel. Annie slowed to a halt. They seemed oblivious to the fact that they were blocking her access to the clothes soap.

Just sixteen, Daniel had barreled into his rumspringa full-tilt, as evidenced by his blue jeans, T-shirt, and exaggerated grin. Flexing biceps thick from working on the farm, he picked up a huge box of clothes soap. "I'll carry it. It's way too heavy for a little squirt like you."

"You're such a gentleman." Sarah leaned toward him, a sly grin stretched across her pretty face. "I love a man with good manners."

He stuttered and red blotches formed on his cheeks and neck. "Anything you need carried, I'm the man for you." His long hair flopped on his forehead as he swiveled his head, apparently searching for more big boxes to carry.

Sarah giggled. The high infectious sound that didn't ring true in Annie's ears. That was the giggle that had snared her brother in a briar patch. Packages clutched in her arms, Sarah stood on tiptoes and kissed Daniel's cheek. The splotches on his face grew until his face turned brick red. "What...what...what was that for?"

"For being so sweet." She started down the aisle, but stopped when she saw Annie standing in her path. Her smile faded, but she turned back to Daniel. "Be a sweet pea and help me check out and take these packages to the buggy, will you? Mayor Haag wants me to mop and vacuum the entire house this evening."

"Sure, no problem." Daniel looked from Sarah to Annie and back. "Anything for you, Sarah."

Sarah patted his hand, but her gaze was on Annie. "Hello, Annie. How are you?"

"I'm fine."

Daniel shifted from one foot to the other. The silence stretched. Sarah patted her kapp in a self-conscious gesture. "Well, I have to get these groceries to Mayor Haag's house—"

Annie knew she should let her go without saying anything. That would be the proper thing to do. What would Luke want her to do? What would Emma say? Emma would protect Josiah and anyone else in their community who stood to be hurt, that's what she would do. "What are you doing, Sarah?"

"What do you mean?"

Annie turned to Daniel. "I'm sorry, I don't mean any offense to you."

Daniel's forehead crinkled, making him look like a confused puppy dog. "About what?"

Annie focused on Sarah. "You can't do this."

"Do what? Can't buy groceries?"

"Can't do this to another boy."

"I'm not a boy," Daniel bristled. "I'm sixteen."

"You're starting it all over again."

"I don't know what you're talking about." Sarah whipped around Annie and headed toward the front of the store. Daniel trotted after her, still looking like a faithful puppy following his owner.

"Sarah—"

"Let it go." Annie found herself in the powerful grip of Josiah's big hand. "Stop."

"I can't. She's doing it again." She struggled, but he wouldn't release her. "I'm sorry, but you have to see she's not what she pretends to be. She never has been. Don't you see what she's doing?"

"I do. Get the groceries. Get one of the boys to take the bags to the buggy."

His tone said he expected no argument. Josiah had grown up. He might be younger than her, but he was a man. His hand dropped. Annie rubbed her arm. "I'm sorry—"

"Don't be. I'm older and wiser now. Get the groceries."

She watched his back retreat on the same path through the store that Sarah had taken.

Thank You, God, for helping him grow up.

⊱⊰

Josiah knew the exact feeling that flowed through Daniel Blount at this very moment. That sense of euphoria. There had been a day when Josiah would've walked off a cliff for Sarah without questioning why. Run to the ends of the earth to save her. He'd been sixteen when he met Sarah at the very first Englisch party of his rumspringa. Something about her red hair and blue eyes. Something about the way she looked at him, like he could do no wrong. Something about how sweet and innocent and in need of a protector she seemed.

A sick feeling crept into his stomach. If she couldn't have him, she'd snare another man. Another young boy who would get caught in that web and spend years trying to reconcile his life in this community with the burning desire for something he couldn't have and shouldn't want. Josiah couldn't let that happen.

"Sarah!"

She stood waiting in line at one of the cash registers. She turned and smiled as if she were delighted to see him. "Josiah. I should've known. You and Annie are still two peas in a pod, aren't you?"

Daniel edged a little closer to her, his arms weighted down with her packages. "Hey, Josiah."

"Could I talk to you, Sarah?" He jerked his head toward the door. "Outside."

"I have to buy this stuff for Mayor Haag."

"I'm sure Daniel will hold your spot in the line."

Daniel nodded so hard Josiah was afraid his head would fall off. "No problem, Sarah. Honest, I don't mind."

"Thanks, Danny. You're so sweet."

Her shoes making a tapping sound on the tile, she swept past Josiah. "What's up?"

He waited until they were on the sidewalk to answer. "What are you doing?"

"What do you mean?" She brushed at a spot of grease on his shirt with slim fingers. "I'm buying cleaning supplies for the mayor. What are you doing?"

He gritted his teeth, trying to ignore her sweet scent. "I mean with Daniel."

She grinned. "What's the matter? Are you jealous?"

"No. Not jealous." He fought to keep his voice down as an elderly couple squeezed past them, arguing about whether to buy chicken or hamburger for supper. "I'm not jealous because I'm courting someone else now. But I am worried for Daniel. I know exactly how Daniel will feel about you. He's young. He's only started his running around. Sound familiar?"

"If you're courting someone else, it's none of your business who I see. Anyway, he's just carrying my groceries. You're making a big deal out of nothing."

"Am I? You're playing with him. Just like you played with me. Only you went too far. I left home for you. I asked you to marry me. I fell off a balcony and nearly killed myself."

She tossed her head. Her prayer kapp slid down a notch, revealing a swathe of her beautiful hair. He loved her hair. She smiled up at him as if she knew exactly what he was thinking. "I've moved on. I thought that was what you wanted."

"I do. Just not with Daniel or any other boy in our community." He took two careful steps back. "Move on. Back to Wichita. Leave Daniel alone."

"You're such a worrywart." She smacked his chest, a playful smirk on her face. "He's just carrying my packages, Josiah. Chill out."

"You kissed him."

"Is that what this is about? A kiss?"

"You had him hook, line, and sinker, at that moment." Josiah waited for a woman pushing a stroller to pass. She gave them a curious look, but kept going. "At that moment, I knew. You'll never be a Plain woman. Never. Go home."

Her bravado cracked for a second. Scared eyes stared out at him. "No."

"Yes."

"I can't."

"Call your dad. He'll come get you."

"Come with me."

"No."

She stared at him for a long second. Then she picked up her skirt and turned away. "Mayor Haag will think I've run away with her money. I'd better get back."

"Yes, you'd better get back."

The double doors squeaked, opened, and closed behind her.

She was gone. Best to wait for Annie here. He'd tell Luke about Daniel later, let him mention it to the bishop and Daniel's father. History would not repeat itself.

Chapter 42

David rapped on the door and then walked into Doctor Corbin's office unannounced. Once again no assistant sat in the reception area. Not wanting to wait, he bypassed her desk and stuck his head into the doctor's area. Doctor Corbin looked up from the folder he'd been reading. Surprise on his clean-shaven face, he removed his wire-rimmed glasses, tossed them on the desk, and rubbed his eyes. "David, you read my mind. I sent you a note this morning. When I didn't hear from you, I thought maybe you didn't get it. I know you divide your time between the farm and the bakery—"

"Kinsey died."

Doctor Corbin leaned back in his chair, the creases in his forehead deeper than David had ever seen them. "Yes, but I can't—"

"I know you can't talk to me about other patients." David sank into one of two straight-backed chairs on the other side of the enormous oak desk covered with neat stacks of folders. He removed his hat and smoothed his fingers across the rough straw. "I didn't come here for that."

"Good." Doctor Corbin held up a manila folder. "Let's talk about the results from your last test."

David shook his head. "No."

"What do you mean, no?" His face puzzled, Doctor Corbin laid the folder on his desk. "I need to discuss the—"

"I don't want to know what that paper says."

"Why not?"

David searched for the right words to make the man understand. He didn't have control of his life. God did. God had a plan. David didn't need to know what it was. He only had to believe. Whatever happened, God would take care of him. And of Annie. "There are some things you have to take on faith."

"Faith is important to a patient's recovery, I believe that." Doctor Corbin touched the file. "Medicine is important too. Your treatment is important. These test results are important. You'll want—"

"I'm not going to stop receiving medical care. I want to live." Even as he said those words David knew he would do everything in his power to live—for Annie's sake—but in the end, when it was time to go, he would go willingly. "I want to ask someone something and get an answer before I know the results. Because I have faith. I need to know she does too."

"Okay." His confusion still clear on his face, Doctor Corbin cocked his head. "But at some point, we'll discuss these results and the next step in your treatment?"

"Yes, but right now it's a question of faith."

"It's a question of medicine."

"Faith comes first."

Doctor Corbin studied the papers in front of him. After a few seconds, he lifted his gaze and met David's head-on. "Come see me when you're ready."

David wanted to go to the bakery now and talk to Annie, but he wouldn't. He would wait for the right time to have the conversation in private. Quietly. The prayer service would be at the Shiracks' farm this Sunday. Afterwards, they could go for a walk. He'd ask her the question he should've asked her six months ago. He would do this properly. "On Monday. I'll come talk to you on Monday."

"I respect what you're doing. Most of my patients are tearing down my door, trying to get their results. I've had patients stalk me even when they know I don't have their results yet." Doctor Corbin stood and offered a hand to David. "You're a brave soul."

The thought of not knowing whether the chemo had worked or whether he faced more excruciating treatments didn't sit as heavy on him as it once had. David accepted the doctor's hand. "I'm not brave. I have faith."

✻

Annie laid the last dish on the rack and dried her hands. All the dishes were washed, but no one was in sight to dry them. Leah was putting the twins to bed. Charisma hadn't come home from the restaurant yet. Annie glanced at the clock. Eight o'clock. Almost bedtime. It would only take a few minutes to dry the bread pans and cookie sheets and put them away. Ignoring a sudden weariness, she wiped the towel in her hands across a pot. At least it was quiet. She needed time to absorb the news Luke had brought to the supper table. Kinsey no longer suffered. She lay in the arms of her Savior. Annie couldn't keep her thoughts from going to David. She wanted to go to him, but uncertainty held her back. He wouldn't want her to witness his sadness. It would be a painful time of letting go for him. Like losing a daughter.

If he had one. The thought pierced her heart. David would see his own passing in Kinsey's. All the lost days. All the lost chances to be a husband and father. Hot tears burned her eyes. She mourned those lost days too. She mourned her lost opportunity to be a wife to David and to be a mother to his children. She bowed her head and prayed. *I'm selfish, God. Please forgive me for not understanding. Help me accept this as Your will. Thy will be done.*

Determined to look forward from now on, she grabbed another wet pan. They would have lots of work to do in the morning. They had the prayer service on Sunday, which meant Saturday would be spent scouring the place from top to bottom. Mark could mow the grass. Josiah and Luke would pick up the benches and get them set up with help from the onkels and Thomas.

Tomorrow would be a full day, as would Sunday.

She counted the loaves of bread. Two zucchini, two banana, two pumpkin. And fifteen dozen peanut butter, chocolate chip, and oat-meal-raisin cookies. A good start. With all the desserts others would bring, there should be plenty.

"It smells really good in here." Charisma traipsed into the kitchen, Luke David in one arm, the diaper bag in the other. Gracie trundled along behind her, humming a song Annie didn't recognize. "Look at all these cookies."

Tossing the bag on the floor, she plopped down in a chair and reached for a cookie. "It was nice of your brother to come pick me up, even if he did keep his mouth shut the entire trip home. You'd think I bite or something. Hmmm, I'm starved."

"You didn't eat at the restaurant?"

"Employees get a fifty percent discount, but I didn't want to use my tip money for that. I won't get a paycheck for two weeks, and I have to pay Sadie's daughter for watching the kids." Charisma talked with her mouth full, making the words garbled. "She's so nice, she practically refused to take the tips I made today."

"Deborah is sweet. Not like her brothers." What made her say that? Annie wiped harder on a cookie sheet. "I mean she likes to help. Not that her brothers don't."

"Whatever." Charisma stole another cookie. "Guess who came into the restaurant this afternoon after you left."

"I don't know. Shall I warm up the brisket for you?" Annie pulled leftovers from the refrigerator. "There's fried potatoes and green beans."

"Sure, sure." Charisma handed Gracie a cookie and snatched another one from the tray. "Sergeant Parker came in. I served him at the counter. I think he sat there because it was part of my station."

"What makes you say that?"

"The hostess was going to seat him in Bertie's section, but he asked for me."

"Maybe he wanted to see how you're doing."

"Yeah, he did. But he also wanted to tell me they have room for Logan at the prison after all. He's being moved to Lansing on Monday."

Her voice didn't betray any particular emotion. Annie turned to look at her. Charisma seemed very interested in the oatmeal-raisin cookie in her hand.

"Will you visit him before he goes?"

"Sergeant Parker says Logan asked him to tell me he wants to see me."

"Are you going?"

"I don't know. No."

"Why not?"

She laid the half-eaten cookie on the table. "I can't. I can't face him. He'll want me to promise to wait for him and I can't. I just can't."

"Then you should tell him the truth."

"I did that last time and he practically had a meltdown."

"He's going to jail for five years, Charisma, for something he did for you."

"Don't you think I know that? I wake up at night and think about it." She shifted Luke David to her other arm. With a delicate finger, she traced the sleeping baby's nose and chin. "But I didn't tell him to rob you. I didn't tell him to do anything. He could've worked. Like I'm doing now."

Annie didn't bother to point out that Charisma had one day under her belt as an employed waitress. She had a long way to go to prove she could support her children. A long way before she could live on her own with them. Far longer than Leah would like.

She set the plate of food in front of Charisma and sliced a hunk of bread for her. "Don't judge him. He loves you." Annie held out her arms. Charisma handed over the baby. "He loves his babies. That kind of love is a precious thing."

"I know." Charisma picked up a fork, then laid it down. "I wish I could feel it, but I can't. He'll get over it."

Annie stared out the window over the wash tub. Charisma spoke like someone who had never really been in love. It wasn't her fault. She'd been robbed of the chance to have those feelings by a father who lifted a hand in anger instead of offering it in love. *God, please heal her heart. Let her feel love as it was meant to be. Smooth the scars left by her father. She deserves love.*

Everyone deserved love.

Chapter 43

Josiah adjusted the space between the two benches in the third and fourth rows. Mark had shoved them too close together. In a barn this big, there was no need to be stingy with the space. He straightened and surveyed his work. The men needed more room for their long legs and big bodies. No one liked to sit too close to the man next to him for a three-hour service. It was mighty uncomfortable trying to squeeze into a space more suited to a woman. Especially on a hot July morning. He wanted everything to be ready so he could take a quick trip out to the road to look for Miriam. He needed to see her. He needed to talk to her.

"Looks fine." Luke slid his hat back so it rested high on his head. "Everything's ready. Which is good. The bishop just arrived, and the deacons right behind him."

"Is the food ready?"

"Jah." Luke smiled. "Leah has been a whirlwind since before dawn. I don't think there's any room for the food people will bring."

The Glicks and the Beaches sauntered through the open barn doors. The women were chattering like a flock of birds, and Luke hurried off to greet them. His brother felt the weight of responsibility more than Josiah did. He figured the point was the prayer service, not all the trappings. It was important to get it right, but it was more important to be in worship. Of course, if things didn't go smoothly, Luke would be the one to hear about it, not Josiah.

He dodged the now steady stream of people flowing into the barn and made it out to the corral. The field beyond it housed a dozen buggies and more were arriving. It almost felt like a celebration. Thankful for a slight breeze, he inhaled the warm, moist morning air. Miriam and her family should be here soon. Maybe they could get away for a walk by the creek after the service. He could tell her she didn't have to worry about Sarah anymore. He was ready to be baptized. Ready to move on.

"Josiah, there you are."

One hand up in a wave, Sarah picked her way across the field. She wore a long dress, apron, cape, and prayer kapp, the picture of a Plain woman. Except she wasn't. Not even close. Josiah swallowed a groan. "What are you doing here? I told you to go home."

"Don't be like that." She skirted the corral fence until they were face-to-face. "I didn't get a chance to tell you at the grocery store that I met with Deacon Altman earlier in the week. He said I could sit in the back and observe. It's important for me to see how you worship before any decisions are made."

"You still plan to join the community?"

"Yes."

Josiah paced the fence line. "Did you tell the bishop about Daniel?"

"No. Daniel's just a friend." She stepped into Josiah's path, forcing him to stop. "He's not very old, but he's mature—like all you Plain men."

He dodged her and resumed his pacing. "You think you'll get me back by doing this. You won't."

"I know you love me, but that's beside the point." She folded her arms, looking every inch an Amish woman. Never had looks been so deceiving. "I want to be a part of this community."

"You never did before. How did this happen?"

Sarah put both hands on the top railing of the fence and leaned in to it. "I watched your sisters at the hospital in Wichita. They were so into their faith. They didn't even think about cheating. You know, like watching TV or listening to music or using the microwave to make popcorn. They wouldn't even read the magazines in the waiting room. They weren't even tempted. They believe so much. I want to believe too."

Josiah had almost no recollection of his time in the hospital, but he believed what Sarah said about his sisters. They were strong in their adherence to the Ordnung. Unlike him. "Then leave Daniel alone."

"You're so jealous. You're still into me." She reached up and touched his cheek, a feather of a touch. "I'd dump Daniel in a heartbeat if you'd come back to me."

"It's not jealousy. It's concern for Daniel's feelings."

"He'll get over it. Tell me you'll come back to me, and I'll ignore his flashlight in the window."

"You'll not have the chance." Deacon Altman strode toward them, his long skinny legs pumping. "Daniel Blount's father came to see me this morning."

"Daniel's father?" She had the good grace to flush. "What did he want?"

"You know perfectly well what he wanted." Deacon Altman panted a little. He stopped, shoulder to shoulder with Josiah. "Your invitation to join us for the prayer service this morning has been revoked. We've spoken among ourselves, and we don't feel you are truly ready to join our community. Give it a year and if you still feel convicted, come talk to me again. In the meantime, please go about your business."

Sarah's chin rose, then fell. Without another word she whirled and stalked away, an exit made difficult by her shoes sinking in the dirt. The burden on Josiah's shoulders slipped away. No regrets lingered. The sun seemed brighter and the sky bluer, his sight clearer. He met the deacon's gaze head-on. "Danki."

The older man clapped his shoulder. "Come, we don't want to be late."

Together they walked toward the barn. At the door, he let his gaze roam across the women's side. *There.* Miriam sat with her mother and sisters. At that moment she glanced up. After a covert peek at her mother, she raised one hand an inch over her lap and gave him a tiny wave. Conscious of the crowd, he bobbed his head. She smiled and dropped her gaze to the floor.

"Glad that's finally resolved." David stood next to him. He'd come up so quietly Josiah looked to see if he was barefooted. "It took you long enough."

"Courting is private."

David grinned. "Yes, it is."

Josiah studied his friend's face. He hadn't seen that smile in a very long time. A good day got even better. "You talked to Annie?"

"No."

"Then why are you grinning like a coyote in the chicken coop?"

"None of your business."

Sure his own face would split from the size of his smile, Josiah sank on to a bench. It was good day to give thanks.

Chapter 44

Annie poured tea into three glasses, added chunks of ice from the pile melting in a pan, and handed the glasses to Emma and Miriam. Then she took a sip from hers. The service was over. They'd made it through. She usually enjoyed having the service at their farm, but today it had been full of drama that took her focus from worship and the fellowship that followed. Word had spread quickly of Sarah's dismissal by Deacon Altman. Josiah had looked distracted during the prayer service and she was sure she'd seen David nod off.

His terse request after the service to talk to her "later" bumped around inside her head, making it impossible to concentrate on anything. Why wouldn't he tell her about the test results? What did he want to talk about? "It's terrible to say, but I don't think I heard a word the deacon said this morning. Does that make me awful?"

Miriam stacked plates without looking up. "I found it hard to concentrate too."

"Because of Sarah?" Emma set down her glass with a clunk. "She's gone for good."

Miriam picked up a towel and wiped at the counter. "After Friday night I thought all was well. I thought we were on the right road. Then this morning, I saw them together at the corral. Not looking like anything but a couple."

303

"He was telling her to leave." Annie tugged the towel from her. "I'll dry, you wash."

"Deacon Altman told her to leave. Josiah looked…distracted during the service."

"But he was smiling afterwards. I saw him looking at you, smiling." Annie wanted to do something to wipe that look of uncertainty from her friend's face. "What did he say to you?"

"Exactly what David said to you. He wants to talk to me later."

Annie scrubbed the roast pan harder than necessary. "Let's talk about something else. How are you feeling, Emma?"

"I feel like David must. People are always asking how I am." Emma slid a handful of dirty silverware into the tub. "I'm fine. It's nice that Thomas and I will have the afternoon to ourselves, though. His parents took Rebecca, Eli, and the twins to their house for an afternoon of swimming at the pond. I love them so much, but the peace will be nice."

"I'm glad Thomas's parents have embraced Lillie and Mary. It's like they have another set of grandparents." Annie didn't give voice to the rest of that thought. Daed and Mudder were always present in her thoughts. "It's nice for them."

"Let's get these dishes washed so we can go out to the barn." Miriam passed a casserole dish to Annie. "The sooner we get out there, the sooner David will have the chance to whisk you away on a walk and Thomas can take Emma home for a quiet afternoon alone."

"And Josiah can take you for a buggy ride." Annie grabbed another plate and wiped it dry, moving more quickly at the thought. "This afternoon we all get a chance to see what God has planned for us."

What God wanted. Annie believed He wanted them to be wives and mothers and sisters and friends who were there for each other through it all.

"I'll help. The kids are down for naps."

To Annie's surprise, Charisma stood in the doorway. She had taken the children into town to put gas in the van long before the service started. She said she wanted to start driving to work on Monday. To

Annie, it seemed a waste of her hard-earned tips. She could've spent the money on the children. But it wasn't up to Annie. Besides, Charisma's absence was for the best. Sarah's visit had been enough of a distraction. "We can always use more help."

"I would've served food too if you wanted." A big smile on her face, Charisma lifted both arms and flexed like a fighter. "I'm back in shape as a waitress now."

"No need, but we'll take your help on the dishes." Emma smiled broadly at the young woman. "Let's take some iced tea and lemonade to the men first. They're loading the benches. They'll be parched."

"Maybe I better let y'all do that part." Charisma's grin disappeared, replaced with an uncertain frown. "I don't want to get in the way, being a what-you-call-it, you know, Englischer."

Annie burst out laughing, Emma and Miriam with her. "It's fine. The bishop and the deacons are gone. Only our men are out there loading up. They'll welcome the visit."

Our men. Annie wished it were so. Maybe David would have good news. Maybe they would finally overcome the stumbling block. Have a little faith, he'd said. The words still rankled. As if she hadn't been the faithful one all along. She handed a pitcher to Charisma. "You take the lemonade. I'll bring the tea. Emma, you and Miriam get the glasses."

"Bossy!" Emma's smile belied the words. "Let's go."

Taking the lead, Annie headed for the back door. Both hands on the heavy glass pitcher, she used her shoulder to push through the screen door.

"Stop."

An enormous black gun appeared in her face, the thick snout even with her nose. Its presence blocked out everything. The sun. The wind. The future.

The soft, southern accent registered. It couldn't be.

Logan was in jail.

Annie jerked back and the pitcher slipped from her hands. It crashed to the floor, the noise loud in her ears. Cool, sticky wet liquid lapped around her bare feet.

Not again.

"Annie, look what you've done! Now we'll have to mop—"

The gun swung toward Emma. Annie staggered back and grabbed her sister's arm. "It's Logan McKee."

His face bruised and his nose covered with dried blood, Logan pushed through the screen door. He still wore the orange jumpsuit from jail. One arm hung limp at his side.

"Logan!" Charisma whispered the name as if she couldn't quite be sure he really stood in front of her. "What are you doing here? How…?"

"I came for you." His bloody lips turned up in a smile. "You wouldn't come to see me, so I had to come to see you. Whatever happens now, it's your fault."

"It's not my fault you robbed a bakery." Charisma slapped her hands on her hips and stood firm, her feet spread. "Listen here, Logan Derek McKee, I didn't ask you to do nothing like this. These are good people. You can't be barging in here pointing a gun at them. They took care of me and your babies."

"Don't Logan Derek McKee me." His chin, covered with the wispy beginnings of a dark beard, trembled. "You made me love you. That's what you did."

"I didn't make you do nothing you didn't already wanna do."

"I ain't got time for arguing. I'm gonna get you out of here and I'm gonna take care of you and my babies." He waved the gun around. "Back up, all of you."

Annie wrapped a hand around Miriam's arm. Emma grabbed her hand. Together, the three of them back-stepped into the kitchen. The sense that she had done this before overwhelmed Annie. *Step, step, step.* Finally they were up against the kitchen counter. The ragged breathing, the scent of fresh baked bread, the gun—it was all so familiar.

"How did you get here?" Only Charisma didn't move. She remained rooted to the spot, the pitcher of tea still in her hands, blocking Logan from Annie, Miriam, and Emma. "You're supposed to go to prison tomorrow."

A tear trailed down his bruised cheek. "I had to come for you."

"So you broke out of jail?" Charisma sounded as if she were scolding a small child instead of a man with a gun in his hand. "You idiot. You didn't hurt Sergeant Parker or that nice Officer Bingham, did you?"

"I heard them talking about moving me to Lansing tomorrow. They take turns on Sundays—only Bingham was there and I owed him for messing me up when he arrested me."

"Did you hurt him?" Charisma's voice climbed higher with each word. Annie wanted to tell her to calm down, but she was afraid to draw attention to herself. "He's a police officer. You added escaping and assaulting an officer to your charges. Instead of five years, it'll be a hundred or something."

"He hurt me worse than I did him." Logan pointed at his bruised face. "How do you think I got this? Huh? I jumped him when he came to give me my lunch. Wrestled him down, grabbed his night stick, whacked him a good one, then sprayed him with his own pepper spray. He still ran after me, grabbed his gun from his desk, and grazed my arm."

"How'd you get out here?"

"Hotwired a car in a church parking lot."

"Lord have mercy," Charisma whispered.

Logan eased into the open space between the prep table and the stove. "I'm not going to prison. I came for you and my babies. I'm taking you all far, far away from here. Where are they?"

"They're napping."

"Get them."

"No." Charisma set the pitcher on the table so hard the lemonade slopped over the side and splashed on the floor. More sticky wetness. "You're not the boss of me no more. I'm not taking two babies on a wild chase with a fugitive from the law. I may be dumb, but I'm not stupid."

"Yeah, you will." Logan trained the gun on Charisma's face. "You will. Move. All of you."

Together, they sidestepped into the living room. Annie peeked at Logan's face. He looked so determined, yet so frightened. Sometimes fear made people do awful things. Sometimes love got so twisted around, a person couldn't see the line between good and bad. Logan wasn't bad. Just mixed up. *God, please soften Logan's heart. Don't let him hurt anyone. Especially the babies. He would never forgive himself. He still has a chance to be redeemed, doesn't he? Please God, forgive him.*

She sidled closer. "Logan, are you hungry? Do you need something to drink? I'm sure you didn't get any dinner—"

"What is all this noise? You woke the babies!" Leah stomped down the stairs, a twin on each hip. Esther had a roly-poly fist in her mouth, slobber running down her cheeks, while Martha cried in a high pitched wail. "This is naptime around here…"

She stopped halfway down the stairs. Her mouth gaped open, then abruptly snapped shut.

"Logan is here." Annie almost laughed at how silly that obvious statement sounded. "He wanted to speak with Charisma."

"Speak with Charisma? That's a gun."

"Yeah, it's a gun. I'm sorry, ma'am." He waved it toward Annie and the other women. "Get over there with them…please."

Something about Leah and her bossiness seemed to have reached Logan. He took a step back. Leah passed in front of him, her gaze glued to Annie's. Annie put her arms out to take one of the babies. Leah shook her head, her face white. Annie understood. At a time like this, Leah needed to keep her children close.

"Are William and Joseph asleep still?" Annie asked.

"Jah, they're sleeping." Leah whispered. Her grip on the girls tightened and Martha whimpered. Leah rocked her back and forth on one hip. "I pray to God they don't wake up to this. They'll be—"

"Shut up. Everyone just shut up!" Logan paced the length of the room. "I need to think."

"I only wanted to help," Annie whispered. "I didn't mean for this to happen."

"Nobody could've known he would do this." Leah's voice quivered, but she sniffed and kissed little Esther's curly hair. "No one. What kind of man does this?"

Emma squeezed between them and put an arm around Leah and then Annie. "Whatever happens, God is with us. He has a plan."

The words were as comforting as her sister's presence. After everything Emma had been through she still had a rock-solid faith. Annie clung to that thought as she sought out Miriam's gaze. They'd already been through so much together. "How are you, Miriam?"

Miriam smiled. "No matter what happens, we'll be all right. God is with us."

Annie smiled back. "God is with us."

Seemingly oblivious to their whispering, Logan paced the floor. He plowed to a stop in front of the window. "Where are all the men? Why aren't there any men in here?"

❧

David snatched his hat from his head and flapped it in front of his sweaty face. The morning breeze had given way to a breathless still. He wiped perspiration from his fuzz-covered head, wishing it would rain and be done with it. No work could be done in the fields today, anyway. "It's time to start having these services in the cellar."

"I reckon the one in two weeks at the Blounts' will be in their cellar. Lot cooler down there, but more crowded." Thomas shoved another bench on the back of the wagon. "I could sure use a glass of iced tea to wet my whistle."

"I'm surprised the women haven't been out with some already." Luke wiped his face with a sodden handkerchief. "Mark, go up to the house and see what they're doing. They're probably so busy gabbing they forgot to take care of their share of the work."

"Taking care of us, you mean?" Grinning, Mark hopped down from the wagon. "Maybe they can bring out some more cookies too."

"You must have a hollow leg." David had personally seen Luke's little brother eat at least six cookies, maybe more. That after a full plate of pulled pork on a bun, potato salad, coleslaw, and barbecued beans. "You eat enough for four men."

"He's growing." Luke laughed and slapped Mark on the back. His laugh trailed away. "Who's that coming?"

David followed his gaze out to the dirt road that wound its way from the highway through the Shiracks' wheat, corn, and alfalfa fields to the barn and on to the house. A black and white car with the words BLISS CREEK POLICE painted on the side sped toward them, dust billowing behind it. The car moved much too fast for the pitted dirt road. It bounced and swerved around a curve.

Something about its urgency sent an uneasy ripple through David. He started toward the road. "That's Sergeant Parker from the police department, isn't it?"

"What's he doing here on a Sunday afternoon?" Luke didn't sound too concerned. The Plain people had few dealings with law enforcement, and they liked it that way. "Logan McKee's trial was over almost two weeks ago."

Josiah tossed aside the sliver of grass he'd been chewing on. "Maybe Charisma did something when she was in town getting gas."

"I doubt that. She's a little off, but not that off." Luke started toward the open area next to the corral where buggies parked. "She has children to think about."

Luke was right. David followed him to the edge of the corral. The car slid to a stop, its bumper just shy of the fence. Sergeant Parker shoved his door open and flew out. "Y'all have company?" he barked without so much as a howdy. "Did he show up?"

"Who? What are you talking about?"

Officer Bingham hobbled around the back end of the car. Blood had dried around his nose and upper lip. One hand wrapped around his arm, he limped toward them, looking like he'd fought a bear and lost. "Logan McKee—"

A crack of a single shot and the sound of shattering glass stopped the officer's explanation dead. He spun around and started toward the house.

"Never mind. He's here."

Chapter 45

Annie struggled free from Emma's grasp. She hurled herself toward the row of windows.

"No!" Leah gasped. "Annie, no! Stay back!"

Annie didn't look back. She couldn't. She'd brought this into Leah's house. Her sister-in-law only wanted a peaceful, Plain home for her children. For William, Joseph, Esther, and Martha. And now a little unborn bobbeli. *Please God, please, protect them. And protect our men out there.* It could be Luke. Josiah. Thomas. It could be David. Or Mark. Family. Friends. Through the broken glass she could see Mark cowering on the ground. Had he been hit? *Oh, God, please put Your arms around him and hold him tight.* "Don't shoot. That's my little brother. Please. He won't hurt you!"

His body shielded by the living room wall, Logan peered out the broken window. "Get away! Get back now or I'll blow your head off."

Annie ducked around Logan.

"Go back to the barn, Mark," she yelled. "He wants you to leave."

Mark rolled up in a ball and stopped moving. Probably so scared he couldn't.

Logan jerked Annie back and pulled the trigger again. The blast hurt Annie's ears and the acrid smell of gun powder burned her nose. Leah dropped to the floor and covered the screaming twins with her body, Emma close at her side. Miriam whimpered, then covered her mouth with her hand.

"What are you doing? Stop it! Stop it!" Charisma ran at Logan, her arms flailing. "You can't shoot these people. They helped me. They took care of your baby."

Logan tossed her away with the back of his free arm. She landed on the floor, sprawled like a rag doll. "I said get away from the house!" Logan pounded on the wall with his free hand. "Don't you hear me?"

"Is someone hurt out there? Is it Luke?" Leah bounced up from the floor. "Is it Mark?"

"Get down. Now!" Logan glared at Leah. She backed away, but her expression said she'd like to take Logan to the woodshed. She knelt by the twins. Logan turned his back on the woman and gazed out the window, his gun ready. "Get out of here or I'll shoot again!"

"It's Mark. He's too scared to run." Annie clasped her hands tightly in front of her to keep them from trembling. Somehow she managed to get the words out without yelling. "He's afraid. He's just a boy."

"It's some kind of trick." The gun dipped and swayed in Logan's hand. "Come on, Charisma, get up. Get Gracie and the baby. They'll be coming after me. Hurry!"

"I can't do that. They're babies. They're safe here." Charisma rolled up on her knees and raised her hands. "Can't you see? This is bad, Logan. This is wrong. These are good people. They've taken care of us. They've provided for Luke David and Gracie and me. Please, please don't do this."

Movement in the yard caught the corner of Annie's eye. She peeked over Logan's shoulder. David sped across the open space between the barn and the house. He grabbed Mark under the arms and hoisted him to his feet. Together, they disappeared behind the corral fence. *Thank You, God.*

Next to the corral fence sat a Bliss Creek police car. "They're already here. Look. There's Sergeant Parker's car."

Logan followed her gaze. "How did they know I'd come here?"

"Because they know you love your babies." Charisma slapped a hand to her cheek. "They know you couldn't leave without the people you love."

"That's right. I love you, Charisma." The gun sank to his side and dangled from his hand. "I love you."

Charisma sat in the middle of the living room floor, her hands to her tear-soaked cheeks. "I know you do, babe, but you have to do the right thing. Don't hurt these people. They're the only good people I have in my life now. They showed me how to be a good mom. They showed me how God loves me, no matter how much I've screwed up. They showed me that it wasn't my fault my dad was so mad all the time. Don't you see?"

Calm stole over Annie. It had been worth it. God had provided for Charisma when she most needed His help. Now God would provide for them. She spoke up: "If you love Charisma and Luke David and Gracie, don't do this."

Emma's hand sought Annie. She shook her head, and Annie tugged free. She moved closer to Logan. "This isn't how you show love. You love people by keeping them safe, not by putting them in danger. By doing this, you're making it so you'll never get to be the father you want to be."

"It's the only way left. You, in the green dress, you go upstairs and bring down anyone left up there." The gun reared up and pointed at Miriam. "I want my babies down here now. And anyone else who's up there. You don't come right back, and I'll have to hurt someone down here."

"No, the boys—" Leah's stoic façade cracked a bit. Her voice quivered. "They're just little boys. They're sleeping. Leave them be."

"No. Bring them."

"Don't worry, Leah. I'll take care of them." Her face the picture of calm, Miriam nodded reassuringly. "I'll be right back. It'll just take a second to wake the boys so don't be nervous."

Leah returned the nod, but her breathing took on a ragged sound.

Miriam scampered up the steps. No one moved. Annie wasn't sure anyone breathed. After a few seconds, Leah scooted into the rocking chair, but she didn't rock the twins, who blessedly snuggled against her chest, their crying subsiding. It seemed years, but surely it was only a few minutes before Miriam reappeared, Luke David in her arms and Gracie and the boys clutching at her long skirt as she guided them down the stairs.

"Where's Daed?" William rubbed his sleepy eyes with small fists. "Is it time to eat? I'm hungry."

"Your daed is working." Leah stood. "With me, boys, quickly now."

"Daddy, Daddy!" Gracie crowed. She let go of Miriam's skirt and nearly tumbled down the stairs. Annie caught her by the arms and lifted her to safety. She trotted toward Logan, but Charisma scooped up her daughter before she could reach him.

"No, baby, not now."

"It's okay, baby. Daddy loves you." Logan held out a hand to Charisma. She took it and he hoisted her to her feet. "Everyone back to the kitchen. Move. We'll go out the back door."

David sank to the ground behind Sergeant Parker's car. Each breath hurt his chest a little more. Mark dropped to his knees and huddled next to David. Bewilderment and fear mingled in the boy's face. The smell of sweat permeated the air. David sucked in air. "Are you all right?"

"Who was that?" Mark panted for a second. Shock turned his skin ashen, making his freckles stand out across his upturned nose. He held on to the corral post with both hands, his knuckles white. "Why is someone shooting from our house?"

Shoulders hunched as if expecting another barrage of shots, Luke squatted in the grass next to the boy and put one big hand on his shoulder. "Are you hurt, little bruder?"

"I bit my lip when I threw myself down, but I'm all right." He huddled close to David. "Danki, David. I got too scared to move."

"You're welcome." David hadn't thought much about it. Instinct had governed every move. He couldn't leave a boy out there in the open. Now that it was done, his entire body trembled. "Shots coming out of your own house would've scared anybody."

"Next time leave rescues to the professionals. The ones with guns." Sergeant Parker turned and peeked over the front end of his car. He looked down at David, frustration lining his face. "We could've fired back, given each other cover."

"We don't want you firing back." David rolled up on his knees and planted both hands on the car's warm metal. "That's a house full of women and *kinner*. We'll find a peaceful solution. He's only one man."

"You'll not do anything. This is a police matter." Sergeant Parker slapped a cell phone to his ear. "I'm calling for help. I can have the county sheriff here in about fifteen minutes. He'll bring in half the state if we need them."

Hunched down low, Josiah scurried after him. "Annie and Miriam and Emma are in there—"

"My fraa and the boys and the bobbelis," Thomas broke in. "A houseful of women and kinner. How are you planning to get them out safely?"

"Logan McKee won't hurt women and children." Sergeant Parker ducked through the corral gate and started talking on the phone.

"Unless you back him into a corner." Officer Bingham dabbed at the blood on his lip with an already soaked handkerchief. "He didn't mind whaling on me."

"I don't think he'll hurt them. He just wants to leave with Charisma and his children." David pictured the man who'd robbed the bakery, terrorizing five women. "Let us talk to him."

"He's a desperate man." Officer Bingham winced. His hand went to his bloody face. "Who knows what he'll do? That's why the boss is calling in the troops."

David exchanged looks with Luke, Thomas, and Josiah. They had to be thinking the same thing. Troops. A shootout. Hostages in the middle. The Englischers would use force to get what they wanted.

"This is my home. I've been host to Charisma and her children for almost two months." Luke spoke softly, his tone persuasive. "Let me at least try."

"He took a shot at your little brother there." Officer Bingham shook his head. "We need a professional hostage negotiator and a SWAT team."

David tilted his head toward Luke. He nodded. They edged away from the car, staying low, but moving fast until they reached the far side of the barn. Thomas and Josiah, Mark in tow, joined them seconds later.

"What do we do?" Josiah asked. "We can't let them turn our house into a firing range."

"If we could just talk to him." The lines in his face deepened by concern, Thomas tugged at his beard with calloused fingers. "He's here to get Charisma and his kinner. That's all. He doesn't want to hurt anyone."

"They'll never let him leave with the bobbelis," Josiah said. "He's broken their laws."

"I understand that, but isn't the safety of the women and children more important?" Luke gripped the fence railing. "Isn't resolving this peacefully more important than their laws?"

"They don't think Charisma and his bobbeli will be safe with him." Josiah's time among the Englisch made him the expert in the group, despite the fact that he was younger. "They shouldn't be forced to go with him against their will either."

"You think she doesn't want to go with him?" Luke looked puzzled. "She stayed here all this time, waiting to see what would happen to him."

David shook his head. "I don't know. On that trip we took to Wakefield, I got the impression she was looking for a place to go. Her plan didn't seem to include him."

"Forget waiting for the sheriff." Josiah whirled and started toward the house. "I'll talk to him."

Thomas shot after him. He grabbed his arm and jerked him to a stop. "It's not our way to intervene in law enforcement."

"I'm not waiting for a team of armed Englischers to go in there." Josiah struggled to free himself, but Thomas had the strong grip of a man who toiled daily in the fields. "They'll destroy our home."

"Nobody wants that, but it's in God's hands now."

David couldn't let their wrangling waste any more precious time. He focused on Luke. "Let me try to talk to him, Luke. While you convince the officers to hold off. Let me try."

Luke's gaze meandered to the house in the distance. "We should wait for the sheriff."

How could David explain the feeling that he was meant for this task? "Let me do this."

Luke wrapped long fingers around his suspenders. He blew out air. "We should get the bishop and the deacons out here. See how they feel it should be handled."

"There's no time."

"They might think we should not interfere."

"Not interfere!" Josiah's eyes blazed with emotion. "They're going to interfere with guns. We only want to talk to a man who is in our house."

Luke's hands fisted. When he saw David eying them, he shook them lose. "I should speak with him. It's my house. My fraa is expecting. She's in there with my boys."

"My fraa is in there too." Thomas crossed his arms. "I should go."

"I'm a better talker than either of you," said David. No arguing with that. Luke and Thomas were two of the most taciturn people David had ever known. "I have no children to leave fatherless. I might not even be here much longer myself."

Luke's bleak gaze didn't waver. At last, he breathed again. "Jah. If the bishop has a problem with our actions, I'll take the reprimand."

"We'll all stand together on it." David jerked his head toward the officers. "Keep them talking."

Thomas and Luke edged toward the officers, both engrossed in a discussion with someone on the phone. David eased toward the buggies, the police car, and Charisma's van, all parked on the other side of the corral. If he could get beyond them, he could make his way along the row of trees that lined the road from the corral to the house. It was the most cover he could get.

After a minute or two, footsteps told him he was being followed. He glanced back. Josiah. "What are you doing?"

"Going with you."

"No. I'll not endanger another member of the Shirack family."

Crouched low to the ground, Josiah closed the gap between them. "You endanger no one. I'm responsible for myself. I won't stand by and let something happen to my best friend and the girl I…" He ducked his head and didn't finish the thought.

The girl he loved. David understood that. He prayed God would see fit to bring Annie and her loved ones through this. *God, they're in Your hands. Today was supposed to be a good day. Is it selfish to want more of those days?* "Stay behind me and keep quiet."

"What's the plan?"

"Only God knows. I'm following Him."

Josiah nodded and breathed a soft *amen*.

Together they angled across the road and ducked behind the porch. Birds sang in an elm tree that shadowed the west side of the house. The sweet trilling sound made David think of long-ago picnics in the Shirack yard, making homemade ice cream and playing volleyball. Memories that soothed away the chilled fear that snaked its way up his arms.

Motioning for Josiah to stay out of sight, David edged around the side of the house. The back door stood open. He eased up to the screen door and glanced back. Josiah had his head stuck out so he could see what was happening. David shook his head. *Stay back.*

Josiah glared and disappeared behind the wall.

No new options presented themselves. Drawing himself up to his full six feet, David knocked. Pure and simple. A double rap.

A gun appeared in the doorway. "I've got a gun and I'll use it. Whoever's out there, leave, before I hurt someone."

"Logan, it's David Plank." Both hands in the air, David sidled in front of the screen door. "My mother is Sadie, the woman who owns the bakery. I don't have a gun. I don't have anything at all. I just want to talk to you."

"Get out of here!" Logan McKee trained the gun on David. It shook so hard David couldn't tell if he was aiming for the head or his chest. It seemed unlikely he could hit anything with hands trembling like that, but the fear in his voice said he would likely try. "Do you have a death wish? I've got a bunch of hostages in here."

No death wish. In fact, a desire to live that burned so intensely, David's body shivered with it. "I know. That's what I wanted to talk to you about. The police are out there and they're planning who knows what to bring this to an end." David removed his hat and held it in both hands. "I wanted to see if we couldn't end this peacefully."

Logan shoved the screen door open. "Get in here."

Stumbling on the second step in his haste, David managed to get in the door without a shot being fired. *Danki, God.*

The first person he saw was Annie. She filled his vision. Whole. Safe. So far.

Again, danki, God.

Then she opened her mouth.

"David, why?" Her green eyes stood out against skin so pale it was almost transparent. "Why give him another hostage? Why you? You're sick."

Because you're here, he wanted to say, but he didn't. With God's provision, there would be time for that later. If not, she would come to understand with time. "I'm not so sick I couldn't come here to talk with a man about his troubles. Where are the others?"

"In the living room." Her voice held steady. "Logan didn't want them to get shot if you were the police coming in the back door. He doesn't want to hurt anyone and he knows they won't try to escape."

A polite kidnapper and perfect hostages. Plain women and children who would simply accept the situation as one only God could control. The idea chafed at David for a fleeting second, but then he nodded. "Thank God they're all right."

"They're fine." Annie nodded at him, her tone encouraging. "They'll wait for us."

Time to try to calm troubled waters. He edged forward so he stood between Annie and her captor. "You know your son was named for me and the man who is the head of this house, Luke Shirack. Luke has provided a home for Charisma and your children while you've been in jail."

"I know that. I appreciate y'all taking them in. I don't want to hurt nobody." Logan's gaze fluttered toward the door to the living room. He shifted his feet as if ready to run. "But I'm not going back to jail. I'm leaving here with my woman and my children."

"I'm not your woman and I'm not going anywhere with you." Charisma's firm voice filtered through the door. Not looking the least bit surprised to see David, she stomped into the room, still talking. "Don't be telling people lies."

Don't be aggravating him, David wanted to tell her. Instead, he took a long breath. "You know, you're a fortunate man, Logan."

"Fortunate?" The man snorted. "What are you talking about?"

"You have a son. I'll probably never have a son of my own, so I can only imagine how it must feel. I reckon you'd do anything for him. Anything."

Annie made a tiny, fluttering sound like a bird with a hurt wing. He sought her gaze. Pain radiated from her beautiful green eyes. He tried to speak to her with his heart. *Wait for me. Wait for the whole story. Later.*

She blinked. Tears rolled down both cheeks, but she didn't speak.

Neither did Logan. David tried again. "I reckon that's why you came here. To take care of him."

"Yeah." One syllable, soaked with defiance.

"But you're a man, a father, and you know this isn't what's best for Luke David. You know you want to show him how real men act. Real men own up to their mistakes and they stand up and accept their punishment. They don't take women and children as hostages."

More silence. David took another step toward the door that led to the living room. "Let the women go. Take me instead. You can negotiate a ride out of here with me as your hostage. Take the van. It's parked right out front."

"Charisma's coming with me. And the babies."

"Logan, there are men—police officers—in the front." Emma's voice carried from the living room. "I think they're trying to talk to you. You better—"

A voice amplified in a bullhorn blasted the end of her sentence. Someone demanded that Logan turn himself in immediately.

Emma was trying to help Logan. Helping him run from the Englischers. Were all the women on his side? David didn't have time to think about that. "Turn yourself in. It's the only way to make sure your babies are safe."

Logan jerked the gun toward the living room. "Get in there. Now."

Praying that Josiah stayed hidden, David did as he was told. A quick glance told him Miriam, Leah, Emma, and the children were all there, all in one piece. Leah had her flock gathered around her like a mother hen confronting danger that threatened her chicks. Their gazes met. "Is everyone all right out there? Luke and Josiah? Mark?"

"Everyone is fine, Leah, just fine." David turned to Logan. "Let the women and children go. Please."

"Everyone but Charisma and my babies."

"I'm not leaving Charisma." Annie put her hands on her hips. "If you think—"

"Go. Now." David didn't raise his voice, but he brought all the force to bear that he could. If they had any future together, she would learn to bow to his authority when it really mattered. "Don't argue. Do as I say."

A mutinous look on her face, she swooped down and picked up the little twins, one in each arm. Leah, her expression pleading, herded William and Joseph toward the front door. Emma and Miriam followed. No one cried. No one spoke.

The voice in the bullhorn demanded Logan surrender.

At the front door, Annie turned to Logan. "Please don't do this to Gracie and Luke David," she pleaded. "They could get caught in the crossfire. If you love them, you'll let them go."

"I do love them. That's why I'm doing this."

"No." David stepped between them. "A man who loves his children doesn't put them in danger. He does everything he can to make sure they're safe. Even if that means he can't have them with him."

Annie sidestepped him, putting herself in the line of fire once again. "If you don't answer them, they're going to burst in here."

Logan shook his head so hard his greasy black hair flopped in his eyes. "They won't endanger children."

"They seem pretty set on it." David took Annie by the arm and forcibly moved her toward the door. "They have rules. You broke them. You hurt one of them. Let all of the women and children go, and they'll know you don't intend to hurt anyone else. It'll be a show of good faith."

"Please, Logan, please!" Charisma had her arms wrapped around the baby. Her squeeze must have been too much. Luke David began to cry. "I want our baby to grow up in a real house, not on the run, hiding out, always looking over his shoulder."

Gracie let go of her mother's leg and trundled across the room. "Daddy, Daddy!" Her lips turned down in a pout and big tears appeared in her blue eyes. "Baby cry."

"Get them out of here." His lips twisted in a painful grimace, Logan's tears matched those of his children. "Get out of here. Now!"

Annie threw David a glance of entreaty. He pushed her toward the door. "We're coming out," she called through the broken window. "Please don't shoot us."

David pulled the door open wide enough for the procession of women and children to pass through, one at a time. If Annie's looks could kill, Logan's gun wouldn't be necessary. He tried to pour assurance into his returning gaze. "It'll be all right."

She glowered back at him.

When she disappeared from sight, he shut the door and turned. "Now what?"

Before Logan could answer, Sergeant Parker bolted into the room. Time slowed. Frozen, David knew he should duck behind the couch, but he couldn't move. Logan whirled, but he was too late. Using his own weapon, Sergeant Parker whacked the gun from Logan's hand with one hard chop. "Get down on the floor. Get down!"

The gun skittered across the floor. Reacting without thinking, David kicked it toward the couch. It boomeranged across the floor and disappeared from sight under the sofa.

Sergeant Parker pointed his gun at Logan's nose. "Don't be an idiot, McKee. Get down."

Logan raised his hands, turned his back, and knelt. Tears running down his face, he looked up at David. "I wouldn't hurt them."

"I know."

Sergeant Parker shoved Logan to the floor so hard his chin smacked the hard wood floor. He let out a *woof* sound. "Hey, you don't have to be so rough!"

"You all right?" Sergeant Parker directed the question at David, but didn't give him time to respond. He holstered his gun and slapped handcuffs on Logan. "You shouldn't have done it, Mr. Plank. You shouldn't have come in here like some hero. You could've gotten them killed. You got lucky."

Lucky? Luck did not exist. The outcome rested in God's hands. "I'm sorry we interfered in your plan."

"It's all right." Sergeant Parker pulled Logan to his feet. "Kid, you've done some stupid things in your short life, but this one's got to take the cake. Now you're going up on escape charges and kidnapping."

"We won't press charges." David didn't have to ask Luke or Thomas. It wasn't their way. "No harm done."

Sergeant Parker's furious expression came close to comical. "No harm done? No harm done, he says." He pushed Logan toward the door. "We'll talk about it later."

Josiah rushed through the door from the kitchen, saving David from having to respond. "He wouldn't let me come in. I would've been right behind you, but Sergeant Parker threatened to handcuff me to the tree."

His friend's wild-eyed statement relieved some of the pressure in

David's chest. He managed a smile. "You were much better off outside. Everything is fine now. Sergeant Parker has taken care of business."

Neither of them spoke as Sergeant Parker escorted Logan from Josiah's house. The man sobbed openly. If the scene where Leah, Emma, Miriam, Annie, Charisma, and the children being held at gunpoint by the man didn't keep playing on an endless loop in his head, David might have felt sorry for him. Not now. He might pity him, but he couldn't forgive him. Not yet.

Logan dug in his heels at the screen door. Sergeant Parker tugged at his prisoner. "Let's go."

Logan craned his neck and looked back at David. "I'm sorry." His voice was so thick with tears David could barely make out the words. "I wouldn't hurt them, I promise."

"We forgive you." David glanced at Josiah. Forgiveness started with saying it. "And we'll take care of Charisma and the babies."

"They're safe here." Josiah added. "I'll give your apologies to Annie."

"And Charisma?"

"And Charisma."

Charisma would need her own place and a new start. David would help Annie finish what she had begun with Charisma. And then they would have their own fresh start.

Chapter 46

His legs soft as melted butter, Josiah meandered through the yard looking for Miriam. She'd disappeared by the time he'd come out of the house with David. Surely she hadn't gone far—the police would want her statement. Rounding the corner of the house, he saw her. She sat alone at the picnic table under the elm tree in the backyard. She stared at the cornfields, her hands in her lap, her face placid. Never had he seen a lovelier sight.

"Are you all right?" he asked softly, not wanting to startle her.

She swiveled her head so their gazes met. "I wasn't scared."

"You're a brave girl. Held at gunpoint twice in a few months' time. Who would've thought it possible in little Bliss Creek?" He slipped closer. "May I sit down?"

"Jah." She shifted so he could sit next to her. He faced away from the table and left a proper amount of space between them. "I think that's why I wasn't afraid. I knew God was in charge this time, just like last time. And Logan is a poor, sweet man who has made terrible mistakes. God will forgive him. Why shouldn't we?"

Josiah admired her simple faith. He longed to be as rooted in his. "You're right."

"I think I'll ask my father to let me stop working at the tack shop."

"Why?"

"I teach nine months out of the year." She ran her hands over the rough wood of the picnic table. Her expression was dreamy, like it often had been in school, as if she had gone somewhere else. "I'd like to be at home, with Mudder, cooking, cleaning, and taking care of the little ones. I've had enough excitement for a long time."

"But you weren't afraid."

She shook her head. "No. My only fear was that I'd waited too long to be baptized."

"In September, we'll both be baptized."

Miriam's radiant smile rewarded him. "You're ready?"

"What would you think of having your own house and your own little ones?"

Her oval face creased around a smile that nearly knocked him from his seat. "It's all I think about."

"With me?"

The light faded a little. Doubt crept in and extinguished the smile. "What about Sarah?"

"Gone."

They sat a while, just breathing. Listening to the coo of mourning doves.

"Will you be happy?"

Her question startled him. He wiggled around so he faced the same direction. The sun warmed his face, reminding him of his mudder's hug on a cold morning. "You make me happy."

"Are you sure?" She sounded so uncertain. "You won't change your mind?"

"I may be slow, but eventually I get there. Once I do, there's no getting rid of me. Ever." He let his hand steal across the table and capture hers. "When I started working at the shop, Luke told me to split my earnings and save half for my future. I've been doing that for over a year now. I've been saving for a house."

"Our house?" she whispered, wonder in her voice.

"There's a little plot of land. Ten acres for sale on the outskirts of Bliss Creek. Enough for a garden, a few cows for milk. It's a start."

"A few cows..." Her voice trailed away. "Chickens."

"You want chickens, we'll have chickens." He could see it now, them arguing over who would clean the coop until the children were old enough for the loathsome task. "I still have a ways to go in saving enough money to build our house."

Her grip on his hand tightened. "I have my savings too, from teaching."

"We'll build together."

"You think by November?" Her voice quivered at the idea. "Or maybe another year?"

"I don't know, but I'll sure try for this year." He swallowed and ducked his head. "I've made you wait so long. I don't want you to give up and—"

"That won't happen and you know it. I got here first, remember? I'm the patient one. I'll wait as long as necessary."

She leaned against him. Her gingery scent enveloped him. "You've waited long enough."

Waited for many things. He inched his face toward hers, and she met him halfway. The kiss lasted so long he thought he might forget how to breathe. Miriam pulled away first. Her eyes glistened with tears, but her smile beckoned to him. "You have my heart."

"And you mine."

Then he kissed her again, just for good measure.

❦

David strode across the porch and pounded the steps. He needed some air. He needed Annie.

They could have their talk. Finally.

He found her sitting on a bale of hay in the barn, surrounded by the children. From the rapturous looks on their faces she was telling a fine story. When she saw him in the doorway, she didn't smile. "I thought it was important to give them something new to think about while their mudders give statements. Officer Bingham says mine will be last." She smiled at Gracie, who sat on her lap. "No nightmares tonight. Only sweet thoughts."

David inched closer. "Will *you* have only sweet thoughts?"

"I don't know." She tilted her head. "I reckon I'll dream about bossy men who think they can tell me what to do when they have no claim on me—"

"I saved your life and that's the thanks I get?" He kicked at the straw strewn across the floor. She surely was something else. He didn't know quite what. "You can't be that ungrateful."

"Saved my life!" She clamped her mouth shut, her eyes bright. After a few seconds, she scooted Gracie onto the hay bale and stood. "William and Joseph, show Gracie the new kittens."

"Kitty. Kitty." Gracie rolled off the bale and trundled after the boys. "Want kitty."

Annie stomped toward the far stall where Mooch chewed on feed, oblivious to the drama around him. "You could've been killed." Her voice soft, she glanced back at the children, who were crawling around in the first stall trying to corral half a dozen kittens and giggling all the while. "He could've shot you right there at the back door. What were you thinking?"

"I was thinking I needed to save his life in order to save yours."

"I was doing fine." She glared, but it only made her prettier. "I almost had him talked into surrendering, and you had to meddle."

"Meddle?" She had a funny way of looking at his offering. "You were being held hostage by a man with a gun. I wanted you safe. That's why I was so bossy." David struggled to keep his voice down. The kinner had been through enough for one day. "I'm a Plain man. Like Luke and Thomas and Josiah. We don't rob bakeries or hold people hostage, but we have strong feelings about the people we…the people we care about."

"You're saying you…" Her voice trailed off. "You care for me?"

He brushed a piece of hay from her apron. Her hands fluttered, then clasped at her waist. Their gazes met. "What if the bossy man wanted to make a claim on you?"

Her face turned pink. "So you talked to Doctor Corbin and you've decided you're healthy enough to court me? Is that what you're saying? Until the next bad test result?"

"Not exactly." David moved closer. "I told him I needed some time."

"Time? Why? If you need more treatment, you need to start now. We can't keep waiting. I can't keep waiting."

"I know that. We're not waiting anymore. At least, I'm not."

Her pretty nose wrinkled. "I don't understand."

Every bone in his body weary, he leaned against the stall railing. "When Kinsey died, Willow reminded me of something. She said love never dies."

Annie leaned next to him. Her scent of vanilla wafted over him, sweet and innocent. "She's right. The Bible says so. It's wonderful that she has her love for Kinsey to hang on to, but what does that have to do with your test results?"

"I've been so afraid of dying, I haven't been living."

"I know *that*."

"I realized I don't need the test results. I need you."

"Me?"

The word came out a squeak. David laughed. "Yes, you. Who else, you silly girl?" She began to protest, but David cut her off. "Listen to me. I don't know what the test results are. I told Doctor Corbin I wanted to talk to you first. Having the faith to commit to a life with you was more important. I couldn't make a decision to commit to you based on test results. They don't matter. I'm asking you to take them on faith, just as I am. Whatever happens, happens, but we'll be in it together."

"Together." She whispered the word. "Always together."

He allowed himself to grasp her soft hands in his. "Take a ride with me."

"What?"

"Get Emma to watch the kinner. Take a ride with me."

"Why—"

"Just do it."

Her forehead scrunched, her cheeks wet with tears, she scrambled from the room. Within a minute or two she returned with Emma, who asked no questions.

Annie waited quietly while he hitched the buggy and climbed in without his help. She remained silent until they were out on the road. "Where are we going?"

"You'll see."

"David—"

"It's been a long day."

"It has."

Realizing he didn't intend to say more, she lapsed into silence. David urged the horse forward, anxious to reach the spot. They plodded down the road, a trail of dust behind them, until they left the Shirack property. Once they made it to the highway they moved more quickly. The sun shone on the blacktop between the occasional car. The longest chunk of the journey meandered through Plank property. He pulled along the fence, finally, and stopped.

"What is this? Why are we stopping here?"

He helped her down. "We're almost there."

Together they climbed a small slope of a hill. At the crest, he stopped. "We're here."

"Here where?"

"We're standing where our house will be."

"Our house." She surveyed the scene, her head cocked as if searching for something among the trees. "Kinsey would've liked it here. It's so peaceful and quiet."

"Jah. We rode here once. She asked me if heaven would be quiet like this. I hope it is." David stared at the horizon, searching for the right words. "My brothers have given it to me to start a new life. It's only a dozen acres, but it's enough. Mudder wants to retire to the dawdi haus and she wants me to run the bakery full time. I'll honor her wishes. I can always help my brothers farm if I get a hankering to plow. I'm asking you to help me build us a home so that come November, we can marry and start a life of our own. Regardless of what the test results say. We face the future together. Whatever time I have, I want to spend it with you. The rest doesn't matter."

Her features softened. Tears pooled in her green eyes. He ached to touch her face. He wanted to hold that image in his mind and his heart forever.

She nodded.

He breathed again. "Say it out loud."

"What?" Her voice shook.

He tugged on her arm so she would turn and face him. He could feel her trembling under his fingers. They clasped hands, his warm fingers wrapped around her cool ones. "I want to make sure you understand what I'm asking. I'd like you to say it out loud."

Comprehension spreading across her face, she smiled. "Yes! Yes, I'll marry you." Her voice, always low for a woman's, was husky. "Whatever time I have left, I want to spend it with you."

He nodded. "This is the first of many good days we'll have here."

They turned and faced the tree-dotted land. "One other thing."

"There's more?" She dabbed at her freckled nose with a handkerchief. "I don't think I can bear it."

"I want to help Charisma and her children get their own place. She needs it, and it's only fair to Luke and Leah."

Annie laughed. "I knew it."

"Knew what?"

"She grows on a person."

"Like a dandelion."

"Some weeds are impossible to get rid of, it's true." Annie chuckled. "Together I know we can help her. She has a job now and Deborah to watch the babies. Plus, I think I know someone else who might be interested in keeping an eye on her."

David examined her face and saw only merriment. "Are you matchmaking?"

"You'll see." She slid her arm around his. "I just want her to be as happy as I am right now. In this moment. Finally."

"Hey, it didn't take that long."

"Only two rounds of chemo for you and being held at gunpoint twice for me."

"Well, when you put it that way."

They both laughed. The sound caught and danced in the late afternoon breeze that rustled through the tree branches. The leaves created a jeweled, dappled effect like lace on Annie's face. David turned and tugged her closer. He let his hands slide up her arms until his hands cupped her face. "Are you sure you want to be married to the likes of me?"

Her eyes, wet with tears, widened at his touch. "I'm as sure as I've ever been about anything in my life."

Then he did what he'd wanted to do since that first singing so long ago. He wrapped an arm around her, brought her close, then touched her chin so she raised her face to his. He kissed her, softly at first, unsure. Her response came swiftly and held no uncertainty. The kiss deepened until he knew it must stop.

When he broke away her breathing sounded a little ragged. "David…" She looked shaken, but she smiled. "That was…I'm…I—"

"Me too." He grinned and pulled her close again. "I love you."

"I love you too."

The words were more than reason enough for another kiss. This time she pushed away. "We can't keep doing that. November will come soon enough."

She was right. Still, he didn't let go of her hand as he tugged her toward the buggy. "Let's go."

"What's the hurry?" She glanced back at the hillside. "I love it here."

"It's time to start our lives together."

She quickened her pace. "Together."

Discussion Questions

1. Logan McKee robs Plank's Pie and Pastry Shop at gunpoint. Annie immediately forgives him and begins to worry about what will happen to him and the child he says he needs to feed. Would your first thought be to forgive him? If not, why not?

2. Logan robs the bakery because he needs money to feed Gracie and Charisma. Is it any less wrong if he does it for what he desperately believes is the "right" reason?

3. Annie not only forgives Logan, she takes his girlfriend and child into her family's home. Many of us have served food to the homeless or given money to a homeless person on a street corner. Would you take a homeless person into your home? Why or why not?

4. The Bliss Creek community of Plain folks believes in forgiveness even in a situation where the law has been broken. Mayor Haag believes Logan must be prosecuted to keep all the people who live in Bliss Creek safe. David argues the Bible says we are to forgive seventy times seven. Mayor Haag points out "Thou shall not steal" is one of the ten commandments. Who is right? Can they both be right?

5. What does Charisma's description of herself as "bad news" and a "dime a dozen" tell you about what her life has been like? Do you think she's "bad news"? Do you think her father's physical abuse excuses the mistakes she's made? What do you think of her treatment of Logan after he goes to jail?

6. Annie and David talk about the story of Job and how God allows everything to be taken from him in order to prove to Satan that Job is

faithful. Has there ever been a time in your life when you've felt abandoned by God? What did you do to strengthen your faith?

7. Emma wants nothing more than to have a baby. She's waited a long time for her first child. Then she has a miscarriage. David wonders why a godly woman like her has to go through such a tragedy. How do you respond when tragedy strikes in your life or in the life of someone you love? With anger? Or by drawing closer to God in your moment of need?

8. Can you find examples in your life of times where you know the power of prayer rescued you from a dire situation? What about times when you didn't get the answer you wanted even though you prayed hard and long? How did you react to that?

9. Annie knows there's a chance David will die from the Hodgkin's lymphoma, but she says yes when he asks her to marry him. Do you think David was right to ask her to give him an answer without knowing the results of his tests? Was he right to ask her without knowing the results himself? Why or why not?

10. The Bible says, "This is the day which the LORD hath made; we will rejoice and be glad in it." On days when things aren't going well or something really terrible happens in your life, do you have trouble finding the joy promised in this verse? How do you reconcile those days with the Scripture?

11. When a loved one is sick, we pray for healing. Sometimes we pray for miracles. If David is right and being afraid to die shows a lack of faith, what should we pray for in those times when a loved one's life or our own lives hang in the balance?

TO LOVE AND TO CHERISH

By Kelly Irvin

In author Kelly Irvin's first installment in the Bliss Creek Amish series, readers will find a charming, romantic story of how God works even in the darkest moments.

It's been four years since Carl left. Four years since he left the safety of the small Amish community for the Englisch world. And in four years, Emma's heart has only begun to heal.

Now, with the unexpected death of her parents, Emma is plunged back into a world of despair and confusion. It's a confusion only compounded by Carl's return. She's supposed to be in love with him…so why can't she keep her mind off Thomas, the strong, quiet widower who always seems to be underfoot? Could the man she only knew as a friend be the one to help her to heal?

In a world that seems to be changing no matter how tightly she clings to the past, this one woman must see beyond her pain and open her heart to trust once again.

About the Author

Kelly Irvin is a Kansas native and has been writing professionally for 25 years. She and her husband, Tim, make their home in Texas. They have two children, three cats, and a tankful of fish. A public relations professional, Kelly is also the author of two romantic suspense novels and writes short stories in her spare time.

To learn more about her work,

visit www.kellyirvin.com

To learn more about books by Kelly Irvin
or to read sample chapters, log on to our website:

www.harvesthousepublishers.com

HARVEST HOUSE PUBLISHERS
EUGENE, OREGON
